PIRATE OF
THE PROPHECY

PRAISE FOR THE PILLARS OF REALITY SERIES

"Campbell has created an interesting world... [he] has created his characters in such a meticulous way, I could not help but develop my own feelings for both of them. I have already gotten the second book and will be listening with anticipation."

—Audio Book Reviewer

"I loved *The Hidden Masters of Marandur*...The intense battle and action scenes are one of the places where Campbell's writing really shines. There are a lot of urban and epic fantasy novels that make me cringe when I read their battles, but Campbell's years of military experience help him write realistic battles."

—All Things Urban Fantasy

"I highly recommend this to fantasy lovers, especially if you enjoy reading about young protagonists coming into their own and fighting against a stronger force than themselves. The world building has been strengthened even further giving the reader more history. Along with the characters flight from their pursuers and search for knowledge allowing us to see more of the continent the pace is constant and had me finding excuses to continue the book."

—Not Yet Read

"*The Dragons of Dorcastle*... is the perfect mix of steampunk and fantasy... it has set the bar to high."

—The Arched Doorway

"Quite a bit of fun and I really enjoyed it... An excellent sequel and well worth the read!"

—Game Industry

"The Pillars of Reality series continues in *The Assassins of Altis* to be a great action filled adventure... So many exciting things happen that I can hardly wait for the next book to be released."

—Not Yet Read

"The Pillars of Reality is a series that gets better and better with each new book... *The Assassins of Altis* is a great addition to a great series and one I recommend to fantasy fans, especially if you like your fantasy with a touch of sci-fi."

—Bookaholic Cat

"Seriously, get this book (and the first two). This one went straight to my favorites shelf."

—Reanne Reads

"[Jack Campbell] took my expectations and completely blew them out of the water, proving yet again that he can seamlessly combine steampunk and epic fantasy into a truly fantastic story... I am looking forward to seeing just where Campbell goes with the story next, I'm not sure how I'm going to manage the wait for the next book in the series."

—The Arched Doorway

"When my audiobook was delivered around midnight, I sat down and told myself I would listen for an hour or so before I went to sleep. I finished it in almost 12 straight hours, I don't think I've ever listened to an audiobook like that before. I can say with complete honesty that *The Servants of The Storm* by Jack Campbell is one of the best books I've ever had the pleasure to listen to."

—Arched Doorway

PRAISE FOR THE LOST FLEET SERIES

"It's the thrilling saga of a nearly-crushed force battling its way home from deep within enemy territory, laced with deadpan satire about modern warfare and neoliberal economics. Like Xenophon's Anabasis – with spaceships."

—The Guardian (UK)

"Black Jack is an excellent character, and this series is the best military SF I've read in some time."

—Wired Magazine

"If you're a fan of character, action, and conflict in a Military SF setting, you would probably be more than pleased by Campbell's offering."

—Tor.com

"... a fun, quick read, full of action, compelling characters, and deeper issues. Exactly the type of story which attracts readers to military SF in the first place."

—SF Signal

"Rousing military-SF action... it should please many fans of old-fashioned hard SF. And it may be a good starting point for media SF fans looking to expand their SF reading beyond tie-in novels."

—SciFi.com

"Fascinating stuff ... this is military SF where the military and SF parts are both done right."

—SFX Magazine

PRAISE FOR THE LOST FLEET: BEYOND THE FRONTIER SERIES

"Combines the best parts of military sf and grand space opera to launch a new adventure series… sets the fleet up for plenty of exciting discoveries and escapades."

—Publishers Weekly

"Absorbing…neither series addicts nor newcomers will be disappointed."

—Kirkus Reviews

"Epic space battles, this time with aliens. Fans who enjoyed the earlier books in the Lost Fleet series will be pleased."

—Fantasy Literature

"I loved every minute of it. I've been with these characters through six novels and it felt like returning to an old group of friends."

—Walker of Worlds

"A fast-paced page turner… the search for answers will keep readers entertained for years to come."

—SF Revu

"Another excellent addition to one of the best military science fiction series on the market. This delivers everything fans expect from Black Jack Geary and more."

—Monsters & Critics

ALSO BY JACK CAMPBELL

THE LOST FLEET

Dauntless
Fearless
Courageous
Valiant
Relentless
Victorious

BEYOND THE FRONTIER

Dreadnaught
Invincible
Guardian
Steadfast
Leviathan

THE LOST STARS

Tarnished Knight
Perilous Shield
Imperfect Sword
Shattered Spear

THE GENESIS FLEET

Vanguard
Ascendant
Triumphant

PILLARS OF REALITY

The Dragons of Dorcastle*
The Hidden Masters of Marandur*
The Assassins of Altis*
The Pirates of Pacta Servanda*
The Servants of the Storm*
The Wrath of the Great Guilds*

THE LEGACY OF DRAGONS

Daughter of Dragons*
Blood of Dragons*
Destiny of Dragons*

EMPRESS OF THE ENDLESS SEA

Pirate of the Prophecy*
Explorer of the Endless Sea*
Fate of the Free Lands*

NOVELLAS

The Last Full Measure*

SHORT STORY COLLECTIONS

Ad Astra*
Borrowed Time*
Swords and Saddles*

*available as a JABberwocky ebook

PIRATE OF THE PROPHECY

EMPRESS OF THE ENDLESS SEA

BOOK I

JACK CAMPBELL

JABberwocky Literary Agency, Inc.

To
Lieutenant ("Leftenant") Commander Julie Vitali, Royal Navy,
who would've made one hell of a pirate,
and who wrote the book on Yankees.

For S, as always

ACKNOWLEDGMENTS

I remain indebted to my agents, Joshua Bilmes and Eddie Schneider, for their long- standing support, ever-inspired suggestions and assistance, as well as to Krystyna Lopez and Lisa Rodgers for their work on foreign sales and print editions. Many thanks to Betsy Mitchell for her excellent editing. Thanks also to Robert Chase, Kelly Dwyer, Carolyn Ives Gilman, J.G. (Huck) Huckenpohler, Simcha Kuritzky, Michael LaViolette, Aly Parsons, Bud Sparhawk and Constance A. Warner for their suggestions, comments and recommendations.

CHAPTER ONE

J acksport had a lively nightlife for a place that wasn't supposed to exist. Lanterns and candles lit up the taverns fronting on the harbor, many blazing through sheets of colored glass, causing the waterfront to resemble a cheap courtesan displaying fake jewelry in hopes of attracting more customers. Most of the buildings had been thrown up quickly using raw timber hewn from the inland forests, but even near the rickety piers extending into the water there were sturdier structures being built of stone or brick. Those who were coming to Jacksport clearly meant to stay. But for now muddy paths passed for roads and sidewalks, and dark corners abounded for those who wanted to offer unsavory services or prey on unwary victims.

Breezes coming down off the inland mountains carried the bracing scent of forest, a welcome competition to the fouler smells of the new town. Above, thousands of stars shone down on the world of Dematr, as well as the Twins, endlessly chasing the moon across the sky, far enough behind their quarry that some argued the moon was chasing the Twins.

"Why would anyone come here?"

"They want freedom," Jules of Landfall replied to her friend Ian. The two lieutenants-in-training stood on the wooden deck of the Imperial galley *Eagle Talon*, recently tied up to one of those new piers. "They're common people like us, tired of being slaves to the Great

Guilds." Anyone not a Mechanic or a Mage was a "common." From the Emperor or Empress down to the lowest gutter dweller, they were all on equal social footing as far as the Mechanics Guild and the Mage Guild were concerned.

"The commons aren't slaves," Ian said. "We're all citizens of the Empire."

"Who have to do anything a Mechanic or a Mage tells us to do."

"Why flee the Empire, then?" Ian demanded. "The Emperor protects his people."

Jules couldn't help a low laugh. "The Emperor wants servants, and he knows better than to cross the Great Guilds. No one really protects the common people."

Ian shook his head, frowning at her. "Jules, be careful what you say. You're already…"

"Already looked at askance because I came out of an Imperial orphan home," Jules finished for him. "I fought for this," she added, touching the officer insignia on her dark red uniform. "Just like I've had to fight for everything since I was five years old. I *earned* this." Maybe the goal she'd set her mind on years ago, to reach for the highest prize within her reach, an Imperial officer commission, no longer felt right for her. But that goal had been her way of proving that she, an orphan raised on the Emperor's charity, was as good as anyone else. She couldn't give that up, couldn't accept failure, because the world held nothing else she had any chance of grasping that could replace it as a mark of success, as an achievement that would force others to admit Jules of Landfall was their equal.

Not for the first time Jules wondered at how small an entire world could feel. But then as far as people were concerned, the entire world was confined to the eastern part of the Sea of Bakre and the lands there, all of which had been controlled by the Empire for as long as history went back. Granted, history didn't go back very far, only to the time a few centuries ago when the first emperor, Maran, was credited with ending a period of chaotic barbarism and founding most of the world's cities. Jules was far from the only person to have noticed that the histories made no mention at all of the Mechanics with their strange devices and the Mages with their mysterious powers who together ruled the world. But the inescapable fact remained that for commons the Empire was all there was, and advancement through Imperial ranks was the only option for those like her who wanted to better themselves.

"Yes, you earned it, and you can still lose it," Ian warned. He gestured toward Jacksport. "Don't start thinking like the people who believe they've escaped the Empire just because they've made it to the Sharr Isles. Don't start thinking you can defy the Empire."

She felt a surge of the old, familiar anger that had driven her since the death of her parents. "It's the Empire. It's all there is, so I have to do what I'm told. But nobody can tell me what I'm allowed to think."

"I wasn't—" He sighed. "Jules, there's a reason the Emperor hasn't yet moved against the people who've established settlements in places like Jacksport. No one will talk about it openly, but everyone thinks it's because the Great Guilds have told him not to. Why are the guilds doing that? To let people have freedom? Does that make sense to you?"

"No," Jules admitted. "The Great Guilds are playing some game of their own, using the common people as pawns."

"Just like always," Ian said in a low voice. "Pawns who'll be used and killed."

"Maybe I'm tired of being a pawn. Maybe all of us can be more than just tools for the Emperor or the Great Guilds to use in their games."

Ian's reply was forestalled by a shout from the quarterdeck. "Officers assemble!"

Jules followed Ian along the deck, past the single mast rising from the center of the galley, its sail furled, past the oars carefully stowed inboard, past the rows of crossbows and swords neatly racked and ready for use, around the after ballistae on its mount, and past the crew of legionaries who watched the young officers in training with looks bearing mischief under the required respect. Mounting the short flight of steps to the quarterdeck, Jules and Ian took position behind the line of full officers as they were joined by Dara, the third and last trainee officer aboard.

Captain Yvette usually appeared to be both smug and unhappy, a combination that Jules believed reflected Yvette's self-satisfaction with having climbed her way to higher rank by stepping on anyone in her way as well as the discovery that achieving her goal in that manner hadn't brought her any sense of accomplishment. This night was no different. Yvette glared at the officers before her as if waiting for one of them to utter an incautious word. "We're here to make it clear to these fugitives that the eye of the Emperor is still on them, and that the hand of the Emperor can reach them. Make sure every person you encounter ashore knows that!"

"Are we going to take control of this nest of criminals?" Lieutenant Franz asked, secure enough in the knowledge that he was one of the captain's favorites to risk asking a question. "Just because the Great Guilds are allowing some commons to set up new settlements outside of the Empire doesn't mean the Emperor has to tolerate it."

Yvette scowled. "The Emperor does not choose to take such action at this time. Most of the crew will remain aboard. The officers will go ashore in groups of two to impress our presence upon the locals and keep an eye on each other." Her eyes came to rest on Jules and a thin smile appeared on her lips. "Except you, Lieutenant-in-Training Jules. You're familiar with this sort of coarse environment, aren't you? You'll be assigned two legionaries and will patrol the taverns, ensuring those inside know the Emperor's eye is on them."

"Yes, Captain," Jules said, keeping her voice flat, knowing that Yvette was once again needling her in hopes of provoking a reaction.

A few minutes later, as Jules buckled on her sword belt, Ian paused by her, his expression troubled. "Jules, be careful. I overheard Franz saying that you're going to be assigned a couple of difficult legionaries. If you take those two into any taverns with you they'll find a way to sneak drinks, and you'll get hammered for it when you get back."

"Thank you," Jules said. "I figured the captain was trying to set me up again." She settled the scabbard of her straight sword on her left hip and checked her dagger, sheathed on her right. "She'd like nothing better than to have grounds to fail me in my training evaluation."

"The Great Guilds *are* here," Ian continued. "At least, a few Mechanics have been seen on the streets, and one Mage has been spotted as well."

"The Mechanics will be watching to make sure we're not breaking any of their rules," Jules said. "If someone wanted to try making something new, they'd head for a place like this where the Mechanics might not notice."

"It's not as if commons have any chance of learning how Mechanic devices work," Ian said. "Their weapons, those 'trains,' and everything else seem as mysterious as Mage spells to me."

"Those devices are what let Mechanics rule the world," Jules said. "As for Mages, who knows why they do anything? Are they even human? I mean, they look human, sort of, but…"

"But they don't act human," Ian said. "And they're even more dangerous than Mechanics."

"I'll try to avoid all of the Mechanics and any Mages," Jules said. "Just like any smart common. I'm sorry I snapped at you earlier. Thanks for being a friend I can say things like that to."

He shrugged. "If that's all I am, I'll do my best at it."

She smiled at him despite her exasperation. "I never said that's all you'd ever be to me. I said I needed more time. I'm probably doing you a favor. Imagine how your parents would react if you brought them a girl from a legion orphan home. Especially one with opinions like mine."

"Jules, you can't change the world. No one can. Nothing ever changes. That's just the way it is. The Great Guilds don't permit it. And nobody can fight the Great Guilds."

He was right. She knew it. But it wasn't in her to simply accept what was. "I was also told someone with my background couldn't qualify for an officer's appointment. Nobody knows what the future holds, Ian."

"Mages do," Ian said. "They sometimes speak those prophecies."

Jules felt an odd sense of foreboding that she shrugged off. "That doesn't have anything to do with me. I'll be fine."

Back on deck she found the ship's centurion waiting with two legionaries in armor, one armed only with a short sword but the other also carrying a crossbow. Jules recognized both of them, troublemakers just as Ian had warned.

"Your escort," the centurion told Jules.

She waited, her eyes on the centurion.

"Your escort, Lieutenant," the centurion said.

How much of such testing of her was due to her status as an officer in training, and how much to the disdain with which those from the homes were treated? Jules couldn't tell. She'd already shown the crew her willingness to push back when tested, but it hadn't stopped, probably fueled by the captain's open scorn. "Come on," she told the two legionaries.

Once on the pier, though, she stopped them. "Let's get one thing straight. I know that in combat unpopular officers sometimes suffer accidents, getting stabbed by one of their own legionaries."

The two legionaries exchanged grins.

Jules drew her dagger, the broad blade that curved to a point at the end glinting in the light of the lanterns on the galley behind them. "It'd be a shame if anything like that happened to either one of you," she said. "If I get too upset, if any trouble occurs, I might get confused and stab the wrong target. But as long as you don't give me any trouble, and obey all orders, you probably won't suffer from any accidents."

The smiles on the faces of her two legionaries faded as they stared at her and the dagger.

"Are we clear?" Jules said.

"Yes, Lieutenant!" the legionaries chorused. Their postures, which had been relaxed, straightened into attention.

She led the way down the pier, no longer quite as worried to have those two at her back.

Just before leaving the pier to step onto dry land, Jules looked up at the stars again. She hadn't told anyone, but it was her twentieth birthday. Jules had been tossed out of the orphan home the day she'd turned eighteen, and like just about every other man and woman ejected from one of the homes had walked straight to a legion recruiting office. But instead of enlisting, she'd been able to pass the rigorous tests giving her a chance for an officer appointment. After two years of training covering everything from how to fight, how to march, how to handle a ship, and how to climb the rigging, she got to spend her birthday leading a pair of unhappy legionaries through the mud and dark corners of Jacksport.

The taverns were only a short way back from the waterfront, lined up ready to separate the unwary from their money in exchange for various legal and illegal entertainments. Jules walked past the doors of the taverns, feeling self-conscious in her Imperial uniform. Except for some of the insignia, her fleet officer uniform was the same as that of the Imperial officers who commanded legionaries ashore. The armor of the legionaries following Jules was different, not as heavy as that of legionaries who fought on land, but it still carried the same menacing message to those who saw it.

The sounds of revelry grew subdued as Jules passed, growing again in her wake, as if Jules were some sort of Mechanic device or Mage spell that suppressed celebrations. "You'd think we were Mages," one of the legionaries remarked.

"If we were Mages," the other legionary said, "they'd be doing a lot less. No one wants a Mage to notice them."

"Saw a guy get noticed by a couple of Mages once," the first legionary said. "A man and a woman, I think. It's hard to tell sometimes in those robes they wear, and they had their hoods up. Those two cut that guy to pieces. Just because they could. Didn't look like they cared. Or like they was having fun. They just did it."

The second legionary gave an angry snort. "At least when Mechanics spit on you they look at you like you're a person, not a bug."

"That's enough," Jules said, thinking that she ought to stop the chatter. "They're the Great Guilds. We're the commons. Everybody knows it."

"The Emperor ought to—"

"That's enough," Jules repeated, putting more force into the words. It'd be awkward if those legionaries openly wondered why the Emperor who reigned in Marandur didn't act. Because the only truthful answer was that the supposedly all-powerful Emperor had to do what the Great Guilds demanded.

The two legionaries subsided for only a moment. As they walked past a particularly garish entry with the sounds of drunken gaiety coming out, the first legionary spoke up again. "Lieutenant, are we going into any of the bars?"

"I am," Jules said. Not that she was looking forward to that. "You two have to stay outside." She ignored the low groans of despair from the legionaries which confirmed that Ian's warning had been accurate. If those two got into a tavern they'd find ways to sneak drinks, and she'd get blamed for it when the three of them got back to the ship.

A shout came from someone safely anonymous inside a bar as they passed. "Go away! We're free here!"

Free. Jules glanced inland, where the Mechanics Guild had already begun construction of one of their Guild Halls, demanding the work of local laborers and artisans.

"Freedom? I saw some Mechanics here already," the second legionary said, unknowingly echoing Jules' thoughts. "Swaggering around in their dark jackets like they own the whole world."

"They do," the first legionary said. "Don't know why Jacksport would welcome them and give us the fisheye."

Jules knew the answer to that, too. Jacksport would welcome the Mechanics and provide forced labor to build that Guild Hall because, as much as the common people detested Mechanics, they wanted the technology only the Mechanics could provide, and the people here knew that the only power on Dematr that could keep the Empire away was the Mechanics Guild. If it wanted to.

The Mage Guild could do that as well, of course, and the Mages would also come here, because Mages went wherever they wanted to go. But no one chose to interact with Mages, and no one could predict what they'd do. Except for the certainty that Mages regarded the lives of common people as worthless.

It had always been that way, though no one seemed to be sure just how long "always" extended into the past, and it always would be. As Ian had pointed out, how could anyone fight the power of the Great Guilds? Mechanic or Mage, they had abilities the common people couldn't match.

"I'm going in here," Jules said, looking for something to distract her from her thoughts. "You two wait right where you are." The tavern, with a wooden plank nailed above the door advertising BOOZE, REAL STUFF seemed to have no name. It didn't look like the sort of place that would welcome someone in an Imperial officer's uniform. Which was exactly why she was going in. *Face what you fear,* her mother had said, not long before dying in childbirth. Jules thought her father would have agreed, but he'd died when his legion was sent to chase bandits in the mountainous Northern Ramparts.

Which had left only her. To endure the harsh environment of a home for legion orphans, to fight and learn and not give up until she qualified for one of the few openings for officer training available to the orphans, to end up here in the muddy streets and raw taverns of Jacksport.

She shoved open the door, striding inside.

Jules had taken barely three steps into the tavern, just enough to wonder why the place felt so quiet, when she abruptly found herself facing a Mage.

She froze, her eyes fixed on those of the Mage, wondering if she was about to die. The Mage looked back at her, his gaze reflecting the total lack of interest that Mages directed toward all others, as if those others meant nothing at all. His hood was down, giving her a good look at the rough, unwashed hair hanging in hanks alongside his face. The Mage's expression, if a lack of any apparent feeling could be called an expression, could have been that of a dead person. The tavern had gone totally silent, all of those here watching with mingled dread and anticipation to see what the Mage would do to this young Imperial officer.

But in the moments while Jules stood paralyzed with fear and uncertainty, some feeling came into the Mage eyes looking into hers. Could that be surprise?

"This one sees and hears," the Mage said, his eyes locked on Jules, his voice hoarse and low. "This one sees that one, and hears a voice inside say the day will come when a daughter of your line will unite Mechanics, Mages, and the common folk to overthrow the Great Guilds and free the world. A daughter of your line will someday do this."

Jules stared at the Mage, a different, vastly greater terror taking the place of her earlier fears as his words sank in.

Following the words of the Mage the silence in the bar had become almost a physical thing, smothering all sound.

Someone finally broke the silence in a whisper, as if afraid to speak the words. "Her daughter will free us?"

"A daughter of her line," another said. "Granddaughter, maybe. Great-granddaughter. But it's a Mage prophecy! You all heard it!"

The voices broke her paralysis, though the Mage still stood as if frozen by shock at what he had seen, and everybody else in the tavern seemed afraid to move. Knowing only that she had to get out of there, had to find a place to hide, Jules scrambled backward—away from the Mage who would kill her as soon as he recovered from his surprise, away from the other eyes—out the flimsy door to where her legionaries waited. Oddly enough, even in the midst of the near-panic filling her, Jules felt an obligation to ensure those legionaries weren't left exposed to any danger pursuing her.

"Get back to the ship!" Jules yelled at the two legionaries. "*Go now!*"

Without another word, she spun about and raced away down the waterfront, trying to lose herself in the crowd. Her guts felt like a hurricane had come to rest in them. Her mind filled with only one thought: that the Mage had pronounced a death sentence on her and any children she might someday have. Because the Great Guilds would never let that prophecy come true if they could prevent it by killing her.

Her churning thoughts and feelings, only partly numbed by fear, settled on one certainty. How hard would it be to learn the exact identity of an Imperial officer who was in Jacksport this night? That Imperial officer had to cease to exist before that Mage shared his prophecy with the Guild. Her future, the one she had worked and fought for, had just become a deadly trap that would have to be forgotten.

Finding an alley, Jules ran down it, trying to get away from the crowds and heedless of the mud splattering her boots and pants. In the dark, she saw a prowling figure lunge toward her and barely got her dagger out in time to swing at the other. The mugger or murderer dropped back, vanishing into the murk again as Jules ran on.

She came out of the alley one street back from the waterfront. Here few lights or people could be seen at this hour. Shuttered stores lined the streets, their interiors as dark as the night about them. Jules spotted a sign with a tattered shirt hanging from it and ran that way. Clothing. Yes. Do that first. She needed something a lot less easy to spot than this uniform.

Not wanting to break in the front door where someone could see, Jules ran to the alley alongside that building, finding a side door whose lock was stout enough to resist breaking. The same couldn't be said of the door. She kicked viciously until the door cracked and she could force it open and get inside. Crates of clothing were laid out inside, forming haphazard rows. Quickly choosing the sort of shirt and pants that any sailor would wear, Jules stripped off her uniform and pulled on the other clothing. Her boots and sword and dagger could still betray her, but she needed those.

A small canvas bag proved big enough to hold her uniform. Jules rolled up her uniform jacket and pants, feeling a sense of loss as she sealed the bag. She paused to stare at the bundle, thinking of how proud she'd been to first put on that uniform. Where could she dispose of it where it wouldn't be found?

When she walked out onto the well-lit waterfront again, no one took notice of her even though she thought her fear must be obvious. But Jules heard the buzz of gossip racing down the street and

being repeated by dozens of people in tones too low for any passing Mechanic or Mage to overhear. She heard the word "prophecy"
repeated over and over, confirming what the feverish discussions were
about.

Jules walked along the waterfront feeling as if everyone around was
staring at her. The bag holding her uniform felt like a huge red flag
that everyone must surely notice. How could she get rid of it without
people seeing? Jules held onto the bag and kept walking, not knowing
where she was going, trying to figure out what to do next.

The Mage didn't know who she was. No one in the bar had known.
But if she didn't get out of Jacksport fast, someone would recognize
her. And that would mean her death. She had to get out of this harbor,
and out of the Sharr Isles, as soon as possible. These areas were sparse-
ly-settled enough that she'd stand out as a stranger no matter where
she went. Even the growing town of Caer Lyn on another island was
too small, and too close to the Empire, to be safe.

Running again would attract too much attention. Settling on a
goal, Jules walked at a pace that she hoped wasn't so quick as to be
suspicious toward a pier she had noticed earlier, where a few merchant
ships were tied up. One of those ships would have to be her way out
of Jacksport.

Her path took Jules back past the pier where the Imperial galley
Eagle Talon rested, the deck of the ship illuminated brightly enough
by lanterns to show figures in dark red uniforms moving about. Her
ship. Her *former* ship. At least she'd no longer have to feel conflicted
about forcing others to bow before the same Imperial authority she
herself chafed at.

Jules realized that a pair of officers from the *Eagle Talon* were coming down the pier toward her. Blazes. Why now? Jules scrunched her
head into her collar, keeping her gaze lowered, letting her gait go a
little loose like a sailor with too much alcohol under her belt, hoping
the Imperial officers would pay no attention to her.

They were even, they were past...

"Jules?"

Her head came up and she looked back, recognizing the voice. Lieutenant-in-Training Ian and Lieutenant-in-Training Dara. Of all people to encounter.

"What are you doing?" Dara asked, her shocked gaze on Jules. "Where's your uniform?"

"I'm leaving Imperial service," Jules said. "Forget you saw me. Please."

"You can't just—" Dara began, shocked.

"What happened?" Ian interrupted, coming closer, concerned for her.

"I have to disappear," Jules said, the words tumbling out. "Or else I'll be killed."

"By who? Who wants to kill you?"

"Every Mage and every Mechanic on Dematr." Jules rubbed her face, already regretting having told them that much, seeing that now she'd have to explain. "I encountered a Mage. He… he looked at me, and said that a daughter of my line would someday overthrow the Great Guilds and free the world." Both Ian and Dara stared at her, their jaws hanging loose in amazement. "The Mage didn't know who I was. I lost him. I need to make sure they don't find out who I am."

"You won't last a day if they do find out," Ian said. "Both Great Guilds? Your daughter will overthrow both of them?"

"A daughter of my line," Jules said. "Who knows how far down the line that will be? It could be centuries."

Ian stared at her. "Do you think it's true? What the Mage said?"

"It's a Mage prophecy," Dara said, sounding joyful. "That means it will happen. Jules, this is wonderful!"

"Wonderful?" Jules asked, wondering why "wonderful" felt so terrifying.

"Yes! The Emperor will protect you! Hide you! Come on back to the ship."

Jules wavered. "Hide me?" Could he? Even the Mages and the Mechanics might not be able to find her if the Emperor…

What would the Emperor do?

She thought of everything she'd heard of the Emperor and the Imperial court. Ruthless, everyone said. The only morality was winning by any means possible. "Hide me? Lock me up somewhere, you mean."

"Somewhere *safe*," Dara emphasized. "The Emperor wants the Great Guilds overthrown, too! If he knows a daughter of your line will… you don't have any children yet, do you?"

"No!" Jules said. "I…" It hit her then with the force of a blow, her fears fanned again by the knowledge of what would happen to her. "He'd make me marry him. Make me his consort. And force me to have children with him."

"Who?" Ian asked.

"The Emperor! If my children were also acknowledged as his he'd be able to claim Imperial credit for whatever they did!"

"I hadn't thought of that!" Dara said. "Jules, you're so lucky!"

"Lucky? How is that lucky?"

"To be the Emperor's consort! To bear the heirs to the Empire, and those who will eventually overthrow the Great Guilds!" Dara smiled broadly.

"Do you think I'm Mara?" Jules demanded. "Willing to sell my humanity so I can sit beside the Emperor's throne?"

"Jules, what's the matter with you? The Emperor keeps us all safe. Even if you don't appreciate that, you swore an oath to the Emperor!" Dara insisted. "You have a duty to come back with us, and to go to Marandur, and to do whatever the Emperor asks of you. Having his children would be an *honor*."

Jules shook her head, a certainty rising to accompany the earlier fear. "Then you have them! I won't spend the rest of my life locked away someplace safe! I'd rather die than become a brood mare for the Emperor, or any other man! I'll marry the man I want when I want, and then I'll have children, if children I have, because I want to!"

"It sounds like you're definitely going to have at least one child," Ian said.

Jules stared at him, only now feeling the force of that. A child was no longer merely a possibility. Someday, at least one child of hers would be in this world.

And the Great Guilds would be doing all they could to kill that child.

Dara's voice, gone cold and authoritative, shocked her out of that dark reverie. "Surrender your sword, Jules. Ian, take her sword."

"You're arresting me?" Jules asked, incredulous.

"You have a duty!" Dara repeated. "Not just to the Emperor but to every common person on Dematr who needs your descendent to someday free us."

Jules hesitated, not wanting to fight Ian and Dara, but seeing no other way out. Ian didn't seem happy, though, even while he listened to Dara's orders. "All right," Jules told Dara, drawing her sword backhanded as if to surrender it. "But first we need to deal with them," she added, nodding back the way she'd come.

Dara and Ian turned to look, but no one was visible nearby. "What—?" Ian began.

Jules slammed the guard of her sword against Dara's head, dropping Dara senseless. Spinning the blade about, she held the tip slanted toward Ian, who hadn't drawn his own sword. "Don't make me hurt you. Please," Jules said.

Ian nodded, stepping back. "You should probably hit me, too, so I can have a good excuse for not stopping you. Dara's just trying to be a good citizen."

"I know," Jules said. "I don't want to kill her."

"You should probably kill both of us," Ian said, his voice cracking. "To keep your secret safe."

Jules looked at him, at the sword in her hand, then shook her head. "No. My life isn't worth that. I won't murder either of you to protect myself."

Ian sagged with relief. "This time I'm glad that you're not taking my advice. All right. I understand why you're doing this. Maybe someday we'll meet again. Good luck, Jules." Ian turned away, standing stoically.

Jules hit him hard enough to raise a lump, dropping Ian to his knees, but not hard enough to knock him out even though he could claim she had.

Then running again, here where it was dark right along the water, the brightly lit taverns well behind her, the night covering her movements. Running through the gloom until she reached the last pier, and out along it, slowing to a walking pace, studying the three ships here. Trying to think as her heart pounded and her breath came quick from the run and from renewed fear.

One of the three ships flew an Imperial flag. A prosperous-looking ship. She knew the type. Owned by someone in the Imperial court, benefiting from the insider connections and trades those facilitated. She couldn't trust anyone aboard a ship like that.

The second ship looked like any other wooden sailing vessel, but flew the flag of the Mechanics Guild, indicating that it was leased or owned by Mechanics to carry cargo. Mechanics would let commons do the work on such a ship, but they would rule every action taken. Even though Mechanics might not believe in Mage prophecies (*did* they believe in Mage prophecies?) they'd probably still kill her just to be safe.

The third ship, though, looked to be decently maintained and also an independent trader. It offered a slim hope, but the only hope there was to be had this night.

Jules went up the gangway, finding a drowsy sailor sitting on the deck. "Is your captain aboard?"

The sailor blinked up at Jules, plainly unhappy at being roused. "Who's asking?"

"Me."

"Why?"

"Why don't I talk about that to the captain?"

"Then you'll wait," the sailor said. "Cap'n said no waking him until dawn unless an emergency. Are you an emergency?"

"Maybe. I came off that Imperial galley." What would get the attention of this sailor? Jules remembered some of the other officers eyeing this ship and discussing what they might do. Why not assume they would? Because a search of every spot on this island would certainly happen once Dara recovered and spoke to the captain of the *Eagle Talon*. "The Imperials are planning to search this ship as soon as the sun rises tomorrow. Maybe even before dawn."

Her partial bluff worked, the sailor getting up and eyeing her narrowly. He was a big man, a bit over a lance tall, the sort who could cow opponents just by looking at them. "You're in the Imperial fleet?"

"I *was*," Jules said. "Are we going to talk to the captain?"

The sailor hustled along the deck to the cabin under the quarterdeck, rapping his knuckles on the door, the sound unnaturally loud at this hour. "Cap'n? We got an emergency."

Less than a minute later the door cracked open. Jules saw a single eye looking out. "What is it?"

Jules answered. "The Imperials are planning to search this ship at first light. Maybe earlier."

"Blazes. Ang, get the crew rousted and send some ashore to get anyone in the taverns. Move fast."

"You believe her?" Ang asked.

"Move fast!" the captain said. As Ang ran off the captain opened the door fully and stood in the doorway, studying Jules. Roused from sleep, he wore only trousers. He was nearly past middle-age, Jules guessed, seeing even in this dim light that his skin was rough from long years at sea. A heavy mustache sprinkled with gray crowned his lip and heavy eyebrows hovered above shrewd eyes.

"An Imperial officer," the captain finally said. "I can see the sword. What brings you here?"

She wasn't about to tell the truth again. "I have my reasons."

"Do you?" The captain looked her over again, something about his appraising gaze making Jules' face warm with embarrassment. "You caught the eye of some Imperial official, I'm guessing. Someone who doesn't have to take no for an answer."

That was close enough to the truth, Jules realized. Though that Imperial official would be the Emperor himself. "Yes."

"So you found your virtue and decided that coercing others wasn't such a fine thing after all," the captain added with a sour look. "Well enough. Some folks don't find that out until they're a lot older than you, and have done a lot worse than someone your age could've yet managed. What do you want from this ship?"

"A fast way out of Jacksport," Jules said.

"It's like that, then? You're that worried about being taken back?"

Tell him the truth and give him a hold on her? Or lie and risk the lie showing in her face or words? Jules inhaled deeply, then nodded. "Yes. I'm that worried."

The captain shook his head. "There'd be a reward then. It would've been smarter to lie, girl." He held up one hand to pause her grab for her sword. "But the Imperials probably have a reward out for me as well, so this time you're fine. Find another story, though. You'll be safer that way. Can you work sails?"

"I'm… I *was* a lieutenant-in-training. I can do anything on this ship," Jules said.

"Ah. We'll see about that." The captain looked about as his crew began rushing onto deck, some of them running down the gangway and toward the town to collect their shipmates. "Do you know how a free ship works?"

"I know how a ship works," Jules said. "You're the captain."

"This is a free ship," he repeated. "I'm captain as long as the crew supports me. If I make enough mistakes, act too high and mighty, they can vote me out and someone else in. Don't *you* be a mistake, you hear me?" The sudden menace in the captain's voice made clear the threat wasn't an idle one.

"I hear you," Jules said.

"I'm Mak of Severun. What's your name?"

"My name is J—" Jules choked off her words, realizing that she shouldn't tell anyone the truth of that. "Jeri. Jeri of…"

"Say Landfall," Captain Mak advised. "Your accent tells anyone you're from there, so stick to a story you can carry off."

"Thank you," Jules said, suddenly aware of how much she didn't know about being on the run from… from everyone. "Jeri of Landfall."

"All right, Jeri. Welcome to the *Sun Queen*. You can climb rigging?"

"Yes, sir."

"Get out of those boots and drop your sword and belt. I'll keep them safe for you. Keep the dagger. Ask Ang for a belt sheath for it from the ship's chest."

Jules leaned against the deckhouse, tugging off both boots, feeling a surge of worry as she unclasped her sword belt and handed over the weapon. But she still had the dagger in her hand, and while Mak didn't seem especially warm he did appear to be helpful. "Can you do something with this?" Jules asked, abruptly realizing she also still had the bag holding her rolled up Imperial uniform.

"What is it?" Mak glanced inside. He raised an eyebrow at her, but didn't ask any other questions. "It'll be in this cabin. In case you need it again."

"I seriously doubt I will." She found Ang, who offered Jules a scornful look before taking her to the chest holding extra clothing and other items anyone on the ship might need. Jules dug until she found a leather belt sheath that would hold her dagger, but there weren't any belts that would fit her. Without her sword belt, the pants she'd stolen kept slipping down over her hips, so going without a belt wasn't an option.

That was a familiar problem from her childhood, though, with a familiar solution at hand. "Is it all right if I cut off some of this?" Jules asked Ang, hefting a length of line. He nodded, she measured out a length with her arms, sliced it free and after putting the knife sheath on it slipped the line through the belt loops of her pants and knotted it.

"You've done that before," Ang said, his gaze gone from hostile to curious.

"Legion orphan home," Jules said, having decided to stick with that part of her past. There wasn't any shortage of people who could claim similar upbringing, and she'd have a hard time convincingly talking about any other kind of childhood.

"Ah." Ang nodded. "Landfall?"

"Yeah."

"I was in one at Sandurin. The Emperor's generosity didn't extend to luxuries like decent clothing, did it?"

"No," Jules said. "And the food was only fit for a Mage."

"On good days." Ang nodded again. "If you need anything, sister, you tell me."

"Thank you, brother."

That had been one of the unwritten rules of the orphan homes. The others there were sisters and brothers, perhaps the only family some of them had ever known. And they all knew it was them against a world that saw them as a burden at best and thieving pests at worst.

Back on deck there were sailors rushing about to ready the ship to get underway, and others racing up the gangway having returned from the taverns. "Something weird's going on back there," one called as she came up off the dock. "Mages going around checking every young woman and young man. They're not saying a thing, just staring and moving on."

"Move fast!" Captain Mak called down from the quarterdeck, where he stood fully clothed, a cutlass by his side. "The Imperials and the Mages are both acting up! We want out of here before the Mechanics join in!"

Jules ran over to where some of the crew were bringing in the hawsers that had tied the ship to the pier, lending a hand as they hauled on the rough, heavy lengths of braided hemp fibers. Other members of the crew were pulling in the gangway even as a last sailor ran up it.

"Get aloft!" Ang called. He gestured to Jules. "Foremast!"

She ran again, joining the others racing up the ratlines and shrouds to the yard where the fore-mainsail was furled. Edging out along the rope strung under the yardarm, Jules helped loosen and unfurl the sail, the heavy canvas fighting her efforts.

The sail dropped, filling with a soft rumble as it caught the breeze.

The *Sun Queen*, drifting slowly away from the pier, picked up speed as the sails were unfurled and caught the wind, her bow coming about to head for the harbor entrance.

Jules paused to stare that way, remembering that Jacksport as yet had no marked channel to follow, and no lights on the headlands marking either side of the harbor entrance. Getting out without running aground would take both inspired seamanship and at least a little luck.

Back down on the deck, Jules joined one of the gangs of sailors hauling on the lines to shift the sails to best catch the wind as the *Sun Queen* swung about. She looked forward, seeing the vague, shadowy shapes of the headlands hard to make out in the night, then back toward the quarterdeck, startled to see Captain Mak apparently looking off to the side. "What's he looking at?" she gasped without thinking.

One of the nearest sailors glanced back at the captain. "You don't know that trick? Something dim at night, you can't see it head on. But if you look out of the corner of your eye, you can spot it. Mak's looking for the surf around the sides of the harbor entrance."

Of course. Jules turned her own gaze aside, catching the faint glimmer of white surf, growing and fading as the swells beat against the rocks.

It seemed a very small and vague thing on which to risk the safety of this ship and the people on it.

Including her.

Jules looked down at herself, in rough sailor clothing, a rope belt, bare feet, on the deck of a ship she didn't know surrounded by men and women whose motives and morality she had little sense of, heading for what might well be a hard grounding on jagged rocks that would tear the bottom out of this ship and spill the crew into the waves slamming into the rocks. There had been little time tonight to think. No chance to really consider what choices she had. Did this make sense? Had she simply run from one form of death to another?

Looking back toward the waterfront, getting farther away as the *Sun Queen* headed for the harbor entrance, Jules made out the shapes of crowds rushing about. Were there dark red Imperial uniforms among them? Hard to tell from this distance. But the Mages had already been looking for her. By now the crew of the *Eagle Talon* might be searching as well.

A boom like that of thunder brought to ground echoed across the harbor, followed by several more booms in a ragged volley.

"Mechanic weapons," one of the sailors said, staring back at Jacksport. "The Mechanics are out, and they're shooting."

"Shooting at who or what? What the blazes happened?" another asked. "Mages acting weirder than usual. The Imperials moving in. I've been to Jacksport a dozen times and never seen the like of this."

"I heard someone say there'd been a prophecy. A Mage made a prophecy."

"About what? The end of the world?"

Jules looked forward again, trying to catch a good look at the rocks and surf around the harbor entrance that the ship was rapidly approaching.

Dangerous as those rocks were, they were the safer choice tonight. And daring them her only chance of living to see the dawn. If she was going to live, she couldn't just stand around waiting for others to save her.

CHAPTER TWO

J ules broke into a run, heading forward past startled other
members of the crew. She reached the bow and kept going, out
along the bowsprit extending from the bow, holding on to the
stay lines until she'd gone as far as she could, the dark waters of the
harbor racing beneath her as she balanced unsteadily on the bowsprit, reaching back to grasp the closest rigging, feeling the tension
in the stay line as it helped hold the masts against the strain of the
wind.

She knelt, staring into the darkness, scanning from side to side,
catching glimpses of white surf from the corners of her eyes. There.
And there. "Surf less than one point to starboard!" she yelled back.

Jules heard her report echoed by others, relayed to the quarterdeck,
and felt the ship swing slightly to port, rocking her on her precarious
perch. Grateful that she had bare feet gripping the bowsprit instead
of the leather soles of her boots, Jules breathed as softly as she could
through her open mouth, listening as well as looking for surf. "Surf
one point to starboard!"

The *Sun Queen* swung a bit more to port.

"Surf two points to port!"

"Surf three points to starboard!"

"Surf just off the port bow!"

The ship swung harder, heeling away from the danger. Jules' foot slipped, leaving her partially dangling over the water for a moment as she clung to the stay.

Both feet on the bowsprit again, looking anxiously ahead, Jules heard and saw the closest surf this time. "Surf one point to starboard!"

The *Sun Queen* rolled a bit to port, threading the needle of the channel entrance. Jules held on, staring at the waters ahead, feeling the motion of the ship change to a long roll and pitch.

"Hey."

Jules looked back, seeing Ang calling to her from the foot of the bowsprit.

"We're out," Ang said. "Get your butt back on deck before you take a swim."

She found it unexpectedly hard to stand fully and make her way back along the bowsprit without falling, surprised by how stiff her muscles were. Hands reached to help her onto the deck. "Who the blazes are you?" one of the sailors demanded.

"J- Jeri. Of Landfall. I just came aboard." She looked at the faces around her, trying to judge their mood in the dimness.

The sailors parted like the waters of a sea as Captain Mak came through them. "That was you up front calling the surf?"

"Yes, sir," Jules said.

"Smart," Mak said. "I should've thought of that myself. Ladies and Sirs of the *Sun Queen*, I give you our newest proposed crew member, Jeri of Landfall! Give her a hand for getting us out of Jacksport in one piece."

Fists punched Jules in the shoulders, knocking her about, the blows friendly rather than intended to harm. Most of the blows still hurt a little, though.

A cheerful woman at least twice Jules' age put her arm about Jules' shoulders. "That's enough, you louts! You'll get your chances tomorrow!" She led Jules out of the circle of grinning sailors, leaning close to talk in a lower voice. "I'm Liv of Marandur. Ang tells me you're a sister like me."

"Yes."

The woman looked over Jules' hair, which despite the events of the evening still bore the styling expected of an Imperial officer. "Looks like you found a better place in life for a while at least."

"I didn't find it," Jules said, her pride stung. "I fought for it."

The woman grinned. "Well done, sister. Listen up. There'll be an initiation tomorrow. To see how tough you are. Ang and I can't help. You'll have to stand on your own."

"I can do that," Jules said.

"Yeah, I expect you'll do all right. I just wanted you to know why Ang and I will be standing by instead of back to back with you. Get on below, now. Let's get you a hammock. Do you need any other gear?"

"I left my last ship in a rush," Jules admitted. "I couldn't go back to get anything." Not that she'd had that much in the way of personal possessions. But simple things like a spare set of underwear fell under the category of necessities.

"No need for details," Liv advised. "A lot of us left our last place in a rush and would rather not share the reasons." She led the way down a ladder into the below decks, where many of the crew were gathering. As was usual below decks on a ship, the overhead was low enough that tall men and women stooped to ensure their heads didn't make painful contact with wooden beams.

Jules gazed around, surprised. "How large is the crew?"

"Forty-seven in all, now you're here," Liz said.

"That's... very large for a merchant ship this size."

"We sometimes have need of extra crew, isn't that right?" Liz called to the others.

Jules heard the laughter in reply. She knew of only one reason why such a ship would need a crew this large.

She'd fallen in with pirates.

* * *

The night had been an uncomfortable one despite the swaying of her hammock to the roll of the ship. Jules lay awake for a long time, feeling the hammocks strung close to either side of her, other sailors sleeping around her making the sort of noises that she'd learned to ignore while in crowded quarters in the orphan home. She stared up at the rough wood of the overhead, but she didn't see those planks. All she could see before her were the burning eyes of that Mage, fixed on hers, as he pronounced her doom.

A daughter of her line. How weird to think of that. She'd barely begun to consider children some day, and certainly had no idea who she'd want them with. But here it was, a Mage prophecy that said she *would* have them. At least one, anyway. Who would be her partner in that? Someone who was truly a partner, or a man chosen to serve a need and nothing more? Would she ever get so desperate that any man would do?

She thought of Ian. A good man, not much older than she, from a good family close to the Imperial household. About as far as anyone could get from a girl out of one of the legion orphan homes. But he'd made clear that if Jules happened to become interested in him, he'd be interested in her. She'd been sorry at times not to feel more toward Ian, but now counted her luck. That kind of entanglement would have only hurt both of them more when the prophecy was spoken.

Would it have meant that Ian would've been the man who fathered the child who'd continue her line?

Jules frowned, her jumbled thoughts for some reason fastening on that idea. Who would the father be? The prophecy almost made it sound as if that didn't matter. It would be *her* line that produced that daughter. As if something about *her* was special.

Apparently overthrowing the Great Guilds and freeing the world would demand a woman with a sharp temper and more stubbornness than common sense.

What would these sailors around her do if they knew about her and the prophecy? Jules gazed into the darkness, feeling very alone despite being surrounded by others. She'd have to avoid blurting out her secret again. Bad enough that Dara knew.

Ian had been right. She should have killed Dara.

But she couldn't have. Jules knew she couldn't take a life just to keep a secret. Not even this secret.

Pirates killed people. They were criminals, like the gangs Jules had known growing up in Landfall. The children of the orphanages had stood together against those predators. Had Ang and Liv joined such a group? Wouldn't they have warned her?

Jules knew that if she'd judged wrong, if she'd ended up in the hands of a gang such as those that had haunted the dark alleys of Landfall, then she might soon be wishing she'd let the Mages kill her. Such a death might be merciful compared to what such gangs had done to their victims.

Only exhaustion finally allowed her to sleep.

And now, after a short breakfast of boiled potatoes and onions washed down with tepid water from a cask, Jules found herself standing on deck alone. The sky above was bright blue, flecked with high, white clouds, the breezes mild, the swells the ship rode long and gentle. A beautiful morning.

Except that the crew had formed a rough circle about her, smiling with anticipation.

Captain Mak appeared on the edge of the quarterdeck. "We have a new candidate for the crew! Shall we test her?"

The men and women around Jules shouted their approval.

Jules' hand clenched as she fought to avoid drawing her dagger.

The crew moved out of the circle, forming two equal lines that faced each other, leading from the foremast to the quarterdeck. Jules saw sailors massaging their hands to loosen the muscles. Saw marlinspikes and clubs held by others. And knew what she faced.

Mak leaned forward to call to her. "Run it, girl. When you reach the quarterdeck, you'll be crew."

She'd felt the fear of pain and of failure, and of losing all she cared about. Of succeeding, and being told by others that she'd been given a special break, hadn't really earned it. She'd been here. Running gauntlets all of her life between people who thought she wasn't good enough.

Jules walked back to the foremast, turning to face down the gauntlet, seeing everyone grinning in expectation of the fun to come. The cold came into her, the same cold that she'd felt when told her mother had died, the cold that had kept her going after she entered the orphan home.

No one was going to stop her.

She looked up at Mak. "I'll reach the quarterdeck," she yelled back.

Then began walking, not running, down the gauntlet.

After a moment of surprise, those on either side began hitting her. Jules felt herself slammed from side to side by the blows. Most of the sailors weren't easing up at all, striking her hard as she walked.

A fist to her face rocked her head. She shook it and walked on. A slam across her back dropped Jules to her knees. She struggled up and kept walking.

Another blow to her left shoulder knocked Jules into the sailors on the right side of the gauntlet. She shoved off of them, getting back to her feet in time for another hit to hurl her to the left.

She kept walking, trying to keep her eyes on the quarterdeck as her body rocked under repeated blows. The sailors had been cheering when Jules had entered the gauntlet, but had fallen silent as she walked between them and endured hit after hit.

Another strike in the back knocked her down to her hands and knees. Jules, breathing heavily and hurting all over, got one knee up and then the other, managing to get to her feet again. She could taste blood in her mouth, feel blood on her arms and legs where strikes had broken skin. One eye felt swollen, limiting vision that was already bleary.

Almost there. She staggered onward, a final strike knocking her against the ladder leading up to the quarterdeck.

She held on to the ladder, trying not to fall.

"You have to get up the ladder," a familiar voice told her. Liv didn't have to speak loudly to be heard. The crew was watching silently.

Jules pulled herself up the ladder step by step, breathing heavily, leaving bloodstains on the steps. At the top, she couldn't get up to her feet, dropping to her hands and knees again on the quarterdeck.

She could barely make out when Captain Mak knelt beside her, a blurry image to one side. "Are you that crazy, then?" Mak asked.

Jules had to spit a gob of blood and saliva before she could answer. "I don't... give up... I don't... quit."

"You've made that clear." Mak's hand grasped her arm, pulling Jules to her feet. She stood, wavering, hoping that she wouldn't throw up, as the captain yelled to the crew. "Does she pass?"

The crew roared its approval, the men and women who'd just beaten her rushing up the ladder to grab Jules and cheer.

* * *

Jules clenched her teeth in pain as the bucket of sea water splashed across her back and rolled along her arms and legs, salt stinging in the cuts, the cold somehow making the developing bruises feel worse.

"Doesn't look like any broken bones," someone said. "This girl must be made of iron."

She was rolled onto her back, someone's hands going over her limbs with firm and sure movements.

Liv's face came into Jules' view. "This is Keli, our healer. He's not going to feel any parts on you he shouldn't."

Jules nodded slightly, not wanting to move her swollen lip and sore jaw.

Keli was an old man, Jules saw, but his hands were strong and his gaze still keen as he looked closely into Jules' eyes. "No sign of brain trauma. Doesn't look out of her mind, either, though why anyone in a right mind would walk a gauntlet instead of running it I don't know."

"She's a sister," Liv said. "Landfall Legion Orphanage."

"Oh. That makes 'em tough or breaks 'em, doesn't it? Is that where you learned to walk a gauntlet, girl?"

Jules nodded slightly again.

"Did you think the crew'd go easy on you because you were walking?" Keli pressed.

Jules shook her head. "I can... take it," she whispered.

Keli leaned closer to her, speaking slowly and clearly. "You can also get harmed for life, hurt so bad you can't think straight any more or use your legs. You're young, girl, not invincible. That body of yours can take a lot of punishment, but too much and it'll break. Next time *run* the blasted gauntlet."

"She's proven herself," Liv said. "You don't understand, Keli. A girl out of the orphan homes, no matter what she does, there're those who say she only got it because she traded her body for it. I know how Jeri feels. She didn't want anyone to be able to question that she passed that gauntlet test. And no one can question it. She won't have to run another."

"Ha!" Keli stood up, pointing to Jules. "That one? I know the likes of that one. She'll spend her life running gauntlets. Or walking them. Trying to prove she's as good as anyone no matter what it costs. Sometimes folks like that grow into fine people. Usually they end up dead long before their time."

Jules thought about that, about risking death, when the Great Guilds already wanted her dead and the Emperor would want her as his slave. Despite the pain she smiled at the absurdity of it. She saw the others staring at her, but Jules kept smiling.

* * *

It took two days before Keli let her get up. By then her bruises had all blossomed and her joints stiffened, so that every movement brought twinges of pain or worse. Liv and Ang helped Jules up on deck, where the fresh air was a welcome respite from the stuffiness below decks.

She sat on the deck with her back against one bulwark, looking up at the sails. "Tell me the truth," she asked Liv and Ang. "Is this ship a pirate vessel?"

"Depends what you mean by that," Liv said, grinning.

"Do we sometimes relieve other ships of cargo and money?" Ang said. "Yes. Do we smuggle items ashore in the Empire, or out of it, without paying the taxes the Emperor's many hands demand? Yes. But we've got rules."

"Such as?" Jules asked.

"No rape," Liv said. "No murder. If someone fights us, we can do what we need to. But no killing beyond that. No taking from them that are worse off than us."

"We're a free ship," Ang said. "We've all escaped Imperial rules, but that doesn't mean we're lacking rules. That's what they claim, isn't it? Without the rules and laws of the Emperor we'd all run amuck and chaos would rule, right? We want to prove that wrong, that men and women can have the right to make their own decisions and still make good decisions."

It sounded very strange, but Jules nodded, wincing slightly as her neck muscles protested the movement. "I can get behind that. What if I hadn't?"

"After your walking of the gauntlet? We'd put you ashore someplace safe."

"How'd you end up in the orphanage?" Liv asked. "Me, my father died of a fever, and my mother supposedly died in an accident. But I was old enough to know an Imperial official had his eye on her, and she didn't want to play. Maybe it wasn't such an accident. But she was dead and I was alone, so into the orphanage I went."

"My mother died in childbirth," Jules said. She didn't have any trouble talking about it. The orphans had their secrets, but always shared the reasons they'd ended up alone. "I was five years old. All I knew was she went into labor, and the next day they came and told me something had gone wrong and she and the baby had both died. They never even told me if the baby had been a brother or a sister to me. I was handed off to another family in the legion camp because my father was on campaign, but when we heard that he'd died in the Northern Ramparts it was off to the orphan home for me."

Jules paused, remembering. "The funny thing is, my mother and my father died on the same day. I didn't know until we received the news about Father."

"A Mage killed my mother," Ang said. "Mechanics killed my father. I don't know why. Maybe he said the wrong thing when they gave him an order." He gazed at the sails above them. "The Great Guilds made me an orphan. I hate them worse than most people do."

Jules looked up as Captain Mak approached.

He stood, looking down at her as if once more appraising her. "Can you walk, Jeri of Landfall?"

"I can walk," Jules said, but she needed a little help from both Liv and Ang to stand before following the captain into his cabin beneath the quarterdeck.

Mak waved her to one of the chairs at the small table, sitting down in the other and watching her lower herself into the seat with careful movements. "I'm trying to decide if you knew what you were doing," Mak said.

"What do you mean?"

"I mean that walking the gauntlet was the sort of act that gave you status. Do you know that? You're not just a new member of the crew. You're that girl that walked the gauntlet." Mak finished speaking, watching her again in a way that made Jules uncomfortable.

"Is that why you wanted to talk to me?" Jules finally said.

"No." Mak waved off to the south. "Back in Jacksport, something happened. We have a rule, that no one needs tell of why they came this ship. But I've talked to some who were ashore that night. Some just heard rumor of a Mage prophecy as being behind the uproar. But a few heard the words of the prophecy."

He paused again.

Jules tried to shrug as if unconcerned, an effort undone by the muscle aches that caused her to wince with pain. She hoped her that the accelerated beating of her heart wasn't obvious to Mak. "Why… do you mention that?"

Mak leaned forward, his forearms resting on the table between them, his eyes on her. "Because, Jeri of Landfall, what those few heard was that a Mage had looked at a young woman in Imperial uniform and prophesized that her daughter would overthrow the Great Guilds."

"A daughter of her line," Jules said. "Not her daughter. That's what I heard."

"Oh. That's a vast difference, is it?"

"It is," Jules said, feeling the frustration and anger come into her voice. "That means it could be a long time before that happens."

"I see," Mak said. "But that young woman has to live with the burden of it, even though she'll never benefit from it. Is that what you mean?"

"I guess. I mean, yes, sir."

The captain sat back in his chair, his eyes still on her. "I'm thinking that the Mages will kill her if they find her. Do they know who she is?"

"No, sir," Jules said. "I don't think so."

"Both Great Guilds? That daughter of her line will overthrow both? So the Mechanics wouldn't want her to live, either."

"I guess not. I don't know how Mechanics think."

"I'm wondering what sort of woman could have such a daughter," Mak said. "The sort who walked a gauntlet, maybe. The sort who came aboard this ship with an Imperial officer's uniform hidden in a bag."

Jules sighed, meeting his eyes and dropping all pretense. "My life is in your hands, sir."

"Your life?" Mak got up, walking a couple of steps to look out the windows that gave a view over the stern of the ship. "The Great Guilds rule us all. They do what they please, and we have to endure it. They'd pay a lot for that young woman, I'm guessing. But could they pay enough? Because someday a girl born of her line will free the children or grandchildren or great-grands that I and every other common person on Dematr might have. How much would their freedom be worth? You tell me that."

"I can't," Jules said.

"Why didn't you run to the Emperor?"

"I knew what he'd do to me."

Mak snorted. "There are advantages to growing up in a hard place. It wears off illusions and any belief that ideals will protect you from those without ideals. A girl who'd been raised in a happy, whole family might well have trusted in the Emperor."

"I wouldn't know," Jules said, hearing the cold come into her voice.

"I would." Mak kept his eyes out the windows as he spoke. "My daughter was taken from me by the Mechanics when she was ten years old. They said she had the inherent skills they needed. The Emperor I'd trusted to protect me and my family did nothing. My wife fell ill after. The healers said it was a sickness the devices of the Mechanics might be able to heal, so I wrote to my daughter and begged her help. I never heard a word back from her. And my wife died. Of a broken heart at losing her daughter as much as any other ill, I've always believed. And then, with my wife dead and me as good as dead to the girl who'd been our daughter, I knew I'd been lied to, and I went West."

Jules watched him, hearing the old pain in his voice. "I'm sorry."

Mak shook his head. "Sorry doesn't bring back what's lost."

"What are you going to do, sir?" Jules asked.

"About what?"

"About me."

He looked at her again. "I don't remember anything special about you, Jeri of Landfall. Nothing at all. You're just another member of the crew. Right?"

"Yes, sir," Jules said.

"I don't know what course you'll have to steer. You're sailing a path no one else knows. But you have nothing to fear from me." Mak jerked his head to indicate outside. "There are some in the crew, men, who might try to force their way into that prophecy, if you know what I mean."

"Yes," Jules said. "The same sort of thing the Emperor would do, but without any façade of legality."

"Just so. The rest of the crew would see them hanging from a yard-arm afterwards, but that might be scant comfort to you. And there are some women in the crew who might see the profit that betrayal would bring. Keep it close for now. Once you're really part of us, after you've been aboard a while, the odds that anyone would cause you harm will be much less. And I've already mentioned in passing to everyone that you came aboard early enough that you couldn't be that woman the Mage saw."

Jules got to her feet despite the pain that caused. "Thank you, Captain Mak."

"I've done nothing as far as anyone but us two is concerned. To others I just wanted to see if you're all right," Mak said. "Healer Keli says you're doing fine."

"Healer Keli knows what he's doing, but I'm not sure 'fine' is the right word for how I'm feeling at the moment."

Mak grinned. "Tell Keli to give you a shot of rum at bedtime for the next few days. That'll help a little."

"Thank you, sir." Jules headed for the door but paused when Mak spoke again.

"Jeri."

"Yes?"

"Live, girl. Have your children. For all of us."

"I'll try," Jules said, for some reason not wanting to disappoint this man.

* * *

Within another day Jules was working alongside the rest of the crew, still hurting with almost every movement but knowing she had to keep stretching and using the muscles or they'd stiffen on her.

With the winds coming out of the uncharted west, the *Sun Queen* sailed north on a beam reach that was nearly at right angles to the wind. Without the need to tack against the wind, the crew only had to adjust the angle of the yardarms occasionally to best catch the wind as it shifted about.

Captain Mak had called the crew together, putting down on the deck between the foremast and the mainmast a map that was partly a chart in the eastern portions and mostly guesswork in the west. A cutlass held down the head of the chart and a pair of wooden marlin-spikes weighed down the bottom corners. As everyone watched and listened, Mak pointed to the chart. "We're heading up toward the north shore of the Sea of Bakre because there's word of another settlement along the coast that could use the cargo we're carrying. The people I talked to in Jacksport say a woman named Kelsi is running the place."

"Kelsi of Sandurin?" Ang asked.

"Maybe. You know of her?"

"Met someone who sailed with her. Mostly smuggling runs." Ang thought as he balanced on the shrouds to look down on the map. "Sharp captain, he said. Not someone you'd want to cross."

"But a fair dealer?" Mak said.

"Yes, Cap'n. As far as I heard."

"Good enough." Mak pointed to the western part of the Sea of Bakre. "There's a chance we'll encounter a ship going to or coming from Altis when we cross the waters between there and Sandurin. If it looks like a decent prize, we'll get close enough to judge if we want to take it."

"Altis is way out there? How'd a city get so far west?" another sailor asked.

"Don't ask that of me," Mak said. "I've no knowledge of it."

Keli spoke up. "Altis has always been there. It's as old as Landfall."

"But the Emperor hasn't taken over Altis," Mak said. "Which means the Great Guilds have told him hands off. It also means we check out any ship from Altis closely to make sure there're no Mechanics or Mages aboard before we capture it. We don't need the Great Guilds putting us on their agendas. Any more discussion? No? Ang, call the vote."

"All in favor of the course of action proposed, raise your hand and say aye," Ang shouted.

Jules, watching and listening in amazement, raised hers along with everyone else. "Aye."

"The course of action is approved by vote of the crew," Ang told Mak.

"Thank you," Mak said, rolling up the chart/map.

Baffled, Jules watched the captain walk back to his cabin. "We all had a voice in that? The captain really can't do whatever he wants just because he's in charge?"

"That's right," Liv said, smiling as if amused by her confusion. "We all get to say whether we support his plan or not."

"But, that's... what is that?"

Ang laughed. "It's nothing you'll see on Imperial soil, where those in charge don't have to worry about what those under them think. People who've escaped the empire... and we've all done that, haven't we? They always have trouble believing it."

"What happens if we see a ship?" she asked Ang and Liv. "Do we vote again on whether to attack?"

"No," Liv said. "We've approved the captain's plan, so he's responsible for making it work. If we see a ship, he'll make the call on whether to attack it."

"So sometimes he's the captain, and sometimes he needs to ask the crew if he can do something?"

"Pretty much," Ang said.

"That seems a little bizarre," Jules said.

"Nah, not really. We want to control what happens to us, so we get to vote on the big plan. But we know someone has to be in charge when things are happening, so we let the cap'n have that authority. It's, uh, what do they call that, Liv?"

"A compromise," Liv said. "Sometimes compromises make sense."

Jules leaned back against the lower shrouds, looking out at the restless waters. "Sometimes they don't, though."

"Right. Sometimes they don't. Hey, if we might face some trouble, you need to practice with a cutlass. You ever used one?"

"Not really," Jules admitted. "I do know a straight sword."

"Forget all that, sister," Ang said. "Straight sword is like that dueling stuff. Fancy games. Cutlass work is different."

Jules soon learned what he meant. Unlike the nicely balanced straight swords she'd learned to use during Imperial officer training, the cutlasses had shorter but heavier blades. Holding it straight out, the blade pulled at her wrist, the tip dipping. And precise moves suited to a well-balanced sword either didn't move the clumsy cutlass enough or resulted in over-corrections as the weight of the cutlass blade threw off her movements.

"Hack and slash," Liv said. "This isn't a dance. Keep your feet grounded, put your strength into the blow, let the weight of the blade knock aside your opponent's defense, and bury it in their head or neck or arm or whatever. Try not to get it stuck, though. You get your cutlass lodged in someone's bone and it'll get yanked from your hand when they fall, leaving you with empty hands facing their friends."

But there was still skill involved, Jules discovered. Just like normal sword work, anticipating your opponent's moves let you counter them, and a well-timed, strong parry would knock aside your foe's blade and leave them open to your attack. She'd always been good at that, reading her opponent's intentions and figuring out how to negate their strengths while optimizing her own attacks. "You have to get inside their heads," she explained to Liv after surprising her with a blow that could have been deadly if Jules hadn't pulled it at the last moment. "I can do that."

"How?" Liv asked, massaging her shoulder where the flat side of Jules' blade had hit.

"I don't know. I learned it at the home, to defend myself. I just look at their eyes and watch them move, and after a little while I can tell what they'll do."

Captain Mak spoke from behind her, startling Jules. "Can you do that with a ship?"

"Do what?" Jules asked, turning to look at him, letting her cutlass drop to point at the deck.

"Watch another ship maneuvering, and anticipate his next move."

Jules hesitated, thinking. "I don't know, sir," she finally said.

"Find out," Mak told her. "Ang, next time we're around any other ships, keep Jeri off the sails and the lines. I want her watching those other ships and seeing if she can tell what they'll do next."

"All right, Cap'n," Ang said. "That'd come in handy, wouldn't it?"

"It would," Mak said.

"I can't see the eyes of whoever is commanding another ship," Jules protested.

"Maybe you can get inside their head anyway," Mak said. "You can sense wind and wave, right? Any good sailor can. Could knowing those be like seeing the eyes of that other captain?"

"It might," Jules said. "I'll try."

"Sail to port! Four points off the bow!" the lockout called down.

"Destiny has sent us a chance to find out," Mak said. "Follow me up, Jeri."

She scrambled up the shrouds behind Mak as he climbed to the maintop where the lookout stood pointing to port. When she reached the top, Jules held on tightly to the nearest stay, only one foot on the small top platform that was already crowded by Mak and the lookout, her other foot hanging out over the deck more than a dozen lances below them.

Mak squinted to port, where Jules could see the barely visible vertical lines that marked the tops of two masts. "I wish we could get our hands on a Mechanic far-seer," he commented.

"A far-seer?" Jules asked.

"I saw one once. Didn't get to look through it," Mak added, shading his eyes with one broad, flat palm. "Supposedly they make distant things look close. Some Mechanic trick. What do you think, Jeri? How's that other moving?"

Jules squinted as well, trying to get a feeling for the movement of the other ship relative to the *Sun Queen*, a task complicated by the swaying and rocking of the *Queen* that was exaggerated by her position near the top of the mainmast. "On this course we're going to pass behind them," she finally said.

"I think so, too," Mak said. "What's your recommendation?"

Jules spent a few more moments watching those distant masts, judging their movement. "I think we should come two points to starboard to meet them up ahead."

Mak nodded. "What if you're wrong? What if we cross their course ahead of them?"

"If we're ahead of them?" Jules looked again. The *Sun Queen* was still headed nearly north. The other ship, which must be coming from Altis, was traveling east, running with the wind. "We'd have to back down. Or come about a full circle. Or furl some sails to lose speed and drop us back to a slower meet-up with him."

"Yeah. And those are all bad ideas, to lose speed when you're trying to close on another ship. If we did any of those things and he maintained his own speed, he could maneuver around us while we're wallowing."

"I see." This was just like training in the Imperial fleet, though without the scorn that normally accompanied pointing out mistakes. "We want to be sure we close on them from their beam or just aft. How fast is this ship?"

Mak and the lookout grinned. "She's fast," Mak said. "We'll aim for the beam of that one. A point and half to starboard of our current course?"

"Yes, sir, I think so."

Mak yelled the course change down to the quarterdeck. By the time Jules had followed him back down to the deck the *Sun Queen* was already on the new course, breasting the swells as if eager to catch her quarry. "We'll see what he's like!" Mak called out to the rest of the crew. "And if he seems overly burdened with valuable cargo, we'll be good citizens and relieve him of some of the weight!"

As the crew laughed, Mak turned to Jules. "Jeri, you don't need to call me sir. This is a free ship."

"I'd feel weird *not* calling the captain sir," Jules said.

"Suit yourself," Mak said, walking aft to the quarterdeck.

"How does he find time to train everyone like that?" Jules asked Liv, who was leaning against the mainmast.

Liv laughed. "He doesn't. *You're* getting that attention."

"I am?" Jules looked toward Mak again, a heavy feeling in her gut. "He's…interested in me?"

"Not that way," Liv assured her. "Mak's a forthright type. I'm sure if he wanted to be your man, he'd say so upfront and let the dice fall as they may. I haven't seen him acting that way around you, sister. No, he's seen some talent in you and he's trying to find out what you're good at and how much better you can get. That's part of how he got elected captain, by paying attention to people and figuring out who was good at what, and who could be good at something with a little work. That's a skill a captain needs."

"That's true," Jules said, relieved. "You're sure Mak isn't giving me special attention?"

Healer Keli answered her as he walked past the mast. "Captain Mak lost his wife before he came west. He says she was the only one for him. When it comes to the heart, I've never seen him look at another woman."

"Some men are like that," Liv said. "I hope I find one before I'm too old."

"I'm always there for you," Keli said.

"I know what you want, and it's not a wife! Get away from me, ya shark!"

"Jeri!" Mak called from the quarterdeck. "Get back up to the top and help keep an eye on that ship!"

Even though the second climb tested her still-sore body, Jules went up as fast as she could until she stood once more next to the sailor on lookout. Ferd, who'd already been sitting up this high most of the morning, gave her a nod. "He's keeping to course, I think."

Jules squinted at the masts again. "Yeah, I think so."

"Jeri, mind if I ask a personal one?"

"Depends what it is."

"Why'd you walk the gauntlet? I mean, you impressed us all. But I don't think that's why you did it. I saw your face when you walked it and it seemed you was doing it for you, not for anything to do with us."

Jules shrugged, a gesture that almost didn't hurt by now. "Truth is, I was trying to be sure I earned what I got. I mean, if I was to be accepted as one of the crew, I didn't want anyone questioning that I'd earned that."

"Why didya think anyone'd question you?" Ferd asked. "You're not some lazy lout."

She glanced at him, judging the older man's face and sincerity. "Because I came out of a legion orphan home. Hadn't you heard?"

"Yeah. So?" He must have seen her puzzlement. "I'm not what they call socially aware. Or so I've been told. I don't get things, you know? I guess other folks know something about them orphan homes that I don't?"

"They think they know something," Jules said. If Ferd was lying, he was better at it than anyone else she'd ever met, so she decided to be candid with him. "It's what other people think of us who came out of the orphanages. The boys are all thieves and predators, you see, and the girls like me are all sluts and predators. Just about all of us go into the legions or the Emperor's fleet because no one else will take us."

Ferd's already wrinkled forehead creased further in a frown. "Ang and Liv are out of those places, too, I heard. There's nothing wrong with you three."

"Thanks," Jules said. "But you're judging us as *who* we are, instead of because of *what* we are."

"Oh, I get it. Well, Jeri, ain't no one on this ship doubts you earned being a member of the crew. Blazes, if I was half my age I'd be hitting on you, I would! But you've nothing to fear from me these days. A girl like you doesn't need an old wreck like me."

Jules gave him another glance, this time accompanied by a smile. "I'm sure there are plenty of women nearer your age who'd like you."

"Point them out if you see them!" Ferd gazed out to sea, wistful. "I expect in a few more years when I get too old for a ship I'll find a place ashore with some girl from the bars who's also too old for her trade. We can keep each other company once no one else wants us."

"It wouldn't bother you to be with a woman who'd worked the streets her whole life?" Jules asked.

"Why would it? She wouldn't have had a trade like that if not for men like me. And I'm no pure flower, Jeri. I've done my share of wrong, I have. You stay away from men like me, you hear me? We're no good. Not until we're too old to be bad."

"I'll remember that," Jules said, her eyes once more on those distant masts, which showed a little higher above the horizon as the two ships slowly drew closer to each other. "You don't seem so bad to me."

"I won't talk of things that would make you think different. Jeri, some ships are bad, full of people you couldn't trust at your back. But the *Queen* is a good ship. We keep it that way. Just a few days before you came aboard we let a fella off the ship who'd been thieving from his shipmates. Caught him after he tried forcing himself on one of the girls, who broke his nose."

Jules gave him another quick look. "He attacked one of the women, you caught him stealing from other crew members, and all you did was let him off at Jacksport?"

Ferd grinned. "We was a coupla days short of Jacksport when we let him off. Gave him a short walk off the side and a long drop to the water."

"You killed him?"

"Could've killed him. Gave him a chance, though. Small chance, with no land in sight, but better than someone who betrays their own shipmates deserves." Ferd's voice went pensive. "The one who broke his nose didn't want him put off, said she'd already given him his due by that, but the thieving sealed his fate. Women are like that, aren't they? They might be as forgiving as a gentle rain, or as vengeful as the stormiest sea. A wise man doesn't risk finding out which he'll face."

Jules laughed. "Is that what women are like?"

"Yes! You, too! We've all seen it. Fella said to me, anyone who crosses that girl better be ready to pay the price. She'll rip out their heart and eat it while they watch, she will."

"That's what people think?" Jules asked, surprised.

"That's what we see," Ferd said.

She didn't reply, squinting again as the distant masts moved, seeming to come closer together. "He's turning."

Ferd shaded his eyes, studying what could be seen. "Yeah. Turning away, I think."

"Yes," Jules agreed.

"Fool. If he'd put on more sail he could have run with the wind and might've outpaced us. But he's hoping we haven't seen him yet and is trying to open the distance enough to lose us. Heading north will bring him up against the coast before long. We'll have him."

"Why would he run when he had no idea who we were?" Jules asked.

"Must have something good aboard him!" Ferd said, grinning. "And that'd mean some guards, too. Maybe former legionaries hiring themselves out. You ready for a fight, girl?"

"Yeah," Jules said. She kept her eyes on those distant masts as Ferd called down to the quarterdeck about their quarry's change of course.

CHAPTER THREE

Jules stood by the bow rail of the *Sun Queen*, cutlass by her side. Other crewmembers stood nearby, some with cutlasses and a few with crossbows, though most were crouched down so they couldn't be seen from another ship and all kept their weapons out of sight below the rail. The easterly wind coming from nearly dead astern tossed her hair lightly. Occasionally the bow broke through a swell in a welter of foam that tossed spray high enough to wet Jules' lips with the taste of salt.

After a long day's chase, Ferd's prediction had proven true. They'd caught up with the other ship as it reached the northern coast of the Sea of Bakre and been forced to turn east again. Both ships had every sail set, catching all the wind they could, but the *Sun Queen* had better legs and drew steadily closer to her prey.

Behind them to the west, the sun was close to setting, casting a long, long shadow of the *Queen* and her masts and sails ahead of the ship. The top of that shadow was nearly even with the other ship.

"Why are we still hiding most of the crew and our weapons?" Jules asked Ang. "It's obvious that we're chasing them and they're running from us."

"Got to play the game right," Ang said. "We don't want them getting so worried they do something crazy, like run their ship ashore to avoid us. We want to let them think that even if we catch up they'll still be able to beat us." He pointed upward. "He's flying the flag of a rich merchant from Sandurin, so we know he'll have some choice cargo aboard. Of course, that also means the crew is likely to put up a fight."

She gazed ahead at the deck of the other ship, at the men and women gathered there, swords and crossbows openly displayed in warning.

There had been brief moments in the last few days when thoughts of the prophecy had been momentarily forgotten. Very brief moments. But as Jules looked at those armed defenders, she wondered again about it.

Could she die? If the prophecy *would* come true, didn't that mean she was fated not to die before she had at least one child? Or were Mage prophecies things that might happen, but could be changed by accidents of fate? It wasn't like she could ask a Mage. No one else could, either. Only Mages knew. Jules felt certain that no matter what Mages believed of their prophecies, they'd do their best to change this one. People were like that, fighting even the seemingly inevitable. And Jules had looked into the eyes of a Mage and seen the person that Mage tried to hide. Despite what she'd heard, Mages could still feel, were still human. They just kept it hidden, perhaps even from themselves.

The *Queen* rode up a swell and down the other side, her bow digging into the trough and flinging up spray as her bowsprit came even with the stern of the other ship. The two ships were now perhaps five lances apart, the narrow strip of water between them churning.

Captain Mak called from the quarterdeck, cupping his hands about his mouth to project his voice. "Ahoy the other ship! Drop your sails and let us aboard and none will be harmed! You have my word on it!"

The shouted reply came back, faint against the wind and the sound of the water rushing past two hulls. "If you come aboard you will be harmed! You have my word on that! Break off!"

"Stand up, sirs and ladies," Mak told the crew. "Let them see the odds now that we're too close for them to get away."

The rest of the crew stood, crowding the rail, brandishing their weapons. The two ships were close enough that Jules could see the expressions of the defenders of the other ship, seeing the resolve in them as well as the uncertainty.

The *Sun Queen*'s bow had reached the midships of the other vessel as they overtook it. Jules judged the movement of the two ships, thinking that Mak would wait until the bow was a bit ahead of the other ship's bow before swinging the two ships together.

"Surrender and none will be harmed!" Mak shouted again.

"Go to blazes!" the shout came back.

Jules grabbed the rail as the bow of the other ship suddenly swung to starboard, angling to collide with the *Queen*.

"They mean to ram!" Ang shouted. "Hang on and get the grapnels across!"

Both ships shook as the bow of the other slammed into the side of the *Sun Queen*, the wood of their hulls groaning, the bowsprit of the other ship stabbing over the rail of the *Queen*, one of the other ship's stays close enough to Jules for her to grab.

She did, reaching up and seizing the stay, feeling herself lifted off the deck of the *Sun Queen* as the other ship's bow rocked a little higher, hearing the *spang* of crossbows firing on both ships, the thud of a bolt hitting the foremast behind her, seeing lines being hurled across the gap between the ships, metal hooks on their ends latching onto the rails of the *Queen*'s prey.

Jules pulled herself the rest of the way onto the other ship's bowsprit, drawing her cutlass as she balanced and ran forward. She hoped other members of the crew were following her, and more attacking over the side, but couldn't pause to look around. Noise filled her world, men and women yelling and screaming, wood screeching and cracking, another crossbow firing somewhere close ahead.

A figure appeared on the deck at the end of the bowsprit, racing to intercept Jules, cutlass raised. Knowing that she couldn't fight well while balanced on the bowsprit, Jules kept running, jumping forward and down, taking the blow of the defender's sword on her own cutlass, the force of her leap driving them together so that for a moment their chests almost touched, the two swords pinned between them.

They both shoved, breaking contact, Jules flinching as her back hit the railing of the other ship. She got her cutlass up in time to parry a swing at her, following up by leaning into her momentarily unguarded opponent, punching the guard of her cutlass into his jaw, hearing the sickening crunch of his jaw bone breaking, seeing him falling, ducking as movement out of the corner of her eye warned of another blade coming at her, stumbling, frantically parrying again as the new foe attacked, falling back against the rail once more, another parry, the woman fighting her reversing her blade to cut at Jules' side.

Knowing she couldn't manage another parry, Jules dove sideways, the other's blade slicing through the side of her loose shirt in a moment of heart-stopping fear. She rolled, getting back to her feet just as the other swung again. Jules caught the blow on her cutlass, the two of them swaying for a moment, swords locked together, each straining to overpower the other.

Ang came off the bowsprit in a rush, hitting Jules' opponent and knocking her to the deck. Jules stared about, frantically searching for more threats, but the deck of the other ship seemed filled with men and women she recognized from the *Sun Queen* and the noise of swords clashing was rapidly subsiding.

"Yield!" Mak called again.

The enraged voice of the other ship's captain called back. "All right! We yield! You promised no killing!"

A hand grasped her shoulder. Jules spun around, starting to raise her sword, seeing Ang glaring at her. "Are you trying to get yourself killed?" he demanded.

"What? I had a way to board them. I thought everyone else would follow."

"Yeah, we followed you," Ang said, his glare turning into a reluctant smile. "Good job, sister. They weren't ready for someone coming over their bow. It threw off their entire defense. But you're lucky you weren't killed before more of us could get aboard."

Jules saw a man still lying on the deck, Healer Keli working on his face, and recognized the man she'd struck down. She knelt by him. "Is he going to be all right?" Jules asked Keli.

Keli nodded his head in reply, keeping his eyes on his work. "He'll be drinking his meals for a while, but it should heal all right."

A rough grip on her shoulder shoved Jules back and away from the man, so that she sprawled in a sitting position, staring up in surprise at the woman she'd clashed swords with.

"Get away from him!" the woman snarled.

"I just wanted to see if he'd be all right," Jules said, momentarily bewildered.

"I've seen those kind of fighting moves before and I know where you learned them!" the other woman said, her face an angry mask. "Legion stray! Have you already worked your way through all the men on that ship so you're trying to get a taste of someone new?"

Jules felt a restraining hand on her arm and only then realized that she was on her feet again, her cutlass blade raised toward the woman.

"Get her out of here!" Liv yelled, relaxing her grip on Jules' arm. Several men from the *Queen* moved forward, shoving the woman roughly back into the group of sullen defenders. "Sorry," Liv muttered to Jules. "Other women are the worst. Most men'll hesitate to say it to your face, but other women will just come out with it."

Jules tried to get her racing heart and her anger under control. "If she says that to me again I'll hurt her," she said, hearing the rage in her voice.

"You'll have to wait in line," Ang assured her. "Why don't you get back to the *Queen*?"

"No! I can handle this." Jules glared at the group of prisoners. "I can handle anything." For a brief moment she felt like shouting at them, telling them what she knew. *A daughter of my line will overthrow the Great Guilds! My line! None of you think I'm good enough because I grew up in a legion orphan home but it's my blood that will free this world some day!*

But that would be a crazy thing to do.

Jules turned away from the prisoners, looking at Mak as he called out orders to some of his crew to search the ship. "Find out what they've got. Look for hidden compartments. You know the game." Focusing on Jules, he waved her over. "Jeri, you probably saved us a few nasty injuries by coming over their bow like that. You'll get an extra share for it."

The nearest sailors from the *Sun Queen* made noises of approval, shoving Jules to show their agreement with Mak.

Feeling oddly tired, Jules went to the rail, looking across at the *Sun Queen*. The two ships were drifting, locked together by numerous lines, the winds still bearing both east. She was startled to realize that the last portion of the sun's disc was still barely visible above the horizon, its red rays painting the sails above her in the color of blood.

She would have killed that woman, Jules realized. Killed her before she'd even realized she was doing it. Where had that come from? Anger at insults because of her background was a familiar presence, but she'd long since learned to let such words roll off of her back. This time, though, the contemptuous words had pierced her as easily as if they'd been the blade of that woman's cutlass.

Jules looked about her, seeing mostly crew from the *Queen*. Men and women who had accepted her as she was, who hadn't cared about her past. It had been very easy to grow used to that in just a short time, to let her defenses down so that verbal blows could get through.

But there was something else different, too. Something inside her, Jules realized. The prophecy had changed how she saw herself. Had made it harder for her to ignore insults and slurs. Because now she knew she was more than could be seen by those who looked down on her.

She knew that, didn't she?

Or was she worried that the prophecy had confirmed that she as a person didn't matter and every effort she put into making more of herself didn't matter? That it was only her ability to found a blood line, to have one or more children, that made her matter? Did her anger grow from new confidence in who she was, or fear that the prophecy had declared that who she was meant nothing?

She searched her inner feelings and couldn't find any clear answers.

Was that an answer in itself? That she couldn't tell? Because how could greater confidence in who she was make her more easily stung by insults?

Lanterns were being lit and hung from yardarms to illuminate the deck. Jules tried to find something to do, something to distract her from her thoughts.

"Hey, Jeri, help us search!"

She joined that small group gratefully. One of them.

Down below decks it was even darker, the lanterns two of the group carried not offering enough light. The leader of Jules' group, a man named Gord, paused when they reached a stout door with a heavy iron lock on it. "This looks interesting. I've got the keys from the captain of this ship. Let's see if one fits."

One key did, the lock opening so they could pull it off the hasp and push open the door, lanterns raised to see inside the closet-sized strong room.

A man wearing a shirt, pants, and boots sat on the floor, blinking in the light from the lanterns. The room was otherwise empty but for a bucket serving as a chamber pot. He had the unshaven look of a man denied access to a blade for at least a week, and the rumpled, worn appearance of someone confined in a small space for the same period of time. But even in the uncertain light of the lanterns the quality of the clothing was easy to see. His shirt was fine linen, not rough wool, his pants tough but well made, and his boots new enough to have few signs of use.

"A prisoner," Gord said. "And not a member of the crew, from the clothing you wear. Who are you?"

The man squinted at them, apparently unimpressed by what he saw. "None of your business."

"Oh? And why are you locked up here? Is that our business?"

The prisoner smiled slightly. "I talk too much. That's my crime."

"Jeri," Gord said. "Go up to Mak and see if the captain of this ship can tell us anything about this guy."

Jules ran up the ladder to the main deck, pausing only to glower menacingly toward the other prisoners before finding Mak.

"A prisoner down below?" Mak turned to the captain. "Who is he?"

"I don't know," the other said. "I got paid good money to take him to Sandurin, no questions asked."

"Who's supposed to collect him in Sandurin?"

The other captain hesitated before answering.

"Let's not make this too hard," Mak added.

"Mechanics," the other captain admitted. "That's all I know."

Ang had been listening. "Maybe the Mechanics would pay us to get that guy back. Or maybe he's an enemy of the Mechanics who we should free."

"I think he is a Mechanic," Jules said, realizing something. "He's not wearing the jacket, but he's got that attitude. Even as a prisoner."

"If he is," Ang said, "we should tie something heavy around his neck and toss him into the sea."

"We might do that," Mak said. "After we find out how much he might be worth to us."

"You don't want to risk being targeted by the Great Guilds," the other captain warned.

Jules started laughing. The man stared at her, but she couldn't stop. "No," Jules said sarcastically. "That'd be awful, to have the Great Guilds after you!" She headed back below deck, still laughing, hoping it didn't sound like the mirth of a crazy woman. Because her dilemma wasn't exactly a laughing matter. But maybe laughing was a better outlet for the stress inside her than screaming, which she had felt like doing when the full weight of the prophecy came to rest on her mind.

"Mak wants him on deck," Jules said when she reached the others again. "He's someone the Mechanics wanted delivered to Sandurin." She watched the prisoner get up and walk to the door to the strong room, seeing enough of a familiar swagger to confirm her suspicions. "Yeah. He's a Mechanic, too."

The attitudes of her fellow sailors toward the captive immediately shifted from wary helpfulness to shoving-along hostility. Jules felt a small twinge of guilt as Gord delivered an especially hard push, but only a small twinge. She'd been shoved aside enough times by Mechanics to have no sympathy for them.

On deck, Mak was examining a small chest whose contents glittered in the lantern light. "Gems and crystals from mines near Altis," he announced. "We'll also take four barrels of the smoked fish. And your prisoner, and half the contents of your money chest. You can keep the rest."

The captain of the captured ship glowered at Mak. "How generous."

"Be glad you got to keep the ship," Mak said. "Say hello to the Emperor for us. And your Mechanic friends, too. Let them know we'll be contacting them about our prize."

"Which ship should I tell them to look for?" the other captain asked.

Mak grinned. "Do you really think I'm that stupid? If they ask, tell them it was the ship *Mara's Mirror* that took your prisoner."

Nearby sailors who'd overheard the conversation laughed. The mirror of Mara was a legend in the Empire, something with supposed magical powers that no one had ever been able to find.

Tackle was quickly rigged from a yardarm to lift and swing the barrels of smoked fish over to the *Queen*. Jules, who'd already grown a little weary of potatoes, onions, and salt pork, expected that she'd soon be even more tired of smoked fish. As she prepared to climb over the rails to return to the *Sun Queen*, she hesitated, thinking she ought to go back and punch out that woman.

But Liv put a firm hand on her arm again, urging her to the *Sun Queen*. "I know what you want to do, because I've wanted to do it. You'd feel better for a very short time afterwards," Liv warned, "and then you'd hate yourself for a long time. There's no satisfaction to be found in hurting those who can't defend themselves."

"What if I gave her back her sword and then punched her out?" Jules asked.

"You're serious, aren't you?" Liv shook her head. "They've surrendered. The *Sun Queen* and her crew would look bad if you did that, provoking another fight just so you could beat up someone."

"But—"

"Captain Mak would also look bad."

"Oh. I wouldn't want that. Thanks for the good advice, sister," Jules said, climbing over the rail and back onto the deck of the *Sun Queen*.

The lines were let go and the ships veered apart. Jules stood watching the lanterns hung on the other ship dwindle like a receding flock of fireflies.

"Congratulations," Ang said, handing her something.

Jules looked down at it. "A sailor's knife?"

"It's traditional, after your first act of piracy," he explained. Ang turned, watching the Mechanic prisoner be hustled below. "I'd still like to tie a large stone to him and toss him over the side."

"If it was a small stone," Liv said, "he might struggle for a while before he sank."

Ang's face lit. "Good idea."

"I wonder what he did to cause his fellow Mechanics to arrest him?" Liv said. "He's not saying. Hey. Got another idea."

"Stand by for trouble," Ang murmured.

"This is another good idea. That guy's not talking. The captain gave orders to take him down to the safe hold," Liv said. "He'll be chained to the bulkhead down there. But we can assign a guard."

"A guard?"

"Yeah. A guard that a guy like that might talk to." Liv looked at Jules. "What do you say, Jeri? Want to see if he'll spill his guts to impress a young lady?"

"Me?" Jules asked. "You think he'd talk to me?"

Ang nodded, eyeing Jules. "Yeah. Good one, Liv. He'll want to impress you, Jeri. You're the right age and everything for him to want to make you think he's everything wonderful with a big hunk of chocolate on top. Want to try?"

"Guys can be stupid," Jules said. "I know. Especially if encouraged. But he's a Mechanic."

"Yeah. A male Mechanic. It'd be a service to the ship if you tried."

* * *

Which was how Jules found herself with a cutlass once again in hand, sitting across the safe hold from the prisoner, who was now chained to the opposite bulkhead, a little more than a lance from her. The chains wouldn't let the Mechanic move more than half a lance, so she was perfectly safe, but Jules kept the cutlass on her lap anyway.

The prisoner sat, pretending not to look at her. He said nothing, the only sounds the creaking of wood, , the faint murmur of water alongside the hull, and occasional sounds of feet overhead or voices raised in loud banter.

She'd been encouraged to strike up a conversation, but while Jules had spoken to many boys and men in her life, they'd all been commons. She had no idea what to talk to a Mechanic about. And it was hot down here in the unventilated space, making the environment both emotionally and physically uncomfortable. Finally Jules unbuttoned the top two buttons of her shirt, spreading the opening a bit to get some relief from the heat.

The Mechanic looked over at her, his gaze obviously directed below her face.

Oh, blazes. In that much at least Mechanic males were the same as other men.

"At least they gave me a guard who's pleasant to look at," the Mechanic said.

"Um… thank you," Jules said, instead of how she'd usually reply to something like that. She forced herself to say more. "I'm… Jeri. Of Landfall."

"Sir Mechanic Karl of Altis," the Mechanic said. "You can call me Karl," he added, smiling at her upper chest.

Oh blazes, oh blazes. She was going to kill Liv for suggesting this. "Hi... Karl."

"I suppose that you know you're very attractive."

"I know that guys usually tell me that when they're drunk," Jules said. She sought for something else to talk about. In her experience, asking a man to talk about himself usually got results. "How did a Mechanic end up a prisoner?"

"That's not important," Karl said, looking away.

"It's not? Because...I think it's interesting."

"Is it?" He looked back at her, flashing another smile. "I told you earlier. I talk too much. I talked about what I thought were flaws in the way the Mechanics Guild did things. I talked about how things should be done differently. I said these things to friends." The smile turned hard. "One of them wasn't. I got turned in, and arrested for disloyalty to the Guild."

That did sound interesting. Jules tried to look intrigued. "Things? What things?"

"I shouldn't talk about it," Karl said, waving off the question, the chain on that arm clanking. "And it's probably a bit beyond your grasp."

She managed not to glare at him. Jules tried changing her expression to fascination. "Why? I'd... really... like for you to... explain it to me."

Karl's eyes rose from her chest and he gave her an appraising look, followed by a bigger smile as he apparently reached a decision. "All right. I think the Guild is making a mistake allowing commons to set up new cities outside the already-settled areas. Some Mechanics think it's a good idea to establish new centers of power that we can play against the Empire to keep it in check. I think we just need to apply the old tried-and-true approaches that have kept the Emperor answering the Guild's orders. There's too much change going on, and no one can predict how that might shake out."

Jules nodded, trying to keep her exaggerated look of fascination going. "You seem to understand things better than the others."

"That's very sharp of you to see that," Karl said. "Some Mechanics say we should permit the new cities because the Mages are moving into them, and we can't have another… I mean, open conflict with the Mages wouldn't serve our interests. But the Mages shouldn't be allowed to act as if they're our equals. Did you know the commons call the Mechanics Guild and the Mage Guild the Great Guilds, as if we were on the same level?"

"I have heard that," Jules said.

"Oh, right. You're a common. But an uncommonly smart one!" Karl added, looking pleased with his own wordplay.

Feeling a bit like a pony being praised for carrying out a new trick, Jules smiled again. "So the Mechanics Guild actually arrests someone as… aware of things as you are? Just because you have better ideas?"

"Politics," Karl said. "I'm not as good at that as others, I guess. I really shouldn't say any more. About anything." He smiled at her again, this time the intent behind the smile clear as his gaze once more lingered below Jules' collarbone where the top two buttons of her shirt were open. "There is something I'm told I am pretty good at. If you'd like, we could try that to pass the time."

Could he really be suggesting that? Why would he think she'd be interested in such a come on? Rage threatened as memories of the woman on the captured ship rose to the fore, but Jules controlled it. This Mechanic didn't know she'd come out of one of the orphan homes. Maybe Mechanics didn't even know that girls from the orphan homes were looked down on as sluts by Imperial society. Apparently he tried this sort of thing on all women who were commons. Would he even know if she made fun of him?

Jules gave the Mechanic an innocent look. "You mean play cards? Dice?"

"No," Karl said, smiling indulgently. "This is your chance."

"My chance?"

"To experience the love of a Mechanic. Most common girls would do anything for the opportunity."

"They would?" Jules smiled as well. "Why?"

"Why?" Karl seemed puzzled by the question. "It's an honor, of course."

"An honor, for me?"

"That's right. And you might have a child from it, who could inherit the Mechanic skills. A child of yours might be a Mechanic!"

"How wonderful," Jules said, unable to keep her voice from becoming as flat as the land around Umburan.

"That doesn't excite you?" Karl asked.

"No."

Karl stared at her, then laughed softly. "Oh, I see. You're smart enough to hold out for more."

"That must be it," Jules said.

"I didn't misjudge you," Karl said, with another smile. "I think you and I could do a lot together."

Jules shook her head at him. "What does that mean?"

"If I… I mean, if *we* get out of this. If somehow…" He paused to wink at her. "Somehow I were to escape, maybe when this ship reaches port, how would you like to be married to a Mechanic?"

Startled, Jules took a moment to respond rather than simply hurling an angry *no* back at him. In that moment, she realized that Karl hadn't actually proposed to her. He'd just asked how she'd feel about being proposed to, which was a very different question, and left him open to later deny having made any sort of commitment to her. "Marry a Mechanic?" Jules said. "Even though I'm a common?"

"Yes," Karl said, nodding. "It's a lot of work for a Mechanic to marry a common. There's a long and complicated process to get approval, because we're supposed to only marry other Mechanics. Keep the blood lines clean. But I've heard that lately it's become a lot easier to get approval, and you seem the type to fit in well with Mechanics. Become one of us! What do you say to that?"

Jules pretended to think about it. How many common women had fallen for such a not-really-a-proposal-or-a-promise from Mechanic Karl? Because he still hadn't proposed to her. He was still speaking in general terms. "You're promising to marry me if I help you escape?"

she pressed, trying to see how he'd deal with a demand for a clear commitment.

He hesitated. "If we escape," he finally said.

She laughed at the evasion in his answer. "That's one great offer," Jules said. "But I'll pass on the honor."

Karl gave her another puzzled look. "But your child might—"

Her temper shot up as Jules thought about this man toying with her, trying to use her. Her anger gave life to words she knew she shouldn't speak but couldn't stop. "I know what a child of mine will do. I doubt any of them will ever be Mechanics, but if they are, it won't be the greatest thing that child does," Jules added. "Not even close."

"What could be greater than being a Mechanic?"

"You'll never know."

His gaze on her grew perplexed. "You're a very unusual girl."

"You have no idea," Jules told him, turning her face from Karl and scowling.

"How did you come to be a pirate?"

"I had to make a sudden change to my life plans, and piracy seemed the least hazardous option," Jules said. "Plus it gives me the chance to chain up guys like you."

Karl grinned. "You like that sort of thing, eh?"

"Oh, stars above. If you're an example of the average Mechanic..." Jules sat back, shaking her head. "You're supposed to be superior, but you don't seem all that special to me."

He frowned at her, apparently lost for words. Finally, Karl spoke again. "I'm a Mechanic."

"I know," Jules said. "I'm not impressed."

"How can you not be impressed? We know things! Things commons like you can't even conceive. We came from the stars!"

"Yeah," Jules said. "I've heard that boast. Everyone has heard Mechanics claim that about themselves. Which star? Or did you come from a lot of stars?"

Karl shook his head at her. "It's a secret. A big secret."

"Sure," Jules said, letting her skepticism fill the word.

"Look, I know this stuff," Karl said, appearing baffled by her lack of belief and respect. "You don't."

"So you say."

"I don't have to tell you where we came from!" Karl insisted, his pride obviously stung.

"You don't know, do you?" Jules said.

"It's a secret! But there are people who remember. Just a few."

"Sure," Jules said. "How did Mechanics get here from another star?"

"I don't know, exactly. That's also a secret," Karl insisted.

Jules rolled her eyes at him, wondering how many more secrets Karl didn't know and couldn't be provoked into saying. "If you came from another star, why do you look just like everyone else? Why can you have kids with common folk?"

"I don't know," Karl admitted. "Everyone looks the same on Dematr, don't they? Why shouldn't people from other stars also look the same?"

"Or maybe we all came with you," Jules said to provoke him.

Karl only smiled at the idea, though. "That's ridiculous."

"No more ridiculous than what you're saying. Why'd you come here from that star? Is that also a secret?"

"I... don't know. Maybe to help you people."

"HelÏΩp us?" Jules said. "Rule over us, you mean."

"We're superior to you," Karl said. "We can do things you can't. Listen... Jori..."

"Jeri."

"I've made you the sort of offer that common women rarely receive. But I'm beginning to lose interest in the idea of you becoming my secret lover and helping me escape. Unless you want to toss aside this opportunity, you might want to consider your words more carefully."

"Yeah." She rebuttoned her top two buttons with one hand while still holding the cutlass. Jules got to her feet, being careful not to get any limb within Karl's reach, and opened the door to the safe hold. "Somebody get Ang!" she shouted. "I am done guarding this guy!"

Ang appeared quickly enough that he must have been nearby. "Are you sure?" he asked. "You know it's important—"

"Ang, do you want that guy alive when the sun comes up? Because if you make me stay in here with him he will not live that long. I *will* kill him."

"All right, Jeri. All right. Go up and talk to the cap'n while I get someone else down here to watch him."

* * *

Mak, obviously tired after a long day and the late night, nonetheless listened attentively as Jules reported what the Mechanic had said. "Too bad he didn't tell you the name of the star the Mechanics supposedly came from."

"It's supposedly a big secret," Jules said, waving one hand dismissively. "I think all that talk of stars was because he wanted to impress me so I'd help him escape and think he was serious about offering to marry me."

"Sorry you had to put up with that," Mak said. "He's a Mechanic. We have to call them Sir but there's nothing of gentlemen about them."

She saw the pain in him as he said it and knew the cause. "Sir, I'm sure your daughter isn't like that."

He brushed off the words with an abrupt gesture, changing the topic. "The information you got might be worth a lot of money. The Imperial court would likely want to hear what he said about the internal disputes of the Mechanics Guild."

"I'm not going anywhere near the Imperial court," Jules said.

"No. Naturally not. But I know some intermediaries who can carry the information there and deliver the payment to us. Can you write down as much as you remember, Jeri?"

"All except the come-ons," Jules said.

"Yes, leave those out. I also doubt the Imperial court will care about his claim of secrets. They're probably as tired as everyone else is of hearing Mechanics boast about coming from the stars." Mak gazed at nothing for a moment. "What do you think we should do with him?"

"Karl? I mean, Mechanic Karl? Why are you asking me?"

His eyes focused on her. "Because you're smart."

"You're sounding like that Mechanic, Captain."

"Not the same, Jeri, and you know it." Mak leaned on the table between them, his eyes on her. "That daughter of your line, whenever she comes, will inherit something from you. Something you've already got. I'm seeing it. I want to know what you think we should do with him."

Jules paused, not wanting to be part of the decision. But she owed Mak, without whom she'd have probably been caught or killed days ago hiding in the hills above Jacksport. "Sir, I'd say let him go to make trouble for the Mechanics Guild."

"You think he would?"

"He's one of those guys who thinks he's really smart, but isn't," Jules said. "I don't know if other Mechanics would listen to him, but if they did it could cause problems for whoever is in charge of their Guild."

Mak nodded, his eyes intent with thought. "He's very confident of himself?"

"Ridiculously so."

"I know the type. Mechanics as a rule are like that, but he seems an extreme case. The sort of person whose confidence in himself can lead gullible followers to mistake self-confidence for competence. I'll consider your advice, Jeri." Mak paused again, his gaze distant. "Those things he said about it being possible, but difficult, for Mechanics to marry commons. Yet now it's becoming easier. Do you think that was true?"

"I think so," Jules said. "His lies tended to be vague, but that was pretty specific. Do you think that's important?"

He took another long moment to answer, his gaze on one corner of the cabin. "When my daughter was taken, it was a surprise in part because few boys and girls had been taken by the Mechanics Guild in previous years. I looked into it, and found the numbers varied quite a bit. And I wondered, did the ability the Mechanics sought vary so much with each year? Or were they like a military unit, seeking to keep their overall number the same, and so seeking more recruits one year and fewer the next?"

She looked away, feeling uncomfortable at being present when Mak discussed his daughter, but trying to think through what he meant. "Do you think allowing marriages to commons might be the same sort of thing? That their Guild makes it harder when they have plenty of Mechanics and easier if there's a shortage?" Jules hesitated as a thought came to her. "The Mechanics Guild is building new Halls in places like Caer Lyn. They'll need more Mechanics, unless they spread themselves thin. And if they're also getting rid of Mechanics like Karl, that'll make their numbers even lower."

Mak nodded. "All of which would mean more approvals for commons to marry into the ranks of Mechanics, and more children forcibly swept up by Mechanics to join their Guild. Their precious bloodlines don't count as much when they need more men and women, boys and girls, to fill out their ranks. Jeri, I hate to keep you up longer, but could you write everything down now before you go to sleep?"

"Yes, sir. Including that last about the Mechanics maybe sweeping up more children?"

"Yes. Other families should be warned, though they may not be able to do anything about it."

Jules used paper, ink, and pen from a drawer in the captain's cabin, writing carefully until she had put down everything she thought was important. She'd devoted a lot of time learning to write well, every letter neatly done, every thought clear, because she'd realized that other people would judge her by those things. She couldn't change her past or her looks or her accent, but anyone reading something she'd written would see the Jules she wanted them to see.

By the time she finished writing, Captain Mak was snoring lightly in his bunk, so she left quietly.

Outside, the ship had that special hush that only came very late, when the whole world felt like it was slumbering. Aside from the sailor at the helm on the quarterdeck and the lookout watch, the rest of the crew was already asleep. Jules stood for a moment, gazing up at the stars.

Among the many things the Mechanics Guild banned was any study of the night sky. No one knew why. Sailors had learned to use some stars to guide them at night, but furtively, keeping their knowledge hidden. Otherwise, like so many other things in the world, the stars held only questions and unknowns.

But she had far too many other things to worry about, even if she'd known any way to find answers to those questions.

Jules went down to her hammock, trying to stifle a huge yawn.

* * *

Five days later, a while before dawn, the *Sun Queen* eased close to the eastern coast of the Sea of Bakre, north of the Imperial port of Sandurin. The longboat was put over the side, several crew boarding it to handle oars, and Mak in charge. Karl was brought up from below and placed in the longboat as well.

Jules hung back as Karl was brought up. She hadn't seen him since that bit of guard duty, and didn't want to run the risk of having to talk to the Mechanic again. But as she saw the longboat heading toward the beach, Jules felt a pang of disappointment that she wasn't helping on the oars. The Empire, after all, had been her home. She regretted not having the chance to touch its soil again, even if only that of a beach far north of Landfall.

When the longboat returned, Karl wasn't on it. Hopefully he was on his way to find friends and make trouble for the leaders of the Mechanics Guild.

But Mak wasn't aboard, either.

"Where's the captain?" Jules demanded.

Ang jerked a thumb back to indicate Imperial territory. "He's heading for a town a little ways off along the Imperial coast road. There's someone he knows who can tell the Imperial police we've got information they'd want to have, and who can work the deal to get us payment for that. We'll pick up Mak again tomorrow night."

"What do we do in the meantime?" Jules asked.

"Head out to sea so we don't get spotted by the coastal patrols during the day," Ang said. "Then back in close when night falls and send the longboat to get Mak."

"What about the Imperial galley that patrols this area looking for smugglers?"

"The galley patrols don't go out over the horizon," Ang said.

"Yes, they do!" Jules said, drawing a surprised reaction from those around her. "They were going to start sweeping out over the horizon because they'd realized how many ships were lurking out there waiting for night so they could run in to the coast."

"How do you know that?" a sailor named Marta asked, her voice wary.

"I came off that Imperial galley at Jacksport. You all know that! They were talking about it. The officers." Would she have to reveal that she'd been one of those officers, even if only one in training?

"How far out, Jeri?" Ang asked. "Do you know how far from the coast the galleys were going to sweep?"

She'd had to work the navigational problem as part of her training. "Three thousand lances past the point where the coast dips below the horizon, then either north or south for eight thousand lances and then back toward the coast."

"That's trouble," Liv said. "They'd see us. If we go out far enough we can't be seen we won't be able to get back to the coast to pick up Mak and out to sea again while night lasts. Jeri should have been part of the planning for this! I said so!"

"Yeah, you did," Ang said. "We need a new plan. What's the name of that town where Mak was going?"

"Saraston," Ferd said.

"Is it on the water? Does anyone know?"

"Check the chart," Jules said. "Mak's chart."

Ang slapped his forehead. "Lucky we've got you thinking while I'm being stupid. Liv, you and Jeri check that chart. If the town's along the coast road there's a good chance it's on the water and has a pier."

"So?" Marta asked.

"So instead of lurking about like suspicious smugglers, we head for Saraston, and when the galley questions us, we tell them we're going there. The galleys don't waste time searching ships headed for Imperial ports because they know the inspectors in the ports will take care of that. Right, Jeri? That hasn't changed, has it?"

"Not that I heard," Jules said.

"Check that chart."

Jules followed Liv into Mak's cabin, where the rolled-up chart was easy to find. Unrolling it on the table, Liv studied the coast north of Sandurin. "There it is. Saraston. No harbor, but… what's that say?"

"It's got a pier," Jules said. "Fishing boats."

They brought that news out on deck, gaining a nod from Ang. He looked about at the rest of the crew. "We'll vote on it, because this is risky. I propose we sail for Saraston, tying up there and buying some provisions from the locals. If they've got a pier and fishing boats, they'll have provisions for sale."

"What about the Imperial inspectors at Saraston?" Healer Keli asked. "We'll need to bribe them. That'll cost the ship."

Jules spoke up. "I got a double share from the last ship. You can have all of it to pay the bribes."

"We do things fair," Keli told her. "Equal contributions from everyone for the bribes, if we vote for it, though we'll be happy to take that from both of your shares."

"Tying up in an Imperial port is dangerous," Ferd said. "If the Imperials get suspicious we could have a cohort coming aboard before we could get the lines loose."

"That's true," Ang said. "We'll be running some risk to get the captain out of there. And it'll cost the ship the bribe money as well as whatever we spend on provisions. But we've got a rule that no one in the crew gets abandoned. I want to stick to that, because next time it might be me or you that needs the ship to come get us. And this is

Mak who needs us to come get him. Show me hands. Who says we do it?"

Jules shoved her hand as high as it would go, waiting tense as Ang counted. "That's a big majority," he announced. "Do we need a count of who's opposed? No? Let's get it done."

* * *

They sighted an Imperial galley at mid-morning as the *Sun Queen* beat southeast toward Saraston. This morning the crew had hoisted the flag of a modestly successful Imperial family trading company, and painted over the name *Sun Queen* on the stern with a new one. The galley approached, its oars moving like wide wings to bring the ship against the wind far faster than a sailing ship could have done.

Jules stood in the captain's cabin, watching cautiously through the aft windows as the galley drew close, her heart pounding with tension. Several other men and women were with her, also deserters from Imperial service who didn't want to risk being recognized even from a distance.

It felt incredibly strange to know that she could have been on that galley. That former friends of hers might walk its deck at this moment. If she hadn't come face to face with that Mage…

The galley eased up several lances from the *Sun Queen*, matching her course, the two ballistae on the galley's deck loaded and ready to unleash their projectiles if ordered.

Jules heard the captain of the galley shouting across the gap. "What ship and where bound?"

Ang, on the quarterdeck, called back. "The *Slim Quarter* out of Altis, bound for Sandurin by way of Saraston."

"Why Saraston?"

"I know some people there. I can get better deals on provisions than in Sandurin."

Jules dared to relax a little. Everything was going just as it should. There was nothing suspicious about the *Sun Queen*. Nothing to prevent the galley from waving off the ship so the galley could continue its customs patrol.

A moment later she felt as if her heart had stopped as another hail came across. "Do you have any passengers?"

"No, sir!" Ang called back.

"Why are they asking that?" Marta wondered. "That's not normal, is it?"

"No," Jules said. Why would the galley need to know that?

Unless they'd already been told to watch for her.

"Furl your sails!" the captain of the Imperial galley ordered. "We need to check everyone aboard your ship!"

CHAPTER FOUR

J ules stared out the aft windows, wondering if she should dive out of them and try to drown herself. Because the galley's crew would surely be looking for her. There was no other reason for them to be searching the ship. She caught a glimpse of a bag still sitting in one corner of the cabin and felt a rock come to rest in her guts. Her uniform. It was still in here. They'd find it, they'd know who she was, and when they got her Jules knew she'd be sent to Marandur to become the involuntary bride of the Emperor, to be raped on her wedding bed and again as many times as necessary to produce as many children as possible with her blood and that of the Imperial family intermingled. Surely death would be preferable.

She took a step toward the windows as Ang called back.

"Aye, sir. We will furl our sails. It will take a little while, because we're short-handed due to the fever. Half the crew is out with it."

A pause, then the galley's captain shouted back. "Fever?"

"Yes, sir. Something we picked up out West, it seems. Half the crew is down."

"How many deaths?" the galley's captain demanded.

"Only… two," Ang answered.

Marta laughed softly. "The man is a genius. They're not going to want to board a plague ship."

"Will they let us tie up at Saraston?" Jules asked.

"Sure. They're going to want healers to check us to see if we're carrying some new bug and where we might've picked it up. We'll be quarantined on the pier, but Mak should still be able to get to us past a couple of local police."

Jules relaxed slightly, but stayed tense as she waited for another reply from the Imperial galley.

"Proceed to Saraston!" the hail came. "Tie up there, send no one ashore, and tell those on the pier you're under quarantine until cleared by Imperial healers."

Ang called back. "Yes, sir! We'll do as you say! Thank you, sir!"

"Don't lay it on too thick, Ang," another of Jules' companions muttered.

Jules saw the galley drop back, swing about nimbly as the oars on one side dipped and pulled, and head back into the wind, rowing out to sea.

"They're going out farther, all right," Marta commented. "Good thing you warned us, Jeri."

Once the galley had dropped below the horizon except for the sole mast still rising to mark its location, Jules and the others came back on deck.

Jules was leaning on the railing, gazing at the water, when Ang came to stand beside her. "Hey, sister. I heard you were thinking of ending it when the galley said they'd board."

"Was it that obvious?" Jules said.

"People on this ship aren't used to seeing you look scared." Ang leaned on the rail, also looking out. "You don't have to tell me, but do you have a death sentence on you?"

Jules thought about how to answer that before deciding it was substantially true, at least as far as the Great Guilds went. "Yes."

"That bad? You did kill him?"

"Him?"

"We figure some Imperial official tried to force you and you gave him what he deserved."

"That's… partly so," Jules said, thinking of what must be the Emperor's intentions toward her.

"He must have been pretty high up if they're searching ships for you. You didn't knife a prince, did you?"

Jules couldn't help laughing at the idea. "A prince?"

"Why not? Or was it the Emperor himself you put a mark on when he disrespected you?" Ang grinned.

"That's it, brother. You've guessed it. The Emperor himself can't wait to get me into his bed." How could she joke about that? But the idea did sound absurd, and it would be, if not for the prophecy.

Ang's expression and his voice went serious. "Whatever it really is, you're safe among us."

"I know that." Jules looked up, toward where land was visible on the eastern horizon, and realized that some of her disquiet was due to Mak being gone. "I guess I'll feel even safer when we get the captain back."

Ang nodded, his eyes on Jules. "Mak told me to keep an eye on you in particular if he didn't make it back. He likes you."

Jules felt that tightness inside her again. "Brother, do you think he likes me more than he should? The truth now."

"No," Ang said without hesitating. "You know about Mak's daughter? The one he lost to the Mechanics?"

"Yes."

"The way he looks at you, he's seeing her. What she might have been. You should feel safe around Mak."

Jules stared at Ang, then back at the water. "Are you sure?"

"Yeah, Jeri, I'm sure. That's not your burden, mind you. It's his."

"I still owe him," Jules said. "For taking me aboard." She tried to make a joke to mask her fears. "Even when a certain sailor wanted me to go away."

"I knew you'd be trouble," Ang said, smiling. "Was I wrong?"

"No," Jules admitted. "You were right. I'm trouble." *More trouble than you can imagine*, she added only to herself.

* * *

From the water, in the light of late morning nearing noon, Saraston had the look of any Imperial town, laid out with geometric precision, the stout stone pier projecting straight out into the water with the strength of something meant to last. When the Imperial government decided to build something, it was built well, and it was built to the same plans and in the same ways with the same materials as earlier such things. Because even if the Great Guilds had permitted any changes, the Imperial government wouldn't.

Jules and most of the crew stayed out of sight again as the *Sun Queen* came alongside the pier, still pretending to be short-handed with a fever aboard.

When the ship was tied up, Ang came down to join them, looking worried. "They've got legionaries at the end of the pier. Just a single hand of them, but it's not local police blocking access to us."

"Does Mak know we're here?" Keli asked.

"I don't know. Something feels wrong about this town," Ang said. "I don't know what. Something. There's no inspector shown up yet. That's odd. And the legionaries at the end of the pier."

"Should we cut lines and run?" Ferd said.

"I don't want to do that yet. We can handle five legionaries if they rush us. But... I don't know."

Liv frowned. "Ang, you're not the skittish type. If it feels dangerous—"

"Do we know where Mak is?" Jules asked.

Everyone looked at her. "I have a name," Ang said.

"If it's dangerous out there," Jules said, frightened of what she was saying but forcing the words out anyway, "then Mak will be staying hidden wherever he is, right? He won't be out where he can see that we're at the pier. Someone's going to have to find him and let him know."

"Someone?" Gord said.

"I know the latest Imperial procedures and rules," Jules said. "Better than anyone else here. I should do it."

"I thought the Imperials were looking for you," Ang said.

"They are." Jules swallowed before she could speak through a throat tightened by worry. "But I'm Mak's best chance."

"It won't do anyone any good," Liv said, "if both of you end up trapped in Saraston."

"I owe him! I pay my debts!" Jules looked around her. "Let me do this. Please."

"All right," Ang said. "You've earned the right, and unless someone gets word to Mak he might be trapped here with the Imperials stirred up. All I know is that Mak was going to the place of a guy named Xan. Good luck."

"But we're going to be ready to cut our lines and head out if more legionaries show up," Marta warned. "You have to know that, Jeri. The good of the ship counts more than whatever happens to you and Mak."

"I understand," Jules said.

"How are you going to walk through that town and not get stopped?" Liv demanded.

"I have something that will help," Jules said.

As she had recently noticed, the rolled up Imperial uniform still rested in the bag in the corner of Mak's cabin. Jules pulled it out and unrolled it, unhappily eyeing the creases and the dried splashes of mud from the streets of Jacksport that had never been cleaned off. "Liv? Can we make this presentable really, really fast?"

"Let me see what we can do. Do you need all this junk on it?"

Jules looked over the rank markers and unit shields, pulling off the ones that had marked her as an officer-in-training and one assigned to the Imperial fleet rather than the legions. "I need the rest."

"Wait here."

Jules paced nervously as she waited, remembered that she also had to find her boots and sword, and looked through the cabin until she found where Mak had hidden them. The boots were muddy, of course, the dirt caked on and dried. Cleaning them gave her something to do as she waited.

Liv came back in, the uniform held carefully. "How's that?"

Jules ran her hand over it, feeling the heat from a hand iron still lingering in the cloth. "Fantastic."

"Are you going to put it on here?"

"No. I'll need to sneak ashore. Do you think I can swim without being spotted?"

"How well can you swim?"

"Well enough," Jules said. That had been part of the required training to serve on Imperial ships.

"Come up on deck." Once up, Liv gestured, keeping the movements small in case anyone was watching. "Go out the stern windows so the legionaries at the land end of the pier can't see. I'll lower you by rope so you don't make a splash. Swim around the other side of the pier. See that low dock just beyond? You should be able to climb up that unnoticed and from there get into the town without the sentries seeing you."

"Thanks, Liv. Do we have a waterproof bag I can put my stuff in?"

"I think so." Liv put her hands on Jules' shoulders, eyeing her. "Sister, are you sure you want to do this? Mak's a fine man and a fine captain, but this could be the death of you if they find you pretending to be an Imperial officer."

"Technically," Jules said, "I won't be pretending. I doubt my resignation was accepted."

Liv stared at her. "Jeri—"

"We're wasting time, Liv. Please, sister."

Jules stripped down before climbing out the stern window and grabbing onto the rope that Liv and some of the other sailors held to lower her. The trip down felt too fast, but she slid silently into the water, gasping at the cold. Another line lowered the waterproof bag. Jules untied it, waved up to anxious faces looking down at her, and began swimming around the end of the pier.

She didn't have to worry about being totally silent as she swam, since the swells of the sea were splashing against the pier on the far side. But that carried the threat of those swells pushing her into the pier. Unable to fight the force of the waves, Jules let one carry her to the pier, turning to catch herself with her feet as she reached the stone supports. Bending her legs, she managed to take the shock without hurting anything, though the impact stung.

Lower down under the water she saw the sharp edges of sea shells where marine life had taken root. If she hit those, even with her feet, they'd cut her badly.

Making her way down the pier to shore turned into a repeated trial of advancing and retreating waves that alternately threatened to pull her out where the legionaries on guard or someone else might see her, or to slam her into the stone pier again.

By the time Jules reached the low dock, she felt exhausted from the struggle. She lay for a moment in the cold water, her muscles trembling. She'd swallowed enough salt water for her stomach to be upset as well.

Moving again took an act of willpower. She pulled herself up on the dock cautiously, eyeing the legionaries whose attention was on the ship down the pier. Rolling onto the wooden surface of the dock and wincing at the scrape of the rough wood against her bare skin, Jules crawled into a shack on one end of the dock, the early afternoon sun warm on her back. Inside, she found a mess of old fishing nets and line, the smell of rotting hemp almost overpowering.

There wasn't anything in here to towel off with, so Jules had to wait, shivering, until her skin was dry. Pulling on her clothes offered warmth, but also a different kind of worry. The uniform that had once been a source of comfort and belonging now felt alien and dangerous.

Jules pulled her boots on and stood up, buckling her sword belt. She ran her hands through her hair, which had grown since Jacksport, deciding to braid it in back, pinning the braid with a pin from one of her discarded insignia. She couldn't carry the waterproof bag with her, so Jules stuffed it in among the rotting ropes.

All right. She was an Imperial officer again. She knew how to do this. Act like she had every right to be here. They hadn't seen any Mages or Mechanics in this town, so the Great Guilds wouldn't be a problem. Find out where Xan's house was. Collect Mak and both of them figure out how to get back to the ship without being spotted. Easy.

Don't think about what could go wrong. About what would happen if she was caught. Concentrate on what needed to be done.

Jules walked out of the shack as if she owned it, turning onto land and striding along as if sure of her destination.

It felt like a strange dream, to be in an Imperial town, to be in uniform, to be walking past people as if she had no particular cares, the citizens yielding way to her as an Imperial officer, not knowing she'd grown up a legion orphan. Horse-drawn wagons rattled down the streets, the horses clopping along with the steady determination of draft animals knowing the day would hold a lot more work before they got their grain and a rest. Scents carried from an open market, spices and fresh plants and soil clinging to the plants. Another wagon passed, doomed chickens clucking in their cages on their way to the meat market.

No problems. Easy.

She was about to stop a citizen to ask where Xan lived when a deferential but powerful voice called out.

"Lieutenant!"

Knowing she couldn't ignore that hail, Jules turned to look. A centurion with perhaps twenty legionaries in his wake, all of them with swords at their sides or crossbows in their hands. The centurion walked to her, speaking respectfully. "Were you looking for the temporary headquarters, Lieutenant?"

Saying no might sound suspicious. A lieutenant being lost, on the other hand, wouldn't surprise any centurion. "Yes, I am."

"I can lead you there," the centurion said. "We've been expecting new personnel to show up. I just collected this batch from the road."

Blast. She couldn't possibly say no without generating a host of questions to which she might not have good answers. "Thank you, Centurion." Jules fell in beside the centurion as they walked down the streets, trying to keep track of where they turned. A pair of tired legion couriers rode by on lathered horses, the sort of sight that screamed of an emergency. It gave Jules an opening to ask a question. "What's going on?" she said to the centurion. "Something special?"

"I don't know, Lieutenant. Something's up. Are you from the Fifth Legion at Sandurin?"

"No," Jules said, afraid that the centurion might know some detail of Sandurin that would trip her up. "I'm from Landfall. Second Legion. I was on my way to Umburan for a temporary assignment but got stopped and told to come here."

"The rest of us, too," the centurion said. "On the way to somewhere else but told to come here. Colonel Yosef has been assigned as the garrison commander. All he's saying is to be ready for trouble."

"Where could trouble be coming from in Saraston?" Jules asked.

"That ship that came in this morning, I'm thinking. You ever have any dealings with Mages, Lieutenant?"

Jules hoped her reaction hadn't shown on her face. "Not if I can help it," she said, her voice short.

"You and me both, Lieutenant. I did hear something about Mages warning about trouble here. Supposedly a few of them are on their way."

Jules swallowed to ensure her voice sounded calmer than she felt. "Oh? When are they supposed to arrive?"

"Coming on a galley, I hear. Up from Sandurin. Sometime today."

Mages. And an Imperial galley. And legionaries being diverted into this town. All she needed now was for some Mechanics to ride in.

They reached a large manor that had been taken over by the incoming legionary forces, the broad open court in the front already trampled by many passing feet. The centurion led Jules and the soldiers to a side building. "Temporary quarters," he apologized to Jules. "I'll check-in with Colonel Yosef and see if he has an assignment for you, Lieutenant."

"Thank you," Jules said, wondering how she could escape this place without everybody noticing. She couldn't walk out now. The centurion would be right back and might find it suspicious that a lieutenant had wandered off while supposedly waiting for orders.

"Sit down," the centurion told the legionaries who'd come in with him, his voice no longer polite. "Wait for assignment!"

Jules stood near the front of the room. It was some sort of store-room, high-ceilinged, bare walls, cleared of goods, a large room with a few high windows that let in plenty of afternoon light. Legionaries slumped against the walls or sat next to them, others seated on the open floor. It felt like any other place where soldiers gathered, waiting for a long time to be told why they'd been brought there in a rush.

She was the only officer present, which was a blessing since it meant no one tried to make small talk with her. But it also meant she was standing alone in the front of the room.

Stars above. She was trying to sneak through this town and she was in a room full of the soldiers who were probably looking for her and Mages were on their way here and so was an Imperial galley. Way to mess up the assignment, Jules.

Already nervous, Jules began to notice curious glances at her, the sort of furtive looks that spoke of trouble. Why? Was there some-thing wrong with her uniform? But the centurion would have noticed that. Centurions were death on problems with uniforms. A legionary would have been chewed out, but since Jules was an officer the cen-turion would have found a way to mention anything wrong to her so she could fix it.

More of the legionaries were glancing at her. And looking again. Talking softly among themselves. Why?

Jules followed other looks, to the far wall, and saw a picture posted there.

It wasn't a great likeness. Someone had apparently copied from a copy of a picture made by an Imperial police artist. But it still looked like her, except for the hair. Jules had it styled differently now with the braid, and that helped disguise her a little. But not nearly enough.

What could she do? At least some of the men and women in here had already spotted her resemblance to the woman on the poster. Trying to distract them from that, trying to make a hasty departure, would just attract further attention.

The last thing she needed was more attention on her.

Unless…

What was the last thing anyone would expect the woman on that poster to do? Take notice of it. Draw attention to that resemblance.

Jules set her expression into annoyance just short of rage, glaring around the room. "*That again?*" she growled in her best imitation of a centurion she'd trained under, pointing at the picture. "If one more fool tells me that looks like me, I'm going to put them on work detail until their fingers are worn to the bone and the bones are worn to sticks! *You!*" Jules cried, pointing to one legionary who'd seemed particularly interested in the resemblance. "Do you think that looks like me?"

"No, Lieutenant! It doesn't look anything like you!"

"What about you?" Jules snarled at another legionary. "You seem interested in my looks!"

"No, Lieutenant!" the legionary denied. "Not me. I wasn't looking at anything!"

No one was looking at her now. Every legionary had found something else to fix their eyes on, trying to avoid her attention. Jules gave a final glower around the room as the centurion returned, casting a curious glance about at the tense legionaries and clearly deciding that whatever had happened the lieutenant must have dealt with it. "Lieutenant, Colonel Yosef doesn't have time to meet with you. He wants you to take ten soldiers to search the south end of the town. All structures. All rooms in those structures."

"What are we looking for?" Jules asked, glad that she knew exactly what questions to ask.

"Anyone who isn't supposed to be in Saraston, Lieutenant."

"Where's the south end begin?"

"South side of the town square," the centurion said.

"Are you going to assign ten or am I going to pick them?"

"I have just the ten for you, Lieutenant." The centurion indicated a group of men and women sitting together on one side of the room. "All of you. Get up. I'd better not hear this officer had any problems with any of you."

Jules led her newly-assigned group back out into the courtyard. She'd managed to not only attract a lot of attention to herself but had also acquired ten legionaries who'd be following her around. Even for a lieutenant that was an impressive amount of screwing up in a short time.

Unable to think of anything else she could do, Jules led her patrol south, the sidewalks clearing before her as citizens made way for the group of soldiers. The town square resembled those in countless other Imperial towns laid out using the same plans, the same central government building with the same bell tower topping the building making it easy to identify. Wracking her brains for some way to ditch her faithful patrol of soldiers, Jules led them to a house fronting on the south side of the square. "Start here."

One of the soldiers knocked heavily on the door, shoving his way inside when it was cracked open. Jules followed, waving the remaining soldiers inside. "Search the place. Check everyone's papers."

A nervous woman holding the hand of a young child stood by the door. "Is there any problem?" she asked. "We're loyal citizens of the Empire. We haven't done anything. There's no contraband here. We have tax stamps on every item in this house."

Jules gave her the cold look an officious Imperial officer would show. "Then you have nothing to worry about."

"If you tell me what you're looking for—"

A mother with her child. The sort of thing Jules had lost at the age of five. And if Jules ever had a child of her own, *when* she had that child, he or she would be in constant danger of death. Neither this mother nor this child knew how fortunate they were. She gave the woman an angry glance. "I didn't ask you to speak."

The mother fell silent, giving Jules a chance to feel guilty for being jealous of her and time to think about what to do next. If only she knew where Xan lived.

Oh, blazes. *Use your head, Jules.* "Is there someone named Xan who lives nearby?" Jules snapped at the woman.

"Three houses down this street," the woman said. "I only know him as Xan. I don't know where he's from."

"Thank you," Jules said as her legionaries returned one by one to report having found nothing untoward.

She had to search the next two houses as well, not seeing any way to skip them without arousing too much suspicion. Every moment seemed a moment too long, wondering when the Mages and the galley would get here.

Jules had far too much time to think and worry while her legionaries searched the homes. How had the Mages known that she'd be here today? Could the Mages really predict that she would be in Saraston before Jules herself had known, before she'd decided to come into the town to get Mak? How could she avoid being killed by men and women with those kinds of abilities?

Fortunately, the Mages apparently hadn't learned she'd be here in time to reach Saraston before her. But she had no idea how much longer it would be before they did arrive.

Finally they reached the third house down, Jules shoving her way inside. "Who are you?" she demanded of the man at the door as her soldiers followed.

"Xan of Pandin," the man said, showing just the right amount of concern and curiosity and innocence at the presence of Jules and the legionaries.

"I saw someone else enter here," Jules said. "Where is he?"

"Yes," Xan said, not quite hiding his surprise this time. "In there. Come out!" he called.

Mak came into the room, his hands slightly spread and open to show he carried no weapons. As his eyes lit on Jules she saw the shock in them, but otherwise Mak revealed no sign of knowing her.

"Search the house," Jules ordered her soldiers. "I'll handle these two. Papers!"

She barely glanced at Xan's before handing them back and taking the identity documents that Mak offered.

Jules scowled as she studied Mak's false papers. "You didn't come off that ship, did you?"

"Ship?" Mak asked, his voice wary.

"The ship that's tied up at the pier! It came in just before noon! You know nothing about it?"

"No," Mak said. "Why would a ship visit Saraston?"

"They must have had a reason," Jules said, her eyes on his. Wait. This didn't sound right if anyone else was listening. Jules let impatience show. "Why are *you* asking *me* questions, citizen?"

"I'm sorry," Mak said, displaying a convincing amount of worry. "I didn't mean any disrespect."

"Then watch your step! You're already on shaky ground!" How much more blatantly could she warn Mak that there was trouble brewing? Oh, blazes, why not spill it all to let him know how bad it was? "There's an Imperial galley on the way here from Sandurin with Mages aboard, and legionaries being diverted into town to deal with that ship. I don't need any more trouble!"

Mak stared at her. "No," he said. "That sounds like plenty of trouble."

Xan was doing a worse job of concealing his nervousness. Jules frowned at him as her soldiers returned from searching the house. "You don't know this one? He just ducked in here when he saw us coming, like I saw?"

"That's right," Xan said, picking up on the leading questions.

"There's something wrong about this," Jules announced. "I'm taking this one back for questioning. You," she told her legionaries, "start searching the next building and go on from there. I'll meet you back on this street."

"Lieutenant? But—"

"Is somebody questioning my orders?" Jules almost shouted. Having always regretted the poor officers she'd been exposed to during her training, and ill-qualified workers at the legion orphan home with little patience for the children they were supposed to care for, she now felt grateful that they'd given her models for poor leadership and poor decision-making. She'd already been abrupt with her soldiers and everyone else they'd encountered. This latest display of ill-tempered authority was perfectly in keeping with her role as a pompous and touchy junior officer.

The legionaries had obviously seen their share of such officers. They stiffened to attention, saluted, and headed for the next building as Jules shoved Mak ahead of her in the other direction. "Get going. I need to get back here quickly," she announced loudly for the benefit of her still-within-earshot legionaries.

They walked down the street, moving as fast as they could without looking as if they were running. "What the blazes are you doing, Jeri?" Mak asked in a low voice.

"Saving your life," she replied.

"You shouldn't have risked this."

"It's my fault. They're looking for me."

"You don't know—"

"Yes, sir, I *do* know! There's a poster up with my picture on it. And that's why the Mages are on their way. Somehow they knew I'd be here."

"Blazes. Where are we really going?" Mak asked.

"To the pier."

"Then we need to turn left here." Mak waited as they took the corner, then spoke again. "The legionaries are probably waiting for that galley to arrive so the ship can't get away when they rush it from the land side. Why'd the crew bring her in to port?"

"Because we knew you needed us."

"It was a stupid thing to do, Jeri."

"Yes, sir. Thank you, sir."

"We'll talk about it later," Mak said. "If there is a later."

The sentry post at the end of the pier came into sight. Jules kept walking toward it, keeping her confident stride, Mak staying with her.

"I'm guessing you know how to get past those soldiers?" Mak muttered.

"I have a plan," Jules said, hoping that this particular plan worked better than her other plans so far today.

The five legionaries at the sentry post came to attention at her approach. Jules returned their salutes with casual precision. "At ease. I'm to take this healer to the ship to check the fever cases."

The legionaries exchanged glances. "Lieutenant," the corporal in charge said, "our orders are not to allow anyone onto that pier."

"My orders are from Colonel Yosef!" Jules said, trying to sound like a jerk junior officer again.

"So are our orders, Lieutenant!"

The corporal clearly wasn't going to give in to pressure. Fortunately, she'd thought of a way to use persuasion. Jules leaned closer and lowered her voice. "We're going to rush that ship later, right? You've heard that, haven't you? Don't you think Colonel Yosef is smart enough to send a spy aboard before we attack to see how many enemies of the Emperor are aboard?"

"Oh." The legionaries saluted again. "Forgive us, Lieutenant."

"That's all right. You're following orders, just as you should. Now keep quiet. We don't want to alarm anyone or make them think anything unusual is happening. Understand?"

"Yes, Lieutenant!"

As Jules led Mak down the pier she heard him laugh very softly. "Jeri, you're even more dangerous, and even more crazy, than I thought you were."

"I'm actually really scared at the moment," Jules whispered in reply. "Actually, I've been really scared since I came ashore." She could see Ang on the deck of the *Sun Queen*, looking down the pier at her and Mak approaching. Hopefully the rest of the crew was poised to get underway as quickly as they could.

They reached the gangway, Mak holding out one hand to pause Jules. "Those legionaries watching us won't expect you to go aboard with me. That wouldn't happen if we were supposedly worried about fever. Wait here."

"Yes, sir." Mak was in charge again. Someone she trusted. Jules felt relief dampening the fear that had been riding her most of the day.

Mak went aboard, speaking to Ang and others who gathered about. Jules waited, her hands clasped behind her as sailors ran about on the deck of the *Sun Queen*, staying low beneath the rail so they wouldn't be seen by the legionary sentries. Trying to look confident and calm,

Jules couldn't help casting occasional glances down the pier to the legionaries still watching alertly.

During one such check, Jules saw a much larger group of legionaries, maybe thirty or forty total, at least one officer among them, run up to the sentry post from the land side. Words were shouted, slightly too faint for her to make out at this distance, arms gestured angrily, and the officer suddenly led the entire batch of legionaries charging down the pier. "Captain Mak!"

"Get aboard, you fool!" Mak shouted from the quarterdeck.

Jules ran up the gangway, sailors hauling it in along with her. Other sailors were racing up the rigging to unfurl the sails. She heard the thud of axes as the lines tying the ship to the pier were cut, the shouts of the legionaries running this way, the twang of crossbows releasing their bolts.

The *Sun Queen* moved away from the pier as the sails unfurled above, but slowly. She was still only a few lances from the pier. The legionaries were lining up on the pier, reloading their crossbows, aiming at the figures on the ship's quarterdeck.

Jules hesitated for only a moment before racing up the ladder to the quarterdeck, standing at the rail facing the crossbows, her body between the legionaries and Mak and the woman at the helm. She stood as tall as she could in her dark red Imperial uniform, letting her face be clearly seen. *Here I am. The one you're looking for.*

The legionaries on the pier stared at her.

The officer shouted orders.

The legionaries raised their crossbows.

CHAPTER FIVE

"What the blazes are you doing, Jeri?" Mak shouted angrily behind her.

"They probably have orders not to hurt me!" Jules called back over her shoulder. She hoped so, anyway. The Emperor wouldn't want a badly injured, or dead, reluctant bride and brood mare.

Of course the legionaries might not know who she was even though she was wearing her Imperial uniform. But if she moved, they'd have a clear shot at Mak, and at the woman at the helm. This had all happened because of her. She wouldn't let someone else take those crossbow bolts, even though her grip on the wood of the quarterdeck's rail was slick with sweat as she waited fearfully for the impacts that might end her life.

"Get down, you idiot!" Mak yelled.

"No! Get this ship clear!" Jules yelled back, realizing on the heels of her words that she'd just shouted an order to the captain of the ship.

The legionary commander, who must be Colonel Yosef, glowered at her across the water separating them, his anger strong enough that Jules could almost feel the heat even across the growing distance to the pier. "Follow your oath to the Emperor, Lieutenant!"

Jules shook her head. "The Emperor will never have me."

"He will!" Colonel Yosef snapped orders to his soldiers holding crossbows, who shifted their aim to the sailors in the rigging. But as the legionaries fired, the *Sun Queen* suddenly yawed, throwing off the aim of the crossbows and making the bolts go wild. Some sailors lost their balance as the masts jolted beneath them, but their shipmates caught them in time to keep any from falling from the yardarms.

Jules glanced behind her, seeing that Mak had ordered the helm jerked over to cause the ship to yaw at the right moment. But the crossbow carriers were reloading again, and the *Sun Queen* was still well within range of those weapons.

She stood at the rail, shifting her position as the *Sun Queen* moved and the angle between the legionaries on the pier and their targets behind her changed.

Liv charged up to her and pulled Jules down before she knew what was happening. Jules managed to break away from Liv and stood up again. "Leave me alone!"

"This is even more stupid than walking a gauntlet!" Liv shouted at her, reaching for her again.

"Get down!" Jules ordered Liv as the crossbows readied again.

The *Sun Queen* rolled, coming around fast, the sails filling, sailors at the lines swinging the yardarms to catch the wind, a flurry of crossbow bolts flying harmlessly past as their targets moved too quickly for good aim. Jules looked around as the *Sun Queen* steadied out, seeing the legionaries and the pier were now on the opposite side of the ship, off the stern quarter.

She'd only taken one step that way when a furious Mak blocked her. "Don't! Or I swear that I'll personally knock you out with a marlinspike and have you dragged below."

A last volley of bolts chased the *Sun Queen*, some thudding home in the stern. "Yes, sir," Jules said.

"You'll follow orders, Jeri, or you'll be off this ship!"

"Yes, sir." Jules nodded toward the south, wondering why her mind felt so calm when her body was shaking. "Don't forget there's a galley coming from that way."

"Get the blazes off this quarterdeck!" Mak told her. "Liv! Get her below deck!"

"Yes, Captain." Liv took Jules' arm, leading her down the ladder to the deck. Once there, she paused to give Jules an amazed look. "You're not hurt? Why didn't they shoot you?"

"The Emperor wants me alive," Jules said.

"Blazes, girl, what'd you do?"

"I was in the wrong place at the wrong time," Jules said.

"Sail to the south!" the lookout called.

Jules broke free from Liv and ran to the shrouds, racing up them to the main top. She stood, balancing, one hand on a stay, staring to the south.

One mast. One sail. "It's the galley."

Mages were on that ship. Could they tell where she was? She needed to warn Captain Mak.

Liv appeared beside her. "Jeri, if you don't get your butt down below deck right now, Captain Mak will probably toss that butt off the stern the Imperials to pick up. And the rest of you with it. He's that unhappy with you."

Jules felt herself sagging with exhaustion, her energy suddenly spent. "All right. I'm going. Tell Captain Mak…" How could she pass the message about the Mages through Liv? "Tell Captain Mak there's something I have to tell him that I can only say to him. But I'm going below deck now because he ordered that."

She made it down to the deck and staggered toward the closest ladder down, only to have a firm hand grab her shoulder. "What is it?" Mak asked, his expression stony, his eyes still angry.

"Mages on that galley," Jules muttered. "They knew I was going to be in Saraston. They might, somehow, be able to tell where I am."

He eyed her, nodding. "All right. Thank you for reminding me. What's the matter? Did you get hit?"

"No, sir. I'm just worn out."

"I wonder how that happened. Get below. If we need you to deal with the galley and the Mages I'll call you."

She thought maybe Mak was being sarcastic, but wasn't certain.

* * *

Jules passed out while sitting at one of the mess tables, waking up finally in her hammock where someone had carried her, still wearing the Imperial officer's uniform. Apparently they had managed to avoid the galley since she hadn't heard any sounds of fighting. Jules managed to get up to use the head, change back into her sailor clothing, and get some food, planning to go on deck to help work the ship, only to have Ang tell her she was confined below by order of the captain.

All right. She'd disobeyed orders. She could understand being punished for that. Even if she had saved Mak's ungrateful life.

Her banishment lasted until sunset, passing crew members expressing muted admiration for what she'd done in Saraston. Finally, Ang came down. "The cap'n wants to see you in his cabin."

"Fine," Jules muttered. She held up the uniform. "Is it all right if I toss this overboard?"

"I wouldn't do that," Ang said. "It came in real handy. We might need it again."

She dropped the uniform on the table and walked up on deck, then to the door to the captain's cabin. "Jeri of Landfall, reporting as ordered."

"Come in."

He still sounded mad. She went inside, closing the door behind her, but staying standing near it.

Mak, sitting at the table, gave her a glower. "What the blazes was that about?"

"Could the captain be more specific, sir?"

"Everything that happened today. In Saraston."

Jules held herself at attention. "It was about saving your life, sir." Let him complain about *that*. "And repaying a debt."

"You could've easily been killed or captured!"

"You're welcome, sir."

He jumped to his feet, coming closer, his eyes almost glowing with anger. "Jeri, this isn't a joke! Putting yourself between me and those crossbows! What the blazes were you thinking?"

"I knew they wouldn't hurt me, sir," Jules said.

"You knew nothing of the kind!"

"I can't die, sir," she said, her voice growing rough. "You know that. I have to have at least one blasted child first!"

"You don't know that!" Mak said in a low growl, his face nearly touching hers. "The Mages wouldn't be wanting to kill you unless they thought the prophecy could be stopped with your death! So don't tell me you're invincible! You're just as likely to die as any man or woman! And I won't have your death on me!"

He spun away, walking back to the table, his back to her. When Mak spoke again, his voice held forced calm. "Jeri, I've got enough deaths on me. People I should have protected. Don't make yourself into another memory of failure for me."

"I wasn't going to let you die," Jules said.

"Why not? What am I to you?"

"My captain. And the man who gave me safe harbor when I needed it."

He turned again, his eyes studying her. "Don't you go thinking I'm more than that to you, Jeri. My life was meant for one woman. I had her, I lost her, and there'll never be another."

Jules felt words momentarily caught in her throat. "Sir... I... you mistake my... feelings, sir. It's not that."

"You're sure?"

"Yes. I don't... You're a fine man. I admire you as a leader. But I can't imagine you... and me... like that. You're..."

"Old," Mak said.

"No! I mean, not old. But older. Too old for..."

"A woman your age. We're in full agreement on that." Mak finally relaxed. "You scared me, Jeri. Scared me with the risks you took and scared me with what you might be thinking. And feeling." Mak sat down, running one hand through his hair. "You're crew, Jeri. I have a responsibility to look out for you."

"What if I weren't crew?" Jules pressed.

He studied her again for a moment. "You'd still be a lot less than half my age, and deserving of a man close to your own age."

"Thank you, sir," Jules said, feeling her own tension subside. "I'm relieved to know that."

"Have I given you any reason to think I'd do otherwise?"

"No, sir. You haven't. Experiences with other men have given me reason. I'm sorry I judged you based on experiences I'd rather not explain further."

"That's all right. I've probably heard about similar experiences. That's one of the reasons I resolved not to be a predatory old fool. And I'm sorry I misread your motivation. It seemed far more than I deserved." He surprised her with a sudden laugh. "But I've never heard of anything like today! Stars above! How'd you do it? I saw you walking into that house with a bunch of legionaries answering to you and I thought I must've been slipped one of those mushrooms that make the world go strange."

"Sir, I was just making it up as I went," Jules confessed.

"Don't do it again," Mak said. "I mean that, Jeri."

Her temper flared as she thought of how he'd gotten into trouble to begin with. "Make me part of the planning next time and I won't have to! Sir!"

He smiled. "You'll be part of the planning next time. I guarantee it. And Jeri, my name is Mak. This isn't the Imperial legions. You don't have to call me sir."

"Yes, sir."

"Get back to work, Jeri."

* * *

Several years before, a captain named Kelsi had been shipwrecked on the north coast of the Sea of Bakre. She'd made the best of it, getting her badly damaged ship into a natural harbor with an open valley before it. Though hemmed in by the Northern Ramparts mountains, the harbor was a good one, and the valley broad enough for settlement. Kelsi used the wreckage to construct the first buildings there, and within a few years men and women seeking escape from the domination of the Empire had swelled the numbers of her settlement into a small town.

The *Sun Queen* hadn't been able to get food or water at Saraston, so Captain Mak had taken them north and west to Kelsi's settlement, a remote-enough spot that they were unlikely to find any Imperial presence there. The ship had tied up at a newly-built pier that seemed sturdy enough to hold her even if the weather rose. Searching the city from the maintop, Jules didn't see any sign of Mages or Mechanics. Apparently neither of the Great Guilds had yet taken notice of this place.

"Come ashore with me," Liv urged her. "I'll keep an eye on you. Unless you'd prefer I turn a blind eye to whatever you want to get into. You might meet a handsome fella. You never know."

Jules laughed at the idea. "I'm not into casual encounters," she said.

"That's your call. But at least get a drink and maybe a decent meal. It's not healthy to stay aboard the ship all the time."

"I was ashore at Saraston," Jules said.

"Doesn't count. You were too busy having fun to have any fun."

"Fun?" Jules said, following Liv off the ship. "Has the captain told you anything about what happened?"

"Just about you ordering around half the garrison in town," Liv said. "This place looks good."

The waterside bar didn't exactly look good to Jules. Rough exterior of reclaimed timber, a couple of small windows, and a door that had come from some other structure. As she stared at that door, she couldn't stop thinking about what had happened the last time she'd walked into a tavern.

But there was no good way to explain to Liv being afraid to enter a bar. And she'd always prided herself on not being afraid to try, on being able to take anything.

Jules set her mouth and walked behind Liv into the dim interior, her eyes taking a moment to adjust after the glare of the late afternoon sun.

There were other sailors in the tavern, scattered at a variety of battered tables that hosted a variety of chairs that looked used and abused. Two of them, Gord and Marta, were off the *Sun Queen*. Jules and Liv took a pair of seats at the small bar, whose top was an uneven, solid slab of rock. Sawdust covered the floor, giving off a fresh scent to war with less savory smells that were probably reminders of unfortunate outcomes from prior customers who'd overindulged. A girl far too young to actually partake of the bottles behind the bar poured them two glasses of clear liquid and took a coin from Liv in payment.

Liv sniffed the liquid. "Rum. About as raw as it comes. Here's to freedom and adventure on the great blue sea."

Jules clinked her glass with Liv's and took a cautious sip. "Raw" was probably as good a way as any to describe the feel of the alcohol as it ran down her throat. This rum was only one step up from the rotgut sold in the alleys of Landfall, and a long ways down from the booze sold in the respectable bars that she'd visited with other officers in training over the last couple of years.

Liv finished her first glass and ordered another as Jules nursed her drink. "You ever have a serious man, Jeri?" Liv asked as she took a swallow of the second drink.

"Not really," Jules said. "There was a guy who let me know that if I wanted to be serious, he did, too. Does that count?"

"Not if you didn't return it. Did you?"

"No," Jules said, taking a drink, her eyes on the surface of the bar, feeling moody as the rum brought up memories. "I felt bad about that. Ian was a good guy, from a good family."

"A good family? Did he know you were out of a legion orphan home?"

"Yes."

"And he let you know he'd still want you?" Liv shook her head. "Why'd you let him go?"

"I told you. I didn't feel that way about him," Jules said, draining the rest of her glass in a rush and feeling the alcohol hit her. "Maybe I would've, someday, if... I should've killed him, Liv. Him and Dara both."

"What?" Liv stared at Jules. "What're you drinking, girl? Did you take anything with that? Not those blue pills. Did you take one of those blue pills?"

"No. I'm sorry. I shouldn't have said... forget it."

"How many people is it you think you should've killed?" Liv asked, as if uncertain whether to be wary or amused.

"Just those two. And that woman on the ship we captured. And maybe Karl the Mechanic. And that Mage." Jules felt her jaw lock with fear. What had she just said?

"Which Mage?" Liv asked, her voice soft and sympathetic. Encounters with Mages usually resulted in painful memories for anyone who survived. Everyone knew that.

Jules got down off of her chair, stumbling slightly, appalled by how much the drink was affecting her. It was because she was in a bar again, she realized. The unrelieved stress of her last experience in a bar, the Mage staring into her eyes, was rising out of the depths of her mind and hitting her with all the fear and confusion that Jules had been forced to put aside during that first frantic night of flight. "I'm not saying anything else. I need to get out of here. Back to the ship. Right away."

"All right, Jeri, all right. Take it easy. I'll walk you back safe. You're in safe hands, sister. You know that."

"Thank you." Jules managed to walk to the door without stumbling, pausing to glance down the street and jerking herself to a halt in the doorway so abruptly that Liv slammed into her back.

"What's the matter now?" Liv asked.

"Two Mages outside," Jules whispered. "They weren't out there when I looked before."

Liv took a cautious look. "They're way down the street. Three or four hundred lances, at least. We can steer clear of them."

"They could see me," Jules said. "Us, I mean. They could see us."

"From a ways off, yeah." Liv's curious look grew concerned. "What'd Mages do to you? Something that makes even the sight of them unbearable?"

"No. I…" Jules tried to think. "Liv, I can't let them see me. Even from a distance. I don't know how close they have to be to… see something. To know where I am. Like they did at Saraston, Liv. They knew I was going to be at Saraston. What if they knew I was going to be here?"

"They knew you'd be at Saraston? Jeri, you only had the one drink. You're sure you didn't take anything else?"

"Blast it, Liv, those Mages might be after me! If you care for me at all, help me figure out how to get back to the ship!"

"All right. Trust me." Liv nodded slowly, worried eyes resting on Jules. "Slump over. Act like you can't stand. I'll hold you up. Hey! Gord and Marta! Get us a plank to carry Jeri on. She got some bad booze and can't walk."

Trusting in Liv, Jules kept her eyes mostly closed, acting like someone drugged who was barely conscious. She felt herself being laid on a plank of wood not really wide enough to hold her, her arms and legs dangling off each side. Liv draped her coat high up on Jules' chest so that Jules' face was covered as well. She felt the plank lifted, Liv's hand keeping Jules from sliding off to one side or the other as Gord and Marta carried the plank back to the *Sun Queen*. Jules found it very difficult to lie still as the plank jolted under her, sometimes causing her head to rise enough to whack back down painfully hard. The buzz of the alcohol made it worse, dizzying her so that Jules started to wonder if she'd throw up.

Were the Mages watching? Could they see her? Could they tell where she was? How far off could one of them tell? The one who'd spoken the prophecy had been looking into Jules' eyes, but did other Mages have to be that close once the prophecy had been made? No one who wasn't a Mage knew anything about Mage spells except that they were terrible and strange. Supposedly a Mage could make someone's heart disappear from their chest, or an arm or leg suddenly vanish.

That's if they didn't appear out of nowhere before anyone knew they were in danger, slashing with those long knives the Mages favored.

Gord and Marta set down the plank. "You need her carried aboard?" Gord asked, sounding a little out of breath.

"Nah, thanks, I can get her down below deck," Liv answered. "Thanks, shipmates. Have your next drink on me."

Jules heard Gord and Marta walking away, but waited until Liv picked up her coat and urged Jules up. She got up fast, scrambling up the gangway, onto the deck, and down below without looking around. If the Mages were watching and she faced them, would that give her away? If they saw her face at a distance?

Shaking with relief, Jules sat down at the long mess table, trying to get her breathing and her fear under control.

Liv came down the ladder slowly, walking over to sit next to Jules. "I told the watch at the gangway to keep an eye out for any Mages heading this way. There's no sign those two followed us, though."

"Thank you," Jules muttered.

They sat close together, Jules staring ahead, aware of Liv sitting by her, feeling the questions the older woman was holding inside. What could she say to Liv? How could she say it?

Liv spoke up in a low voice. "Most times, you're a brave girl. Foolhardy, even. But there're things that spook you bad, Jeri."

Jules nodded, not answering with words.

"There's been talk, Jeri. Since you came aboard. Because of when and where you came aboard, and because of the things you've done. Because of that bit where the Imperials didn't shoot their crossbows at you, and you having that Imperial officer's uniform that fit you so well everyone knew it was yours. And the Emperor wanting you, like that legionary officer shouted from the pier in Saraston. That's not… normal. Captain Mak tells anyone who speaks of it that you couldn't be that woman who was in Jacksport, that you were aboard this ship before the Mage saw that girl and spoke the prophecy. But there's been talk."

Jules moved her hand, grasping Liv's hand tightly. "I am her," she said in a whisper. "The Mage in Jacksport spoke to me."

She heard the quick intake of Liv's breath, and then a long pause before Liv finally breathed again. "It's true, then," Liv said. "Not a rumor."

"It's true," Jules said. "A Mage prophecy. A daughter of my line will someday overthrow the Great Guilds."

"Stars above, girl. No wonder you're so worried about meeting any more Mages. Who else knows?"

"Captain Mak. You. A couple of my fellow trainees from the Imperial ship."

"What? Imperial soldiers? And they know it's you?"

"Yes." Jules finally looked at Liv, seeing her concern. "Ian and Dara. I should've killed them, I guess, like I said. To keep the secret. But I couldn't. So, the Emperor knows. The legionaries wanted to get me at Saraston. I saw a poster with my likeness on it."

"So that's the way of it. The Emperor'd love to get his hands on the girl who's going to have that daughter, wouldn't he?" Liv murmured. "Why'd you go ashore at Saraston, knowing that?"

"I didn't know they'd be expecting me! And the captain needed me. He wouldn't have survived that trap. A trap set for me."

"I see. You did think it was something that you were responsible for." Liv suddenly smiled, a fierce look. "A girl out of a legion orphan home. And it's her line that will free us. I wonder what all the fine ladies of Marandur who look down their noses at those of us from the homes would say if they knew that?"

"Liv, who I am has to stay secret. The Mages know I exist. If they know who I am, where I am…"

"You'll die," Liv said. "They can tell if they look at you? Even from far away?"

"I don't know."

"Of course you can't. How could you? You can't ask a Mage. Mechanics, too, right? They wouldn't want you alive."

"I don't know. I'd rather not risk it," Jules said.

"Your secret is safe, sister. But I ask if I can tell Ang. He's our brother, and he'll have your back when I might not be able to."

"Liv…"

"Just Ang. No one else, Jeri. I promise."

"All right. You tell him. Make sure no one can overhear." Jules looked at Liv again. "The Emperor is looking for me. And so are the Mages. My life's not my own, Liv. Not anymore. It got taken from me. Now it's about that daughter, whoever she'll be. It's about the future. I don't count, except as the seed for something that will someday grow."

"Don't say that," Liv urged. "Your life is still yours. You still count. I've seen enough of you to know that."

Jules smiled a bit to humor Liv. "Thanks. Only tell Ang, Liv. No one else."

"You've my word on it." Liv blinked away tears, surprising Jules. "It's true," she whispered. "Someday our people will be free. Thank you, Jeri."

"I'm not doing anything except trying to stay alive," Jules said.

"You're doing something," Liv said. "Someday, when it's safe, everyone'll know who you were. And they'll believe the prophecy, because they'll look back at you and say, yeah, *her* daughter could do that."

Jules surprised herself with a low laugh. "I have a lot of trouble believing that will happen."

"Then the rest of us will believe for you."

* * *

Mak had been off the ship, returning that evening with a woman of indeterminate middle age in a sailor's coat and decent boots. She had eyes that seemed to catch everything going on around her, and a dagger at her belt that was perfectly positioned for a rapid draw and a quick stab. Jules eyed her suspiciously, not pleased to see someone like her with Mak.

"This is Captain Erin of the *Storm Rider*," Mak said to those gathered in his cabin. He and Captain Erin sat at the small table, Ang, Liv, and Jules standing around them. "We were talking about working together for a little while, her ship and ours. I wanted to discuss ideas before we bring it to the crew for a vote."

Captain Erin nodded to Ang and Liv in greeting, her eyes lingering on Jules. "That girl seems a little young to be part of your strategy council," she commented to Mak.

"I'm twenty," Jules said.

"Ah. Old enough to have seen something. The question is, how much have you learned?"

"Not near enough," Jules said.

Erin grinned. "Good answer."

"That girl got me and this ship out of Saraston despite part of a legion, an Imperial galley, and some Mages trying to make sure we never left," Mak said.

"So? What's your name, young sailor?"

"Jeri of Landfall," Jules said.

"Have we met?"

"No."

Erin frowned. "You look familiar, though. Wait." As Jules looked on, her heart sinking, Erin pulled a paper out of an inside pocket of her sea coat, unfolding it and looking at the picture drawn on it. "Ah." Turning to Mak, Erin raised an eyebrow. "You're carrying some hazardous cargo, Captain."

"I know, Captain," Mak replied.

Erin looked at Jules again. "Imperials were handing these out at Marida's harbor. It says there's a big reward for locating you, and a bigger punishment awaiting anyone who hides you. What it doesn't say is why the Emperor wants you so badly, girl," she said, rustling the paper. "But people have been saying there's a big reason. What's the truth of it?"

Jules gazed back at her. "I walked into the wrong bar."

"Sure you did." Erin shook her head at Mak. "I was going to go along with you to prey on the shipping around Landfall. We could pick up some rich prizes together. But not if you're carrying that. Half the Empire will come down on anyone they think has her. Put her off, and we'll talk."

"That's out of the question," Mak said.

"And why is that? Because it's a death wish you have?"

"She's part of the crew."

"Part of the crew?" Captain Erin asked. "And does the rest of the crew know about that woman? About what the Mage said of her?"

"I know of it," Mak said.

"That's not answering the question." Erin stood up. "I like working with you, Mak. But I won't as long as she's aboard your ship drawing Imperial galleys like blood draws sharks."

"It's not like you to be so scared of the Empire," Mak said, making it sound like both surprise and a taunt.

"Of the Empire?" Erin leaned down, looking at Mak. "Some important news, given freely because of past association. We came from Marida's harbor. Mages were there, Captain Mak. Stopping every young woman and looking at each one as if reading their deepest secrets before moving on. What do you suppose they're after? *Who* do you suppose they're after? I'll face the Empire, Mak. But the Mages, too?"

Ang spoke up. "Captain Erin, one of her line will free us all."

"Oh, to be sure," Erin said. "Some day. A Mage prophesized that, the stories say. But when will that be? She doesn't look to be expecting anytime soon." Her eyes went to Jules again. "Is that daughter already on the way?"

Jules felt her face grow hot with mingled anger and embarrassment. "No. And it's a daughter of my line. There's no telling how many generations it might be."

"So it's no one that's going to help us today. Or tomorrow, when the Mages and the Imperials come knocking. I pity you, girl, I do. But I won't die for the promise that long after I've left this world some girl in your line will come along and do what no one can do." Captain Erin walked toward the door. "Put her off, and we'll talk, Mak. Keep her, and no one will work with you."

"She's crew," Mak repeated, his voice hard.

"And what about the rest of your crew, Captain? Do they know what they're carrying? Do they know what's going to come looking for her and what'll happen to them if they're in the way?" Erin shook her head, her hand on the door. "I have a responsibility to my crew, Captain Mak. And you have a responsibility to *all* of your crew."

"Are you going to betray her?" Mak asked. "Tell the Imperials and the Mages where to find her for the reward?"

Captain Erin paused, looking at Jules. "No. She's got burden enough, and will probably die soon enough. I want no part of that."

"Thank you," Jules said between clenched teeth.

"I told you I pitied you and I meant it, girl. But if you care for any other person on this ship, you'll leave it. I don't know when you'll carry that child, but I do know that today you carry death with you."

Erin left. Mak sat silent.

Jules inhaled a shaky breath. "She's right. I'll go."

Mak looked up at her. "No, you won't."

"It's my choice," Jules said. "I'm poison for the rest of the crew."

Ang and Liv started to object but Mak stopped them. "You'll go? Here? And just wait until they come for you?"

"I'll go somewhere else," Jules said. "Overland."

"Where?" Mak waved north. "Kelsi's settlement is surrounded by mountains. There are some paths inland, but they've barely been explored. How much do you know about survival in the wilderness, Jeri?"

"I heard there's a pass in the mountains, leading west," Jules said.

"West to what? Has anyone followed it yet? Answer me, Jeri, can you survive in the wilderness?"

"I can't survive anywhere!" Jules clenched her fists, staring at them, ashamed of her outburst. "Mages can't be killed by normal weapons. Everyone knows that. Sooner or later, they'll find me. Do you want to die with me when that happens?"

Mak shook his head. "What we want is to ensure that daughter of your line gets born. Maybe we're willing to risk some danger for that. And for you."

"Captain—"

"I won't put you off. And I won't let you leave this ship here."

"Because of her? That daughter of my line? I don't even get to decide how I die because of her?"

Mak's mouth formed a tight, unhappy line. "You'll ride with us, remain crew, until we reach a better place to disembark. Caer Lyn, maybe. I heard Dor of Emdin was planning to head along the south coast of the sea, looking for a good place to set up a town far from the Emperor's reach. And far from where Mages are looking for you. We can find him. You can join him."

Jules stared at Mak. "So it's not my choice."

"All of our hopes ride on you," Ang said. "You're important."

"I am? I'm important? No, I'm not. That's not what you think. *She's* important, isn't she? That daughter of my line. That's what you all really think." Jules closed her eyes, taking a deep breath. "Liv?"

"Yes?"

"You told me my life was still my own. You lied."

Opening her eyes, Jules stormed out of the cabin, slamming the door behind her. Though she stood for a moment to let her eyes adjust to the dark, none of those inside tried to follow her.

The deck was shrouded in darkness that the lanterns of the town beyond only served to emphasize. Aside from a single, small lantern near the gangway, nothing but the stars overhead illuminated the ship. Most of the crew were ashore, so the deck was deserted except for the gangway watch, who was apparently trying to avoid getting involved in whatever drama had occurred in the captain's cabin.

Jules walked as far forward on the ship as she could, feeling trapped, knowing that there was no escape from what her life had become. Seeing the cathead projecting outward, she crawled out along it to the very end, the anchor suspended below her. She sat on the end of the cathead, her legs dangling, looking down at the harbor water, seeing nothing in the black surface. Not even her own reflection. The sounds coming from the town mocked her, speaking of normal things she could no longer share.

Why did you do this to me? she thought to that distant daughter of her line. *What did I ever do to deserve this?*

I had a life.

I was going to do so many things. Be so many things. I worked hard for that.

And it's all gone. Because of you. Because of you, I'm so important that I don't matter any more. Because of you I carry death for anyone near me. Because of you I'll never again know a moment of peace.

What will happen to my children if I survive long enough to have any? Children who also won't be you. Who also will be so important that who they are no longer matters. How will I be able to protect them when I can't protect myself?

Will they be children from someone I choose, or children forced upon me? Will I be able to love them if that happens?

Why did this have to happen to me?

Jules stared down at the water, trying to pick up any trace of her reflection, any sign of herself.

Who will you be, daughter of my line?

You took my life from me. But I'll never get to see you. I'll never get to hold you. I've never see your smile or touch your hand or watch your first steps or comfort you when you're hurt or frightened. I don't even know what you'll look like. Who your parents will be. Will they be good to you? Who will be there when you need someone? Will you have to face the world alone as I did?

Will there be any trace of me left in you?

Why have you done this to me?

Why can't I hate you?

She watched her tears fall, dropping to mingle with the salt water, vanishing into the harbor as if they'd never been.

* * *

In the morning, the *Sun Queen* sailed out of the harbor. Jules stood on the yardarm of the mainsail, watching the other ships as the *Queen* passed them. There was the *Storm Rider*. Captain Erin stood at the stern rail, her eyes on the *Sun Queen*.

Jules stared at Erin, hating her, yet admiring her for speaking a hard truth to people who didn't want to hear it.

Jules straightened to attention, standing there on the yardarm, and saluted Erin.

Captain Erin returned the salute, her expression impossible to read at this distance.

I decided to salute you, Jules thought at Erin. *I decided that. No one made me do it.* She might be carrying death, but she'd do it with dignity. And she'd pretend that what she did still mattered. Because anything else would make whatever remained of her life impossible to endure.

* * *

Two days later, with the *Sun Queen* beating just east of south toward Caer Lyn, Jules sat in the maintop as the sun rose, finishing her watch as lookout. She hadn't said much to Ang or Liv or the captain in the last couple of days, carrying around a cocoon of isolation that others in the crew could sense and didn't try to pierce. Solitary duty as a lookout suited her mood perfectly.

She squinted to the northeast, where a low-lying cloud skirted the horizon, lit by the rising sun. An odd cloud, it seemed to be growing longer and larger on one end. As the sun peeked over the eastern edge of the sea, Jules caught a momentary glimpse of a dark object below the larger end of the cloud before the brilliance kept her from seeing more.

Oh, no.

"Ship to the northeast!" Jules called down to the quarterdeck. "I think it's a Mechanics Guild ship!"

Within a few minutes her once-lonely perch was crowded with Ang, Captain Max, and Marta. "Marta," Mak said. "You've seen one of those Mechanic ships underway. Is that what we're dealing with?"

"Yeah," Marta said, squinting. "See that cloud? What's it make you think of on land?"

"One of those Mechanic trains," Ang said. "What's that thing on the front that pulls the train?"

"A locomative. Something like that," Marta said. "Someone told me once they thought that whatever makes the Mechanic ships go is the same thing that makes their trains go. I don't see how that can be, but they do put out the same sort of smoke."

"He's heading this way," Ang said. "He must have seen us. The sun's lighting up our sails as it rises."

"Still happy to have me aboard, sir?" Jules muttered to Captain Mak.

He looked at the approaching Mechanic ship for a moment longer before answering. "Yes."

"We can't outrun him," Ang said. "They don't need wind. They don't even have sails. Those ships are faster than we are even when we're running straight out before a strong wind. On a reach like this he'll be on us by mid-morning at the latest."

Jules leaned close to Mak. "Drop me off in the small boat. Once they have me, they'll leave you alone."

"No." Mak looked at the others. "If he keeps coming, we'll meet him together. One ship. One crew."

"Sir," Jules said. "I'm begging you. Give me up."

He shook his head. "I lost one girl because I stopped trying too soon. I won't do that again."

"This won't bring back your daughter, Captain!"

"No. But I won't give up before I have to." He met her eyes with his. "A girl who'd walk a gauntlet should understand that. She's still here, isn't she?"

"You don't have to walk it with me, Captain."

"Yes, I do. If you'll let me, Jeri, I'll stand beside you against them."

"And if I won't let you?"

"I'll be there anyway." Mak called down to the deck. "We're going to be intercepted by a Mechanics Guild ship! Make sure there's nothing they can find that could cause us trouble."

She stopped Mak before he could go down the mast with the others. "Captain. You know what they'll find when they board us."

He gazed back at her again, pain and resolve deep in his eyes. "If they do, they'll have a fight."

"No. You can't win that fight. Ang, Liv, you, you'll all die. For nothing. Because the Mechanics will have me anyway."

"What would you have me do, Jeri?"

"Let me decide."

"Jeri—"

"Blazes, Captain, I have nothing left in this life! Except possibly the right to decide how it ends! Give me that! If you care for me at all, give me that!" She saw him wavering. "That's the greatest gift you can give me. And I know it'll be a hard one for you. But give me that, sir. Please. Let me decide."

"Jeri, you can't give up," Mak said, looking at her with a pleading expression.

"Who said I want to give up? I don't quit, remember? Trust me. Give me a chance. I got out of the legion orphan home. I got out of Jacksport. And I got out of Saraston. Give me the chance to get out of this, without seeing you all die."

"And you walked the gauntlet." Mak nodded. "All right, Jeri. If this is the end, I'll give you the right to decide how it goes. And the chance to make something else of it."

CHAPTER SIX

The Mechanic ship overtook them as easily as a young man striding to catch a man hobbling with a broken leg. Jules stood with the rest of the crew as the strange vessel came even with the *Sun Queen*. The *Queen* was about forty lances long from the tip of the bowsprit to the stern, among the larger sailing ships on the Sea of Bakre, but the Mechanic ship seemed to be more than twice that, looking to be about one hundred lances long. A few wooden accents gleamed in the sunlight, but everything else about the ship seemed to be metal, gray or white by nature, or painted those colors. Instead of tall wooden masts, two stubby metal spires with metal supports rose amidships and a bit farther aft. Two big tubes also rose up from the deck, smoke coming out of their tops. Above the deck, buildings seemed to have been stacked on, rising in layers for three stories. On the front, another tube rested, this one level, behind a big metal shield.

Jules had seen similar ships in the harbor at Landfall. The Mechanics Guild had four metal ships like this, it was said. She knew the tube on the front was some sort of weapon, a much bigger version of those the Mechanics carried to kill anyone who opposed them.

A hail carried across the water from the Mechanic ship, unnaturally loud. "Furl your sails and await a search party!"

"Get the sails in," Mak told the crew. "Mechanics don't repeat orders. If we don't obey they'll sink the ship."

Jules helped bring in the sails and the *Sun Queen* coasted to a halt, rocking on the swells. The Mechanic ship easily matched her speed changes even though no means of propelling the craft was visible.

She watched a long boat being lowered by the Mechanics, figures in dark jackets crowding it, the angular shapes of their weapons visible at this distance.

"Jeri," Liv whispered. "There's a hiding place—"

"No," Jules said. "I'm going to face this. If it ends here, it ends here."

"But the daughter of your—"

"If she's all that special, maybe she'll finally do something for me!"

The Mechanics came up the rope and wood ladder that the *Sun Queen* put over the side, a device that for unknown reasons was called a Jaykob Ladder. But then most things on ships, like the catheads, had names that no one knew the reason for.

Jules watched, feeling curiously detached from everything, as Mak greeted the Mechanics with stiff formality. She could only imagine how he felt to be speaking with those of the same Guild that had stolen his daughter.

"Line the crew up," one of the Mechanics ordered in a loud voice.

Jules joined the line, refusing to come to attention, standing with her arms crossed as the Mechanics spread out and started looking over everyone.

One of the male Mechanics, a middle-aged man with a paunch on him, stopped in front of Jules, staring at her. He pulled out an all-too-familiar sheet of paper, looking from Jules to the picture on it. "Hey, look what I found," he called to the others.

Two other Mechanics came over, looking from the paper to Jules. "Sure looks like her," one said. "What's your name, common?"

"Jeri. Jeri of Landfall."

"I bet. Hey, Gin, look at this girl. Is it her?"

A female Mechanic walked up to them, also comparing the image on the paper to Jules. "Yeah, that's her. The report from Kelsi's was right."

The report from Kelsi's. Someone had betrayed her. Had it been Captain Erin, after all? The Mechanics were known to have a means of sending messages over long distances apparently with no delay, though no one knew what that means was. But they must have used it this time.

"Do we shoot her?" another Mechanic asked.

"Why? Because a Mage said she's dangerous? We take her back to the ship so Senior Mechanic Liz can decide what to do with her."

"Gin's right," the first Mechanic said. "We don't decide this. Come on, girl. You're taking a boat ride."

Jules saw Captain Mak step forward as if unable to stop himself, and saw two of the Mechanic weapons leveled at him. "Captain!" she yelled. "Don't! You agreed!"

"But, Jeri...!" Liv called, her face working with grief.

"If it's really true, I'll be fine. Let me walk this one!"

The Mechanics had been waiting, listening, with the relaxed attitude of people who didn't think any danger could threaten them. One of the Mechanics pointed to his ship as he spoke loudly to the crew. "We're faster than you, and that gun on the bow can blow this ship to splinters. Don't give us an excuse for target practice."

"Maybe we should kill a few just to remind them," another suggested.

"Give it a rest," a third said. "Get in the boat, common," he told Jules.

"Jeri," Mak called. "Good luck!"

"Thank you!" she shouted back before descending the ladder into the Mechanics' boat.

The Mechanics hauling the oars looked younger than those lounging in the seats. They reminded her of the officer trainee she had once been. Jules sat alone in the bow, the Mechanics facing her, feeling occasional spray strike her back as the boat made its way back to the Mechanic ship. The fact that she'd been allowed to decide to come with the Mechanics without the crew starting a hopeless fight was a very cold comfort at the moment.

"Hey," one of the women Mechanics said. "Did any of you geniuses check her for weapons?"

The female Mechanic named Gin leaned forward, yanking at the bottom of Jules' shirt. "A dagger and a sailor's knife. On a rope belt. See that? They can't even make enough leather to keep themselves clothed."

"Leather belts are expensive," Jules said.

One of the male Mechanics leaned forward as well, casually slapping her. "Shut up unless we ask you a question."

She wanted to hit him back. Pull out her dagger and make this a last, glorious fight. But that would be giving up. She wouldn't do that.

Her choice.

"Yes, sir," Jules said, the side of her face stinging. *I can take this.*

He slapped her again. "What did I say?"

"Unless you ask a question," Jules said. *I can take this.*

A third slap. "Unless who asks a question?"

"You, Sir Mechanic." *Someday I'm going to kill you.*

"You got it right that time," he said, smiling. "See?" he told the other Mechanics. "They can learn."

Mechanic Gin took Jules' knives, stuffing both into one of the big pockets on the outside of her dark jacket. She and the other Mechanics began talking in low voices about some work they were doing on the ship, ignoring Jules. Occasional unfamiliar and incomprehensible words came her way when the noise of the oars subsided for brief intervals. "Condensate... recirc pump... wiring... generator... voltage..."

Jules watched them, staying silent, feeling the tingle on her face from the slaps, imagining the many ways she would choose from someday to kill the male Mechanic who'd done that.

As the boat reached the side of the Mechanic ship, she faced another rope and wooden plank ladder leading up. Jules went up it, wishing she were wearing her Imperial uniform boots instead of bare feet. All of the Mechanics wore stout work boots as if they were part of some uniform, leaving Jules feeling once again like the orphan without the things more fortunate people enjoyed.

The deck was metal, cold and hard to feet accustomed to the warmer and softer feel of wood. She had little time to marvel as rough hands shoved her toward a doorway with rounded edges on all four sides, then inside the metal structure on this level, into a passageway with metal on all sides, some sort of tubes and cables that weren't rope snaking along supports overhead. Glass fixtures glowed with a strange, steady light that brightly illuminated the inside. It all felt alien, something not of this world.

Maybe the boasts of Mechanic Karl hadn't just been empty words. Could a ship like this actually go from one star to another?

She was shoved along a short distance to another door, through it into a room perhaps three lances on a side. A large table dominated the room, metal chairs scattered about. Jules was pushed into a chair against one wall, the Mechanics standing around as if waiting for someone.

A woman with the unmistakable air of command walked in, pausing only a moment to look at Jules. She sat down, the other Mechanics following suit.

Lady Mechanic Gin spoke respectfully to the new woman. "The information relayed from that tavern keeper in Kelsi's was accurate. We found her on that ship."

A tavern keeper. One of the eyes of the Mechanics among the common people, taking small sums of money to betray their fellow commons. At least Jules knew that Erin hadn't broken her word.

The new woman eyed the paper, then Jules. "Is this you?"

That was a question. Jules decided that if she was going to have any chance of getting out of this she'd have to be honest when she could. "Yes."

"Yes, *what*, common?"

"Yes, Lady Mechanic."

"Yes, Lady *Senior* Mechanic," the woman said with a glare.

"Yes, Lady Senior Mechanic," Jules repeated. What was a Senior Mechanic? Apparently that was the title for the Mechanics who bossed around other Mechanics.

"Why does the Emperor want you?"

"Because of the prophecy the Mage made in Jacksport, Lady Senior Mechanic." She heard derisive snickers from the other Mechanics at her mention of the Mage.

The Senior Mechanic leaned back, her eyes on Jules. "Tell me what it said."

Jules met that gaze. "That someday a daughter of my line would overthrow the Great Guilds and free the world." That wasn't the whole thing, but the Senior Mechanic hadn't asked for *everything* the prophecy had said.

"Great Guilds," another Mechanic complained. "Why haven't we wiped out that saying?"

The Senior Mechanic ignored him. "Not your daughter? A daughter of your line?"

"Yes, Lady Senior Mechanic."

"Why would a Mage say that to you?"

Jules hesitated, not certain how to answer that. "He was looking at me, Lady Senior Mechanic. That's all I know."

"How many children do you already have?"

"None, Lady Senior Mechanic."

"You're not pregnant?"

"No, Lady Senior Mechanic," Jules said, feeling her face warming at the intrusive question. She'd never imagined so many people caring about her physical condition, nor how unpleasant it would be to have them all wondering if she was expecting a child yet.

Another Mechanic laughed. "I guess she didn't start as early as most common girls."

The Senior Mechanic kept her eyes on Jules as if trying to read her truthfulness. "Why didn't that Mage kill you?"

"I ran, Lady Senior Mechanic."

"She's got some common sense," Lady Mechanic Gin said.

The Senior Mechanic snorted, looking around her at the other Mechanics. "The Mages are worried about a baby who's going to be born to a baby that hasn't even been conceived yet."

"Are they? Or is this all some sort of theater to convince us that they're worried about that?" the Mechanic named Nat wondered.

"Why would they do that?"

"Maybe to get us to waste time chasing her?" Nat suggested.

"That'd hardly be worth the amount of effort the Mages are putting into this," the Senior Mechanic said.

"She doesn't even have the kid yet," Gin said. "Why are we bothering with her?"

"If this baby is going to be so special, maybe we should make sure it's part Mechanic," Nat said, grinning. "I'll bet a lot of guys aboard would enjoy contributing to the effort."

"I would, too," another one of the men said, though some others looked uncomfortable or unhappy.

Jules sat, rigid, as the meaning of that hit home.

"It's against Guild rules," the female Mechanic named Gin said, her words short and sharp.

"She's a common, Gin."

"Rape is rape, Nat. It's against Guild rules."

"What? You'd turn us in?" another man complained. "You think the Guild Masters would care? They'd probably reward us."

"They'd reward you with the inside of one of the new cells at Longfalls," the woman Senior Mechanic said. "Drop it."

"But she's just—"

"We're not Mages," a third male Mechanic interrupted. "We don't do that."

"We're not *supposed* to," a fourth male Mechanic mumbled, looking discontented. "That doesn't mean some don't do it anyway."

"Are you going to press charges against anyone?" Mechanic Nat demanded of Gin and the other men.

"*I* might," the Senior Mechanic said, instantly ending the argument. She looked at Jules again. "It's not just the Mages. The Emperor wants this girl. Do you know why he wants you, common?"

Jules met her eyes. "To take over the prophecy, making it part of the Imperial family line."

"You don't want that?"

"No. The only way the Emperor will have me is if he does the same thing those other Mechanics were just talking about doing."

"Speak with respect or you might still get that."

She managed to answer in a level voice. "Yes, Lady Senior Mechanic."

The Senior Mechanic studied Jules again, her eyes thoughtful. "You've got spirit, but you've also got brains. How did you do on the Mechanic tests?"

Jules hesitated. "I don't know what a Mechanic test is, Lady Senior Mechanic."

"They're given in all the schools! How could you be ignorant of them?"

A male Mechanic, one of those who had objected to the idea of raping her, spoke to Jules. "Where did you go to school when you were growing up?"

"I was in the legion orphan home in Landfall, Sir Mechanic."

He gestured to the other Mechanics. "One of the orphan homes. We don't test there."

"Why not?" the female Mechanic named Gin asked.

The Senior Mechanic answered. "There didn't seem a high probability of finding good candidates in that setting. But maybe the Guild should revisit that decision. We may have missed an opportunity with this one."

One of the other male Mechanics eyed Jules. Was it her imagination that she saw some sympathy in those eyes? "The Emperor is devoting a lot of resources to looking for her. That's good for us, right? It'll keep him too busy to give us any more trouble about new towns being founded outside his control. And the Mages are so busy looking for her they're not interfering with anything we want to do. As long as she's alive, she's doing us a service. As long as she's free, the Mages and the Empire will be devoting resources to catching her."

"The Emperor might take over those new towns to try to get her," Lady Mechanic Gin pointed out. "We need to get Guild Halls built in those locations before the Imperials try to move in."

"Why not just hand her over to the Emperor?" another Mechanic said. "As a trade for him doing as we say? If he believes in this Mage garbage, and apparently he does like the other commons, he'll be preoccupied trying to get as many kids out of her as he can. And if the Mages know he has her, they'll start making serious trouble for him and the Empire because they want her dead before she has any kids."

Jules listened as most of the Mechanics spoke of her fate as if she wasn't even here. She might have been another chair for all the concern they showed.

She knew that feeling. She'd experienced it many times in the orphan home, at the hands of administrators who saw the orphans as names and numbers but not people.

Mechanic Karl had seemed like any other boorish man. These Mechanics were speaking like the bureaucrats Jules had known. They weren't special, she realized. They were as flawed and human as any of the commons they looked down upon. But they were also separate, speaking a language and sharing ideas she sometimes had trouble grasping.

"We don't want a war between the Mages and the Empire," the sympathetic Mechanic said. "What if the Mages win?"

"They can't!"

"The Mages have power over the commons as long as the commons believe in that Mage nonsense."

"Lock her up in Longfalls then."

"If we lock her up we're telling the commons that we believe in that prophecy junk, too," Gin said. "They'll take that as confirmation that this baby factory is important to them." She nodded toward Jules.

"How about just killing her then?" Mechanic Nat asked.

"You mean, do the work of the Mages for them?"

The Senior Mechanic, listening to the debate, looked at Jules. "What about you? Why do you think we shouldn't kill you?"

Jules, startled by the sudden interest in what she thought, chose her words carefully. Was the Senior Mechanic simply looking to have Jules condemn herself with her own words? "Because I'm valuable to you alive, Lady Senior Mechanic."

"Why? You're supposed to have this daughter that's a big threat to us, aren't you?" the Senior Mechanic asked in a mocking voice.

"A daughter of my line, Lady Senior Mechanic. Not my daughter. It could be a long time before that daughter appears." Why not make something that tormented her into something that might help instead? Would these Mechanics pick up on the ways they could try to use her uncertain future, or would she have to spell it out even more clearly?

The Senior Mechanic's eyes narrowed in thought. "A long time. While the commons wait for her. I see. It would work to prevent uprisings against the Guild. The Guild Masters want to prevent uprisings by the commons. Uprisings waste resources."

The sympathetic male Mechanic smiled. "Then this is perfect, isn't it? They think some kid she has way down the line will overthrow the Mechanics Guild. So the commons will stay quiet while they wait for this mythical hero to show up and save them. Which will never happen."

"But she's going to have children," Lady Mechanic Gin said. "What if the commons decide one of them is that hero predicted by the Mages?"

One of the Mechanics who'd seemed supportive of raping Jules shrugged. "We'd have to kill any kids she has, right? To keep the commons from rallying around one of them, which might force us to kill a lot more commons."

"Killing a lot of commons would teach them a lesson," another Mechanic said.

"Do we have that much ammunition?" another man asked. "There was that quality-control problem—"

"If the Guild would give a waiver authorizing one-time mass production—"

"Unthinkable," the Senior Mechanic said. "If the problem is severe enough, the Guild has access to special weapons that can suppress any common rebellion."

"We do?"

"Even I don't know the details, but I'm told that if they're needed they'll be brought out and employed. But the Guild wants to avoid extreme measures that could also destroy Guild Halls and create problems with contaminated areas. I think you're right," she told the Mechanic who'd suggested freeing Jules. "If we don't have custody of her, anything that happens to this common girl will be laid at the feet of the Mages. The commons will blame them." She tapped one finger on the table, looking at Jules. "If she's free, the Empire remains distracted, the Mages are occupied trying to find her, and the common folk remain focused on that daughter of her line, waiting for her to show up. She seems smart enough to stay free and keep causing trouble for our enemies."

"We still ought to kill any kids to make sure they don't become rallying points," another Mechanic complained. "Even if we let her go, the Guild wouldn't have much trouble finding her again, right? Just like we did this time."

"Why would we kill the boys?" Gin asked. "Obviously none of them could be a daughter of her line."

"Fine," Nat said. "We kill her girl kids. But we ought to kill the boys, too, because when they grow up they might have girls. They're just commons. They're having too many kids as it is. That's why we're having all these problems, isn't it? The population of commons inside the Empire is too big, and they're spilling out looking for new places."

"If the Emperor would crack down on commons trying to escape his lands—"

"He is," another Mechanic said. "But the Empire's like a boiler with too much pressure on it. Commons are escaping it, and that's a good thing because otherwise the pressure might get too high."

"You think it could blow?" Gin asked, skeptical. "The Empire?"

"Yeah. And then where are we? Having to pick up the pieces and rule the commons directly?"

"If we killed some of the kids," the Mechanic named Nat complained, "maybe when commons have more than two, the pressure would come off, and—"

"I'm uncomfortable with talking about killing kids," the sympathetic Mechanic said. "Adults can make their own decisions. Children have no voice in what happens. Or who their mother happens to be."

"You're too soft! Next thing you know you'll want us teaching them how to use tools! As if they could ever learn!" Nat pointed at Jules. "Senior Mechanic Liz, do we want her free, and alive, if she's smart? We don't want commons getting ideas."

Another Mechanic raised her eyebrows at Nat. "Are you scared of her?"

"I don't think we should reward a common who's smart enough to figure that stuff out!"

"We can't use a common who's not smart. She'd just be killed by the Mages in no time. They're liars and fakes, but they know how to kill their enemies."

"And do we want the Mages killing her?" another female Mechanic asked. "If they do, yes, the Mages get the blame, but the commons stop hoping this hero will show up to save them, and maybe start causing more trouble right away."

"Good point," the Senior Mechanic said. "We want her alive. For now, at least. And she's obviously smart enough to be obedient when her life is on the line instead of striking out blindly like a frightened animal as many commons do. She could be a valuable resource for the Guild." She looked at Jules again, smiling in a way that was meant to look encouraging but instead sent a chill down Jules' spine. "We can use her. How would you like that, common? If you do what we ask, the Mechanics Guild can help you. And protect you."

Jules breathed in and out before replying. This kind of outcome was what she'd hoped for. But... "And kill my children."

"Does that idea bother you?"

"Yes, Lady Senior Mechanic, it does."

The Senior Mechanic smiled again. "But if you have any children, they'd give us a handle on you, wouldn't they? The commons will listen to you. If you're compliant, if your children are compliant, we can use all of you to preach compliance to the other commons. And if you and your children tell the commons to submit to the authority of the Mechanics Guild, there would never be need to kill the children. Everyone wins. We just have to see to it that right now you have a means to deal with any Mages who corner you." The Senior Mechanic stood up abruptly. "I need to call—" She glanced at Jules. "I need to talk to some others. Everyone wait here."

After the Senior Mechanic left, Jules waited along with the Mechanics, most of whom engaged in low conversations among themselves. Only occasionally did one of them take a brief look at Jules. She sat straight in the chair, knowing she looked nervous and deciding that was probably for the best. Looking too confident might anger the Mechanics.

She wondered who the Senior Mechanic was talking to. Were there more high-ranking Mechanics on this ship? But, if so, why weren't they at the meeting?

After what felt like a very long time, the Senior Mechanic returned, her expression giving away little. Sitting down again, she gestured to one of the male Mechanics. "Give her your pistol and four rounds of ammunition. Don't load it."

"Honored Senior Mechanic—" the man began to protest.

"The Guild Masters approved this. Don't forget *your* place," the Senior Mechanic said.

The man scowled, bringing out an object that he put on the table and shoved across it toward Jules.

She stared down at it. A thick, hollow metal tube on one end about the length of one hand and its extended fingers, a curved wooden handle of some sort at the other end, and what looked like a metal cylinder and other objects in the middle. Jules had sometimes seen Mechanics with such things in their hands, and knew it was a weapon. She'd never seen a Mechanic weapon so closely before, though. The Mechanics Guild had decreed it would mean death for a common to possess or to use one.

"Hold it like this," the male Mechanic closest to Jules said, grasping the wooden handle. "It's called a revolver. This is the trigger. Pull it to fire the weapon. Four cartridges. Here. Load them like this. Pull out the cylinder, slide them in, close the cylinder. Point it at someone, pull the trigger, this hammer comes back, slams forward, hits the round in the chamber lined up with the barrel, and bam. There's no safety like there is on a rifle because the revolver uses a double action trigger pull so an accidental shot is almost impossible, though I guess commons might manage it."

"That's not exactly a firearms safety course," Gin commented.

"If she accidentally shoots a friend it's just another common." The Mechanic set the weapon down in front of Jules again, along with the four "cartridges," cylinders rounded at one end and flat on the other.

"That is a Mechanic weapon," the Senior Mechanic said to Jules, speaking slowly as if to a child. "A revolver. It's far more powerful than any weapon commons have. With this, you can defend yourself against the Mages. But you only have four rounds for it. That means it will only work four times. If you want more ammunition, you'll need to do what the Mechanics Guild tells you to do."

The cartridges must be like the bolts for a crossbow. Without them the revolver would be useless except as a club. Jules looked down at the weapon, then back at the other woman. "I understand, Lady Senior Mechanic. This... I'm permitted to have this?"

The Senior Mechanic nodded. "For this purpose, and for you alone, the rule against any common having a Mechanic weapon in their possession is waived. Don't let any other common touch it. Understand that we're not giving it to you. It's a loan, for as long as you serve the purposes of the Mechanics Guild."

"Yes, Lady Senior Mechanic."

"Don't let her load the weapon before she gets back to her own ship," the Senior Mechanic told Gin. "Oh, and, common, what's your name again?"

"Jules of Landfall."

"If you try to use that weapon against Mechanics it will explode and kill you. So don't. Kill Mages with it. Or other commons. We want the attention of the Mages focused on you, and we want the Emperor to stay busy trying to catch you. The weapon is so that you can stay alive for those purposes. If you want to continue to live, if you want your children to live, do as you're told."

"Yes, Lady Senior Mechanic."

"Take her back to that ship," the Senior Mechanic told Gin. "She'll do our bidding, and create more problems for the Mages and that troublesome Emperor."

Jules sat, not believing, until Lady Mechanic Gin gave her a glare. Jules got up, but Gin stopped her with a push and pointed to the Mechanic weapon. Jules picked it up carefully, as well as the four… cartridges? She thought that was what they'd been called. She held the weapon awkwardly as Gin pushed her out of the room and along the metal-lined passage again until they emerged into daylight.

Surprisingly little time had passed. Jules blinked at the sun, not ready to accept that she wouldn't die today.

They went back down the ladder into the boat, the younger Mechanics once again pulling the oars. This time the only Mechanic not pulling oars or handling the rudder at the stern was Gin in the bow with Jules.

Jules looked at the female Mechanic. "May I have my knives back, Lady Mechanic?"

Gina started at the reminder, scowled, then dug into her pocket and pulled out both knives, looking over the dagger before giving it back to Jules. "There's some nice metallurgy there in the blade, but the handle isn't great quality."

"It's all I could afford," Jules said. "Thank you, Lady Mechanic."

"They're yours," Gin replied without turning her head to look at Jules.

"Not for returning the knives. For stopping the others from harming me."

That earned her a very brief glance from the female Mechanic. "I didn't do it for you. How they treat common women affects how they think of all women. If they get away with mistreating you, they won't respect me. I did it for me."

"Thank you, anyway," Jules said, knowing her voice sounded sharper.

"Don't get uppity, common," Gin said. "I'm an engineer. You're a common. A common whose sole claim to fame is that she's going to have a baby."

"I appreciate your support as a fellow woman," Jules said, her emotions beginning to boil as she thought back over the meeting and her treatment by the Mechanics.

The female Mechanic finally focused fully on her, an angry glint in her eyes. "Watch your mouth. A daughter of your line. That's what it says? So what does that make you?"

"Nothing," Jules said, feeling that answer deep inside her and trying not to show the pain it caused.

The other woman hesitated, her eyes on Jules, before turning away. "No mother is nothing," Gin muttered. "Each one is something. Don't let anyone tell you otherwise. What do you do on that ship?"

"Anything that needs doing."

"Anything? Can you navigate?"

"Yes, Lady Mechanic. I was an Imperial officer trainee before the Mage spoke the prophecy."

Gin eyed her closely. "You might be too smart. It's a good thing for you that Senior Mechanic Liz didn't know that part about you."

Was that a subtle warning not to share that information with other Mechanics? Or was Gin saying out loud her own misgivings regarding Jules? "I don't understand you, Lady Mechanic," Jules said.

"You're a common."

"I don't think that's the reason."

"If you say one more word before we reach that ship, I'm going to take you back to ours.. Got that, common?"

Jules nodded.

She climbed up the ladder onto the deck of the *Sun Queen* again, turning slightly just before reaching the top to see the Mechanic boat already returning to their ship.

"Jeri?" As Jules reached the deck of the ship she saw Captain Mak looking at her in disbelief. "Are you free? They're letting you go?"

"Yes, sir."

"How did you manage that, Jeri?"

Jules inhaled slowly, seeing the rest of the crew staring at her. "Sir, we need to talk privately." She realized she still had the Mechanic weapon in one hand and held it up, bringing a gasp of shock from more than one of those watching. "About this, and other things." She couldn't help adding one more thing. "I told you to trust me."

* * *

Mak sat thinking after Jules had described the conversation between her and the Mechanics. She sat on the other side of the small table in the captain's cabin, the "revolver" on the table between them. "Jeri, this changes a lot of things." He nodded toward the weapon. "That changes a lot of things. *You* changed a lot of things."

"How?" Jules asked him. "I got through that, I got released by playing on what the Mechanics wanted, but I'm not sure what happens now. That revolver can only kill four people. Then if I beg and promise to do what the Mechanics tell me to do, they might give me enough, uh, cartridges to kill four more."

"It's not just the means to kill Mages," Mak said. "It's the symbolism." He reached a finger toward the revolver, not quite touching it. "Do you know what this says? It says the Mechanics Guild is backing you. You're one of their players."

"I know," Jules said. "That's how it looks. How many common people are going to hate me for that?"

"That depends on what they hear from us. And now we have a chance to talk to them. Captain Erin was worried about you being aboard this ship because the Empire and the Mages wanted you and there was no way we or any other group of commons could stand against those two powers. But the Mechanics Guild *can* stand against them. You've got backers powerful enough to turn you from a dangerous liability to a very desirable asset."

"Like I'm a game piece," Jules said.

Mak hesitated. "A game piece who gets to make her own decisions."

"That hasn't been happening a lot lately, sir."

"I let you decide to go to that ship," he said in a low voice. "Do you think that was easy? But you said that was what you wanted, and I listened, even though it hurt a great deal to see you go."

That was true. She sat staring at the weapon. "Between you and me, sir, I'm not sure how I managed it. Part of it, maybe a lot of it, was saying just enough to let the Mechanics believe what they wanted to believe about me. And then prodding them in the direction I wanted. But I'm very much out of my depth now. I feel a little stupid saying this after insisting I should make my own decisions, but I'd really appreciate some advice from you, sir. On what I should do."

"I think we should take this ship back to Kelsi's settlement, where I know the *Storm Rider* was going to be for a while to fix some damage, and show Captain Erin that weapon. And then we plan to hit Imperial shipping off Landfall while the Emperor's galleys are chasing around the Sea of Bakre looking for you everywhere else."

"What about the Mechanics?" Jules asked. "They want me to do things that will help them. But I don't want to help Mechanics. I'll try to find ways to undermine them and their purposes. How do I keep the Mechanics happy while working against them?"

"You play them, Jeri. Just like you did in that meeting on their ship. They think you're their pawn. But you're nobody's pawn. You're the Emperor piece."

"Right," Jules said. "Sure."

"I'm serious." Mak nodded to her, smiling. "And that's what we'll tell other commons, that you're actually working for the common people. Since you're the woman who was told the prophecy, other commons will believe you. But the Mechanics will think that's you fooling the commons. They won't believe you're playing *them* under the table because they can't imagine a common being smarter than they are. And the Mechanics haven't realized yet what a powerful piece you are. They're so busy plotting against the Mages and the Empire, and being smug about their own status, that they're not even considering what you might do."

"You mean, have a baby?" Jules asked. "Yeah, they're counting on that happening at some point."

"No. That's not what I mean." Mak paused. "I haven't figured this all out yet. But I'm thinking. Jeri, have you wondered why the person who's going to overthrow the Great Guilds is going to take a while to show up? Why she's a daughter of your line instead of, say, you?"

"Because it's ridiculous to think I could do that, sir."

"Others might disagree."

"Sir, that ship… it's hard to describe. It's so different from the *Sun Queen* or any Imperial galley. And the Mechanics have four of them! They're too powerful, sir."

"That's my point. Why not you or your own immediate daughter?"

Jules shrugged, fighting the depression that question brought to mind. "I figured it was just part of a cruel joke on me, sir."

"No. I think it's part of a very big plan," Mak said. "Though I can't imagine what force is driving that plan. Yes, the Mechanics are immensely strong. But, listening to those Mechanics, did you think they sounded like people who were strong and getting stronger?"

"No," Jules said. "They sounded like people concerned with maintaining the power they had."

"Yes. Maybe the Great Guilds are like people, Jules. I was pretty strong once. Young and vigorous. But as I aged I lost things. I got weaker."

"Sir—"

"Listen. Maybe that's going to happen to the Great Guilds. The devices of the Mechanics will wear out. Something will happen to the Mages. It will take time. Maybe centuries. And the daughter of your line will appear when the Great Guilds have become weak enough that a sufficiently amazing woman can overcome them."

Jules stared at him. "I never thought of that. Nothing has changed in my lifetime. But you're right, someday the Great Guilds could get weaker."

"Or the commons will get stronger," Mak said. "It's already starting. Kelsi's settlement. Marida's harbor. Caer Lyn. Jacksport. And I've heard rumors of similar things happening inland, of towns being founded in the Northern Ramparts beyond the Empire's reach, and convicts working the Imperial salt farms escaping to form a settlement in that southern area beyond the Waste. If commons can plant and grow new cities, we'll be stronger by the time things happen. More people. Bigger armies. Maybe big enough to finally defeat the weakened Great Guilds—if led by that daughter of your line."

The vision of it staggered her. Jules had to breathe in and out slowly to calm herself. "So maybe there's a reason."

"Maybe."

"Shouldn't we be turning the ship and heading back to Kelsi's settlement, sir?"

He grinned. "Excellent idea, Jeri. Is that your decision?"

Jules found herself smiling back at him. "Yes, sir. That is my decision."

* * *

"And then I—"

"Hey, Don! Get up here and help with this rope work!" Ang called.

"I gotta go," Don said to Jules. "See you later, Jeri."

"Yeah," she said in a noncommittal voice. She stayed leaning on the rail amidships as Don went to help Ang near the bow. The sun had set some time ago, the last traces of its light vanished, darkness all about the ship, the sea gone black and mysterious under the starlight. Aside from the sailors at the helm on the quarterdeck, most of the crew were below deck, already sleeping, but Jules had lingered up here. She suspected that Ang had deliberately called away Don to give her some private time.

They'd be back at Kelsi's settlement tomorrow morning. She hadn't had much time alone to think.

Liv and some of the others had sewn together a sort of hard leather sheath for the Mechanic revolver, shaped to the weapon like those sheaths some had seen Mechanics wearing. When done it was sort of a combination sheath and scabbard. Leather straps at the top could be tied to ensure the weapon wouldn't fall out. They had also crafted a leather belt for Jules despite her protests that it wasn't necessary. The revolver sheath fitted on it along with the sheaths for her knives. The Mechanic weapon rested on her hip, its weight slowly becoming familiar, because the captain had said she needed to get used to having it with her. And she wore her boots, polished leather, because Mak had advised Jules that she needed to stop looking like any other sailor.

She was hiding from the Mages and the Empire, but she had to look special, stand out next to others. Apparently that made sense.

Jules almost groaned when another man came to lean on the rail right beside her. But when she looked she felt relieved to see Mak. "Good evening, Captain."

"How are you doing, Jeri?" Mak asked.

"I'm fine, Captain."

"Don seemed to be spending a lot of time with you."

Jules paused, thinking, surprised at the observation coming from the captain. "I guess."

"Is there anything going on?"

"Between me and Don?" Jules asked, feeling a curious mix of aggravation and affection over Mak's interest in her life. "No."

"All right." Mak didn't do a very good job of hiding the relief in his voice. "I just felt I should let you know that Don isn't the finest man in the world."

"Don isn't the finest man on the *Sun Queen*," Jules said. "He's not even the finest man with a name beginning with D on the *Sun Queen*. But, I'm on a pirate ship. My social prospects are pretty much limited to pirates."

Mak chuckled. "There are a lot of good men ashore, Jeri."

"Yes, sir. Living in places where bad men and bad women can find me and kill me or kidnap me for the Emperor." Jules glanced over at Mak. "In case you're worried, there hasn't been anything physical between me and Don. I have to think about the future, you know." She heard the bitterness that came into her voice on the last words and regretted saying them.

This time Mak responded with a sigh. "Jeri, I really wasn't thinking about that."

"I didn't think you were," Jules admitted, looking down at the dark waters of the Sea of Bakre. "Sir, can I ask you something? About men? You don't have to answer, but I don't think I'd be comfortable asking anyone else about this."

He paused. "Certainly."

"When I started carrying this Mechanic weapon, this revolver, I thought people would steer clear of me because of it." Jules frowned at the passing water. "But it's like it's having the opposite effect, especially on guys. Young guys. The last couple of days they won't leave me alone. It's like… this is going to sound weird. It's like years ago when my chest grew, and the sort of guys who'd never seemed to think I was interesting all of the sudden wanted to spend time with me. Do you have any idea what's going on?"

"Um…" Mak began, sounding a bit uncomfortable. "I can only speak with certainty for myself, but I know that when I see a woman carrying a sword, she looks stronger, and more dangerous, and that is… more attractive."

"Because you can tell she can take of herself?"

"Not exactly. It's the danger itself, Jeri. The strength and the danger. Men, young men in particular, tend to be attracted to dangerous things."

"Oh. I knew that. Women, young women especially, are like that, too. Dangerous men are… you know."

"I hope you're not—" Mak began.

"Not me! I don't need to be burned to know I shouldn't put my finger in a flame! I've seen other girls get burned." Jules gasped a brief laugh. "Sir, I know you're a man, too, but guys are really strange some-times."

"I admit it," Mak said, smiling wryly. "Which is why I wanted to ask if you were all right. I don't want to overstep my bounds. You're a grown woman. But I've seen the extra attention you're getting and I know the sort of mistakes people can make. I hope I can help you avoid making some of those."

"You don't seem to have that same interest in the other women aboard," Jules said.

"You're younger."

"Not that much younger than Reya or Lana."

"No, you're not," Mak said. "I did talk to Lana once about Don's history, not that she seemed all that interested. People get to be eigh-teen, or twenty, and they think they've learned all the important things. It's hard for them to realize how much is left to learn, and how easy it is to make a single mistake that can change your life for the worse."

"I know all about that already," Jules said. "This one time I walked into a bar, and my whole life get wrecked."

"Jeri..." Mak looked around for anyone close enough to hear. "Do you realize how important it was that the prophecy was made in a bar where a lot of other people could hear it?"

"No. You mean to be extra double sure my life was wrecked?"

"Jeri, you know how it feels for everyone," Mak said. "Slaves to the Great Guilds. Whatever they say, we have to do. The way those Mechanics treated you. And not a trace of hope that we could ever change that. Mechanic or Mage, they have powers we don't. How could they ever be beaten?"

He paused. "But now, there's hope. People heard it. People are repeating it. They know that someday one of their own will do the apparently impossible."

Jules lowered her head, staring at the dark waters. "So I got to lose all hope and it was given to everyone else."

"Is that really how it feels?"

"Yes. Sometimes… sometimes I want to throw myself off the ship and sink to the bottom of the sea."

Mak took a long moment to respond. "Jeri, I know I made some mistakes in how I dealt with things, but I never wanted you to feel like that. No one does."

"It's not anything you can help doing," Jules said. "It's the way it is. I don't matter. I'm not going to do anything anyone cares about. Except have a kid. And someday some child down the line will do that great thing. That's who matters. But me? I'm just the mother hen. I'll lay the egg that someday hatches into the hero. A daughter of my line. She probably won't even know my name. She'll have no idea who I was. But the entire rest of my life, which may be really short, is going to be about nothing but her. That daughter."

Mak didn't answer. She looked over at him, seeing the darkness in his eyes so deep that even the starlight could pick it out. Her ranting about a daughter. And him thinking of the daughter he'd lost. "Oh. Captain. I'm sorry. I'm really, really sorry."

He blinked, looking away for a moment. "We're both haunted by daughters, I guess," Mak said in a low voice. "The past, and the future."

"You didn't do anything wrong," Jules said.

"Neither did you. That didn't change our fates, did it?"

"You came out here to see if I was all right, to make me feel better, and I made you feel terrible," Jules said.

"That's all right, Jeri. It's all right. Can I ask a favor of you?"

"Anything, sir."

"Don't throw yourself off the ship."

She fought the smile, but it came anyway. "Yes, sir."

"And don't think you're not going to be anything," Mak said. "That prophecy didn't say you'd be nothing but the ancestor of that girl. It said nothing about what you will do beyond your having at least one child to carry on your line. Who *you'll* be has not been prophesized."

"But—"

"Listen to me, Jeri. We can create the future we most fear for ourselves if that's all we dwell on. Or we can create the future we want by working toward it. Think of what *you* can do. Think of who *you* can be. And then become that. Before, during, and after having that child."

She looked at him, feeling hope where little had been, a possibility of purpose where none had been. "Thank you, sir. Do you really think I can?"

"Yes. I told you that I think you're the Emperor piece. I think you can change the game. Not overnight. Not as fully as that daughter of your line will someday. But the commons have to grow in strength. I really believe that you can help that happen. That you can help provide the things that daughter of your line will need if she's to succeed. And if you do, she'll know who you were. She'll treasure the memory of you, no matter how many years pass between now and then."

Jules looked down again, blinking away tears. The dark waters were still there, but this time she saw the stars reflected in those waters. "Captain Mak…"

"Yes?"

"I… I don't know. Just… thank you. Your words mean a lot to me. I needed to hear them, but I also needed to hear you say them. I don't know why. Thank you."

"Thank you," Mak said.

* * *

They walked onto the *Storm Rider*, Jules and Captain Mak, the Mechanic revolver swinging at her hip. Jules could see the stares resting on the weapon before going to her face, could feel the stares at her back. Those stares had followed her from the moment she walked onto the pier where the *Sun Queen* was once again tied up, and across to the pier where the *Storm Rider* still rested. The whole way, Jules held her expression calm and composed, as if she was so confident and so strong that she didn't need to fear anything. It was an act, but she hoped it was a convincing one.

Captain Erin met them outside the *Storm Rider*'s stern cabin, her eyes also going from the weapon to Jules' face. "Can I ask where you got that?"

"Some new allies gave it to me," Jules said loudly, hearing the muted cries that followed from many of those listening.

"Allies?" Erin looked at Mak, the meaning behind that question clear.

"It's on terms I'm comfortable with," Mak said.

Erin stepped closer, her voice low. "You're comfortable working with the Mechanics? You? Why, Mak? I know you can't be bought. What's the deal?"

He smiled. "They think they're steering the ship, so they're happy."

"And who is steering it? You?"

"I am," Jules said.

Captain Erin nodded slowly, her eyes on Jules. "I thought you were dangerous, but you're far more so than I realized."

"People keep telling me that," Jules said.

"Maybe they're on to something." Erin nodded again, to her and to Mak. "Allies. Very powerful allies. Are you still willing to discuss mutual endeavors, Mak, or did you just stop by to let me know you've no need of the likes of me anymore?"

"Jeri made the decision to come back here and speak with you," Mak said.

"Did she?" Erin said, looking a question at Jules.

"You were blunt," Jules said. "But honest. You spoke your mind, and you were looking out for your crew. I know the value of people like that."

"Then you're wise beyond your years and I give you full credit for that," Erin said. "What is it you want to talk about?"

Jules smiled. "I'm supposed to keep the Emperor's attention focused on me. Captain Mak has suggested some ways to do that which should profit all of us."

Erin grinned. "Oh, yes. I can think of ways that should profit us greatly. Come into my cabin, honored guests. Let's have a drink together and talk business."

Two days later, the *Storm Rider*'s repairs complete and both vessels stocked with enough water and food to last a while, the two ships sailed away from Kelsi's settlement, bearing south and east together toward the sea lanes along the Imperial coast. Jules stood alongside Captain Mak on the *Sun Queen*'s quarterdeck, cutlass riding on one of her hips and the revolver on the other, her boots shining from a fresh polish, the wind blowing her hair.

Her life had been taken from her that night in Jacksport.

It was time to start taking it back.

CHAPTER SEVEN

The merchant ship was big and riding low from what must be a heavy cargo. He had been heading toward Landfall along the southern sea route from the salt marshes west of Imperial territory. As the *Sun Queen* swooped down on him from upwind, the other ship put on more sail, but it made little difference. In the rough seas, with a stiff breeze at her back, the *Queen* bounded from swell to swell like a wolf closing on a fat, slow cow.

The Imperial sloop that had been patrolling this area had been drawn off in a prolonged pursuit of the *Storm Rider*, Captain Erin repeatedly teasing the sloop with apparent chances to catch her ship before slipping away again. Both ships were somewhere back to the west and south, beyond the horizon.

Jules stood on the quarterdeck, checking the revolver. She'd been practicing with the strange weapon, removing all of the cartridges and watching how using her finger to pull the trigger caused the hammer to first come back and then slam forward, how each time that happened the cylinder that held the cartridges rotated one increment to place another empty hole or cartridge under the hammer. But she'd yet to shoot the weapon, since she had only the four cartridges and might never see another one.

Fortunately, she wasn't dependent on the Mechanic weapon. In addition to the dagger at her belt, she kept her cutlass loose in its scabbard, ready to be drawn.

"Jeri," Captain Mak said. "You don't have to lead the boarding party."

"Yes, I do." She smiled at him. "It's part of showing everyone that I'm someone."

"You can get hurt. You can die."

"I know." Jules flexed her legs. "It'd actually be safer to go barefoot than to wear these boots."

"You have to look the part, Jeri."

She held the revolver in one hand and drew her cutlass with the other, standing next to the railing as the wind whipped at her. "How's this look?" Jules asked.

"Dangerous," Mak said. "Any young men on that ship will be eating out of your hand."

"Maybe one of them'll be cute," Jules said, turning to look at the other ship as it strained to escape, spray flying about its bow. "Don't pirate girls get to love 'em and leave 'em?"

"If they want to live that way," Mak said.

She heard the note of disapproval, of concern, in his voice that he couldn't quite hide, and turned to grin at him. "Don't worry, Captain. I'll be a good girl as I run my cutlass through anyone who resists and help ransack that ship."

He smiled at her. "You do need to set a good example for that daughter of your line." Coming closer, Mak nodded toward the other ship. "Don't get so far ahead of the others this time. You want shipmates on either side of you, protecting you at the same time that you protect them. Are you sure you want the Mechanic weapon in your hand? You could drop it."

"I need to have it ready to use," Jules said, looking down at the deadly object. "If it's at my belt and not tied in, it might fall out. And if I'm holding it the people we're facing will see it and not put up as much of a fight."

"I can't argue with your reasoning," Mak said. "Blazes, Jeri. Be careful."

She gazed back at him, serious, and nodded. "I will be. Captain, I have to do this."

"I promised to let you decide," he said. "Go get that ship."

Jules slid her cutlass back into its scabbard and went down the ladder to the main deck, where most of the crew were gathered. Most already had cutlasses in hand, but some held lines with grapnels on the end to hook over the rail of the other ship. Ang and Liv gave her somber looks, unhappy with what she was doing, but she wouldn't let fear keep her from being who she had to be.

She climbed up, balancing on the rail facing the other ship, one hand gripping the nearest shrouds. The boots offered only a precarious balance on the top of the rail, so Jules held tight to the rigging with her free hand. The *Sun Queen* corkscrewed through the bottom of another swell, bounding up the other side to the crest, her bow hurling out a cloud of spray that pelted Jules. She squinted at the other ship, seeing a line of defenders at the rail, naked blades in their hands. The ships were only about twenty lances apart now, the distance shrinking rapidly as the *Sun Queen* closed from aft on the other ship's port side.

Jules leaned out, shouting against the wind. "Heave to and yield! We're coming aboard!"

She heard the reply shouted back at her. "We'll see you dead first!"

"Better than you have tried!" Jules yelled. Feeling a strange exhilaration mixing with the fear that had her heart pounding faster, she turned her head to call to her own shipmates. "Come on, ladies and sirs! Let's show this lot how real sailors fight!"

Sailors of the *Sun Queen* came to the side in a rush, some balanced on the rail and holding onto the rigging, others poised to leap up and over. Jules watched the gap between the ships shrinking fast, the *Sun Queen* still overtaking so that their bows were nearly even as the distance between the two ships dwindled to nothing and hulls grated together with the groan of tortured wood.

A few moments before the impact Jules had let go her hold on the rigging, balancing as she yanked out the cutlass again. As the two ships struck she let the force of the collision help toss her over the rail of the other ship, her cutlass held in front of her, broad blade held flat across her chest to catch the swords of the defenders as she leaped into their midst.

She knocked aside one sword blade, barely turned a second before slamming into the two sailors holding those weapons, knocking them and her to the deck. Rolling to one side, Jules got to her feet, the Mechanic revolver clasped so tightly that her hand ached. She got the cutlass up again just as another blade came at her, the impact of cutlass on cutlass causing Jules to stumble backwards, the ring of clashing metal in her ears and her hand stinging from the force of the blow.

The *Sun Queen* had rebounded from the glancing blow and was swinging back to make contact again, another wave of boarders waiting to jump and join Jules and the others who were fighting with the defenders in an intermingled mess of bodies. Fortunately, the other ship's crew were all fitted out in neat, identical outfits, making it easy to tell who was friend and who was foe.

Jules parried the next attack, getting her feet firmly set, and rammed her cutlass' guard into her opponent's stomach. As he reeled backwards, another defender thrust at her with a short sword. Jules twisted aside and beat at the defender's blade, but as she tried to swing her cutlass up the ship rolled, the deck tilting under her so that Jules staggered back against the rail. Her foe, in the act of raising his sword to chop at her, over-balanced as the deck tilted and fell against her, pinning her to the rail.

She swung up the pistol and hit his head with it, dazing the man and giving her a moment to position her leg and knee him hard. As the ship rolled back, the deck tilting the other way, the man stumbled backwards, bent over with pain.

Jules brought her cutlass grip down on his head, taking him out of the fight.

She looked for a new opponent, seeing defenders grappling with pirates on both sides of her before the ship twisted over a swell, causing the crowd of defenders to part momentarily as everyone sought firm footing.

Through the gap, Jules saw someone in the suit of an Imperial official near the quarterdeck, pointing toward her. A big man in full legionary armor who'd been standing next to the official responded by charging straight at her, a short sword in one hand and a shield in the other. A quick glance to either side told Jules that she was hemmed in by other combatants, leaving no room to dodge the assault except by diving backwards off the ship. But if she stood and took that charge, the big man in armor would slam her back against the rail hard enough to break her bones.

She'd resolved to save the Mechanic weapon for an emergency. This seemed to qualify.

Jules raised the revolver, pointing it at the charging foe, her finger on the trigger, wondering what aside from a very loud noise would happen when she shot the weapon.

The legionary was almost on her, his shield held like a battering ram, his sword raised to chop down on her. The end of the revolver was nearly touching the shield when Jules pulled the trigger.

The *boom* of the weapon blanketed the other sounds of fighting. The weapon bucked in Jules' hand, shoving it back with surprising force, just as the shield hit her and she yielded to the attack, ducking under it and letting the shield and the legionary behind it roll over her and slam into the rail at her back.

Jules came up again as fast as she could, her wrist aching from the force of the Mechanic weapon, but her cutlass held ready for the legionary's next attack.

It took her a moment to realize that no one was fighting. Instead, everyone was looking at her with varying expressions of shock, surprise, and on the part of the *Sun Queen*'s crew, elation.

The legionary tried to get up, rolling to his side. A hole was visible in his shield, another in the armor covering his torso, red blood spilling out. He lay, staring at her with a bewildered expression.

Jules raised her revolver into the air. "Who wants to be next?" she shouted.

Blades hit the deck as the defenders dropped them, holding out empty hands, the triumphant sailors from the *Sun Queen* rounding up their prisoners.

Jules walked toward the quarterdeck, revolver in one hand and cutlass in the other. "Do you yield?" she yelled at the captain of the ship.

The captain seemed to be having trouble believing his eyes. "Who are you that carries the weapon of a Mechanic?" He looked about as if searching for Mechanics with her.

"Jeri of Landfall," Jules said.

"Where did you get that weapon?"

"I have friends. That's the last question about me that I'm going to answer. I'm going to give you one more chance to answer mine. Do you yield?"

"Will you spare my crew?"

"You have my word."

The captain reversed his sword, extending the hilt toward her. "On your word, Jeri of Landfall."

"Wait," someone else cried. Jules looked, seeing the man who'd ordered the legionary to attack her. This close she could see the fine quality of his Imperial suit, speaking to both his wealth and status. His eyes studied her, amazed. "That's her! The one the Emperor seeks! Your name isn't Jeri. We know your true name, pirate."

"Then speak it if you dare," Jules said, holding the revolver up. "No?"

The captain gazed at her with a different sort of surprise, extending his sword hilt again. "I yield the ship to you, Lieutenant."

"Good," Jules said, ignoring the use of her Imperial rank. What next? "I also need you to yield your money chest and the key to it. Show this man your cargo manifest," she added, pointing the tip of her cutlass at Ang. "Get enough of your crew in the rigging to furl your sails." She looked over at the bleeding legionary. "And this man needs a healer."

"He failed," the man in the suit said, glaring at the legionary. "The healer is in my employ and will only aid those honorably wounded in the fight."

Jules shook her head. "I said I'd spare the crew. You're not part of the crew. You'll have your healer help him first or you'll need the assistance of that healer yourself."

The tone of his reply held the same arrogance as that of the Mechanics when they'd spoken to her. "You wouldn't—"

She'd been forced to endure that from the Mechanics.

Jules held herself still, realizing that she'd moved in a flash without thinking, her cutlass blade pressed against the neck of the official in the fine suit, pressed hard enough for the edge to draw a trickle of blood. The official stared at her, frozen in fear. "Go ahead," Jules said. "Finish what you were saying. What? I can't hear you."

She stepped back from him. "The healer. Now. I won't ask again."

As the Imperial official frantically waved a middle-aged woman into motion toward the fallen legionary, Jules turned her back on him, walking away. "Ang, could you keep that guy away from me?"

"Sure." Ang eyed her. "Was that really an act? It sure was a good one. You even had me believing that you were about to shove that cutlass halfway through his neck."

"Yeah," Jules said flatly. "It was an act."

The money chest proved to have a substantial sum inside, even considering that they'd have to split it with the *Storm Rider*. Most of the cargo proved to be salt blocks harvested from the waste to the west of the southern reaches of the Empire. Valuable, but heavy.

"Who does the work?" Jules asked, feeling uneasy as she gazed at the rough blocks that had been hewn from mines. "Cutting these out of the ground?"

"Felons," Ang said. "You never heard where the salt on your table came from?"

"We didn't get much salt in the orphan homes," Jules said. "Remember? Where's Captain Mak? Why haven't I seen him yet?"

"Still on the *Sun Queen*."

"Why? Doesn't he usually come over to supervise looting the captured ship?"

Ang had the expression of someone eager not to be caught between duelists. "Captain Mak told me, and Liv, to inform anyone who asked that you are the captain of the *Sun Queen*."

Jules brushed by him, going to the rail to look over at the *Sun*

Queen's quarterdeck. "What are you doing, Captain?" she yelled across.

"Following orders, Captain," Mak yelled back. "I think following orders is important."

"So is understanding them. What am I doing?"

"What your new allies want you to do. We want them to be happy, right?"

"How much of this salt do you want us to send over? Liv's supervising the rigging of some tackle to lift blocks over to the *Queen*."

"Keep sending it over until we tell you to stop!"

Feeling like the "captain" should be supervising things, Jules set out to check out everything on the captured ship. She almost immediately saw the healer wrapping up a cut arm on one of the defenders. "Where's the man I shot?"

The healer looked up, her face hard with anger as she looked at Jules. "He'll live. We need to get him to one of the hospitals in Landfall, though, to ensure he recovers fully."

"Good. What are you mad about?"

"People who attack other ships and give me far too much work to do."

Jules nodded to her. "If I was still serving the Emperor, I'd be doing the same thing, wouldn't I? Only I'd be doing it to add to the fortunes of people like your employer."

"Is that how you justify theft and murder?" the healer said as she worked on the injury.

"Yes," Jules said. "Where's the injured legionary?"

"Over there by the foremast. You can gloat all you want. He's too weak to hurt you."

Jules crouched down to look directly into the healer's eyes. "I fought him when he was at his full strength. And I let you speak like that to me without doing anything to you in response, even though I could have. Remember both of those things." Without waiting for a reply, she stood up and walked to the foremast.

A pallet lay next to the foremast. On it was the legionary, stripped of his armor and weapons, his upper torso naked except for the bandage the healer had wrapped tightly around him. Jules hadn't had time to really look at him before. He had strong features and a thin beard, even looked a little familiar. Maybe she'd met him during her training in Imperial service. His torso was well-enough proportioned and muscled to remind her of her joking comment to Captain Mak about finding a cute guy on the captured ship.

Jules knelt by the pallet. "How are you, soldier?"

The man's eyes moved to rest on her. This close, she could see the pain riding him from his injury, and the weakness his blood loss had caused. "I will live, I am told," he replied in a Landfall accent.

"I'm sorry I shot you without warning," Jules said. "That wasn't a fair thing to do."

"You were in a fight. It was the smart thing to do. Don't fight fair, Lady Pirate. Fight to win. Fight to live."

Lady Pirate. She smiled down at him. "Good advice. I'm glad you'll live."

"Thank you, Jules."

She gave him a stern look, thinking he must have seen the name on those Imperial posters with her picture. "Don't call me that."

"I called you that in the legion home in Landfall, when you were a little demon of a girl and would ask to ride on my shoulders so you could see over the wall and watch people on the street."

Jules stared at him. "Shin? You're Shin?"

"A little bigger, a little older, but yes."

"You joined the legions. How'd you get assigned to this ship?"

"That fine suit among your prisoners. He demanded a personal bodyguard, and my commander was eager to please. So here I am."

"I don't believe it," Jules said. "I'm so glad that I didn't kill you."

"I'm glad that I didn't kill you," Shin said, his eyes searching her face. "I wouldn't have tried if I'd known who you were. There's a story going around, Jules. About a prophecy."

"It's true."

"But… it's you? It's truly you?"

"Yes," Jules admitted.

Shin paused, his eyes watching her with awe. "A daughter?"

"A daughter of my line," Jules said. "Stop looking at me like that. That daughter might take more than a few generations to get here. I'm going to try to lay the groundwork for her, though."

His smile grew slowly. "Then you'll need strong fighters," he said. "Take me with you."

Jules smiled in return, warmed not only by meeting Shin again but also by his response. "Thank you. But the healer says you need to get to a hospital to recover. There aren't any hospitals to speak of west of the Empire yet. Go back to Landfall and get well. I just hope you don't get punished for failing to kill me."

"I was felled by a Mechanic weapon. Even a centurion would say there's no shame in that," Shin said. "Jules, will you tell me, why do you have it?"

She let her smile grow conspiratorial. "Because a certain Great Guild thinks I'm going to do what they want."

"Fools. I'd know better than to trust a tricky girl like you."

Jules felt her smile become hard. "The Mechanics don't know what being from a legion orphan home means about a person."

"It means you're a sister to me. I heard you called Lieutenant. Is that true?"

"I managed to get an officer appointment," Jules said, feeling embarrassed to tell Shin that. It felt like boasting. "Before I had to go on the run."

"An officer? One of my sisters from the home? Jules, I'm so proud. How will I find you again?" Shin took a quick breath as a wave of weakness washed across his features. "I know others who will come with me if I go west."

"Deserting from the legions is a death offense," Jules reminded him.

"You mean like you did?"

"I didn't have a choice." She reached out to touch his shoulder. "I don't know where I'll be. Go west, ask for me in ports you stop at. Even if I'm not there, I'll hear you were asking for me."

Shin moved his head slightly in the faintest nod. "Please stay alive until I can join you, Lady Pirate."

"I'll do my best," Jules said. "Sneaky, unfair stuff. And you please get strong again. Are you and Beryl still a thing?"

"That didn't work out," Shin said. "But there's another."

"Good. For now, you shouldn't seem too happy with me. When I get up, yell something threatening. Can you yell?"

"I'll try."

Jules straightened up.

Shin yelled at her in a weak voice, but one strong enough to be heard by many of those on deck. "I will find you again! I'm not afraid of you and your weapon!"

Jules smiled mockingly down at him. "Next time I'll kill you." She winked once, very quickly, before turning away, wishing that she had more time to speak with him. But appearing friendly to Shin wouldn't be doing him any favors.

The other prisoners were gathered on the fo'c'sle under guard. Liv was busy getting salt blocks swung over to the *Queen*, a usually simple procedure with the help of the tackle hung from a yardarm but complicated today by the rough seas that had the ships rolling and rubbing against each other. Ang saw her and walked up, holding out some keys. "We should search the captain's cabin, Jeri. Look for any hidden boxes. These are all the keys he had on him."

The stern cabin was nice enough to seem luxurious to Jules. She and Ang went through it, searching for any concealed boxes or drawers, Ang finally spotting a slim case fastened under the table. One of the keys fit it, revealing not money or jewelry, but documents. "I'll look these over to see if there's anything important," Jules told Ang, who headed back out of the cabin to check on things elsewhere on the ship.

The top document proved to be the captain's sailing orders from his company, consisting mostly of lists of places to stop at and the expected times for the ship to reach those destinations. As long as ships depended on wind, trip times could only be educated guesses. She didn't see anything useful in those orders.

The next paper down was different. Jules unfolded it to see a familiar drawing of herself staring back at her. Below the picture were several lines of text.

Lieutenant-in-Training Jules of Landfall. So that was why the captain of this ship had called her Lieutenant. Apparently the Empire had yet to revoke her status as an officer. *All efforts must be made to capture her ALIVE.* That "alive" was reassuring in an all-capital-letters way. *Avoid harming her unless necessary to achieve capture, ensuring that HER ABILITY TO CONCEIVE AND BEAR CHILDREN REMAINS UNDAMAGED.*

Jules sat staring at those words. There it was, laid out in black and white, the letters emphasizing her worst fears. As far as the Empire was concerned, she had only one purpose in this world.

The page didn't contain any reference to the Mage prophecy, though. Why was the Emperor trying to avoid telling his citizens about that? From what Shin had just told her the word was getting around inside the Empire anyway.

But then Shin's reaction had been to help her. Maybe that was why the Emperor didn't want his people knowing about the prophecy.

The rest of the write-up listed her height and weight as of the time of her physical when reporting for officer training, eye and hair color, build, complexion, and noted her "lower class" Landfall accent. *Moderately skilled at sword. Minimal crossbow skills. Capable at basic tasks on ships. Rudimentary leadership skills. Average intellect.* They certainly made her seem like a prize, didn't they?

Following that, a warning. *ANY MAGE WHO SEES THIS WOMAN WILL SEEK TO KILL HER. SHE MUST REMAIN HIDDEN FROM ANY CONTACT WITH MAGES. IF MAGES ATTACK HER, ALL IMPERIAL CITIZENS ARE EXPECTED TO MAKE ANY SACRIFICE TO PREVENT HER DEATH.*

That would have been comforting, if not for the fact that even the most loyal Imperial citizens might balk at sacrificing themselves in hopeless fights against Mages, and that the only reason they were being called on to make that sacrifice was so that the Imperial police could haul her living self to Marandur in chains.

At the bottom, another all-capital letters warning. *ANY PHYSI-CAL VIOLATION OF THIS WOMAN WILL RESULT IN DEATH FOR ALL INVOLVED.*

That was sort of nice to see, in a very creepy way. The Emperor wanted to ensure that any of her offspring were his.

She wondered what the guys hitting on her would do if they knew success on their part would mean an Imperial death sentence. Maybe she ought to spread the word so they'd leave her alone.

Jules imagined herself with someone, saying to him "oh, by the way, before we go any farther there's something you ought to know."

She laughed as she put back the paper and looked through the remaining ones, finding only routine documents related to the ship's license and inspections.

"What's so funny?" Ang asked as he came back in.

"I'm not sure I want to explain it. Is something wrong?"

"The cap'n wants to talk to you as soon as possible."

Jules replaced all of the papers in the case, working quickly. After returning the case to its hidden location, she ran out onto the deck and up to the quarterdeck. "Yes, Captain?" she called across to the *Sun Queen*, leaning across the railing.

"We've got the *Storm Rider* in sight," Mak called back. "Captain Erin is flying a flag and pennant that tell us the sloop is heading back our way. We'll probably see their masts any moment now. Drop everything and get everyone back aboard."

"Yes, sir!" Jules turned to pass on the order, but paused as a wild thought came to her. A crazy thought, really. She spun about to face Mak again. "Captain? Captain, I have an idea."

"What is it?"

"It's insane. It really is."

"Tell me."

"What if we captured that Imperial sloop?"

Mak cupped one hand to his ear. "What did you say?"

"We could capture the Imperial sloop, sir. Lure it in close and board it."

"That's…" Mak paused, gazing downward. "Possible. Lure it in using the captured ship, you mean?"

"Yes, sir! If we get enough people on his deck, it won't matter how agile that ship is."

He hesitated. "It's a big risk."

"But if we can capture an Imperial sloop," Jules said, "we'll be able to use it. With that sloop and the *Sun Queen* and the *Storm Rider* we could probably go into a fight with an Imperial galley!"

"We're not going to do that even if we take the sloop!" Mak called back. "I have to decide this now. There's no time to think about it. Do you think it can work?"

"Yes, sir, I do!"

"All right. We'll keep just enough crew aboard the *Queen* to handle her. If for some reason that sloop doesn't get lured in, steer the ship you're on south and run it ashore so you and the others can escape overland to a place where we can pick you up."

"Yes, sir! Ang, Liv! We've got another fight on the way!"

Soon afterwards, the *Sun Queen* broke away from the captured ship. She veered off to the north, only a small portion of her usual crew handling the sails, Captain Mak himself steering at the helm. Not having worked out in advance any signal for trying to capture the Imperial sloop, the *Queen* was flying the flags indicating an attack on the sloop, hoping that Erin on the *Storm Rider* would be able to figure out what was happening.

Jules stood on the quarterdeck of the captured ship, gazing to the west-northwest, where the masts of the Imperial war sloop were in sight. Barely visible to the north were the masts of the *Storm Rider*. "Get the emergency flag hoisted," she told Ang. "How's the outfit feel?"

He tugged at the collar of the shirt, taken from one of the prisoners who closely matched Ang in size. "A little small. You should get down and hide before there's any chance of them seeing you."

"All right. Let's do this." Jules went down the ladder to the main deck. The sails on the captured ship remained furled, the ship wallowing in the rough seas enough to stress her stomach even despite her sea legs. The prisoners had all been locked below deck.

Huddled beneath the rail on the north side of the ship were a major portion of the crew of the *Sun Queen*, cutlasses in their hands as well as a few crossbows.

Jules crouched down with them, keeping her head up just enough to watch the sloop again for a moment. The Imperial warship had all sails set, swooping closer on the wings of the wind. Small, fast, and agile, the sloop carried a single ballistae between its masts. In a fight with a ship like the *Sun Queen*, the sloop could out-maneuver any attempts to board it, while using that ballistae to hurl rocks at its opponent and slowly pound it to pieces.

Which was why Jules had suggested they try this trick. If it didn't work, they'd be in big trouble, having to run for the coast before the sloop crippled their ship by taking down one or more of the masts. But if it did work, that sloop would be a very nice capture. And the Emperor would be very unhappy.

She ducked down below the port railing, nodding to the others from the *Sun Queen*. Gord gave her a tight grin in reply. Liv seemed lost in thought. Old Ferd wore a pensive look, but nodded back. "Ferd, I thought you were going to stay on the *Sun Queen*."

Ferd smiled at her. "I'm not too old to take part in the fun. Not yet."

Should she order him to stay on this ship? Ferd looked even older than he usually did. But he held his cutlass with a firm grip, and his gaze on her almost pleaded with Jules to not object to his presence. "All right."

The wait seemed interminable as the ship rocked in the waves. Jules, unable to look at the fixed horizon to fight her looming seasickness, tried staring up toward the sun as clouds swept majestically past above.

Finally, she saw Ang, alone on the quarterdeck, waving off to port. "What is your emergency?" Jules heard, the hail from the sloop hard to make out as the words were battered and tossed by the wind.

Ang cupped his hands around his mouth to yell back. "We were attacked while you were away. We managed to fight off the pirates, but we lost a lot of crew dead and wounded. Including our healer. We have a lot of people that need medical help. Can you come alongside and send over your healer?"

The reply sounded a little louder. The sloop must be veering closer. "We only have a healer assistant on board, but we'll send him. Do you need crew to handle your sails?"

"Yes," Ang called back. "If you could send some after you send the healer assistant."

"Hang on," Jules said, feeling her heart racing. Her grip on her cutlass tightened, the hilt of the sword slick with sweat from her palms.

Three cartridges left in her revolver. Hopefully she wouldn't have need of them. They were supposed to be saved for Mages. She'd tied the revolver's sheath closed, not wanting to risk losing the weapon.

Jules saw the tips of the sloop's yardarms come into sight above as the warship came in close. She heard and felt the bump as the two ships came together.

"Now!" Jules shouted, jumping up and onto the railing. Less than a lance below her, the deck of the sloop was crowded with Imperial sailors, some of them already starting to climb up to board this ship. They had just begun to stare upwards in shock at the sailors from the *Sun Queen* who had suddenly appeared along the railing.

Jules leaped down and out, crossing the small gap made as the hulls of the two ships had rebounded, her cutlass guard advanced so that as her boots landed on the deck of the Imperial sloop the guard crashed into the skull of an Imperial officer.

Other sailors from the *Sun Queen* dropped down, falling on the surprised Imperials.

Jules almost lost her balance as the sloop swerved wildly away from the other ship. She cursed as she saw that about a third of her own sailors hadn't made it to the sloop's deck by the time the two ships were too far apart. The sloop's commander had been smart enough and quick enough to do the right thing almost immediately, leaving her with fewer sailors to attack the sloop's crew. Now they were rapidly recovering from their surprise, grabbing marlinspikes and cutlasses of their own and fighting back. Even worse, the pirates with crossbows were still back on the captured ship, leaving the boarding party with only cutlasses.

"Take them! Before they can rally!" Jules shouted over the clanging of metal on metal and the horrible crunching of bones hit by marlin-spikes or sword guards. She beat aside the blade of an Imperial sailor who'd just managed to grab a cutlass, swinging a cut that felled her opponent. Jules led the other pirates in a rush to clear the foredeck of the sloop.

But the Imperials were trained fighters, whereas her pirates were a slapdash collection of men and women with varied skills and experience. Despite her efforts to keep the attack going, the pirates faltered in their rush as the defenders armed themselves and fell back together toward the stern. Jules saw the Imperial crew forming a line across the deck even with the sloop's mainmast, sailors shoulder to shoulder facing her pirates with bared weapons and grim resolve. The ballista stood between the two groups, where neither side could hope to reach and tension it before the other side hit them.

She had to break that Imperial line before it firmed up. Raising her cutlass, Jules ran at the Imperial sailors. "Come on!" she called to the pirates.

Many of the pirates followed, but Jules had to fall back as multiple cutlasses slashed at her. The other pirates recoiled from the defenders as well. Despite having taken down many of the crew, the boarding partly was only roughly even in numbers with the defenders, and the defenders had the advantage of being disciplined and well-trained.

Jules looked past the heads of the line of Imperial sailors, seeing the sloop's captain standing by the helm. Could she hit him from this distance with the revolver? It seemed very unlikely. The way the weapon kicked had been a surprise, and she'd barely hit Shin when he was right next to her.

"Pirates, throw down your weapons!" the sloop's commander ordered. "Only your leaders will be executed!"

The pirates with Jules looked at her, anxious, hoping for orders.

Blazes. She'd gotten them into this. How would she get them out?

Jules took a step forward from the gaggle of pirates facing the firm line of Imperial soldiers. "Throw down your weapons!" she called. "I promise mercy to all!"

She saw the mocking grins that answered her demand. The Imperials weren't having any of it. She'd been one of them. She knew why. Their pride and resolve wouldn't crumble so easily.

"Line advance!" the sloop commander ordered his sailors.

The Imperial line began moving forward, a wall of cutlasses facing the pirates who fell back before it. But there was only so far to fall back. Jules glanced behind her, seeing the bow not far off, knowing that if they got packed into the bow they'd be unable to fight effectively against the Imperials.

She reached down to untie the straps holding her revolver. Only three shots, but maybe these Imperials would crumble in the face of that threat.

She got the revolver free as the pirates retreated past the foremast, holding it up to point at the Imperials. "Line hold!" she shouted, just as if she was in command of the sloop's crew.

The Imperial sailors halted their advance, immediately obedient as they'd been trained and momentarily confused at hearing the order called out in proper form by their opponent.

"Who dies first?" Jules demanded, slowly swinging the Mechanic weapon from side to side so that it pointed at the faces of all the Imperial sailors facing her.

"It's a bluff!" the sloop's commander shouted. "Line advance!"

CHAPTER EIGHT

The Imperial sailors hesitated, their fear of the Mechanic weapon momentarily countering their obedience to orders.

What would have happened next, Jules never found out.

She suddenly saw the bow of another ship coming up behind the stern of the sloop, very close, felt the thump of the two ships coming together, and saw pirates leaping down onto the sloop's quarterdeck, led by Captain Erin.

The *Storm Rider* had ridden the winds back quickly enough to lend a hand.

Jules saw the sloop's captain cut down as he turned to face the new threat. Erin's pirates cleared the Imperial quarterdeck in a sweep, rushing forward to hit the rear of the line of Imperial sailors as they belatedly tried to shift their formation from facing only Jules and her pirates.

As the Imperials wavered in confusion, trapped between two forces, Jules shouted again. "Drop your weapons and mercy will be shown!"

"Hold-!" an Imperial centurion began to yell before she fell to one of Erin's crew.

Cutlasses began hitting the deck as Imperials dropped them and raised their empty hands in surrender.

Jules stood watching the pirates cheer as they rounded up the Imperial sailors, feeling oddly detached from it all, as if this was a dream that would soon shatter into reality. Someone bumped her, and as she regained her balance Jules felt the world becoming real again. She carefully put the revolver back into its sheath before walking toward Captain Erin, weaving her way between the pirates and the captured Imperials.

"There she is!" Captain Erin called down from the quarterdeck, grinning. "The dangerous one! Give her a hand, everyone!"

Cheers and applause erupted around Jules, but she didn't feel elated. Or deserving. "Thank you for arriving when you did," she told Erin as the tumult subsided.

Erin leaned on the front rail of the quarterdeck, smiling down at Jules. "What's the matter? An Imperial sloop of war isn't a big enough prize for you?" What was wrong with her? Jules looked about at everyone else celebrating.

This didn't feel like a victory that she'd earned. It had nearly been a disaster. She'd been over-confident and reckless. She'd nearly led the pirates from the *Sun Queen* to their deaths.

But before she could try to form those feelings into words, Liv touched her arm. Looking over, Jules saw a somber look on Liv's face.

"It's Ferd," Liv said.

Jules followed Liv forward, seeing Ferd's body lying still. She knelt by him, seeing that it was far too late to call for the healer even if such wounds could have been survived. Even a young, vigorous man wouldn't have been able to live with those injuries. Old Ferd hadn't had a chance. "I should have ordered him to stay on the other ship. I thought about doing it and I didn't."

"He's happier this way," Liv said. "Ferd never really wanted to leave the sea, for all his talk of getting a place on land. He's been getting more careless of late, heedless of dangers, but I don't think it was because of his age. He wanted to die out here on the waves."

"That one killed him!" Gord said, pointing an angry finger at an Imperial sailor.

"It was a fair fight," Jules muttered.

"No, it wasn't! Ferd was down. I saw it! He couldn't move. And that one ran him through twice more!"

Jules' head came around to stare at the Imperial singled out by Gord. "You murdered him?"

"It was combat!" the Imperial sailor protested, his voice high with fear. "We had orders to show no mercy!" He looked to either side at his comrades for backing, but they avoided his gaze.

Jules walked up to face the sailor, her eyes on him. For a moment she couldn't feel anything, an emptiness shadowed by violent emotions ready to rush in. "I know Imperial orders. Your commander said only leaders would be executed. That's not a no-mercy command. Is it?"

The sailor didn't answer, shaking.

"*Is it?*" Jules yelled, anger filling that emptiness as she glared at the other captured Imperial sailors. "You murdered an old man who couldn't defend himself! Is that what the Emperor expects of his servants? *Is it?*"

"You promised mercy," the Imperial sailor said, his voice quivering. "You promised mercy."

Jules looked to Captain Erin, who had come down from the quarterdeck and was standing to one side, watching.

Erin shrugged. "The prize was taken jointly, but that man there murdered one of your crew. The decision of what to do with him is yours alone."

"You did promise mercy," Liv muttered as she gazed at the sailor with death in her eyes. "That doesn't mean I can't kill him, though."

She should wait until Captain Mak brought the *Sun Queen* back. Let him pass judgment. But she had been in command here, and Ferd had been murdered while answering to her orders. Jules felt a cold, clear certainty wash through her, sweeping away the heat of her anger but leaving no compassion in its wake. "No, Liv. I promised mercy. He'll get mercy."

"Jeri?" Liv stared at her, having heard something in her voice that had alarmed the older woman.

Jules looked at the Imperial sailor and pointed off to the side, where only open water could be seen. "The nearest land is that way. Just head south. You can't miss it. If you're a strong enough swimmer to cover the distance and beat the currents, and if you manage to avoid the sharks, you'll come ashore on the Bleak Coast, and if you're very lucky and very strong you'll survive there until you reach safety."

"I won't have a chance!" the sailor cried.

"Yes, you will. A small chance. A very small chance," Jules said.

"You promised mercy!"

"I did. And you're getting it. Instead of killing you out of hand, as you deserve, I'm giving you that very small chance. More of a chance than you gave the old man you murdered." Jules came closer to the sailor, knowing her face showed that cold certainty and little else. "No one murders one of mine. No one."

She turned away and gestured to her crew. "Over the side with him."

Jules turned back in time to see several of her pirates toss the struggling Imperial sailor over the side of the sloop. The sailor's despairing wail ended in a splash, resuming again but diminishing as the sloop and the *Storm Rider* drifted away from where the sailor struggled to stay afloat.

"Thank you, Jeri," Liv said.

"Yes, thank you," Gord said. "Ferd would be happy."

Jules faced the Imperials, trying to control that coldness still filling her, seeing the fear in their eyes as they waited for whatever she would do next. "Who's the senior surviving member of your crew?"

Hands pointed to a figure sitting against the mainmast, holding his head. It was the officer Jules had struck down when she first leaped aboard.

She crouched down to talk to him. "Your ship has been taken."

The officer looked back at her, confused as he tried to recover from the blow to his head. "Captain Tod—"

"Is dead. Has the healer seen you?"

"I don't... know."

The cold vanished. There was a young man sitting before her, hurt and unable to think. A young officer who could have been her, had Jules never walked into that tavern at Jacksport.

Jules stood up. "Where's the healer?"

"On the other ship," Liv said.

"This one has a healer's assistant. Where's the healer's assistant?"

A young man was pushed forward from the ranks of the captured sailors. "I'm... I'm..."

"Why the blazes aren't you working?" Jules demanded. "We've got cuts and broken limbs and this officer might have a head injury. Get to it!"

This she could do. Organize things. Tell people what to do. Make sure all the injured were being taken care of, including the wounded centurion who clearly wished that she still had her short sword handy when Jules stopped to check on her. "All efforts must be made to capture me alive," Jules told the centurion, earning herself a baffled glance in place of the hostility. "You don't get to kill me yet."

By the time the *Sun Queen* rejoined them, the sun was close to setting and Jules felt worn out. Captain Erin and Captain Mak jointly decided to transfer the Imperials from the captured sloop to the merchant ship before letting it go to carry both crews home to Landfall. Jules watched the last of the Imperial sailors being ferried over to the merchant ship, thinking about Shin and hoping he'd be all right.

"The Cap'n asked me to sail the sloop back to Jacksport," Ang told her. "I'll have some of our crew and some of Erin's."

"Good," Jules said. "I guess I should get back to the *Sun Queen*." She staggered as the sloop rolled over a swell. "I can barely stay on my feet."

Pulling herself up onto the *Sun Queen*'s deck took more effort than it should have. "Where's Captain Mak?"

"Still talking to Captain Erin," Liv said. "Get in your hammock, Jeri. I'll wake you for the dawn watch."

"Thanks." Jules got below without tripping on the ladder, paused only long enough to remove the cutlass from her belt, then crawled into her hammock.

She slept like a stone through the night before being roused sometime before dawn to stand her watch on the helm. One day you're boarding ships and fighting with a cutlass, Jules thought, and the next you're standing on a quarterdeck steering a ship as if nothing had happened the day before.

"Hold her north of west," instructed the sailor she relieved from the helm watch. "She's fighting the rudder a little, trying to turn east, so watch for that."

"Got it," Jules said.

The seas had subsided a bit, and so had the winds, giving her an easier watch than she'd feared. As she stood at the helm, the sky to the east slowly paled, giving way to the day. The quiet broken only by the sounds of wind and wave and creaking wood disappeared in a series of routine errands by men and women rising to deal with the challenges of another day at sea.

Captain Mak came on deck right after dawn, scanning the seas, but said nothing to her despite Jules' "good morning, sir." Perhaps he was preoccupied, she thought.

The next watch finally took over. Jules stepped away from the helm, shaking her arms to relax them, for the first time that day free to look around as well.

The three ships were sailing together toward Jacksport, the *Storm Rider* and the *Sun Queen* in front roughly even with each other and a few hundred lances apart, the captured sloop of war bringing up the rear a few hundred lances astern. A few whitecaps still dotted the waves, and a few clouds still swept by overhead. The wind felt fresh and clean, something Jules had always enjoyed since growing up in one of the less fancy portions of Landfall where ash and smoke from coal stoves often sullied the air.

Jules gazed back at the sloop, waving to Ang on the quarterdeck of the captured Imperial ship. When she turned, she saw Captain Mak watching her with a gaze that appeared cold. "We need to talk, Jeri. Follow me."

Worried by Mak's demeanor, Jules followed him down the ladder to the main deck and into the cabin. Captain Mak sat down in one of the chairs, stretching his legs out before him, arms crossed on his chest as he eyed her. Unlike his usual habit, he didn't ask her to take the other chair, so Jules stayed standing just inside the door. "Is something wrong, Captain?"

He nodded, keeping that harsh gaze on her. "I heard what happened to Ferd."

"Yes, sir. He was—"

"I know." Mak's gaze grew a little harder. "And you took it on yourself to decide the fate of his murderer."

"Yes, sir."

"Why?"

She stared back at him, feeling unhappy and angry at what felt like a chewing out. "He was part of my crew."

"Ferd was part of *my* crew."

"He was under my command—"

"You were both under *my* command."

"Sir, I had to act!"

"Why?" Mak demanded. "Why couldn't you have waited until I brought the *Sun Queen* back to join you?"

"I… it felt like… a decision I had to make."

"Really?" Mak waved aft. "Do you want command of the sloop, Jeri?"

"No, sir."

"No?" He seemed surprised by her answer. "Why not?"

"I'm not ready for independent command," Jules said. "I have training, but I don't have experience to match it. And I need to learn more."

"You're not ready for independent command?" Mak asked.

"No, sir."

"But you felt qualified to independently decide the fate of a man who murdered one of *my* crew. You felt qualified to usurp my authority and my responsibility over *my* crew."

"Sir, that's not what happened!" Jules protested, feeling unjustly accused. "That's not what I was thinking."

"It's not? What do you suppose every witness to your actions is thinking? What do you supposed they're telling everyone else about it?"

"I... I..."

He leaned forward, feet flat on the deck, his eyes holding her. "You don't want command of the sloop. Are you angling for command of a bigger prize?"

"Sir, I..."

"You seem to think you're already captain of the *Sun Queen*," Mak said. "How long until you call a vote to make it official?"

She stared at him, his accusing words filtering down through her brain which seemed to have stopped working, until finally words burst from her. "No! No, sir!"

"No, sir, what?"

"That was not my intent! That is not my desire! I did not mean to undermine your authority! I apologize to the captain for creating the impression that I desired anything other than to carry out my orders in the most effective manner!"

The vehemence of her response seemed to mollify Mak a little. He sat back again. "You've got the backing of the Mechanics Guild. Not me. You're carrying that Mechanic weapon. Not me. This is already a delicate situation in terms of authority on this ship. Didn't you realize that?"

"No, sir," Jules said, feeling deflated and miserable.

"What?" Mak seemed genuinely startled by her response.

"You're the captain, sir. How can anyone question who's in charge of this ship?"

"You're serious? It never crossed your mind?"

"No, sir. You're the captain. I'm... I'm sorry."

He shook his head. "Imperial discipline. I hadn't realized it had soaked into you that deeply already."

"This isn't about Imperial discipline, sir," Jules said. "You're the captain."

Mak studied her with growing understanding. "Are you saying that by your choice I'm the captain? That as far as you're personally concerned, it can't be questioned?"

"Yes, sir. I think so." Jules waited, wondering what Mak would say next.

He shook his head. "Here I thought you were undermining me, and instead you were acting the way you did because it didn't occur to you that anyone would question my authority. Jeri, that's not how it works."

"Why not? I thought on a free ship we got to decide who the captain was. And you're the captain."

"That's not written in stone. It's not like I'm the Emperor."

"I'm sorry, sir. I didn't understand. Like I said, I need to know more. I need to learn more. And I know if I stay on this ship, I will. Please… you're not going to put me off, are you?"

"Why would I put you off?" Mak asked.

"For challenging your authority," Jules said. "And messing up so badly when we attacked the sloop."

He gave her a sidelong glance. "You don't see that as triumph for you?"

"No, sir. How could I do that? We were losing. If Captain Erin hadn't shown up when she did. we probably would have all died or been captured. I totally messed that up. My plan was flawed. We didn't have enough fighters on our side, and we needed to have crossbows instead of just cutlasses. I'd told those with crossbows to wait and let those with cutlasses board the sloop first and clear a space before the crossbows boarded. But that meant when the sloop veered off none of our crossbows had reached its deck. It was my fault."

Mak shook his head rapidly like someone trying to order confused thoughts. "You weren't thinking of yourself as the conquering hero?"

"How could I feel that way? I messed up. Badly!" Jules paused, trying to sort out the right words. "Sir, please let me stay aboard so I can benefit from your experience."

Mak spread his hands, as if confused. "What is it you're expecting of me, Jeri?"

"What you're doing. Teaching me. Showing me how to do things. Telling me what I need to think about." She flinched. "Like now.

Telling me what I should have thought about. I don't know what to call that."

"Mentoring? A role model? Jeri. have you ever had an authority figure who was concerned about teaching you and supporting you? Helping you become more of what you wanted to be?"

"No, sir. That's called mentoring?"

Mak sighed, rubbing his forehead with one hand. "I didn't realize. I was trying to look out for you, but I didn't realize how much that involved. You often seem very wise in the ways of the world, Jeri. Experienced beyond your years. But there's a lot you've never learned."

"I grew up in a legion orphan home, sir. And since then it's been discipline and training in Imperial service, doing what I was told when I was told, by officers and centurions who knew what I was and didn't make any secret of what they thought of me because of that."

"I knew that. I didn't know all that it meant, though. I thought Imperial officers were taught to think as well as to follow orders."

Jules shook her head, looking down at the deck, old misery filling her. "No, sir. Not me. I had to do exactly as I was told, and nothing else, or I'd get a black mark. I learned a lot of technical skills, but I didn't dare think, Captain. Too many of my trainers and superiors just wanted any excuse to knock me down into the enlisted ranks where they thought anyone out of one of the homes belonged."

Mak nodded to her. "I've misjudged a number of things. Sit down, Jeri."

"Thank you, sir."

"I think I understand why you rendered judgment on that Imperial sailor. But you need to find ways to make it clear to the crew of this ship that you thought you were acting as I wanted you to act. Not that you were acting on your own to preempt whatever I might decide to do."

"I can do that, sir," Jules said as she sat down in the other chair. "I will do that."

"I can't fault your actual punishment of the man. It was fairly brilliant, the sort of thing that will enhance your reputation. I guess that's why I didn't realize you were oblivious to other aspects of what you were doing."

"It just felt like the right thing, sir. I'm sorry that I—"

"You already apologized, Jeri." Mak looked searchingly at her. "That was a very effective punishment. I'm surprised you could have done it. It takes ice in your heart to make that kind of decision in cold blood."

Jules nodded, feeling depressed. "Ferd was right."

"About what?"

"We had a talk, soon after I joined the crew, and he said the others thought that if someone crossed me I'd cut out his heart and eat it in front of him. I didn't think that was true of me. I guess it is."

Mak smiled. "Jeri, I don't think you'd do that."

"You don't?"

"Not unless you had some salt. I don't think you'd eat a man's heart without some seasoning."

She stared at him, momentarily lost for words. "That's a joke, isn't it? You are telling a joke, right?"

"I'm honestly not sure." Mak gave her a long, appraising look. "All right. You and I have both learned something. If I'm going to keep grooming you for command—"

"What?"

"Didn't you realize I was doing that?"

Jules shook her head. "I thought you were just making use of my Imperial training."

Mak laughed. "That makes perfect sense, doesn't it?"

"What about Ang, sir? I thought he was in line to command the *Sun Queen* if… I mean… when…"

"It's up to the crew who becomes captain after me," Mak said. "There's no line of succession like there would be on an Imperial ship. As for Ang, I've talked with him about command someday. He's not interested. Ang is a very good sailor, and a very good first officer, and that's what he wants to remain. I think he'd be a fine captain, but for reasons of his own he has no desire for the job. I have to respect that. If he ever changes his mind, he knows all he has to do is tell me."

"Oh." Jules brushed her hair back with one hand, thinking. "It never occurred to me that Ang wouldn't want the job. He'd be good at it."

"Jeri, remember how you talked about sword fighting and how you get in the mind of your opponent? You need to do the same thing with your captain. And those you command. Don't just see things from your perspective. Think about how they'll see what you do. Think about what their priorities might be, which might not be the same priorities that you'd have. Get to know your people."

"Is that mentoring?" Jules asked. "Because that was great. Is that how it's supposed to work?"

"Hopefully."

"Will you...? Sir, I don't have any right to expect it, but will you keep showing me these things? Telling me about them. I'm paying attention when you talk to Captain Erin or other captains. But obviously I'm still missing things."

Mak studied her again. "My question is, do you think you could do that getting-in-their-head thing with Mechanics, too? Maybe even Mages?"

"See things from their perspective?" Jules shook her head. "I've tried with the Mechanics. There's something... I don't know. Like a very different... what's the word? For everything about the way people do things and see things?"

"Oh. That's... I've heard talk about the Imperial court being different from the way Imperial citizens are in a place like Dunlan because of... Culture! That's the word."

"Culture? Then the Mechanics have a culture which is different from ours, but there's some overlap. Like when I talked to Mechanic Gin. It was almost like there was a wall there that we could both see over if she'd try, and if she'd help me up, but she didn't want to. Or she'd been taught not to look over." Jules shook her head. "But Mages. I have no idea. How do they think? Who's ever talked to one? I mean, really talked?"

"You're the only person I know who's ever spoken to a Mage," Mak said.

"I did not speak to the Mage. He spoke to me. I didn't say anything." Jules shuddered at the memory of those burning eyes gazing into hers. "I just ran. I wasn't really thinking. I just ran."

"Which was the right thing to do," Mak said. "If you'd given the Mage time to recover from his own shock, he would've killed you. You do that a lot, don't you, Jeri? Respond instinctively in an emergency. You just suddenly know what to do and you do it."

"I think that's a fair statement, sir. That's wrong, isn't it?"

He shook his head again. "No. Obviously not. You've made it this far. Your instinctive reactions tend to be exactly right. But you don't plan well between those reactions. You have long-term goals that you can tackle step by step if those steps have been laid out. But laying out those steps yourself is something you haven't been taught."

"Like the attack on the sloop," Jules said. "I just suddenly knew we should try to capture it. But I didn't do the planning right."

"We both messed up the planning, Jeri," Mak said. "Later on. why don't we go over that and figure out what we should have done differently?"

"Does that mean it's all right? I can stay aboard?" Jules waited anxiously for his reply.

"Jeri, at this point if I tried to kick you off the ship, I'd probably face a mutiny," Mak said.

"And you'll mentor me? Is that the right way to say it?"

"I think I need to, if only in self-defense."

* * *

A few days later, Jules gazed at the shore of one of the Sharr Isles, the island that held Jacksport. The town itself was a good ways off to starboard, too far off to be seen, or for anyone there to see what the *Sun Queen* was doing. The coast here held only a thin strip of beach backed by trees growing on slopes rising quickly to hills. From what could be seen of the island from this spot, there might be no human presence on it at all.

The only other sails in sight were those of the captured sloop and the *Storm Rider*, continuing on toward Jacksport.

"Get going, Jeri," Captain Mak said. "We'll be back for you when business is done. Lay low and keep an eye out for us."

"Yes, sir." Jules waved a farewell to the rest of the crew as she went over the side and down the Jaycob ladder into the ship's small boat, which had just been lowered. The other boat carried by the *Sun Queen*, the longboat, would've been too big for her to handle comfortably alone. She set the oars in the oarlocks, the hull of the *Sun Queen* rising above her.

How are we going to get you into and out of Jacksport again in one piece, Jeri?

Maybe it'd be a good idea if I didn't go into Jacksport at all, sir.

Which is why she was now rowing alone toward the beach. The *Sun Queen* put on more sail, following the sloop and the *Storm Rider*. By the time she grounded the boat on sand just short of the beach, only the *Sun Queen*'s masts were still in sight.

Jules hauled the small boat as high onto the beach as she could, which wasn't nearly far enough to hide it. After running a line from the bow of the boat into the trees and tying it off around a trunk big enough around to hold even against a major storm, Jules gathered what big branches she could find and dragged them out to the boat, draping them on and around it to hopefully create something that looked like a big mound of driftwood.

Retreating far enough into the woods to be sure she couldn't be easily spotted from the water, Jules finally sat down, her back against a tree trunk. She started chewing slowly on a small piece of salt pork, letting the wood-hard meat soften in her mouth, and batting at a couple of gnats that had already taken interest in her. In addition to the revolver she had a cutlass, her dagger, and her sailor knife. There was enough food and water in the boat to last for three days (four if she stretched it), more than enough time for the *Sun Queen* to finish her work in Jacksport and come back out for her.

Which left her with a lot of time to think.

Jules sat watching the water, trying to dredge up memories of her life before her parents died. There weren't many. More like vague impressions, and occasional clear images whose meaning she didn't remember.

Then the orphan home. Life as one of many orphans there, her clothing a shapeless shirt and loose trousers that eliminated the need for any sort of tailoring, the cheap fabric rough on her skin. Getting picked on, learning to fight back, that one fight where she'd nearly strangled a mean girl who'd been pushing her, the mean ones leaving her alone afterwards. Had the darkness inside her come from that, or had it always been there? She didn't have a mother to ask.

Terrible food, and usually not enough of it.

But also friends. People like Shin. And the schooling, where the bottom-of-the-barrel teachers cared so little for their jobs that Jules had been able to read ahead, learn ahead, determined not to have only the choice of enlisting in the legions. Because once a legion orphan turned eighteen the Emperor's charity no longer flowed, and few places other than the legions would accept them.

How proud she'd been to put on that officer's uniform, knowing she'd earned it by her own work, knowing she'd passed every test on her own, with no help from family connections or paid tutors.

While she remembered, the sun had already settled far enough in the west to be blocked by the hills behind her. Jules made sure her food was safely secured in the chest in the boat, then taking a length of line walked into the woods until she found a tree that seemed suitable. Climbing branch by branch, she found one broad enough to sit on. Jules wrapped the length of line about herself, knotting it around the tree trunk at her back so she could sleep without fear of falling to the ground.

It wasn't animals or insects she feared. It was other people. Imperials, smugglers willing to deal with the Imperials in hopes of collecting a ransom for her, and Mages.

Jules draped a sheet of dark cloth over herself, both as camouflage and to protect from the gnats who were swarming out in greater numbers as evening fell.

By the time morning dawned she was full of aches in stiff muscles that made getting down to the ground perilous.

The day went by very slowly.

What was happening in Jacksport? Would she be able to hear if Mechanics began firing their weapons that far off? Would she be able to see the smoke of burning ships or buildings?

Jules sat inside the edge of the trees, watching occasional sails go by, the ships under them hidden by the horizon, and repeatedly imagined the worst things that could befall the *Sun Queen*.

Imagining Captain Mak dying. Feeling her heart pound each time that happened.

And yet she was absolutely certain there was nothing wrong in her feelings toward Mak. Nothing romantic anyway. No physical yearnings. She just didn't want to think of losing him. She admired him and respected him. Whatever that was, it wasn't love.

Jules did a bit of exploring inland from where her boat was beached. She had plenty of time to kill, and as a general principle she thought it would be a good idea from now on to know enough about her surroundings to help her if she suddenly needed to start running for her life. In recent months that had happened far too many times already.

Inland the ground sloped upward fairly steeply, going near vertical in places where trees grew up against the cliffs to mask them. There didn't seem to be any good paths in that direction. To the left and right as far as she explored, the land stayed low near the beach, though the density of the trees varied. A short distance in the direction toward Jacksport, Jules found a stream coming through the trees and emptying into the ocean. It wasn't wide or deep, easily walked through, but the water tasted refreshing after the stale supply she had in bottles on the boat.

She returned to the boat and opened the chest to get some hardtack. It took a blow from her cutlass the break the hard cracker into chunks that could be softened enough in her mouth to eat. Wishing that she'd asked for a bottle of wine to be included in her food supply, Jules went back to the sleeping tree.

The second night seemed a lot longer than the first.

Jules got down from the tree on the second morning almost wishing that a Mage would show up so she could kill him or her with the Mechanic weapon. It hurt to walk. Everything hurt.

The morning was halfway gone when Jules noticed some masts coming closer. Hopeful, she watched the masts grow higher as they grew closer, yardarms and sails appearing. But a lot of ships had that same arrangement of masts and rigging.

As the hull came into sight and grew larger, Jules grinned. That had to be the *Sun Queen*. She stepped out of the cover of the trees, waving.

The ship came about near the beach, but Jules frowned at it. Something didn't seem right. Why couldn't she see Captain Mak on the quarterdeck?

Two longboats were lowered, sailors piling into them.

Two longboats? The *Sun Queen* only had one. And that ship was definitely not the *Storm Rider*.

Jules turned and began running.

CHAPTER NINE

Knowing she was being watched from the ship, Jules ran straight back into the trees. She kept going that way long enough to lose sight of the ship, then turned and began running to her right, in the general direction of Jacksport. Staying on the lower land not far from the beach, she tried to maintain the best pace she could, hearing shouts behind her as the longboats grounded on the sand.

Those weren't shouts. They were orders, and the way the orders were being called sounded very much like legionaries at drill.

Jules went through the stream in two quick steps and on through the land beyond, dodging between trees and trying to stay far enough inside them that the Imperials wouldn't spot her from their ship.

They'd known where she was. Someone on the *Sun Queen* must have talked while the ship was in Jacksport. And this Imperial ship, disguised as just another merchant ship, had come looking for her before the *Queen* could get here.

The shouted orders behind her were growing fainter. With any luck the legionaries had spread out in a search line and then charged straight inland in search of her. Hopefully, by the time they realized she'd gone another way they would have lost a lot of time trying to find a path up those cliffs.

She had to slow down a bit, her breath coming deep and fast, almost slipping as she dodged around another tree.

The beach where she'd been dropped off had been thousands of lances from a turn in the coast that eventually led to Jacksport. How far off was Jacksport? Too far to run.

More shouting of orders. Jules paused for a moment, trying to catch her breath while looking back the way she'd come. Some shouts from inland on her left. Some shouts from her right on the beach.

Blazes. They were spread out and coming this way. The ship must have spotted her when she turned, and gotten word to the legionaries.

Jules began trotting through the woods, trying to keep her pace. She was surprised to realize that the noises from the legionaries behind her quickly faded again, as if they were moving slowly rather than running in pursuit of her.

The reason for that became clear as the trees thinned without warning, giving her a look out onto the water. The ship, sails set, glided along in the same direction that she was going. Also visible was one of the longboats, the rowers pulling hard.

They were going to get ahead of her, land more people, and wait for her to either run into them or try to hide and get caught by the searchers coming behind.

She dropped her pace to a walk, thinking. What would Captain Mak be suggesting? *Plan.* All right. Hiding wouldn't work. She knew how well legionaries handled tasks like searches. Running wouldn't work. She couldn't outpace a longboat and a ship. Going out to sea, swimming, would just leave her easy prey for one of the longboats.

That left trying to go inland. Which meant tackling that high ground even though the cliffs farther back hadn't looked very friendly to climbers. But it was the only way that offered any chance of avoiding capture.

The trees had gotten denser again, blocking her view of the ship and the longboat. Jules veered to her right, heading straight inland at a trot.

The land sloped up quickly for a short distance before leaping upwards into cliffs, just as it had back where she'd started. She walked along the cliffs, looking up for any possible way to climb them. Stay calm, she told herself. Take time to study those cliffs. Look for a path up. Look for…

She'd reached a place where a section of cliff had collapsed, leaving a mound at the bottom and a steeply rising ramp upwards.

Jules stopped at the foot of it. Maybe a hundred lances from top to bottom. Mingled dirt and rocks. But it wasn't a cliff that would require a slow, tortuous climb. She should be able to run up this. If she didn't fall or slip and slide back to the bottom.

She paused, breathing deeply, trying to gather her strength, hearing the shouted commands behind her slowly getting closer.

Jules launched herself at the rise, her legs pumping in an all-out effort. She ran, her feet slipping on the loose soil of the rockfall—*keep going*—rocks and gravel and dirt sliding under her feet, leaning forward enough to keep from falling backwards, grabbing with her hands at new clumps of brush springing up and bigger rocks to pull herself up and aid her legs which were aching and *blazes how much longer could she do this* she couldn't stop to look up and see how far was left to go or she'd fall *where was the top* her left leg almost slipped completely out from under her *blazes recover keep going up don't stop or you'll fall blazes she couldn't-*

She reached the top and sprawled on the narrow ledge of what had been clifftop here, more cliff rising behind it, unable to move for a few moments as her vision hazed from exhaustion over the extreme effort. Still trying to catch her breath, Jules painfully pulled her legs all the way onto the ledge, out of view of anyone below. Finally managing to get to her hands and knees, Jules rolled against the back of the ledge into a sitting position.

Her vision clearing and her breathing becoming less labored, Jules looked to her left and right along the ledge. It quickly disappeared on one side but meandered along the height in the direction she'd come from. Behind her the cliff only went up another ten lances or so, but offered no obvious good handholds on its dirt surface. That made deciding what to do next pretty simple.

Jules got to her feet, one hand on the side of the rise, and began moving cautiously along the ledge, listening for the commands being called below. The legionaries were sure they had her trapped and were hoping to scare her into flight, like hunters beating the underbrush to spook birds into the air.

She put her feet down carefully as the ledge narrowed, trying to avoid sending any rocks or gravel down what had once more become cliffs. If the legionaries heard that they'd know where she was.

"Count off!" The shout came from nearly even with her, rattling Jules. She crouched, unmoving, her eyes on the ground below her.

"One!" a legionary called from near the beach.

"Two!" a bit closer to her.

They kept calling out their numbers until Jules heard one that sounded as if he was right beneath her. "Twenty!"

She tried to breathe silently, leaning as far back as possible, hearing the crunch of feet stepping on fallen branches and leaves. A bit farther off from the high ground, Jules spotted a legionary walking at a slow, steady pace through the woods as she searched to either side and ahead, as well the trees above her. From here, Jules could spot the armor concealed under the woman's sailor shirt. There was a scabbarded short sword at the legionary's belt, but in her hand she held a padded club.

They wanted her alive. Undamaged except for bruises and maybe broken limbs, neither of which would prevent her "wedding" to the Emperor.

Jules waited only a short time after the legionaries passed her spot before moving on at the fastest pace she dared. The ledge varied in width and was descending enough to be dangerously slippery but not enough to offer hope of getting her back near the ground.

The searcher closest to this side would probably spot the marks she'd made running up that steep slope. They'd have to decide whether she'd kept going inland and higher, or if she'd turned left or right. That meant sending someone up to the ledge. She'd barely made it, as lightly dressed as she was and carrying only the revolver and a cutlass. The legionaries had the weight of their armor to contend with.

Jules paused, looking out over what she could see of the water through the tops of the highest trees growing between the cliffs and the beach.

Was that the same ship? Returned because they'd already realized that she'd doubled back?

No. That was Mak on the quarterdeck. It had to be. And the sloop of war coming into view from behind the ship wasn't flying an Imperial flag.

Taking the risk of standing tall, Jules looked back along the way she'd come, making out the masts of the ship that had been chasing her.

Shouts from that direction. Not as calm and confident as they had been. The legionaries had found her path up the slope and realized their prey had found an escape path.

She had to get down to the beach. Climbing down looked too hazardous to risk.

Jules still had wrapped about her waist the length of line she'd used to tie herself into the tree at night. She unwrapped it, wishing that she'd taken a much longer length. There wasn't anything to tie it to. She drew the cutlass and using both hands plunged the sword straight down into the surface of the ledge, putting her weight behind it. It only sank about a third of its short length, but that would have to do. Tying off the line on the cutlass grip, Jules went over the side of the cliff, sliding down as quickly as she dared.

Her fist encountered the knot on the end of the line far too soon, but she was at least even with the tops of some of the trees growing up from the bottom of the cliff. She felt the line jerk as the cutlass slid a bit from its anchorage in response to her weight. No time to hesitate. Jules kicked herself off from the cliff toward a sturdy-looking tree, letting go of the line and grabbing frantically as she hit the tree to stop herself from falling. The first branch she grabbed broke, she dropped, the second branch broke, she dropped… the third held.

Jules tried to look down just far enough to see the branches right beneath her. Fortunately, her experience in the rigging of sailing ships helped her keep her head despite the height.

She went from branch to branch, dropping through them much faster than she could have climbed. Her descent made noise as leaves rustled and twigs snapped, but right now speed was far more important than stealth.

The final drop to the ground was far enough to worry her, but Jules rolled when she hit and got up with only a twinge in one ankle. The legionaries were calling orders a ways back the way she'd come. No hurry. She walked toward the beach, limping slightly, coming out of the trees to see the second legionary longboat already in the water and rowing west toward the other longboat and the ship that had launched both. The small boat from the *Sun Queen* was still there on the beach, though the branches concealing it had been pulled aside.

The *Sun Queen* herself was standing in closer to the beach, her longboat in the water and headed this way.

Far down the beach, Jules saw legionaries come out of the trees, looking her way. They started running, but she knew it would take them too long to get here.

Jules went the edge of the water. "It took you long enough!" she called to Ang as the longboat got close.

"You don't look like you've had any trouble," he called back.

"I lost my cutlass," Jules said. "And you can see that company is coming. Ang, somebody talked. They knew I was here."

"Yeah, we think we know who it was." The longboat grounded lightly. "You two, go get the small boat and row it back," Ang ordered a couple of sailors.

"What about them?" one of the sailors protested, pointing toward the legionaries running this way.

"Do it fast," Ang said. "Get in, Jeri."

"Yes, sir," she said, climbing into the longboat and wincing as she put weight on the hurt ankle. "You think you know who told the Imperials I was here?"

"Yeah," Marta said as she and the others began rowing the longboat back to the *Sun Queen*. "It was Don."

"Don?" Jules looked back at the beach, where the frustrated legionaries had slowed to a walk as it became obvious they had no chance of catching her. "Are you sure?"

"He was flashing a lot of money last night. Claimed he won big at dice. And this morning, no sign of him when it was time to sail."

"He might've been mugged and murdered for that money," Jules said. "Why would he betray the ship?"

"We asked, and no bodies were found this morning," Ang said. "That's when we got worried for you. Didn't I hear you and Don going at it pretty angry the night before we got to Jacksport?"

"I don't know how angry we were," Jules said. "He pushed things, I told him to back off, and he did."

Marta laughed as she pulled on her oar. "Pretty sure I heard a *never* in there during that talk you and Don had, and also something about him losing a hand if he ever tried that again?"

"Yes," Jules admitted. "He was pretty aggressive, and I didn't like it."

"He was talking to those Imperials on the captured ships before we left them," Ang said. "He might've heard something."

About her. Jules made a face as she realized that should have been obvious earlier. "Yeah. I'll bet he did."

"The cap'n has some other things to talk to you about," Ang added as the longboat pulled alongside the *Sun Queen*.

Mak gave her a relieved look as she came up the job ladder. "The *Storm Queen* is keeping your friends off our backs, but we still ought to leave this area."

"The *Storm Queen*?" Jules asked, following Mak to the quarterdeck, favoring her ankle as she walked.

"That's the name we decided on for the captured sloop," Mak explained. "As if it were the offspring of the *Sun Queen* and the *Storm Rider*. We also decided to give command of her to Lars, one of Captain Erin's sailors. Some of the *Queen's* crew went to her, and some from Erin's ship. The rest of her crew is made up of sailors who were in Jacksport and looking for work."

Jules heard a loud *thunk* coming from over the water and turned to see that the newly named *Storm Queen* had launched a rock from her ballistae at the big ship coming back in their direction. The ballistae, resembling a giant crossbow, canted back on its mount as the crew worked to tension its cord and load another rock.

"They were definitely after you?" Mak asked.

"Yes, sir. Padded clubs instead of swords."

"Blazes." He watched the longboat and the small boat being hoisted aboard. "While we were in Jacksport, three Mages came aboard at three different times. We were told that's become common the last few weeks, Mages going aboard ships stopping at Jacksport, searching the ships with particular interest in any women aboard, then leaving. The only ships safe from that treatment are those flying the flag of the Mechanics Guild."

"Maybe we should get one of those flags," Jules said.

"You might ask your friends about that next time you see them."

"They don't actually ask my advice or about what I want," Jules said.

Thunk.

She heard the distant sound of splintering wood as the *Storm Queen*'s ballistae put a rock into the side of the Imperial ship, which veered off in response to the attack. "They were in Jacksport, too?" Jules gestured at the Imperial ship as it wore about to retrieve its longboats, ceasing to close on the *Sun Queen*.

"Yes," Mak said. "When we saw this morning that they'd left before dawn, it worried us, so we got here as quickly as we could and made sure the *Storm Queen* came with us."

"They have legionaries aboard, sir. I wonder why they didn't try to retake the sloop while it was in the harbor?"

"They probably have orders to pursue only one target," Mak said with a glance at her. "Did Ang tell you about Don?"

"Yes, sir." Jules leaned on the railing to take weight off of her ankle, looking aft at the far-off legionaries boarding their longboats. "I should've realized he'd learned who I was. That must be why he pushed me hard on the way to Jacksport for us to become really close shipmates. When I made clear to him that'd happen sometime between never and not a chance, he must've decided to cash in on what he knew by telling the Imperials. But why did they have that ship at Jacksport waiting? And the Mages searching ships? It's like they all expected me to come back there."

"If so, you out-thought them." Mak eyed the other ship. "What would you do now?"

"After escaping this? If I was smart," Jules said, "I guess I'd run and hide."

"And if you were Jeri the pirate?"

"I'd go see what kind of ships might be left unguarded near the Imperial coast while the Emperor's eyes are trying to find me farther to the west."

Mak grinned. "That's a good plan. The crew already voted for it. The *Storm Queen* will keep that ship from tailing us while we go to meet up with the *Storm Rider* south of Caer Lyn." The smile faded as he looked at her. "How was it before we got here?"

"Boring for a long time," Jules said, "then too exciting for a little while. I kept my head, though. I planned things out. But I lost my cutlass."

"Cutlasses can be replaced," Mak said. "You look like you've been rolling in some dirt."

"Thank you, sir. I missed you, too, sir."

* * *

A week later, so close to the Empire's shores that the land showed clearly on the horizon, the *Sun Queen* and the *Storm Rider* ran down their prey.

Their quarry was one of the largest types of sailing ships, bound to have a large cargo but also a large crew to defend it. The two pirate ships came at the big merchant ship from opposite sides, Captain Mak and Captain Erin expertly timing their approaches so that the two ships reached the port and starboard sides of their target at almost the same time.

At Captain Mak's suggestion, Jules stood high on the shrouds as the *Sun Queen* approached her target, cutlass and revolver prominently displayed. It felt fake to her, like an act to impress people. But the show seemed to inspire the pirates aboard the *Queen* as well as frighten the defenders of the other ship.

Jules led the *Sun Queen*'s boarding party over the merchant ship's starboard rail, the defenders falling back rather than fighting. As the pirates swarmed aboard from both sides, the crew put up only a little resistance before dropping their weapons. "Something odd's going on," Ang commented to Jules. "Crews usually try to put up at least a decent show of resistance so the ship's owner can't fault them for not trying to fight off pirates."

"Between us and the *Storm Queen*'s crew, we did outnumber them a lot," Jules said.

"It's not about whether there's a chance of winning," Ang said. "It's about collecting some cuts and bruises to prove they put up a fight."

"Maybe they hate their captain?" Liv wondered. "Didn't want to die for her?"

"Let's get her here and see what she's like," Jules said.

The captain was hauled before her, middle-aged, looking more like a bureaucrat who'd gotten lost and ended up on a ship rather than the commander of a ship at sea. "Do you yield?" Jules demanded.

"Yes," the captain gasped, her eyes looking around the deck as if searching for something.

"I'm the one you're talking to," Jules said. "Who are you looking for? Ang, are we sure there aren't any people hiding below deck? Maybe some legionaries who plan to surprise us?"

"There are no legionaries aboard," the captain protested, her gaze still roaming the deck. "It's… them."

"Them?"

The captain's eyes looked past her, fixing on something behind Jules and growing wide with fear. Jules felt silence spreading rapidly around the deck, both victorious pirates and cowed defenders shrinking in fear.

At something behind her.

She still had the revolver in her hand. Jules gripped it tightly as she turned.

A Mage stood on the deck just outside the stern cabin. His hood was down, revealing a man whose age could be anywhere from his twenties to his forties. Something about him gave a sense of the younger side of that span, though. In the bright light of day, Jules could see a patchwork of scars on the Mage's face, marks of old injuries. A small part of her remembered seeing similar signs of injuries on the Mage she'd come face to face with in Jacksport. As she stood watching the Mage, Jules wondered what the significance of those scars might be.

The Mage looked slowly around the deck, his gaze finally centering on her. With a slow, deliberate motion he drew from beneath his robes the long knife that Mages were infamous for. Jules could see his eyes as they rested on her, see the death they promised with cold, passionless certainty. He'd recognized her, either by her description or through some Mage talent beyond normal human understanding.

The Mage began walking toward her, his long knife out, expressionless face somehow malevolent. Why wasn't he using one his spells against her? Was this a Mage's way of saying that she didn't merit that amount of effort, a last insult? Did he feel so safe that he wasn't worried about she might do? He had a right to feel that way, Jules knew. Common people were aware of the strange powers of Mages and that they couldn't be killed by normal weapons. His inhuman lack of emotion combined with the fear that Mages inspired held everyone silent and unmoving.

Jules felt that fear, too, felt it freezing the blood in her veins, but she had the revolver in one of her hands. In case she encountered Mages. Jules raised the Mechanic weapon, aiming the barrel at the Mage, who kept coming without any visible reaction. She realized that her hand was shaking and tried to steady it, pointing the barrel at the center of the Mage's body. *Don't miss. Don't miss. Wait until he's close.*

The Mage was almost close enough to strike her with his knife when Jules pulled the trigger with a spastic jerk of her finger.

The boom of the weapon filled the sky and the sea.

The Mage staggered backwards, still showing no feeling. A hole had appeared in the front of his robes. A trace of a frown appeared on his face. He took another step toward her.

Despairing, Jules held her ground and pulled the trigger again. The hammer came back, slammed forward with a metallic click, and... nothing.

Had the Mage done something? A spell to keep the Mechanic weapon from working? Had she done something wrong?

Her heart almost stopped with fear, Jules quickly pulled the trigger again.

This time she was rewarded with another crash of thunder, the revolver bucking in her hand.

The Mage jolted again with the impact of the projectile. He stopped moving, his unfeeling eyes fixed on her, a second hole in the front of his robes.

Jules held her revolver aimed at him, her hand steadier despite the fact the Mage was still standing, still apparently a threat. Maybe she had one cartridge left, if the one that hadn't shot worked on a second try. Maybe she no longer had any cartridges that could work.

A trickle of blood came from one side of the Mage's mouth.

The crashes of the two shots had dulled Jules' hearing, so that the world about her felt unnaturally silent as she waited to see if she'd have to shoot again, and whether even a third shot would stop a Mage. Was that why the Mechanics had given her four cartridges? Because she'd need that many to kill a Mage? But she'd wasted one of those cartridges shooting Shin. And one of them hadn't worked the first time she'd tried. As the Mage stared at her, Jules raised the revolver to look at it, rolling the cylinder back to where the hammer would fall on that third cartridge again when she pulled the trigger. Then she waited.

The Mage finally staggered to one side, his eyes still fixed on her, then fell, blood pooling under him.

Jules inhaled convulsively, not even having been aware that she was holding her breath.

A low murmur sounded around her.Ang stepped up beside her, looking ashamed. "I couldn't move. I was scared."

"That's all right," Jules said, feeling numb. "I could barely move."

"You killed a Mage, Jeri. Without anyone's help. Just you and him. You killed a Mage."

She inhaled deeply again, tasting the odd, acrid smell from the smoke created by the Mechanic weapon. Jules looked about, seeing her pirates and those from the *Storm Rider* grinning at her in disbelief and wonder.

The crew of the captured ship still looked scared.

Jules pivoted to face the captain again. "Why are you all still frightened?"

"There's another," the captain said, almost breathless with fear. "Another Mage aboard. He's... he's still in the cabin."

Jules followed the line of the captain's pointing finger, which visibly shook as she indicated the stern cabin.

A hush had fallen over the deck again as the captain's words were repeated among the two pirate crews, the only sounds the sigh of the wind and the water alongside the ship while everyone looked toward the cabin. And looked back to her.

Jules looked down at the weapon she held. One cartridge left. If it would work this time. That would have to be enough.

"We'll go in with you," Ang said, Liv beside him, both of them with cutlasses at the ready. "You won't face a Mage alone this time."

"No," Jules said. "You'd just get in the way. I need to kill him with this."

Her mind screamed at her to run the other way, but Jules began walking toward the door of the cabin, which the dead Mage had left open. She wasn't thinking, just acting. Captain Mak would be angry that she wasn't planning. But she knew that if she really thought about this, she'd never get her feet into motion. She'd stand paralyzed, waiting for the second Mage to come out of that cabin and attack her.

The open door to the stern cabin loomed before her like a dark portal.

Blinds must be drawn closed across the stern windows. No lanterns were lit to dispel the gloom inside.

Jules took two long, slow breaths.

She stepped inside quickly, nerves twitching in fear of being attacked by the knife of the other Mage. Or, worse, having a Mage spell remove her arm, or turn her into an insect. No one knew exactly what Mages could do, but none of the stories circulated among commons were comforting.

Nothing happened. She heard a soft, wheezing noise, gradually realizing it was the sound of someone's labored breathing.

Jules waited, her eyes growing accustomed to the dark inside the cabin, finally making out the shape of the second Mage, who was lying in the bunk. Jules flexed her hold on the Mechanic weapon, forcing herself to walk closer.

The Mage didn't move, didn't seem to be aware that she was in the cabin.

She had to get very close to the Mage to be sure of hitting him with the shot. Jules took two more steps, gazing down at the Mage, who lay with closed eyes on rumpled sheets. The man seemed to be very skinny, bones standing out in the angles of his face.

He wasn't skinny, she realized. He was very old.

The Mage's eyes opened, fixing on her own.

Jules almost froze again, but she raised the revolver to point it at the old Mage.

He didn't react at all, merely looking at her.

She felt a curious mix of anger and reluctance as she looked back. One Mage had ruined her life. Others sought her death. They hurt others and showed no signs of caring.

Why wasn't she pulling the trigger?

Jules glared at the ancient Mage, all of the questions that had tormented her tumbling through her mind. Why had she been chosen for that prophecy? Why did Mages act the way they did? Why couldn't the Emperor protect her instead of being a threat? Why was all of this happening?

But only one word came out of her. "Why?"

One corner of the Mage's mouth twisted slightly. He spoke in a weak voice tinged with distance, as if already halfway gone from this world. "A shadow asks the ultimate question."

Was that really a trace of humor she'd heard in that quavering voice? "What's the answer?"

"There is no answer to *why*, but the answers are so many they are beyond number," the Mage gasped.

"What does that mean?"

"Think on it. Perhaps even a shadow can learn wisdom." The Mage's eyes lingered on her again. "The prophecy was correct. This one sees it. That one's line will produce the daughter who destroys the Great Guilds. This one wonders why that one was chosen."

Jules heard her own voice quaver with pent-up emotions. "I've been asking myself that a lot. Do you know the answer?"

"There is no answer, and the answers are beyond number."

She'd let the revolver droop, and now raised it again to threaten him. "What does that mean? Tell me!"

"Wisdom must be found," the Mage said. "Do not demand it from illusion and shadows. Seek it inside."

Jules stared at him, wondering why this Mage was so talkative, why she kept catching traces of feeling in his voice and seeing them on his face. Perhaps his age was the answer, the Mage's iron control breaking down as his old body and mind finally failed. "I don't understand."

"If that one understands that one does not understand, then that one knows the beginning of wisdom." The old Mage shuddered slightly, his eyes staring upward. "This one will cease soon. Very soon."

Had she really heard the emotion that she thought she had? "Are you afraid?"

"This one is alone, and the last door beckons."

He was afraid. A very old man, on his deathbed, staring into the emptiness. Jules let the hand holding the revolver drop so it was pointed at the deck. She felt a strange and inexplicable desire to comfort the Mage. "You're not alone."

"That one is a shadow. All are shadows. Only this one exists, and soon that will end. What will become of the illusion then?"

"Shadows? You think other people are just shadows?"

"This one knows. Nothing is real."

"Nothing?" Jules waved to the room around them. "I'm standing on a deck on a ship. That's real."

"A shadow stands on an illusion."

"Is that why Mages act the way they do? They believe that people like me don't even exist? That even this ship is just some kind of trick?"

The Mage didn't answer, the slow, shallow rise and fall of his chest as he breathed hesitating before continuing.

Jules glared at him. "Listen, if a daughter of my line is supposed to do something someday, doesn't that mean that everything is going to continue? If Mages can see that future, then that future must exist, won't it? My line—which means somehow I'll still matter, I'll still continue. Somehow. People don't just cease. If they did, that prophecy couldn't be real."

The Mage's eyes sought hers again. "That one sees wisdom this one did not. Can that one understand it?"

"I don't understand anything! How is she going to do it?" Jules demanded. "I can't figure out what you're saying. I can't even talk to any other Mages because they'll either ignore me or try to kill me. How is that daughter of my line going to get Mages to help her? How is that even possible?"

The Mage looked back at her. "That one will learn wisdom."

"That one? You mean the daughter of my line?"

"The shadow asks many questions. The shadow seeks wisdom given. Wisdom cannot be given. Others can show the path. But only that one can walk the path and find what lies…" The Mage paused for a long time before finishing, his words tailing off. "At the end…"

"Do you mean me this time? Why can't you just say what you mean?"

The Mage didn't answer, his eyes fixed and unmoving. Jules, feeling revulsion, reached out to touch him. No one touched Mages by choice.

She nudged him. He didn't react. He'd stopped breathing.

Jules put the revolver back in its sheath, looking down at the body of the old Mage.

She'd finally been able to talk to a Mage, and instead of answers had only gotten more questions.

And yet, for just a moment, he'd felt like another person rather than a monster. Which meant that inside, somewhere under those inhuman exteriors and dead faces, Mages still had something human left in them. But it must be buried very, very deep.

Would the daughter of her line find a way to touch that? To reach the people left somewhere inside Mages?

Outside, the brightness of the day seemed blinding. Jules had to pause again to let her eyes adapt to the glare. She saw everyone still standing on deck, watching her. "The Mage is dead," Jules said.

"We didn't hear your weapon," Ang said.

"I didn't need it."

A ripple of astonishment ran through the crowd as they stared at her. Astonishment and... awe? Was that what she was seeing? What was wrong with people? "He died," Jules snapped at them. "That's all. He died. Just like anyone else."

"We heard talking in there," Liv said.

"Yes. I talked to him."

"You *talked* to him? A Mage talked to you?"

"Yes." She felt a strong reluctance to say anything else. And what could she tell them? She hadn't learned anything. No answers, and answers beyond number. Would she ever be able to forget that? Jules glowered at those watching her. "What are you all looking at? Didn't we just capture this ship? Doesn't anyone have anything they need to be doing?"

Men and women pirates jerked guiltily and began rushing about.

Ang gestured to the body of the first Mage. "What do we do with the Mages? This one and the one in there?"

"Bury him," Jules said. "Bury both of them. Just like you would anyone else. Bury them at sea."

"But they're Mages."

"They're people. Bury them." She walked away, feeling the darkness inside her despite the light of the sun beating down.

* * *

The evening, back on the *Sun Queen*, she laid the revolver on one of the mess tables and used her dagger to pry out the cartridge that hadn't worked. She saw that the silvery round part in the center of the flat end was compressed where the hammer had struck it. That looked exactly like the ones that had worked. Otherwise, the cartridge seemed like the others. It just hadn't worked.

What had one of the Mechanics said when talking about "ammunition"? Something about a quality problem? Was that what he'd meant, that sometimes the cartridges didn't work? But how could that be so? Mechanic devices always worked. She must have done something wrong. Pulled the trigger in the wrong way, maybe too hard or too soft. Or that Mage had managed to do something to this cartridge to keep it from shooting.

Not knowing what else to do with it, Jules put the cartridge back into the cylinder of the revolver along with the three cases left from the first three.

Even if she couldn't make that last cartridge work, the revolver wasn't entirely useless. As long as no one else knew that cartridge couldn't work for whatever reason, it would seem that she had one shot left.

"Jeri?" Ang said, speaking with unusual shyness. "I wanted to thank you."

"Thank me?" Jules said, looking over to see that he had walked up as she worked on the revolver.

"Yes, sister." He sat down next to her, but facing out away from the table, looking out into the below decks. "You know that Mages killed my mother. One of the hardest parts of that has been knowing that nothing would happen to them for that. No one would punish them.

No one could bring them to account. Mages could do whatever they wanted, and we just had to put up with it and bury our dead."

He paused, looking down, his hands tightly grasped together. "But today you killed two Mages." Ang held up a restraining hand as Jules began to deny credit for the old Mage's death. "Let me finish, Jeri. You made them pay. So I wanted to thank you for that."

Jules smiled at Ang, blinking away sudden tears. "You're welcome."

"I just hope," Ang continued, "that they felt it. At the end, I mean. That when you killed those two Mages, they felt the fear of death as it laid hands on them."

She nodded. "I know at least one did."

"Good," Ang said. "That's good. I just wanted to thank you, Jeri."

He got up and walked away, leaving her to think about what she'd done and what it meant to different people. About what it meant to learn that Mages were still people deep inside, but thought all others literally weren't people, literally didn't even exist. No wonder Mages acted the way they did toward others.

What did it all mean?

No answers.

Answers without end.

CHAPTER TEN

S elling the cargo they took from captured ships wasn't simply a matter of pulling into an Imperial port where demand would likely be high. Even out-of-the-way places where inspectors were more easily bribed were too dangerous at the moment for the *Sun Queen* and the *Storm Rider*. So the two ships steered north and west until they reached Kelsi's settlement again, encountering some rough weather the day before reaching the shelter of the harbor.

Meeting a ship on its way out of Kelsi's, they confirmed that no Imperial warships were visiting. "No Mages to be seen, either!" the captain of the departing ship called across the waters separating the ships. "It's like they all went somewhere else!"

Somewhere they expected to catch her? Jules wondered. But it was good news as far as Kelsi's settlement was concerned, allowing her to ride the *Sun Queen* in instead of risking another isolated stay somewhere away from the port.

They'd barely tied up when Captain Erin came aboard, shaking her head at Mak. "That mast cracked again. I've got to get it replaced, Mak."

"Can they do that here?" Mak asked as Jules listened.

"Not here. They can't do that kind of work here yet. I'll have to take my ship east to Marida's harbor. You can't follow me there, not with this girl aboard, and the repairs will take a while." Erin nodded to them both. "We should be fine. There's enough illicit trade flowing through Marida's these days that even our haul won't stand out too much. But if anyone asks about the *Sun Queen*, and about a certain girl who rides that ship, we'll say that we've no idea where you've gone. So don't tell me where you intend heading next. I'd hate to tell a lie."

Jules laughed along with Mak.

"Fair winds," Mak said, extending a hand to Erin. "I hope we can work together again."

"To be sure," Erin said. "Take care, Mak." She looked at Jules. "You, too. I wouldn't want to trade places with you, but you're handling it better than I could."

"I'm just trying to stay alive, free, and feeling like I matter," Jules said.

Erin smiled at her, the sadness in the smile all too evident. "Good luck, girl. You've got some rough waters ahead no matter what happens. A bit of advice from one whose heart has weathered a few storms. Pay no heed to the men who say they love you while they're trying to get you into bed. That's true of any woman, but more so of you because of that prophecy. No, wait until you're having the worst day of your life, when you hate everything and everybody and are biting the heads off anyone who looks sideways at you, and watch for the man who stands beside you anyway. That's how a man really says I love you and means it, by being there for you when you know you're not a joy to be around."

"I'll take that advice to heart," Jules said. She watched Erin leave before turning to Mak. "Where do you suppose the Mages are, Captain?"

"They can be invisible, people say," Mak replied.

"Meaning I shouldn't go ashore?"

"The Imperials have their share of paid agents in this harbor," he said. "Some of whom would doubtless love to get their hands on you to please the Emperor."

"Meaning I shouldn't go ashore." Jules looked toward the ramshackle town that was rapidly putting up new buildings. "My life wasn't all that great, but I miss it."

He sighed. "I'm sorry, Jeri. I can't give you back that life. But I'll lay you odds at this moment every sailor ashore is talking about the young woman who killed two Mages. Not the young woman who's going to establish the line of daughters that fulfills the prophecy, but the one who faced down Mages and killed them. And the one who successfully captured an Imperial warship. Has that ever been done before? By anyone?"

"I didn't do it," Jules said. "I would have caused a disaster, remember? Captain Erin should get credit for that."

"Erin never would have thought of it," Mak said. "Next time you see her, ask her and she'll tell you."

Jules shivered, feeling cold. "I wish I could think of a way to protect my child. Or children. Whichever it turns out to be. It still feels so weird to know I *will* have a child. And that the moment I do, a lot of people are going to want to kill that kid."

"I wish I knew how to protect those children," Mak said. "But I couldn't even protect my own."

She flinched and gave him an apologetic look. "I'm sorry. I keep reminding you of things that make you unhappy."

He smiled at her. "You also remind me of good things, Jeri."

* * *

They spent three days in Kelsi's as Mak arranged the sale of their cargo to people who wouldn't ask questions about where and when the goods had been acquired. The crew spent most of that time trying to spend every bit of their shares on the diversions that every port offered to sailors with money in their pockets. All except for Jules, who stayed aboard and out of sight, which was boring but much safer than risking being recognized ashore. Early on the fourth day, the *Sun Queen* left Kelsi's, her crew poorer but happier than when they'd arrived. The plan had been to head all the way south, to the waters off Landfall again, hoping to throw off any Imperial pursuers or Mages who would've heard that Jules' ship had been seen in Kelsi and would be heading north in hopes of finding her.

But as the dawn just began to touch the sky a few days later as the *Sun Queen* passed east of the Sharr Isles, the lookout called a warning. "Lights to starboard! They look like Mechanic lights!"

Before the sun had risen, one of the metal Mechanic ships had pulled alongside the *Sun Queen*. Jules, standing on the quarterdeck with Captain Mak, gasped when a different light appeared on the Mechanic ship. Intensely bright, it cast a beam across to the sailing ship as if a shaft of the noonday sun had been captured. The light played across the *Sun Queen*, coming to rest on the quarterdeck and then on Jules herself, who had to cover her eyes against the radiance. "I guess we know who they're looking for," she said to Mak to try to hide her nervousness.

She heard that unnaturally loud voice calling across to them from the Mechanic ship. "Follow us into port!"

"Apparently we're going to make a port call in Caer Lyn," Captain Mak announced to the crew, who had all come on deck in response to the arrival of the Mechanic ship. "Come about and follow in their wake," he ordered the helm. "We'll have to tack against these winds. Hopefully the Mechanics will give us some leeway for that. Jeri, you'd better get ready."

"Ready, sir?"

"Either you're going to be hauled off for another interview, or they're going to come aboard. Either way, you want to look your best. Use my cabin. Sponge yourself off. Make sure your shirt and pants look neat, your boots polished. The Mechanics are going to be judging you."

"Like an inspection," Jules said.

"That's right."

She went down the ladder and into the cabin. The captain had a bath pan under his bunk, with a sponge resting in it and a pitcher of water nearby. She stripped down fast and stood in the pan, scrubbing with the sponge. She finished up by pouring the remainder of the water over her head and rubbing some of the rough soap through it to clean her hair.

Jules stood for a moment after she was done, naked in the bath pan. Plenty of men had seen her like this. Modesty was a luxury at sea or in the orphan homes. But she hadn't been touched by them. And now, how could she? Knowing what might happen to any child who resulted from it?

But how could she not some day become intimate with a man? Knowing how important her line was? If she didn't keep it going, didn't have children, the Great Guilds would win.

Her mother had died in childbirth. That's all that Jules knew. What exactly had gone wrong? Was it something that would also affect her? Would having that child be a final act of sacrifice for a future that she'd never see?

Questions without number. No answers.

After cleaning up the bath pan, she dressed carefully, taking time to check the polish on her boots. She took out the revolver and looked it over, seeing rough patches on the smooth surface. What was she supposed to do about that?

Jules brought out the cloth she used to polish her dagger and rubbed it over the revolver. When she was done, it looked better. But there was something dark and sticky where the hammer moved. She remembered seeing a clear fluid there when she'd first been examining the weapon. And the hammer didn't move as smoothly now.

She cleaned off the dark, sticky places as best she could. The parts of the weapon seemed to move more easily after that.

Despite the Mechanic woman's warning that it would explode if she tried, there didn't seem to be anything about the weapon that would prevent it being shot at a Mechanic.

Someday she would try, Jules thought. Someday.

Each of the three cartridges that she'd shot had left behind a cylinder that Jules had looked over. Sort of an empty tube made of brass, open on one end where the rounded projectile had once rested. What was she supposed to do with those?

She removed them from the revolver, along with the one that hadn't worked, placing them all in one pocket.

She went up on deck again, the headlands of Caer Lyn's harbor sliding by on either hand. A small home draped with fishing nets stood precariously on one of the headlands. "That's Meg's place," Ang told her. "At night, ships can find the headland by looking for the lantern in her home. Caer Lyn is growing fast," he added. "Last time I was here it was maybe half this size, and that was only a year ago."

Jules leaned against the railing, gazing at the buildings sprawling through the lowlands and spreading up through the valleys and heights surrounding it. "It's a nice harbor."

"Great harbor," Ang agreed.

Jules' gaze came to rest on a large structure being built in the center of a cleared area some distance from the water. "That's a Mechanics Guild Hall, isn't it? What's the bridge thing leading to it?"

"It's called an aqueduct. The Mechanics always want water brought in," Ang said. "I don't know why. It's a lot more than the people in a Guild Hall should need."

She saw the outlines of another structure farther off. "A Mage Guild Hall. That looks like a Mage Guild Hall."

"I think you're right. I guess the Great Guilds are moving in permanently."

And this ship was going to tie up here. She really, really hoped that the Mechanics had some plan to keep the local Mages from killing her.

The Mechanic ship was tying up at the best pier in the harbor, covered horse-drawn carriages arriving from inside the growing town to meet it. Jules watched figures in the dark jackets of Mechanics coming out of the carriages to meet their counterparts coming off the ship. She also saw with relief a line of Mechanics at the land end of the pier, blocking access. If they had revolvers with them, that ought to keep Mages away.

One Mechanic stood on the stern of his ship, gesturing to the *Sun Queen* to tie up behind the Mechanic ship. "I hope this is just about me," Jules said.

"We won't let them hurt you, Jeri," Ang said.

"Just stay out of the way."

The *Sun Queen* glided in to the pier, some of the crew in the rigging furling the last sails. A bump, lines across for the commons working the pier to tie up to bollards, and Jules was left wondering what she should do.

Mak came down off the quarterdeck, nodding to her. "You look sharp, Jeri. Now what?"

"I have no idea. Wait, there's a carriage coming past the Mechanic ship and on toward us."

"Get the crew lined up," Mak told Ang. "If they see us treating them with respect, the Mechanics are more likely to leave quickly."

"Yes, Cap'n."

The carriage halted near the bow of the *Sun Queen*, three Mechanics getting out of it. Jules saw the weapons two of them carried, much longer than her revolver. The woman and one man carried the weapons. The other man, older, appeared unarmed as he walked with a quick, impatient stride toward the gangway of the *Queen*.

Jules stood at the head of the gangway, hoping she was doing what was expected, and hoping that she'd keep her temper no matter what the Mechanics said or did. This wasn't about her. It was about keeping the crew safe and getting them out of Caer Lyn again in one piece.

The three Mechanics came up the gangway, the older man in the lead eyeing Jules. "That's her, isn't it? Yes. She has the revolver."

"I think that's her," the woman said.

Jules waited, wondering why they didn't simply ask her. Her eyes lingered for a moment on the female Mechanic, who looked to be maybe thirty years old. She seemed vaguely familiar, though Jules couldn't say why.

The older man looked around, seeing the stern cabin. "You," he said, pointing to Jules. "Inside. Tosh, stay out here and keep an eye on things."

She followed them, with a glance to Captain Mak that both warned him not to try anything that might provoke the Mechanics, and sought reassurance in his steady gaze.

The younger male Mechanic didn't seem happy with his assignment, glowering at the crew and brandishing his long weapon.

Jules closed the door behind them as she followed the female Mechanic and the older man into the cabin. Both looked around the interior of the sparse cabin with thinly veiled contempt before the man focused on Jules. "What's your name?"

"Jules of Landfall, Sir Mechanic."

"Sir *Senior* Mechanic."

Why did they all have to do that? How was she supposed to know which was which? "Yes, Sir Senior Mechanic."

He smiled. "You've been busy, common."

How was she supposed to answer that? Was she supposed to?

Apparently not. The older man's smiled faded as he looked at her. "Where did you get that holster?"

"Excuse me, Sir Senior Mechanic? Hol-ster?"

The female Mechanic answered in condescending tones. "The holder for the revolver. It's called a holster."

"The crew made it for me," Jules said.

"They must have seen holsters Mechanics were wearing and copied them," the woman told the Senior Mechanic.

"Trying to imitate the works of their betters? Don't make any more copies of Mechanic equipment," the Senior Mechanic told Jules. "Not even clothing. That's forbidden. If we want you to have something, you'll get it from us."

"Yes, Sir Senior Mechanic," Jules said, knowing that arguing the point would only cause trouble.

"Give me that," the Senior Mechanic added, pointing to her revolver sheath.

Her "holster," Jules corrected herself as she resignedly unfastened her belt.

"Give her yours," the Senior Mechanic told the woman. "If this common is going to be an agent of the Guild she needs to have proper equipment."

The female Mechanic didn't seem happy, but she dutifully removed her own holster, taking out the pistol and placing it in a large coat pocket before passing the holster to Jules.

She took a moment to look at it, seeing how much better designed the Mechanic holster was for its purpose, and how a flap at the top could be folded over and tied down to hold the weapon in place. Working hastily as the Senior Mechanic waited with ill-concealed impatience, Jules slipped the holster onto her belt and put her own revolver into it.

"That's better. Verona, check the weapon."

The woman held out her hand and Jules pulled out the revolver, giving it to her. Verona examined it. "She's kept it clean. Needs a little oil. Otherwise fine."

"Good. Return it to her." The Senior Mechanic looked over Jules as she returned the revolver to her new holster. "You're not pregnant yet?"

Jules had to take a moment to respond, not wanting to sound as angry as that question made her. "No, Sir Senior Mechanic."

"Good. Try to continue controlling your physical urges. We don't want that child appearing too quickly. I hear that you've killed two Mages."

She wasn't about to explain what had happened with the second Mage to these two Mechanics. "Yes, Sir Senior Mechanic."

"Two Mages dead, and the Mechanics Guild can deny giving you orders to kill them. The Mage Guild is working hard to find you. They don't like having a common they've marked for death walking around alive. It hurts their image," the Senior Mechanic said with a smirk. "Not bad. And the Emperor is very displeased by the failure of his forces to find you and catch you. The attacks you've made on Imperial shipping are keeping his attention on you rather than other matters, exactly as the Guild desires." He smiled again, a thin, humorless expression. "For a common, you've been unusually effective in advancing the goals of the Mechanics Guild. Those who do well get rewarded. Give her the ammunition."

The female Mechanic stepped closer, dropping six cartridges onto the table one by one.

"Six," the Senior Mechanic said. "For six more enemies of the Mechanics Guild. Use them well, and there'll be more." He gestured toward the long weapon held by the female Mechanic. "You might even earn one of those rifles. If you keep us happy."

"I understand, Sir Senior Mechanic."

"Pick them up," the female Mechanic said impatiently, gesturing at the ammunition.

Jules gathered the six cartridges, holding them tightly in one hand. "Thank you, Sir Senior Mechanic. Lady Mechanic. Am I supposed to return these?" she asked, pulling out the three empty cylinders from the cartridges that she'd shot and the one that hadn't worked.

"You kept your brass?" the woman commented. "Will wonders never cease. Give them to me."

"Am I supposed to keep doing that, Lady Mechanic?"

"Yes," she said. "You could have figured that out without asking."

Jules wondered if Mechanics were actually taught to say everything to commons in the most insulting way possible.

"Not this one," the female Mechanic said, holding out the fourth cartridge. "Why'd you give this one back? You haven't used it."

"I tried to use it, Lady Mechanic. But nothing happened."

The other woman frowned, examining the cartridge. "It's a misfire."

"Did I do something wrong, Lady Mechanic?" Jules asked, certain that she must have.

"No. I can see where the hammer hit the primer. It's just a misfire. It didn't work."

It hadn't been her fault? She hadn't done anything wrong?

Sometimes the devices of the Mechanics didn't work?

Sometimes the devices of the Mechanics didn't work.

Jules tried her best to hide her surprise and elation at the news. "Yes, Lady Mechanic."

"Use those cartridges wisely," the Senior Mechanic said.

"I will, Sir Senior Mechanic." Jules hoped she still looked calm and obedient. Inside, she was imagining loading the cartridges and shooting both of these Mechanics and then their friend outside the cabin. But better to save them for Mages.

"Oh," the Senior Mechanic added, "one other thing. You're headed for the area around Landfall, aren't you? Don't. They're waiting for you. A lot of Mages and a lot of Imperial warships. They may be working together to try to get you, some sort of bargain among thieves."

How had the Mages and the Imperials known? And, for that matter, how had the Mechanics so quickly known what the others were up to? "Thank you for the warning, Sir Senior Mechanic."

The Senior Mechanic waved a negligent hand at her and walked out, the woman following him. Jules came behind them.

The younger male Mechanic was berating the crew as they came on deck, standing in front of Captain Mak as he complained about their attitudes.

Mak glanced over their way to ensure that Jules was all right.

Jules saw the eyes of the female Mechanic meet those of Captain Mak, and suddenly the resemblance between the two was clear. Mak seemed turned to stone, frozen as he stared at the woman. The woman looked back at him with what seemed a curious mix of anger, love, resentment, and longing.

Mak's daughter. Taken by the Mechanics. One of them now.

The female Mechanic looked away, scowling.

"Hey! Common! When I talk, you look at me!" the male Mechanic facing Mak yelled. Furious, he jammed the end of his weapon into Mak's stomach and did something to a lever on the bottom, causing the weapon to make an odd, metallic click-clack noise. "You commons need an example of what happens when you don't act respectfully!"

Jules stared, horrified, knowing she couldn't load the cartridges and try to use the revolver against that Mechanic in time to save Mak.

"Wait, Tosh," the female Mechanic said, her voice rough. "Should we waste ammunition on him? He's not worth it."

The male Mechanic hesitated. "It's only one bullet."

The female Mechanic looked at Jules, a message in her eyes. *Say something.*

"I need him, Sir Mechanic," Jules said. "Please. He's a... valuable assistant."

"So what?"

The female Mechanic spoke again, as if disinterested. "Don't we want her to stay effective? For the Guild?"

The young male Mechanic hesitated again.

The Senior Mechanic looked aggravated. "Don't kill him. This time. You can consider that another reward," he told Jules.

"Thank you, Sir Senior Mechanic."

"Can I hit him?" the male Mechanic pleaded.

"Go ahead," the Senior Mechanic said, "as long as you don't hurt him so badly she can't use him."

The Mechanic grinned and reversed the weapon, using the other end to hit Mak in the face.

Mak went down without a sound, two members of the crew lunging to grab him before he hit the deck.

Everyone else stood silently, watching the Mechanics.

The younger male Mechanic spoke up again, his voice loud as he looked around the deck of the *Sun Queen*. "The next time some common acts like that, he or she takes a bullet. Got it? You do what you're told!" He turned to stomp off the ship but had to pause and wait for the Senior Mechanic to precede him, somewhat spoiling the effect of his departure.

The female Mechanic followed behind the other two, her weapon held so the open end pointed at the sky. Jules tried to catch her eye again, but she kept her gaze fixed on the backs of her fellow Mechanics.

The sailors who'd caught Mak helped him stand, but he still looked like a man frozen in a moment of pain. "Ang," Mak said in a whisper, "please take the ship out. We don't want to stay here. Too many Mages about."

"Yes, Cap'n," Ang said. "No worry. Get the cap'n to his bunk," he ordered the two sailors supporting Mak. He raised his voice to the rest of the crew. "Prepare to get under way!"

As the other sailors milled about, Jules started running forward.

She ran all the way to the bow, leaning over next to the bowsprit, looking down at the horse-drawn carriage the Mechanics had arrived in. The two men must have already gotten in, the woman in the act of stepping inside. "Lady Mechanic!" Jules yelled.

The female Mechanic paused in the door of the carriage, looking up at Jules, her face a carefully neutral mask disguising her feelings. The woman shook her head once at Jules, then ducked inside the carriage, closing the door.

Jules stood watching the carriage roll away as the driver urged the horses into motion.

"What were you going to say to her?" Liv asked from beside Jules.

"I don't know. That was Captain Mak's daughter."

"I guessed. She didn't want anything to do with him, though."

"She saved his life, Liv. You saw that."

"I don't know that she—"

"She *did*. I could see it." Jules shook her head, remembering the look on the face of Mak's daughter when she recognized him. What had that woman been told once she was taken from her family? How had she been told to think? Why couldn't she reach out to her own father? "How is she going to do it?" Jules whispered.

"That female Mechanic? How's she going to do what?"

"No." Jules watched the carriage turn off the pier and head down a street off the waterfront, vanishing from sight behind buildings. "The daughter of my line. How is she going to talk to Mechanics? Get them to help her? How?"

Liv frowned. "Why would Mechanics help her?"

"That's what the prophecy said, Liv. That she'll unite Mechanics, Mages, and common folk like us to overthrow the Great Guilds."

"She what?" Liv made a derisive noise. "Mechanics? Help us? And Mages? How could anyone get *them* to help? And to overthrow their own Guilds? The prophecy couldn't have—" Realizing who she was talking to, Liv stopped speaking.

"That's what it said." Jules looked at Liv. "I'll never forget a word of it. It said she'll do that. Somehow."

"Nobody's repeating that," Liv said. "I guess because it sounds too hard to believe, and we all want to believe the rest, about the Great Guilds being overthrown someday."

Jules took a final look at the carriage, fast disappearing away from the pier. "That woman still felt something, Liv. Despite whatever the Mechanics Guild did to her, part of her wanted to talk to Mak. Part of her still loves him. I saw it. But she wouldn't listen to any of us."

"Mak's going to be a wreck," Liv said. "You could comfort him, because you mean a lot to him, Jeri."

"We're not like that, Liv. People don't think we're like that, do they?"

"No. I didn't mean that. Mak cares about you. He'll listen to you. Go talk to him. Ang and I can get the ship underway without the two of you."

"But—"

"I'll make it an order, since you're still the most junior sailor on the ship even though you're always on the quarterdeck nowadays calling out orders to the crew like you're the Emperor himself. Attend to the captain, Jeri. Talk to him."

"All right. If you really think I can help."

Jules paused to open the revolver and carefully load each cartridge. Six of them. Each worth far more than if it were made of solid gold.

If that male Mechanic showed up again, he wouldn't get another chance to shoot Mak.

Tying the revolver securely into its new holster, she went aft, weaving her way between the other crew members rushing to bring in lines and make sail, feeling awkward not to be helping. She reached the door to the captain's cabin and paused, reluctant, before finally rapping softly. No answer came, so Jules nerved herself and opened the door.

Mak lay in his bunk on his back, his gaze straight up, his expression the same as if he was still looking at the Mechanic who'd been his daughter.

"Sir?" Jules said. "Can I come in? Can I talk to you?"

He said nothing.

Uncomfortable, her own emotions a swirling mess, Jules closed the door and sat down at the small table, facing Mak in his bunk. "Sir, is there anything I can do?"

He didn't respond.

"Captain, she still loves you. I could see it. They've done something to her, twisted her mind, but she knew you and she cares about you. She argued to keep that guy from killing you, and she prompted me to help. She still cares."

Mak said nothing, his eyes still fixed on the overhead.

Jules sighed, listening to the sounds of the ship getting underway and feeling odd not to be part of it. But she was needed here. Liv was right about that. "Sir, I don't know the right things to say," Jules began in a low voice. "I don't know a lot about having a family. About how that feels. I don't remember much about my father. I was only five when he died on campaign. I remember that he was big, and that he smelled of leather and horse. Because he was legion cavalry. I like to think he loved me and tried his best for me and my mother. I don't know because I have nothing from him except those few memories. But I remember that when he was there I felt… safe."

She sighed, trying to avoid tears that the old memories threatened to bring. "Sir, since he died, and my mother died, I haven't known that feeling. I haven't ever felt really safe. But since I came to the *Sun Queen*, when we're underway and you're in command, it's the closest I've felt to that. Talking to you, I know someone cares about me. I know it's just because I'm crew, but I hope you'd care about what happens to me even if I wasn't crew. I don't know what I'm trying to say there, except that you've made me feel wanted, and not in the way a lot of men have since that prophecy. In a comforting way. Despite knowing about the prophecy and everything else, being on the *Sun Queen* is the closest I've felt to safe since I lost my mother and my father. And I know that's because you're the captain. Thank you, sir."

Mak finally moved, rolling his head to look at her. "Stars above, Jeri, stop calling me sir."

"Yes, sir."

"Is what you just said true?"

"Yes, sir. All of it. I'm sorry I didn't say it very well."

"You said it very well. Thank you, Jeri."

"Sir… my real name is Jules. Of Landfall. You should know that. Because… you should know."

"All right, Jules. That's a good name. A strong, graceful name. It suits you." Mak looked back up at the overhead of the cabin. "You saw it, too? That she still cared?"

"Yes, sir, I did. It hurt her to see you and not be able to talk."

"But there was anger there, too. Anger at me. I saw that."

"Yes, sir. I don't understand what that was about."

"I guess there's no way for us to know, is there? The barriers between me and my daughter have grown too large. Someday that daughter of your line will change that. Change things so the Mechanics Guild, and the Mage Guild, can no longer take children from their parents," Mak said. "No longer turn them against their parents."

"I hope so," Jules said.

Mak rolled to his side and sat up, rubbing his face where he'd been struck. "Jeri… Jules… I long ago learned how little power I have to influence what happens in this world. But this little part of the world is mine, and I will do what I can. Whenever the Mages find you, no matter where or when, I will stand between you and them. You have my promise."

"I can't ask that of you," Jules said.

"You're not asking for it. I'm giving it." Mak looked at her, speaking with firm resolve. "I couldn't protect another girl. I'm going to protect you, no matter the cost."

"But, sir—"

"Blast it, girl, my name is Mak!" He looked up as feet and tackle thumped on the quarterdeck above their heads. "Shouldn't you be out there helping get the ship under way?"

She stood up. "Yes, si- Mak. Captain. Captain Mak."

"That's something," Mak said, waving her out. "Go on, Jules. Take charge up on the quarterdeck until I join you. And stay safe. Neither of the Great Guilds will kill you while I live."

"Sir, please—"

"You have my promise. Get out of here, Jules." He smiled at her. "I'll always be calling you that in my head from now on, even though in public my voice will still be saying Jeri."

"Yes, sir." She ran out and up the ladder, smiling, happy to have heard her real name spoken again by someone who was a friend.

* * *

In light of the Senior Mechanic's warning, Mak had ordered the *Sun Queen* about and headed back north, thinking that Kelsi's settlement would be safe with so much attention focused on the south. Jules stood on the quarterdeck the next morning as the *Queen* beat her way north, trying to occupy her mind with details of the ship and the set of the sails. But her eyes kept going to a patch of the sea off the port side, where the water looked as if it were boiling, seagulls swooping down to strike at fish near the surface. "What's happening there?" Jules asked Keli the healer.

Keli looked over. "There's a big school of smaller fish being driven to the surface as they try to escape bigger fish down below. The gulls see it and know there's plenty of food, so they sweep in, too."

"The small fish are caught between big fish below and the gulls above? Both trying to eat the small fish?" Jules shook her head. "It's sort of like being a common, isn't it?"

Keli nodded. "We're the small fish in the sea, sure enough."

"Maybe not forever," Jules said. "Good morning, Captain," she added as Mak come up onto the quarterdeck.

Keli excused himself, leaving Jules and Mak together. "Captain? I've been thinking about what the Mechanics told me. Why do you think the Emperor and the Mages would work together to get me?" Jules asked. "One wants me, and the other wants me dead."

"You can bet that both are planning to double-cross the other,"

Mak replied. "But the Emperor is being particularly foolish in think-ing he can get away with that. Like the Mechanics, he's seeing what he wants to see. I know the odds against you seem pretty daunting, Jules, but you do have the advantage that your three main foes are all working for themselves and against each other. As long as you can play the Great Guilds and the Empire each against the others, you'll have a chance."

Jules smiled at the irony. "The prophecy says that a daughter of my line will unite Mages, Mechanics, and common folk in one cause. But in order for me to do my part I need to ensure that Mages, Mechanics, and the Empire keep fighting each other. She'll need to unite, but I need to sow chaos."

"I can't think of anyone more qualified for the task of sowing chaos," Mak said.

"Thank you, sir. I appreciate your confidence in me."

When they reached Kelsi's settlement a few days later, the decision to head there seemed to be proven a good bet. No Mages, Mechanics, or Imperial forces were to be seen when the ship tied up. The crew had grumbled a bit at the sudden reversal of course, but cheered up when told they'd have a few more days at Kelsi's to enjoy themselves.

Jules had actually gotten off the ship that morning to run some errands with Captain Mak, surprised to be bothered by the now unfamiliar feel of solid land under her feet. She felt more secure with six cartridges loaded into the revolver, yet also nervous about Mages or Imperial agents, and was relieved to once more return to the *Sun Queen*.

Mak called her to his cabin again as night fell. "Jules, I'm going ashore for a while. I want to see what I can learn talking to people in the taverns. Maybe even figure out which one of them is the one feeding the Mechanics Guild information."

She looked in the direction of the town distrustfully, but nodded. "Yes, sir."

"You'll be in charge of the ship while I'm gone."

"Sir?" Jules pointed out the front of the cabin. "Ang is here. He—"

"I want you in charge," Mak said. "Can't you handle it?"

"Yes, sir," Jules said. "I can handle it."

"Stay up here in the stern cabin so if any big visitors show up you can receive them properly. I'm not sure when I'll be back."

"Be careful," Jules called after Mak. "Sir. Please."

He paused to look back at her, smiling in the flickering light of the lantern hung outside the cabin door. "I'll try. You stay out of trouble."

"I'll try," Jules said.

It felt a little strange to be in the cabin without Captain Mak here. Jules wandered about, fighting the temptation to look inside drawers.

She'd never realized how few personal mementos Mak kept in his cabin. A reddish rock that must have some significance sat near the head of the bunk. A drawing labeled "View of Lake Bellad north of Severun" hung where Mak could see it from his bunk. And a thin book entitled "Wildflowers of the Northern Empire" rested on the small desk next to the bunk. That was all. If not for the promise ring that Mak still wore, there would have been nothing to serve as a clear reminder that he'd once been married.

Since it was lying out, Jules opened the wildflower book to look inside. It seemed to consist entirely of facing pages, one of which showed a hand painted image of a flower while the other contained a description and facts like the range of the plant.

She noticed that some of the pages had long-dried samples of the flowers they described pressed between their picture and the written description. Someone had once collected those flowers.

Jules stood looking down at one of the dried flowers, delicate petals of a blue faded to almost white, the leaves and stem disintegrating to grayish-green dust. She wondered whether it had been Mak's wife, or his little daughter, who had found that flower and pressed it into the book.

She closed the book softly, wanting to be sure she didn't harm any of the contents.

Since the day she became an orphan, her world had felt full of things and people intended to make her cynical and distrustful. That had only gotten worse after the prophecy was spoken. At times she wondered if the world was worth freeing.

But then there was Mak. Loyal still to a love long dead, and to a daughter who'd disowned him. A world with even one man like Mak in it was surely worth sacrificing for. Not to mention people like Liv and Ang. Maybe, if she kept trying, that daughter of her line would be born, and a future Mak wouldn't lose his daughter, and a future Ang wouldn't lose his father, and a future Liv wouldn't lose her mother.

She wasn't sure how much time had passed when a soft knock came at the door. "Jeri?" Ang called through the closed door. "Captain Vlad of the *Star Seeker* just came aboard."

What had brought Vlad here at this late hour? "Tell him that Captain Mak is ashore and we don't know when he'll be back," Jules called.

"I did. He says he has a deal he needs to discuss with you."

Oh, blazes. She and Mak had been over to the *Star Seeker* that morning, at Vlad's invitation. The ship had been neatly kept, but hadn't struck her as happy, and Captain Vlad had spent an uncomfortable amount of time looking at her instead of at Captain Mak as they discussed possibly working together. But Vlad's terms had been too weighted in his favor, so despite the size of the *Star Seeker* and the number of her crew, Mak had politely declined.

And now Vlad was here wanting to speak to her. Jules wanted to tell Ang to send him off, but Mak had been emphasizing to her how important it was to deal fairly and respectfully with other ship captains. And she had been wrong in her first opinion of Captain Erin. It would be wrong to condemn Vlad on her impressions from one meeting. "All right. Send him in, please."

A few moments later the door opened and Vlad came in, dressed in the same sort of fine shirt and trousers and gleaming boots that he'd been wearing this morning. He must have multiple outfits. A two-handed straight sword swung at his side, so long that the scabbard and the elaborate guard came up well above Vlad's waist, something much better suited to impressing other people than it was to fighting in the constricted quarters of a ship. Vlad smiled at Jules as Ang closed the door.

"What can I do for you?" Jules asked. "Captain Mak isn't aboard, and I can't make any deals on behalf of the ship."

"This isn't about the ship," Vlad said, eyeing her with another smile. "What is it you're calling yourself? Jeri?"

The rules of the pirates of the Sea of Bakre were not exactly concerned with fine points of etiquette, but one of them was that no one should refer to anyone else's name as false. The name given was supposed to be accepted, no questions asked and no skepticism displayed. Jules didn't call Vlad on it, though, not wanting to give him any excuse to explore the topic of her real name. "What was it you needed to talk about?"

She'd deliberately avoided inviting him to take a seat in hopes he'd keep the visit short, but Vlad walked to the small table and sat down in one of the chairs, facing Jules. "Who you really are is a poorly maintained secret. You know that, I'm sure. Your actual name, and... the actual Mage prophecy about you."

"I won't discuss either," Jules said, trying to keep her voice polite but firm enough to make it clear the topic was closed. "Is there something else?"

"That's quite a role that fate has in store for you," Vlad continued as if Jules hadn't spoken. "This morning, I was looking at you and thinking how fortunate the man would be whose blood made that prophecy eventually come to pass."

Great. Another man who thought she was irresistible because she'd someday have a child who'd continue her line toward that daughter. And a man who, like the Emperor, wanted to hijack the prophecy by linking his blood line to hers so he could claim credit for the outcome. "I told you I won't talk about that," Jules said, dropping any pretense of politeness from her voice. "You said you had a deal to discuss. Lay it out, or take your leave."

Instead of answering her, Vlad brought out a small leather pouch with a dramatic flourish. He opened the pouch with careful movements, giving her a smile as he did so, then poured out onto the table a half-dozen gems that winked in the lantern light.

She reached to pick up a gleaming emerald the size of a small marble, turning the polished green stone in her fingers. "Impressive."

"All that," Vlad said, waving to the gems. "It should be more than enough."

"For what?" Jules put down the emerald, picking up a ruby that glowed in the lantern light like a large drop of crystallized blood.

"One night for each gem."

She frowned at the ruby, bothered by Vlad's gaze and choosing to avoid it. "One night?"

"It can be for more nights, if you desire."

"I'm missing something," Jules said, finally looking at Vlad again. She saw the smile on his face, a smile that held a quality she recognized and didn't like. "One night of what?" she asked even though that smile held the answer for her. "Playing innocent?" Vlad said with a laugh. "One night of you. Sunset to dawn. I promise you'll find each one a memorable evening, and I'm certain that those nights are all I'll need to ensure myself a place in that prophecy."

Her fingertips tightened painfully on the ruby as Jules tried to control her voice. "You want to buy me?"

"I'm sure that no one else has ever offered so much for you! Or for any other woman!"

Don't lose your temper, she told herself. Don't do anything that would embarrass Captain Mak. Jules put down the ruby, using her forefinger to shove it back with the other gems. "No. I'm not for sale. Not for one night. Not for one moment."

"You're bargaining?" Vlad demanded. "When I opened with an offer like that?"

" 'No' is not an opening for bargaining," Jules said, feeling herself getting angry despite her efforts to control it. "I said no, and that's all there is to it."

"You can't be serious! Just one of those gems would buy me a month with a dozen of the finest courtesans in Marandur!"

"Then I suggest you use it for that purpose," Jules said, giving him a warning look. "Because you're not going to get anything from me for it."

Vlad leaned forward, his eyes on hers. "I know where you came from. You don't have to give me this act like you're some virginal innocent. I don't mind that you probably had a lot of guys before you even left that legion orphan home. All that matters to me is that you're not pregnant now, and I get to put my mark on the child you end up having. I'm offering you a very good payment for that!"

Jules fought to keep from trembling with the anger that filled her. "You'd better leave."

"Wait. Is that it? You're already pregnant? I'm too late? There'll be another, won't there?"

"Get out."

"I won't be treated this way! I've made a very generous offer!"

Her dagger was in her hand even though Jules didn't remember drawing it. She held the point near Vlad's throat. "Leave *now*."

He backed the chair far enough from her dagger to stand, glaring at her as he swept the gems back into the pouch. "You'll regret this. You should be honored that I was willing to offer that much money for something a lot of other men must have already—"

Jules lunged, the dagger stabbing. Vlad leaped backwards, clawing at his long sword, but there wasn't room to draw it in the small, low-ceilinged cabin. Racing two steps to the door, Vlad yanked it open. But instead of continuing to flee, he paused in the doorway, glaring at her. "I'll have you on my terms someday! You'll be tied down and begging for mercy! No slut from the streets can-!"

Jules flipped the dagger blade between her thumb and fingers before hurling the weapon, the motions happening so quickly they cut off Vlad in mid-sentence.

Vlad staggered back a half-step, staring at the dagger buried in his chest.

Crossing the remaining distance between them, Jules grasped the dagger and pulled the blade out in one swift yank. "I'm sorry. Did I miss your heart?" She plunged the blade into his chest again as Vlad gazed at her in disbelief, then yanked it free a second time to let his blood flow without hindrance.

"You… you…"

He fell.

Jules took a long, slow breath, trying to regain control of herself. "I need some help here," she called.

Several crew members came, looking down with mingled surprise and worry at Vlad's body. Ang came to the fore, his eyes on her. "What happened?"

"He wouldn't shut up," she said, stooping to wipe her dagger blade on Vlad's shirt.

"What do you want done with him?"

"Throw him in the harbor. Wait." She picked up the gems that Vlad had dropped when the dagger went into him. Prying open his mouth, she shoved the pouch of gems into it. "Now throw him in the harbor."

"Jeri, this could cause big problems. What—"

Her control snapped again. "NO MAN WILL SPEAK TO ME LIKE THAT AND LIVE!"

She saw their eyes on her, wide in the light of the lanterns.

Ang nodded. "You heard her. Toss him in the harbor. Someone get some rags and water so we can clean up this mess," he added, gesturing to the blood pooling under Vlad's body. Turning back to Jules, he spoke in a low voice. "Jeri, the crew of the *Star Seeker* may want revenge for this."

"Ask me if I care, Ang."

"What are we supposed to do if they show up looking for Vlad?"

Jules ran her thumb lightly down the blade of her dagger. "Tell them where to find me."

CHAPTER ELEVEN

Jules stood next to the stern windows, looking out at the darkness, until the cabin door opened. She heard the familiar sound of Mak's boots on the deck as he walked in, waiting for and dreading what he'd say to her.

"I hear we had a visitor," Mak said. She heard him sitting down in one of the chairs.

"Yes, sir," Jules said, continuing to face the stern windows, afraid to see the look on Mak's face.

"What happened?" Mak asked in a calm voice.

"He..." Jules swallowed, trying to prevent herself from yelling again. "He tried to buy me. He wasn't happy when I turned him down. He... wouldn't shut up."

"What did he say?"

"I'm not going to repeat it, Captain, because if I do I'm going to go looking through the harbor until I find his body so I can kill him again."

"All right." Jules heard Mak stand up. "I'll go tell Vlad's ship."

Alarmed, she spun about to shake her head at him. "No, sir, you won't. His crew might take it out on you. I'll tell them."

He gazed back at her, not seeming angry, but rather solemn. "You don't think they'd take it out on you, Jules?"

"I hope they try."

Mak sighed. "You can't kill his entire crew."

"Yes, I can."

Mak looked at her, rubbing his mouth with one hand as he thought. "Jules, there's a dark streak inside you. A very dark streak."

"Really?" she said. "I wonder where it came from."

"You'd do it, wouldn't you? Try to single-handedly kill every person on Vlad's ship."

"If I had to."

Mak shook his head, grimacing. "Are you the same young woman who told me how ridiculous the idea was that she personally could overthrow the Great Guilds?"

"That's different, Captain. That is so different." Jules paced about the cabin, feeling her nerves jumping, unable to keep standing still. "It's bad enough that every man in Dematr is lining up hoping to be the guy who impregnates me! But half of them seem to think I should be thrilled at the chance to have them do it!"

"That's not true, Jules," Mak said, watching her pace. "There are always jerks. There are always foul-mouthed bottom-feeders who act badly toward others. You're not the only woman who suffers from their attention."

"There's one less of those jerks after tonight," Jules said. She forced herself to stop pacing, her hands knotted into fists. "Blazes, Captain. I've never wanted a lot of male attention. I just wanted the right kind of guys to look at me and say, hey, maybe that girl is the one for me, and treat me with respect, and talk to me like I have dignity, and..." She felt her control slipping again and struggled to calm herself. "Why is that so much to ask?"

"I don't know," Mak said. "You shouldn't even have to ask for it. It should just be that way. But, Jules, flawed as we are, most men try to be the right kind of guys. Don't judge all of us by what the worst of us do."

"I don't," Jules said. "Obviously. I've never stuck a knife in any man on this ship, have I?"

"No, you haven't, though I understand at least two of them were threatened with worse than Vlad got."

"They were smart enough to back off," Jules said. "And one of them was Don, who will get what I threatened if I ever find him. Captain, you're angry with me, aren't you? Will you just say it so I don't have to wait to hear it any longer?"

"I'm not angry with you, Jules. I'm disappointed."

"I let you down, didn't I, sir?" Jules was once again unable to look at him, not wanting to see the disapproval there.

"No, you didn't. I'm disappointed because *I* didn't get to kill Vlad. Not if what he said made you this unhappy."

She turned her head to stare at Mak. "Captain?"

Mak smiled at her. "Let's go inform Vlad's ship of his untimely demise. You and me together. You can keep Vlad's crew from killing me, and I'll try to keep you from killing Vlad's crew."

"All right."

As they walked off the *Sun Queen* to the pier, Jules remembered something. "Sir? Vlad had some really valuable gems with him. I doubt that his crew knew about them."

"What happened to those gems?" Mak asked.

"He ate them."

Mak took a moment to reply, then nodded. "All right. Hopefully we won't get asked about that."

They'd hadn't walked much farther before Mak spoke again. "We can't make it go away, Jules. The prophecy. It's going to follow you, no matter what."

"Meaning I just have to learn to live with it?" Jules said. "I thought that was what I'd been doing."

"Meaning that there will be days like this. Or worse," Mak said. "All your life there will be days like this. I want you to understand that. Harden yourself against the struggle. I think I understand why you have that darkness. A person without it wouldn't survive what you'll face. I've encouraged you to fight to be known as a person, not just as the woman of the prophecy. But you need to accept that the fight will never end, and some days it may seem like more than you can endure."

She realized that Mak had put into words the feelings she'd been dealing with since killing Vlad. "Do you believe I can do it, Captain?"

"Yes, Jules, I do. When it seems like too much, remember I said that. And meant every word of it."

"Thank you." They reached the end of the gangway leading onto the *Star Seeker*, both pausing at the bottom.

"On the ship," Mak called. "Who's in charge while Captain Vlad is gone?"

After a few moments a woman appeared at the head of the gangway. "That's me. You're Mak from the *Sun Queen*, aren't you? What do you need?"

"Vlad is dead," Mak said.

She took a moment to respond. "How? Why? Do you know?"

"I killed him," Jules said. "Because he insulted me and threatened me."

"You can't kill a man for those reasons! Who the blazes do you think you are, girl?" The woman put one hand on the knife at her belt as she came two steps down the gangway to glare at Jules.

"I know who I am," Jules said. "And I'd take it as a favor if you told every sailor on your ship that I'll do the same to any man who propositions me the way Vlad did. And the same to any woman who insults me the way he did."

The woman paused, her eyes on the revolver that Jules wore. "You're that one. How about if I told the Mages where to find you?"

"What if you did? Go ahead."

She came another step closer to Jules, shaking her head. "You'd like that, wouldn't you? You'd be relieved of the burden of the prophecy, and I'd be blamed for your death and the failure of the prophecy."

"That's not why she killed Vlad," Mak said, sounding every inch the captain. "His actions led to his death. You're better off without a captain who had such poor judgment."

"That was our decision to make, not yours! He played straight with us."

Jules laughed. "He played straight with you? Did you know that when he died he had on him gems valuable enough to buy at least two ships like the *Star Seeker*?"

"Gems?" The woman's eyes narrowed. "No. Where are they?"

"He still has them. I had his body thrown into the harbor."

The woman's anger now appeared to be torn between Jules and former captain Vlad. "And not a scratch on you. When we find that body, will all of the injuries be in Vlad's back?"

Jules shook her head. "In his chest. Facing me."

"Captain Mak, you're well known and well respected. You're not the sort to stand by one who doesn't deserve it. But I wonder at your judgment concerning her."

Mak smiled slightly, confident and calm. "No one would want to be her enemy, but to others there's no better friend. I've never regretted taking her aboard, and she's well-regarded by the crew of the *Sun Queen*."

"So you say." The woman turned to yell. "Get the boats launched! We need to search the harbor, starting near the *Sun Queen*!" Lowering her voice again, she addressed both Jules and Mak. "This will lie where it is for now. If we find Vlad, and none of those gems are on him, you'll hear from us."

"Understood," Mak said.

"The gems aren't in any of his pockets," Jules added. "But they are on his body. I wanted to make sure he kept his mouth shut in the future."

Jules didn't like turning her back on the crew of the *Star Seeker*, but Mak walked away without apparent concern so she had to do the same.

"I hope you're not disappointed at not getting to kill them all," Mak said once they were off that pier.

"I'm fine," Jules said, hearing the depression in her voice.

"What else is wrong?"

"Nothing," Jules said. "Except… I'm trouble. We can't keep this up, can we? Operating so close to Imperial territory? And with the

Mages chasing me? Even with the Mechanics trying to use me, the odds are getting worse with every port we visit. Aren't they?"

"I don't know," Mak said.

"Sir, you owe me the truth. Do you think we can keep this up?"

"Yes. How many of those cartridges do you have left?"

"Six. I haven't used any since the Mechanics gave me more. But some of them might not work."

Mak nodded. "Sometimes Mechanic devices don't work. That's an important thing to know. The supposedly perfect, infallible devices can fail sometimes."

Jules stole a glance at him. "I know this may be hard for you to talk about, but do you think she knew how important that was when she said it? That she might have been slipping us important information on purpose?"

He didn't answer for several steps. "I don't know. The girl I knew at ten years of age would've done that. But I don't know if the woman she is now would do it, not after the Mechanics Guild has had her all these years."

"I heard her called Verona. Was that always her name?"

"Yes. Verona." He breathed out slowly. "I'm glad to know she's still using it."

"A name is a hard thing to let go," Jules said. "But hanging on to it means something. I know that."

"How long are you going to stay Jeri? A lot of people already know your real name."

"I know. But I feel like I should stick with Jeri a little longer. What are we going to do now, sir?"

Mak smiled. "I think the tavern where the Mechanics get their information is the Old Bones. I may have mentioned in there that we're heading south again."

"Where are we really going?"

"East to the waters off Sandurin. Do you feel like going hunting again, Jules?"

"Yes, sir!"

* * *

On a day such as this, handling the helm of the *Sun Queen* was a workout, human muscles straining to control the movements of an entire ship through the motions of the wheel that Jules grasped with both hands. Turning the wheel turned the tiller ropes wrapped about the wheel's center spindle, moving the rudder to one side or the other. On any day, the weight of the rudder to be shifted and the force of the water flowing past and the resistance of the ropes made that a task requiring effort. Today it was like battling the sea with her arms and legs and back.

The sun shone down only intermittently between low clouds that scudded past above, the clouds growing in number and size throughout the day. The winds kept shifting as the weather patterns of fall and winter gradually replaced those of spring and summer. And the seas borrowed from the storminess that threatened in the skies, swells racing past capped by white foam as if the *Sun Queen* sailed among a vast herd of dark horses with white manes and tails.

And yet Jules loved this, not only for the feel of the weather, but also for the feel of the ship. She could place her hand on one of the stays and feel the tensions in the masts. Or set her palm directly against a mast and feel the wind striking the sails. Through her feet, Jules could sense the water moving against the hull, the swells rocking it, the rush of the sea going past.

But only while holding the handles of the helm could she feel it all. All of the tensions and pressures affecting the ship, coming together in the wheel and the wooden spokes of it that joined at the axle, to be felt by the man or woman who gripped the handles. On a day like this it was a constant battle to keep the *Sun Queen* on course.

Jules didn't see it as a battle, though. To her, it felt as if the ship and she were working together to ride the elements and use wind and wave. She felt the sea's movements through the wheel, the wind playing with the ship, and the weight of the ship itself. Those couldn't really be fought, head to head. Instead, Jules likened it to sword fighting. Feel the movements of the sword, anticipate what the opponent would do, and use timing and careful movements that merged with the flow of the contest to produce that perfect outcome.

She didn't get to go aloft much any more, or handle the lines herself, because Captain Mak wanted her learning how to give the orders for such things. But he approved of her continuing to stand watch on the helm, saying that would teach her more about the feel of a ship, and how wind and wave could change that feel.

Early this morning they had sighted a small schooner. It had spent a good part of the morning nosing carefully around the *Sun Queen* like a mouse approaching what might be a trap. Finally coming close enough to exchange hails, the schooner had requested permission to send someone over in a boat to talk to Captain Mak. In these waters, the boat's short journey had attracted a number of wagers from the crew on whether it would make the trip successfully or be swamped by the waves.

But eventually a spray-soaked man had come up the Jaycob ladder dropped for him, going into Mak's cabin. He and the captain would be talking right now, both of them in the stern cabin under the deck where Jules' feet stood.

Another of the *Sun Queen*'s sailors, Luke, came up on the quarter-deck. "Hey, Jeri. I'm to relieve you at the helm."

"Relieve me? It's early for that."

"The captain wants you in his cabin. Some sort of meeting. How's she handling?"

"About as you'd expect on a day like this," Jules said. "She's fighting the helm."

"The *Sun Queen* can be tough to order around," Luke said as Jules stepped back from the helm and he stepped forward, grabbing the handles of the wheel. "Stars above, she is giving us a fight, isn't she?"

"I needed to keep some starboard rudder on constantly, but the amount of rudder needed keeps changing. You got her?"

"Yeah, I got her. Hold this course?"

"That's it." Jules went down the ladder to the main deck, flexing her arms to relax them, feeling the weariness in every muscle. Fighting the helm had required the strength of her legs and torso in addition to those of her arms.

Inside the cabin, she found Captain Mak and the visitor dripping salt-water sitting at the table facing each other. Ang and Liv were here, too, standing back and listening. "Reporting as ordered, sir."

The visitor picked up on her phrasing, recognizing the Imperial training behind it. "Is this girl trustworthy?" he asked Mak.

"More trustworthy than you can imagine," Mak said.

"Well, if you…" His voice trailed off as the visitor realized that Jules was wearing the revolver in its holster. "That's her. That's her, isn't it?"

Mak didn't answer him directly. "Jeri, this is Loka of Centin. He has a problem that he's willing to pay us to try to solve. We need your insight on whether it's a problem we should take on."

Loka also spoke directly to Jules. "As I told the captain and the other two, I escaped from the estates of Prince Ostin north of Centin last year. A good-sized group of others recently went on the run from those estates. I was supposed to meet them along the coast and take them to safety in the west. But late yesterday the smuggler who was supposed to help us got a message to me that the others had been captured by Imperial police."

"How can we help with that?" Jules asked. She knew why Loka and the others had fled the prince's estates. Such agricultural laborers were worked hard, and what private lives they had were closely controlled by whichever noble owned the land. They couldn't move, marry, or have families without permission. Everyone in the Empire gave up some freedom for the security the Emperor promised them, but laborers on the estates of nobles gave up more than most.

"They're being held in the detention building near the harbor in Sandurin," Loka said. "Awaiting a ship to take them back south. I wondered if this ship could pretend to be the one intended for them. Impersonate an Imperial chartered ship and rescue my friends."

Jules looked at Mak. "What are you thinking, sir?"

Mak had his fingers interlaced as he watched Loka. "It's not impossible, but it's also not easy. I want to know what you think, because you're the person on this ship most familiar with what problems we might encounter trying to pick up those people and get back out of Sandurin."

"You're confident we can get in to Sandurin?"

Ang spoke up. "You've seen the weather. There's a storm coming from the east. By tonight we're going to be seeing a lot of rain, with clouds to block the light of the stars and the moon, and winds strong enough to make anyone outside regret that they're not inside."

"A dark and stormy night?"

"Just so. Perfect weather for arriving in Sandurin pretending to be another ship. No one will be able to view us clearly. I came out of the legion orphan home here, so I know a little about the city, but not much. I do know the weather."

"Can we do it, Jeri?" Mak asked. "Will we be able to fool the Imperials well enough to get out again with those prisoners? The only way I think it's plausible is if we go in with the evening tide and sail with the dawn tide so we don't have to bluff our way through daylight, but can we do that?"

Jules grimaced, thinking. "We were told in officer training that sentries always slack off in bad weather. I saw that myself when I was supervising guards. We might be able to do it if we can forge a good set of release orders. But the jailers won't surrender those people to a bunch of sailors. They'll expect legionaries assigned to guard the prisoners on the way home."

"We have a dozen sets of legionary uniforms, swords, and armor that we took off the *Storm Queen* about a month ago when we captured her," Liv said. "We can find sailors of the right size."

"Who's going to be in command of them?" Jules asked. "You need an officer."

"Why wouldn't it work to have one of the sailors pose as a legionary?" Mak asked.

"Because the Empire doesn't trust legionaries to do things like that without supervision," Jules said. She knew what that implied, and felt her guts tightening at the thought.

"Then we can't do it," Mak said, shaking his head at Loka.

Loka's face fell.

"Cap'n?" Ang said. "Couldn't Jeri pull that off? Like she did at Saraston?"

Mak shook his head again. "Jeri came very close to being caught at Saraston. The Imperials know that she went back on Imperial territory using that uniform to fool people. They'll be looking for that."

Jules made a face, her common sense agreeing with Mak but her heart urging otherwise. "I'd hate to abandon those people, Captain."

"I'm sure you'd hate being caught by the Emperor a lot more. Sandurin also is home to a good number of Mages."

Liv shook her head. "The only good number of Mages is none."

"Sir," Jules said, "the Imperials will not expect me to try that again in Sandurin because no one with any sense would do that."

Mak raised an eyebrow at her. "You do realize what you just said, don't you?"

"Yes, sir. That's my point. They'll think I have too much sense to try it again."

"Until this moment, I thought the same thing," Mak said. "Jeri, you're the only one aboard who could carry off pretending to be an Imperial officer. You're the only one with an Imperial officer's uniform. But the level of risk is simply too high."

"Captain, would you say that if I was anyone else?"

Before Mak could answer, Loka did. "If she's really... um... if she's..."

"Jeri," Jules said, hearing the coldness entering her voice.

"I can't ask you to risk her," Loka said to Mak. "She's far too vital to the future of—"

"*My* future is *my* business," Jules interrupted. "The captain doesn't make decisions for me. Neither do you."

"But if... have you already-?"

"Don't. Ask. Me. That." The temperature in the cabin seemed to have dropped enough to put a chill in the air. She felt a strong temptation to walk out and leave Loka and his friends to the hands of Imperial fate. But that would mean giving up, acting as if she was also too concerned about her prophesized future to risk herself no matter how important the reason. She wouldn't give anyone that.

Jules shifted her gaze to Ang. "The storm that's supposed to hit tonight—how long will it last?"

"At this time of year," Ang said, "it could easily take days to pass over."

"So we'll have bad weather as a cover for our actions and for each of us personally," Jules said. "And bad weather to cover our escape. I'll do it."

Mak gave Loka an angry glance before answering her. "You don't get to decide whether we do this," he said. "The crew has to vote."

"Then call the vote," Jules said.

"*You* don't give *me* orders," Mak reminded her. "Ang, Liv, could you and Loka wait outside while Jeri and I discuss things?" He waited until the other three had left the cabin and Liv had closed the door behind them. "Jules, what the blazes do you think you're doing?"

Jules shrugged off his anger, standing at attention as she spoke. "Deciding my own destiny, sir. I thought we'd agreed I had the right to do that, sir."

"Rushing into extreme danger just because some man says the wrong thing is not deciding your own destiny! It's letting someone else drive those decisions for you with careless words."

"Sir, you know I was already considering the action before that man spoke."

Mak rubbed his face with one hand. "Why do you want to do this, Jules?"

"Because I don't want to abandon those people, sir."

"That's the only reason?"

"Yes, sir." Jules paused. "No, sir. If we pull this off... I mean *when* we pull this off, the Emperor will be furious and order more security at major cities, which will limit how many forces he has to threaten new settlements in the west, sir. And it'll have the same impact on the Mages, sir, who'll realize they need to keep enough Mages inside the Empire to watch for me there."

"That's true." Mak looked at her. "Have you ever noticed that when we're arguing you call me 'sir' at least once in every sentence?"

"I don't think that's true, sir."

"I must be mistaken." Mak closed his eyes as he rubbed his forehead. "Jules, if you were me, what would you be asking you?"

She hesitated, thinking through the question. "Whether I understood the risks. Whether I was making the decision for the right reasons. Whether…"

"Yes?"

"Whether the potential gain was worth the risks involved."

"And what would you answer to that last?" Mak asked, his eyes on hers.

Pausing again, Jules chose her words with care. "That only I could decide the answer to that."

He blew out a breath that carried exasperation with it. "I know you hate your role in that prophecy, but you do have a role. And it does vastly increase the personal risks to you, and the potential consequences for everyone if the worst happens."

"Sir, can I sit down?"

"Of course, Jules."

She sat in the chair facing him, trying to get her argument stated just right. "Captain, you told me, and I believe you, that my life is more than that prophecy. Please let me finish. You also told me that I could have an important role to play in preparing things for when that daughter of my line arrived. It took me a while, but I realized something, because of something Liv told me."

"Something Liv told you? When she learned the truth about you, you mean?"

"Yes, sir. She said that when that daughter of my line came, people would all believe in her because they'd look back at me and tell themselves that a daughter of Jules' line could do it because of what I did with my life. And at first I just laughed at that idea. But it's true, isn't it? The commons of that time, whenever it comes, have to believe in her. Not just because of the Mage prophecy, but because of what they think of me. What did I do? And this is part of that. Doing something that will be remembered. Doing something that no one else would dare to do, and succeeding at it. Because that's exactly what she'll have to do, and the people then will have to believe that she can."

Mak gazed at her, his expression slowly going from challenging to a frown. "Blazes," he finally said. "I was really hoping you'd make an argument that I could easily knock down."

"I'm right, aren't I?" Jules said.

"Ummm…"

"I'm right. Admit it."

He nodded. "Good captains admit when they're wrong, and when someone else is right." Mak looked out the stern windows at the stormy sea.

"Sir?" she prompted, worried by how distressed he looked.

"I'd be very… sad… if anything happened to you," Mak said.

"It won't," Jules said. "I'll come back from this. And whenever that daughter of my line shows up, she'll know, everyone will know, that I didn't spend my life hiding in fear."

"I'll call the crew together for a vote," Mak said, keeping his gaze fixed out the stern windows. "I imagine it'll be an easy sell despite the risks. Everyone on this ship had to escape from the Empire at some point. They'll want to help others."

"Sir, are you unhappy with me?" Jules said as she studied his expression.

"Why would you ask that?"

"Because when you're unhappy with me you don't say my name."

One corner of Mak's mouth twisted upward in a reluctant half-smile. "I don't think that's true, Jules."

* * *

The great harbor at Sandurin on the northern coast of the Empire was the result of human ingenuity as much as the work of nature. A hook-shaped barrier of sand on the southern side had been reinforced and built up with soil dredged from the harbor until it formed a wide, towering wall on which a legion fort had been built. On the northern side, a breakwater extending out into the Sea of Bakre and angling over to enclose the sheltered water had been created mighty stone by mighty stone, though rumors persisted of some strange Mechanic building means that had helped anchor and support those stones. Inside the harbor itself, dredging had both deepened and extended the port inland, creating sheltered waters well protected from any weather.

Which made the harbor at Sandurin particularly attractive on a day such as this, when a late fall storm was passing over the northeastern Empire and that portion of the Sea of Bakre. With the prevailing winds shifting from summer and spring's easterlies to south-wester-lies, storms born over the northernmost stretches of the great Umbari Ocean on the Empire's east coast brought cold, wind, and rain to the usually temperate lands here.

Jules stood on the quarterdeck of the *Sun Queen*, wearing a long oilskin cloak with a hood to protect her head, as the skies poured down an unceasing torrent of rain that pattered on the sails above her, ran along the yardarms and rigging, and formed streams of falling water that added to the misery of the cold and the wet on the deck of the ship. Ang's prediction of the weather appeared to be uncomfortably accurate.

For all that, she was lucky, as well as nervous, and feeling out of sorts because of both things. A good portion of the crew were up in the rigging, bringing in most of the sails as the *Sun Queen* beat her way toward one of the long, wide piers that offered places to tie up along the landward side of the harbor. The sailors on the masts faced not only the usual hazards of climbing in the rigging and moving out along the yardarms, but the added slickness of wet ropes and wood, and the buffeting of the winds.

They hadn't been challenged at the harbor entrance as the *Sun Queen* rode in on the evening tide. The Empire had never had external enemies, so the defenses of ports like Sandurin were aimed against weather, not attackers. After all, which smuggler or pirate would be so crazy as to sail into an Imperial harbor? Such criminals needed to be chased, which was the task of Imperial galleys and other warships. In this weather, with the sun already close to setting, it was impossible to see whether any Imperial warships were in the harbor, but that worked both ways. Any warships wouldn't be able to see the *Sun Queen*, either. Jules wondered how long it would be before the growing threat from ships operating out of the settlements to the west led to ballistae being mounted near the harbor entrances.

But still, she was down here on the quarterdeck and others ran risks in the rigging. "I should be up there," Jules grumbled for perhaps the twentieth time that day.

"Aren't you miserable enough down here?" Captain Mak asked. Despite the hood of his own oilskin, his face was streaked with water that ran down to fall off the ends of his mustache.

"I'm getting too many privileges," she said, letting her anger sound in her voice. "This is a free ship. The crew has every right to resent that."

"They don't," Mak said. "Because they know what you've done to help earn those privileges, and they know you're going to have the privilege of running the greatest risks while we're in Sandurin." He paused, squinting through the gloom and the sheets of rain in search of landmarks around the harbor. "There's a buoy. Good. We're still in the channel."

The *Sun Queen* heeled over as a gust of wind hit her on the beam, momentarily suspending the crew in the rigging over the water as the masts swung out to starboard. Jules grabbed the rail to keep herself from sliding, bracing herself against the wind and blinking away wind-driven rain. "We're close to the starboard side of the channel!"

"Bring her a point to port," Mak ordered the helm, who braced his legs and strained both arms to move the ship's wheel enough to bring the *Sun Queen* a ways to the left.

A harbor patrol boat appeared out of the murk, sliding along the water close to the quarterdeck, the legionaries on the boat huddled against the storm but still doing their job as legionaries always did. The *Sun Queen* wasn't the largest sailing ship on the sea, but her quarterdeck was a good two lances higher than the deck of the patrol boat. "What ship?" one legionary called up to Jules and Mak.

"*Gentle Dancer*," Mak called back. "Out of Landfall. In port to drop off cargo and pick up passengers. And to ride out this storm!"

"This isn't a storm!" the legionary called back. "Up here in the fall this is a gentle evening rain! Proceed to pier three, straight ahead along this channel!"

Jules breathed a sigh of relief as the patrol boat moved off. The patrols were primarily charged with enforcing safety regulations and other rules, but they did carry legionaries and they could sound alarms.

Mak came close enough to her to speak at more or less normal volume despite the storm. "Have you ever thought about how much harder this would be if so many ships weren't nearly identical? There are three-masters like us, two-masted ships of various kinds, and a few types with four masts. And the galleys with one mast. But all of a type tend to be the same, built to one plan."

"That's the way it is," Jules said. "Isn't that the way it's always been?"

"I suppose. Buildings aren't like that, though. Official buildings are, of course, but others can be built using lots of plans. How did it happen that ship types are as uniform as they are?"

"You're asking the wrong person. I'm only supposed to give birth to a line of daughters who will someday change the world," Jules said.

"You're doing a bit more than that," Mak said. "I'm asking you one more time: Are you certain you want to do this? This is going to be a lot riskier than Saraston was. There are a lot of Mages in Sandurin, plus the number of Imperial troops here."

Jules winced as another gust tossed cold rain into her face. "Captain, we've been over this. I haven't changed my mind and I won't change it. Besides, I think even Mages won't be moving around too much in this weather!"

"Don't bet on it. I've never seen Mages act as if weather bothered them in the slightest. Cold, hot, wet, or dry, they never seem to notice it."

As the *Sun Queen* proceeded toward her pier, Jules caught glimpses through the pouring rain of the indistinct shapes of ships already riding at anchor. Sometimes she could also faintly make out the feeble glimmer of storm lanterns hung as anchor lights on those ships. The sound of the bells hung on the buoys they passed was muffled by the drumming of rain on wood and canvas and on the waters of the harbor. With the sun setting somewhere beyond the clouds parading over Sandurin, the already murky atmosphere grew darker and darker, until Jules worried about their being able to safely find the pier they'd been assigned by the harbor patrol.

The only lights clearly piercing the gloom were those of one of the huge, metal Mechanic ships, glowing with that eerie steadiness and more strength than oil lanterns could manage. Jules took note of where the ship lay, since those lights could serve as a reference later on in the night. She also wondered if it was the same Mechanic ship that she'd once been taken aboard.

A string of shielded lanterns appeared out of the gloom to mark the pier. Captain Mak called orders to furl the already reefed sails and to the helm, slowing the *Sun Queen* and bringing her alongside the pier. Lines were thrown down to the dock workers, miserable in the rain, who looped them around bollards. Jules watched and listened and felt the ship respond to Mak's commands, trying to learn everything she could from seeing him call the orders in this difficult situation.

The Imperial inspector who soon showed up, miserable in his own inadequate official rain coat, and already inclined to skimp on duties because of the weather, accepted a smaller than expected bribe to pass the *Sun Queen* without an inspection so he could hurry back to shelter. The Empire did everything efficiently, even bribery of public officials. "Supposedly there's an official form somewhere laying out the bribes expected by position and rank," Liv commented to Jules as Mak paid out the bribe

"I've never seen that," Jules said. "But I wouldn't be surprised if there was one. I'm going to get dressed, Liv. Let Ang know he and the other legionaries need to get into their outfits as well. I'll come by and inspect them after I get into my uniform."

"Inspect them?" Liv asked, grinning. "Will you be issuing demerits for poor appearance, or will a bribe serve to clear the matter?"

"Very funny. I need to make sure there aren't any discrepancies that would stand out to anyone who sees us."

She changed into her Imperial uniform and checked it over carefully, making sure nothing was out of place. Worrying about the state of her uniform felt strange, as if the last several months had never happened and she was still an officer answering to the orders of the Emperor and his commanders. Imperial uniform regulations were set in stone, as were many things in the world, so Jules didn't worry about any changes that might have rendered her uniform unsuitable. Like the plans for building ships, uniforms didn't change. Weapons didn't change. Armor didn't change. The Great Guilds wanted it that way and kept it that way. But she still had to look the part of the lieutenant she'd once aspired to become.

She buckled on the sword belt, her straight sword swinging where Jules had become accustomed to having a cutlass. But the dagger went where it should, a comfort since any problems tonight should be met with swift, silent death rather than the clamor of a sword fight.

The revolver posed a problem, but she wasn't going to go ashore in Sandurin without it. Any Mages she encountered wouldn't kill her without facing a fight. Finally Jules figured out how to situate the holster on the back of her trousers, hidden under the back of the uniform coat.

Imperial officers and soldiers didn't wear oilskins. Those would hide their uniforms, and in any event the Imperial generals and admirals who sat in warm, dry offices thought their soldiers should be strong enough not to be discomfited by a mere deluge of rain. It was probably just as well tonight, Jules thought. Once her hair was soaked it would make it harder for anyone to recognize her.

Reluctantly leaving the oilskin behind, she dashed from the stern cabin to the ladder below deck. It felt very strange indeed to see a dozen men and women in legionary uniforms and armor, short swords at their sides, below deck on the *Sun Queen*. But up close she could see their faces, clearly uncomfortable in the Imperial get-ups. Jules lined them up, shaking her head at the shaky "line" the sailors formed and hoping no centurion would see them trying to make such a sloppy formation. She walked past each one, checking the uniforms for problems. "Cori, you wear the sword on the left and the dagger on the right."

"But I'm left-handed," Cori protested.

"Doesn't matter. You're supposed to be a legionary, and every legionary fights right-handed."

"That's a stupid rule," Cori grumbled, but shifted the sword and dagger to their proper sides.

"Kyle," Jules said. "You laced those boots wrong. Here." She crouched down and rapidly redid the offending laces. "Everybody else watch how I tie these off. Your knots have to match this exactly."

That elicited more grumbles, but if there was one thing sailors could do well, it was knots. "This is bringing up bad memories of legion boot camp," Marta remarked.

"You were in the legions?" Cori asked. Some of the sailors on the *Sun Queen* offered up details of their pasts, and others stayed quiet about whatever they'd done or been. Marta had rarely shared any information about herself.

But now she laughed. "For two weeks. Then a guy convinced me to desert with him. I wasn't having any fun learning to be a legionary, and the guy swore I was the love of his life, so I went."

"How long did it last?" Ang asked.

"Two weeks. Then he ditched me for a tavern girl." Marta grinned. "Later on I heard that she turned him in for the reward as soon as she got tired of him. So all's well in the end, right? I got the freedom of the sea, and he either got to hang by the neck from the short end of a long rope, or he's spent the years since doing prison labor as he works off his sentence."

"It's good to know you don't hold a grudge," Gord said.

"Nah. If I saw him again I wouldn't hurt him much at all."

Jules stood before them. "All right, listen. There are a few basic rules. No talking when anyone can hear us. If you say something a legionary wouldn't, or say it in a way a legionary wouldn't say it, it'll arouse suspicion. I'll talk to anyone we encounter. Always try to look and act like soldiers. Unlike sailors, soldiers only goof off when they think nobody can see them. We're not going to try to march. Just stay in column like this and follow me. Stay close to each other. In this weather if we lose contact with anyone we might not find them again."

"Maybe anyone who gets separated from the rest should head straight back to the ship," Ang suggested.

"That could create all kinds of problems if they meet anyone. No," Jules said. "No one will get separated from the rest of us."

"What if we get separated anyway?" Cori asked.

Her nerves were already stressed enough. They didn't need this. "If that happens, I'll find you and I'll kill you," Jules snapped in reply.

They nodded, none of them questioning whether she'd actually do so. Jules briefly wondered if that should bother her, but there were too many other things to worry about tonight.

A deep gong belled across the harbor. "Evening watch has been called," Jules told them. "It's time to go. Anyone want to back out? There's no shame in it."

"If you're leading," Marta said, "we're following."

They went up on deck, the wind-driven rain soaking their uniforms through before they reached the gangway.

Mak waited there for them. He held out a waterproof dispatch case to Jules. "We did the best we could on counterfeiting the prisoner pick-up orders."

"Thank you, sir," Jules said, taking the case.

"Be careful, Jeri."

"I'm always careful, sir," she said, pausing to wipe rain from her face.

"That's a good one," he said. "And while you're ashore, stay out of bars. You never know who you might run into in a bar."

He was nervous for her, and joking to cover that. Jules grinned to cover her own apprehension. "Yes, sir. Permission to leave the ship, sir."

Mak leaned close. "Get back here safely, Jules."

"I promise," she said.

CHAPTER TWELVE

J ules led her group down the gangway, making sure they formed a line behind her once they were on the pier. Words from her officer training came back to her in the gruff tones of the centurion who'd been one of the instructors. *Tell them what they're supposed to do, then tell them what to do, then tell them again.* "Remember, stay right behind me, act like soldiers the whole time until we get back, make sure no one wanders off, and don't say anything to anybody unless I say so."

"Should we draw our swords?" Kyle asked.

"No. Legionaries only draw their swords to clean them, to salute the Emperor, or when they intend using them. If I tell you to draw swords, it'll be because we need to use them to fight our way back to the *Sun Queen*."

If anything, the rain had intensified, coming down in what felt like waterfalls dropping from the clouds overhead. Jules slogged through the streets, runoff from the rain swirling around her boots as if she were walking in the bed of a shallow stream. She occasionally looked back at her "legionaries" as she kept sweeping the streets with her gaze in the hopes of spotting trouble before it spotted her.

Fortunately, between the weather and the late hour, very few people were on the streets. But some of those were Imperial police walking their patrols. Citizens avoided the police at such times, knowing that unhappy and uncomfortable Imperial police were more likely than usual to decide that passing citizens needed some special attention. But Imperial military officers were a different matter, so Jules approached one pair of patrolling officers who looked as miserable as she felt. As a junior officer, she and the police officers were of roughly equal status in the Imperial pecking order. "Good evening."

"Isn't it, though," one of the officers replied.

"Yeah," Jules commiserated. "Could you direct me to the detention building?"

"They're not going to deal with routine business at this hour, Lieutenant," the other police officer said, looking her over as a gust of wind howled down the street, staggering all of them.

"I've got a prisoner pickup," Jules said. "I wouldn't be out in this if I had a choice."

"You and me both." He looked over the dozen fake legionaries following her. "Do you have enough muscle with you?"

"These should be plenty," Jules said. "They're well-motivated tonight. The sooner we get this done, the sooner we can get back to the barracks."

"Lucky. We've got the whole night shift. The detention building is over that way. Down that street, left, and then right."

"Thanks," Jules said.

"Hey, word of warning. There seem to be a lot of Mages out tonight."

"Mages?" Jules said, hoping that her voice carried only a normal amount of apprehension at hearing that.

"Yeah," the police officer said. "Don't know what they're up to. Just sort of wandering around. But there're more on the streets than we're used to seeing."

"Hopefully we won't run into any. Thanks," Jules repeated. She headed off in the direction indicated, her disguised sailors in her wake.

"Jeri," Ang said, coming up beside her. "Mages. Maybe you ought to go back."

"You can't do this," Jules said. "You don't know the right way to act or the right way to speak."

"But if a Mage sees you—"

"This weather will protect me. I'm going through with this, Ang. I don't quit."

But though Jules kept an anxious look out, she didn't see any Mages before the storm lanterns burning at the heavy door to the detention facility loomed into sight along the rain-drenched streets.

Inside, it seemed weirdly silent after the tumult of the storm. The sound of water dripping from their clothing felt unnaturally loud as Jules walked to the watch desk, her sodden uniform feeling like a loose, heavy, extra set of skin.

The jailer on duty, working intently on some paperwork, ignored her.

Jules used the scabbard of her officer's sword to rap the side of the jailer's desk.

He looked up, realized this wasn't someone who could be safely ignored, and jumped to his feet. "Excuse me. I didn't see you, Lieutenant."

"We're doing a pickup," Jules said, keeping her words short and sharp. She had the jailer intimidated and wanted to keep him worried.

"A pickup? At this hour? In this weather?"

"Do you think we'd be here now if we had a choice? Prince Ostin wants these people transported back without delay."

"Oh, Prince Ostin's people. I'm glad I'm not one of them. I need to see the pickup order, Lieutenant. That's a rule. I do need to see the pickup order."

Jules opened the dispatch case, handing over the faked document before waiting with obvious impatience.

The jailer squinted at the document. "Somebody forgot a signature, Lieutenant. I can't release the prisoners without that signature."

"A signature?" If one was missing… why not provide it? "Where is the signature supposed to be?"

"Right there," the jailer said, pointing.

Jules took the order back, placed it on the desk, picked up the jailer's pen and scrawled an illegible signature in the indicated space. "There. Now the signature isn't missing."

The jailer scratched his head. "I guess that's all right. You're supposed to pick up the whole group of runaways? They're in the main holding cell. I thought they weren't going to be picked up until tomorrow, though, since Prince Ostin just got into town today."

"Prince Ostin doesn't want to wait," Jules said. "Can we hurry this up?"

The room holding the prisoners, on the basement level, spread across the whole width of the building. The large cell had a few high, narrow windows that offered no possibility of escape but would admit a little air and light during the day. Right now they were letting in streams of water that flowed along the floor to mingle with the refuse of the prisoners. Jules wrinkled her nose at the smell, seeing in the light of the jailer's lantern long rows of men, women, and children chained together. "You're sure this batch is from Prince Ostin's estates near Centin?"

"That's what the receipt says," the jailor replied, offering a sheaf of papers.

Jules looked them over, recognizing a couple of the names that Loka had mentioned. "All right. Eighty-seven of them. They're all in here?"

"Not all. Just eighty-six. One's missing," the jailer offered.

"Where?" Jules said, trying to sound irritated rather than concerned.

"A couple of Prince Ostin's people picked her up earlier. A girl named, uh, Lil of Centin. See, here's their receipt, all signed."

Jules scowled at the receipt. "I'm supposed to pick up every one of the prisoners. Do you know why they took this one?"

The jailer smirked. "If you saw her, you'd know why. Pretty young thing."

Jules resisted the urge to run her dagger through him. "I'll need to account for her. Where she ended up. Do you know where they took her so I can write that in my report?"

"They said they were taking her to the prince at the south fort," the jailer said.

"The south fort. All right. Get the chains off of the rest of these."

"Unchain them? But—"

"I'm getting tired of repeating myself!" Jules snapped. "I don't want this lot shuffling through this rain! They can walk faster if they're not chained." As the jailer went to work on the master locks, she turned to Ang and the others, speaking in a low voice. "Pass the word among them that we're here to free them. Mention the name Loka of Centin. I don't want any of these people running off in the rain when we're trying to help them escape."

The prisoners, slowly, resignedly, got to their feet as the chains were pulled free. The jailer brought her release documents and receipts, the sort of paperwork that the Empire excelled in, all of which Jules signed with the made-up name Lieutenant Spuris of Centin.

"Lieutenant! Please let me speak!" A young man stood before Jules, his clothing as dirty as that of the other prisoners, his eyes dark with worry. "Lieutenant, please, do something for Lil."

"Get back with the others," Jules said, keeping her voice cold and her expression hostile.

"We're engaged to be promised! Please, Lieutenant! I'll do anything. Aron of Centin. I'll be your slave. Just save her."

"I'm not looking for a slave." Jules turned her back on the young man, feeling her guts churn.

"There's nothing we can do," Ang murmured. "If we try to get her, the rest of these people will be caught again for certain. We have to get them to the ship."

"I know," Jules said. "Make sure some of the others talk to him so he doesn't go running off to save her."

"What if he tries anyway?"

"Hit him hard enough to knock him out and let the others carry him. We don't have time for a lovesick fool tonight."

She oversaw forming the prisoners in a column four people across, spacing her legionaries along the sides, the last two legionaries bringing up the rear. "Listen!" Jules shouted, trying to sound as harsh as her role demanded. "You will march where directed! Anyone who falls out will be regarded as an attempted escape and dealt with. No talking.

No singing. No leaving your place in the column. No misbehavior of any kind. Am I clear? *Move!*"

Jules walked out of the detention building and back into the storm. Her uniform, still soaked with water, grew more sodden as she led the group back toward the pier where the *Sun Queen* waited.

She still didn't spot any Mages.

Lil of Centin, taken to the prince.

Enduring the same sort of treatment that Jules herself would at the hands of the Emperor if he ever got his hands on her. She'd had more than one nightmare about being trapped like that.

But there wasn't anything that she could do about it. Sometimes bad things happened. She couldn't fix them all. Not even close.

The rain ran down her hair and her face, through her uniform to join the water in the streets, the darkness around her barely relieved by the flickering flames of street lamps trying to stay lit despite the weather.

She'd known dark nights. Jules remembered her first years in the orphan home, how she'd lain awake in the evenings, fantasizing that her father wasn't really dead. That he'd instead gotten lost in the mountains, or been captured by the bandits, or that he was busy exploring to the west and hadn't heard about her mother dying. But he would, and some day he'd walk in and pick her up in the strong arms she vaguely remembered and carry her home again.

But those fantasies had grown less frequent as the weeks and months passed, and eventually Jules had buried them, refusing to imagine such a happy outcome again. The never-fulfilled dreams of her father returning had been buried deep inside the darkness that Mak had seen within her.

No one had ever come for her.

Jules realized that her fists were tightly clenched as the harbor came into sight just before them.

They reached the head of the pier without incident, the bored pier sentry waving them onward without leaving his guard shack. As the former prisoners filed past on their way down the pier toward the ship, Jules tapped Ang on the shoulder. She didn't realize that she'd decided on something until she heard the words coming out of her. "Tell the captain I'll be back before the tide turns."

Ang stared at her. "Back? Where are you going, Jeri?"

"We're short one prisoner."

"What? No! You can't—"

"Just wait for me. If I'm not back before dawn, get out of the harbor. I'll find another way out if that happens."

"But—"

She turned and began walking briskly inland.

Somehow if felt easier this time. No one else with her, no one following her and depending on her. It was just her, and if she messed up she'd be the only one to pay the price.

She'd pay the price, and so would the future of every common person in the world.

You owe me this, Jules thought at that distant daughter of her line. *You took my life and made it about you. Give me this, so I know that what I do still matters, so that I know who I am still matters.*

As if in sardonic reply, another gust of wind hurled rain at her face, momentarily blinding her as she blinked her eyes clear. When Jules could see again, she spotted on the other side of the street two dimly-seen figures in Mage robes walking the other way.

She took the next corner, turning away from the Mages. Neither one seemed to have taken notice of her.

The south fort. So it was probably to the south, though you couldn't always count on Imperial names matching reality on the ground. Stories abounded of Imperial nobles who acted as if whatever they wanted to believe was in fact hard truth.

Two more vague figures appeared out of the murk, heading her way. Jules reached back to where the revolver in its holster formed a hard lump against her back. Her heart thumped loudly in her ears, almost drowning the noise of the rain.

Police. Jules breathed out with relief.

It was the same pair that she'd encountered earlier. "Oh, it's you again," one of the officers said, squinting as rain poured down her face. "Did you lose your soldiers?"

"No," Jules said. "I found out that I have to file a report at the south fort before I can knock off for the night. What's the quickest way there?"

One of the officers pointed. "See that corner? It turns onto the street where a lot of the biggest hostels are located. Even on a night like this there should be some coaches waiting around in hopes of customers. Using one of them can get you there the fastest. Don't let them charge you! You're on official business."

"Right. Thanks again. Uh, see any more Mages about?"

"Only a few. Either they've called it a night or they all got where they were going."

Jules hoped they weren't heading for the pier where the *Sun Queen* was tied up. But if the Mages were tracking her somehow, that shouldn't happen. Instead, they should be following her back into the city rather than threatening anyone on her ship.

It was odd how something could be both comforting and worrisome at the same time.

Jules slogged her way to the indicated corner, turning it to find only two coaches waiting outside the hostels lining the street, miserable drivers huddled on wet seats while their horses stood with the stolid patience of animals knowing that the barn awaited at the end of their work shift.

Open coaches. So much for hoping for any temporary relief from the storm. She stepped into one, water pooled inside pouring out as the coach shifted to one side under her weight, the driver looking back at her with sudden hope that changed to sullen resignation as he saw she was an Imperial officer. "The south fort," Jules said. "Get me there fast and I'll pay your fare."

The driver perked up and the coach rattled off, sometimes swaying alarmingly in the wind, the open seating no protection at all. In fact, Jules wondered if the forward motion somehow worsened the rainfall she experienced.

Hoping that the south fort wasn't too far south, Jules waited, tense, as the coach kept going. If it was too far, she'd never make it back in time.

Ironically, there was too much time to think about that as she huddled against the storm. Too much time to wonder what the Mages might be doing, or what might happen if more of Prince Ostin's retainers showed up at the detention building looking for the prisoners.

Jules rested one hand on the dagger at her belt, pondering her options if she was trapped.

The coach jerked to a halt. "South fort."

Jules pulled out an Imperial eagle, the gold glinting in the rain. It represented far more than the trip should have cost, but then she'd stolen the coin and many similar ones from Imperial shipping, so it only felt right to spend it here. "Go get some rest."

The driver stared at the coin, grinning. "Yes, Lady! Do... do you want me to wait for you?"

Why hadn't she thought of that already? Plan, Jules! Make a plan! Have you been listening to Captain Mak at all? "Yes. I'll double that if you take me back to the harbor. I shouldn't be long."

The south fort turned out to be a fort that had no walls, being the home of administrators rather than fighters. Jules blinked against the rain and the dark, hailing a passing secretary hurrying past through the storm. "Where's Prince Ostin staying?"

"The grand manor! Straight on! You can't miss it."

Sure enough, Jules soon saw lanterns blazing at the front of a palatial three-story building. Most of the windows glowed with light as well. Worrying about paying for candle wax or lantern oil was for little people, not Imperial princes.

Having undergone mandatory training in Important Person hand-holding at officer school, Jules knew enough about how such things worked to avoid the impressive front entrance where multiple legionaries stood guard. Mere lieutenants were expected to use a side entrance when summoned to duty at this kind of manor.

The legionary huddled against the storm outside the side-entrance sprang to attention when he realized that Jules was an officer. "Halt and identify!"

She walked up to him, once again adopting an officious air. *Act like you belong there*, Ian had once advised her. *Half of having authority is acting like you're in charge.* Even though she felt like a half-drowned animal she was still a lieutenant. Or rather she was still pretending to still be a lieutenant.

She wondered where Ian was, whether he was all right.

"Status?" Jules barked at the sentry, just as the captain of the guard would.

"All's well!" the sentry replied, stiffening his posture a little more.

"Stay alert!" Jules ordered. "I'm going to check the sentries inside as well."

"There's just the one legionary inside this door, Lieutenant. The rest are Prince Ostin's retainers."

"I knew that," Jules said, her voice biting. "The colonel wants to make sure both of you are staying sharp. We don't want the prince complaining about sloppy soldiers on sentry." From what she'd heard, no matter where you went there was always one colonel that everyone wanted to avoid dealing with.

"Yes, Lieutenant. No, Lieutenant."

"Good." The sentry held open the door for Jules, who walked in, grateful to be out of the storm and grateful that the sentry hadn't asked for the colonel's name.

The inside sentry, lounging against a wall, straightened guiltily to attention as Jules walked inside. "You call that standing watch?" she snapped at him.

"Yes, Lieutenant. No, Lieutenant." Apparently the sentries in Sandurin liked to cover every possible correct reply in their responses.

"Where're the prince's quarters? I'm supposed to report to him."

"Down this hallway, left, up one flight, and down to the right," the sentry replied.

"Well done," Jules said. She left the relieved sentry, her soaked uniform dripping streams of water on the fine carpeting inside the manor.

Passing one closed door, she heard revelry inside. Loud voices, laughter, the sound of men and women either drunk or close to it. Making sure no one else was in the hallway to see her, Jules put one eye to the crack in the door, looking inside.

Retainers of the prince, she guessed from the very narrow view. Having a good time inside the warm manor while lesser servants worried about braving the weather. "Is he done with her yet?" one of the men said loudly, generating another gust of laughs.

"Can't wait for our turn!" another replied, leading to a cheer.

Jules relaxed the fist her hand had clenched into as she heard them talk and headed up the stairs.

One flight. Down to the right. A bored guard, one of Prince Ostin's retainers, stood by an ornate double door at least a lance wide. "Is the prince inside?" Jules asked. "I have an urgent dispatch for him."

"No," the retainer answered, not bothering with courtesy to a junior officer, secure in the knowledge that he was protected by his status with the prince. "He headed into town."

"I can leave the dispatch in his rooms."

"No, you can't," the man said with a grin. "The prince has a guest in there."

Hating that knowing grin, Jules smiled at the retainer. "Thank you." One of her palms went over the mouth of the startled guard before he could react, at the same time as her other hand drew the dagger and rammed it home in his chest, making sure it went into the heart.

The retainer stiffened, shuddering, his eyes open and staring at her. She held his mouth closed until he died.

Opening one side of the door, Jules dragged the guard inside and shoved him into the butler's pantry to the left.

The entry opened into an expansive suite, with a seating area that disturbingly faced the wide bed at one end as if positioned for spectator sport. A single lantern burning low gave enough light to see by as Jules walked to the bed.

The girl lying in it had her hands bound to the headboard above her head. She opened her eyes at Jules' approach, gazing at her with stoic misery.

Jules brought her dagger out again, slashing the bonds. "Are these clothes yours? Get into them."

"No," the young woman said, shaking her head. "I can't stop you from doing what you want to me, but I won't make it any easier for you by cooperating."

Jules leaned close to her. "The prince's plans have been changed, though he doesn't know it yet. There's a young man named Aron waiting for you, Lil. I'd hate to disappoint him."

"Aron? How do you know Aron? Why would an Imperial help us? Who are you?"

Resisting the urge to slap the girl to get her moving, Jules spoke quickly. "He's on a ship in the harbor. I'm not an Imperial officer. I'm a pirate. I've got a couple of names I'm going by, so you can call me Jeri."

"Jeri? A pirate? Stars above, you're... you're..."

"Impatient. We don't have much time."

"Yes." Lil got up, wincing, and struggled into her clothes.

Jules found a long, hooded cape in one closet and draped it over her. Just because a lieutenant couldn't protect herself from the rain didn't mean this girl also had to suffer. "Can you walk?"

"Yes."

But Jules found she had to support the trembling girl as they headed for the door.

It opened when they were almost there, another retainer looking into the dimly lit room. "Lerd? Where are you? If you're taking your turn early—"

The dagger in Jules' free hand swept through an arc that included the front of his throat.

As he collapsed, gurgling on his own blood, she used one foot to shove the dying retainer to the side where the other retainer's body lay.

Pausing only to shut the door behind her, Jules helped the girl down the stairs. "We're going to go past two sentries. Don't say a word. I don't want to have to hurt them."

The inside sentry eyed them worriedly as Jules approached. "Is something wrong, Lieutenant?"

"I've been told to take her to the healer," Jules said.

"Oh," the sentry said, the single word carrying a wealth of meaning also reflected in the revulsion the sentry couldn't quite conceal. He held the door for Jules as she helped the girl outside and past the other sentry.

The rain whipped at them as Jules supported the girl along the streets of the fort. To her relief, the coach was still waiting. She helped the girl into it. "The harbor. Fast."

"You got it, Lady!"

She looked up at the sky as the coach jolted down the streets, still nearly empty of traffic, wondering how much time she had left. Rain fell into her face, making it even harder to judge the hour while dark clouds covered the pre-dawn sky.

The coach rumbled to a sudden halt. Jules raised up to look ahead. "Why have we stopped?"

"Some sort of backup, Lady," the driver said. "Something down by the harbor, I think."

Had the Imperials been alerted? Was there already a cordon in place to keep her from getting back to the ship?

"What's that?" the driver called to those ahead. "Mages? Doing what?" He looked back at Jules, fear walking across his features. "It's Mages. A lot of them. They're stopping everyone heading for the harbor. The drivers up ahead say they seem to be looking for someone."

Blazes. They knew she was here. And that she wanted to get to the harbor. If only she hadn't gone to get this girl. Stupid. Stupid. Stupid.

Jules looked over at the girl huddled beside her and realized that she'd be stupid again.

Maybe she could head out of the city. Find somewhere to hide, get word to the *Sun Queen*...

A covered carriage rolled up behind them, coming to a stop as well.

With the window shades down and the doors closed, the occupants were protected from the weather and from being seen. But Jules heard a man inside calling to the driver of the carriage. "What's going on?"

"Some sort of stoppage on the street, Sir Mechanic."

Sir Mechanic? Did she know the voice that had come from inside the carriage? Jules weighed her chances if she didn't try something very risky, and decided that she had nothing to lose. Hopping down from the cart, she approached the door to the carriage, ignoring the driver's silent attempts to warn her away.

"Sir Mechanic," Jules called softly, rapping on the door to the carriage.

The door yanked open, giving her a view of the interior. Only two occupants, both Mechanics. One a woman, one a man. Both were glaring at her.

She recognized the man, the Mechanic on their ship who she'd thought might be sympathetic to her. "Sir Mechanic, I need your help."

He looked back at her in disbelief. "I don't care if you are an Imperial officer. That's nothing to me. Why do you think I'd help a common?"

Jules reached behind her back to draw the revolver, displaying it to the Mechanics. "Because I'm someone you've met before."

"How did you-? Wait. You're her?" He leaned closer, staring at her. "What was the name?"

"Jules, Sir Mechanic. Sir, there are Mages stopping access to the harbor. They're looking for me."

He stared at her a moment longer. "Get in."

"Sir, there's someone with me."

"Then get him and get in!"

Jules got the girl from the coach, tossing another eagle to the delighted driver. "We found another ride. Go home." Pushing Lil into the carriage, and following her inside, Jules closed the door in time to hear the female Mechanic talking to the man. "Hal, what the blazes are you doing? Is this common your mistress? You gave her a *revolver*?"

"Sit over there," the male Mechanic ordered Jules and the girl, motioning to the front seat of the carriage facing him and the woman. "Gayl, she's not my mistress. She works for the Guild."

"A common?"

"Remember? The one the Mages made that prediction about?"

"That's her?" Lady Mechanic Gayl stared at Jules. "So you're supposed to overthrow the Guild, huh?"

"A daughter of my line, Lady Mechanic," Jules said. Water running off of her uniform was pooling on the seat and streaming down to the floor before seeking exit from the carriage through the bottoms of the doors.

"Huh. What's the matter with her?" the woman asked, pointing to the girl. "Is she hurt?"

"Yes, Lady Mechanic. She caught the eye of a prince."

The woman's eyes narrowed in anger. "And what, you're rescuing her?"

"Yes, Lady Mechanic."

"Commendable for a common. What is it you need?"

"We need to get past the Mages searching everyone going to the harbor," Jules said. "Sometimes they know where I'm going to be. But only sometimes."

"Erratic intelligence collection," Mechanic Hal commented. "She's killed two Mages," he added to Mechanic Gayl.

"She could kill some more tonight," Gayl said. "Instead of us getting involved."

"Lady," Jules said, "we need to get to my ship and out of the harbor. If the Imperials realize I'm here, there'll be trouble."

"Why?"

Mechanic Hal answered. "The Emperor wants in on the Mage prediction. And she's been doing the Guild's bidding, keeping him distracted so he wouldn't try to interfere with our ongoing projects."

"We could take her to our ship, then," Mechanic Gayl said. "If she's an agent of the Guild."

Mechanic Hal shook his head. "My understanding is that we're not supposed to show any direct tie with her. The Guild has to be able to deny that it's giving her orders or helping her."

"She's got a revolver! Where was that supposed to have come from?"

"I don't make policy," Hal said. "If I did—"

"Don't," Gayl warned. "You don't want to be associated with Grand Master Bran's faction."

"Bran has some good points about the need to accommodate some changes and—"

"And be less harsh toward the commons! And he's running straight down a track to a collision with Grand Masters Fern and Ulan! You don't want to be one of the casualties when those two locomotives collide!"

"I'm not doing anything wrong," Hal muttered.

"A few people have already disappeared. I don't want you to be one of them." As if suddenly remembering others were present, Gayl cast a glance toward Jules.

But Jules had kept her eyes down to avoid seeming like she was listening.

"Drive around!" Mechanic Hal ordered the carriage driver. "We're going to the harbor and we're not going to wait on Mages!"

At this hour, even in a big city like Sandurin, traffic to the harbor wasn't backed up far. Jules heard other drivers shouting angrily at the carriage driver as he rolled past them, only to be silenced when their driver indicated that he had Mechanics as passengers.

"What are you even doing in this city?" Mechanic Hal demanded of Jules. "I thought you were smart enough to avoid putting yourself in the lap of the Mages and the Emperor."

"I had a task to do, Sir Mechanic."

"What task?"

"Rescuing people who are trying to escape the Empire."

The Mechanic grinned. "Rescuing them right out from under his nose? That'll certainly upset the Emperor and keep his attention on you. You are clever. You're doing that all by yourself?"

"I have friends at the harbor, Sir Mechanic," Jules said. Clever. The sort of thing someone said to a child who'd done something better than expected. Not smart or capable, she thought. Clever. And that was from the Mechanic who seemed most considerate toward her. But then anything short of withering contempt toward a common was considerate for a Mechanic.

"We probably shouldn't know any more about this than we have to," Mechanic Gayl said. "Not if the Guild is officially not supposed to be involved."

"You're right," Mechanic Hal said.

"Stars above, you're actually listening to me for once! This must be a day for miracles."

The carriage halted. "I have orders, Sir Mage," the driver could be heard saying, his voice quivering with fear.

"Let's make sure they don't look in here. Mages should know better than to interfere with Mechanics." Hal went out the door, closing it behind him. As Jules waited, tense, she saw Gayl looking at her. The female Mechanic mimed using a pistol. Jules nodded and drew out the weapon, ready in case it was needed.

The sound of the rain and the wind made it hard to hear what was happening outside. Jules put her ear to the window covering, listening.

"-out of the way now!" Hal was saying.

Then something she couldn't hear, though the emotionless tones came through enough to make it clear a Mage was replying.

"You won't search us and you won't search our carriage. You don't give orders to the Mechanics Guild."

Another short inaudible reply.

"We're driving through. If you try to stop us, there'll be trouble. We're not commons. We're not afraid of your tricks!"

Hal came back inside, sitting down and breathing out heavily. He grinned at Gayl, tense. "Let's see." He glanced at Jules. "You might still have to use that."

"They didn't back down?" Gayl asked.

"I don't know. How can you tell? The one I talked to just turned away. That might mean they won't fight. I saw three or four here. If they've got all roads to the harbor blocked, every Mage in Sandurin must be out and they must have called in extra Mages from elsewhere to help." Hal looked at Jules again. "They really seem to believe their own fortune-telling."

"Lucky me," Jules said.

Hal smiled. "Driver! Go ahead!"

Jules wondered how badly that driver was shaking was fear as he urged the horses back into motion.

They moved ahead, the carriage gradually picking up speed.

She breathed a sigh of relief. "Are you all right?" she murmured to Lil, who was huddled next to her.

"Yes, Lady."

Jules laughed. "I told you that I'm a pirate."

"Yes, Lady Pirate."

The carriage halted. Hal opened the door, looking out cautiously. "We're at the waterfront. No Mages in sight. J— What was it?"

"Jules, Sir Mechanic." Mechanics were supposed to be so smart, but none of them could remember her name.

"You and that other common follow me out. Gayl, watch our backs. We'll go right down to the boat waiting at the landing."

"Go ahead, hero," Gayl said.

Jules reached behind her to holster her pistol and jumped out of the carriage, back into the storm, the cold, the wind, and the slapping rain. She helped Lil down as well, once again helping her walk down stairs. The stone steps leading to the landing were slippery from the rain, forcing Jules to concentrate on her feet rather than looking around. It would have been a lot easier if either of the Mechanics had helped get Lil down the stairs, but neither one did, of course.

A harbor boat at the landing held a couple of miserable-looking rowers and a woman at the tiller. Mechanic Hal waited until Jules and Lil were in the bow of the boat before joining them with Mechanic Gayl. "Where's your ship?"

Jules looked around, trying to orient herself. There were the unnaturally steady lights of the Mechanic ship, impossible to mistake. Up there were the lights of the fort atop the harbor wall. Which meant the *Sun Queen* was tied up... "Over there, Sir Mechanic. I can't see it yet, but it's that way."

"Go that way," Hal told the woman at the tiller.

"Sir Mechanic, your ship is over—"

"Did we ask you to tell us where our ship was?" Gayl demanded.

"No, Lady Mechanic."

The group fell silent except for the splash of the oars, Jules gazing anxiously ahead.

"How's your math?" Mechanic Gayl suddenly asked.

Jules looked, seeing the question was directed at her.

How should she answer? Jules remembered what Lady Mechanic Gin had said after her first meeting with Mechanics. Learning that Jules had more education than the Mechanics had thought, Gin had given her what was either a warning to stay quiet about it or an implied threat of what could happen to a common who was too smart for her own good. Whether it had been a warning or a threat, Jules decided it'd be smart to downplay her abilities to Mechanics from now on. "I know my numbers, Lady Mechanic."

"That's all?" Gayl shrugged, huddled under the rain, looking at Hal. "I don't know what you see in her."

"She's not my mistress," Hal said. "Look at her! Sooner or later she'd knife me."

"Yeah. You can't trust commons. Thank you for talking sensibly for once," Mechanic Gayl said. She glanced at Jules again and caught her looking this time. "You don't like hearing that, do you? But you're our enemy. You're happy knowing that daughter of your line is supposedly going to overthrow our Guild."

"You'll help," Jules said, unable to stop herself.

"What?"

"The prophecy said the daughter of my line will unite Mechanics, Mages, and common folk to overthrow the Great Guilds."

Gayl stared at her. "You believe that?"

"The Mages do. Even though it says they'll also help her."

"Why would the Mages say something like that?" Mechanic Gayl asked Mechanic Hal. "Unless they're referring to internal dissension in the Mechanics Guild that'll open the door for commons to attack," she added pointedly.

"The Mages don't know anything about internal Mechanics Guild matters," Hal said. "And even if they did, it'd be wishful thinking for them that any Mechanic would further their aims, or those of the commons. Every Mechanic is faithful to the Guild, and Mages are all crazy," Hal added. "Who can even talk to them?"

"I did," Jules said, unable to understand why she was saying so much. Maybe despite her worries she wanted these Mechanics to respect her. To feel less smug about themselves and their place in the world. "I talked with a Mage. He was dying. An old man. And he told me things."

"What did he say?" Mechanic Hal asked, hunching closer, rain dripping from his hair and face.

"He said… he said everything is an illusion and everybody is just a shadow."

"That's the sort of craziness I'd expect from a Mage, but I've never heard of a Mage saying even that much to anyone," Hal said. "You're sure he said that?"

"Yes, Sir Mechanic," Jules said.

"What else did he tell you?"

"Nothing. I asked him a lot more but he just kept saying I had to find the answers inside me rather than expecting someone else to tell me those answers."

Mechanic Gayl shook her head. "You must have asked the wrong questions. How do you like that? The only Mage anyone could talk to, and a common got the privilege. If only one of us could have interrogated that guy and gotten more useful information out of him."

"There it is," Jules said as the hull of the *Sun Queen* loomed out of the rain like a wooden wall rising from the harbor's waters, relieved both to reach the ship and to have an opportunity to get out of the helpful but condescending company of the two Mechanics. Still, without them she'd be trapped outside the harbor, facing a cordon of Mages. "Sir Mechanic, Lady Mechanic, thank you. I owe you my life."

"Don't speak of this," Hal warned her.

"Yeah," Gayl said. "We don't need Senior Mechanics giving us loyalty quizzes."

As the boat came alongside the *Sun Queen* on the side away from the pier, Jules called up. "On the *Queen*! We need a ladder!"

Startled faces looked down on her over the railing. "Captain, she's back!"

A Jaycob ladder came down in a fall of wooden steps and rope supports. Jules sent Lil up first, pushing to help her up until those on deck could grab her hands. "She needs to see Keli right away!" Jules called. She put her hand and foot on the ladder, turning back to see the Mechanics watching her. "Thank you," she said again, before beginning her climb, but neither one answered her.

What was the matter with her? Jules thought as she climbed. Confiding in Mechanics. Telling them things she didn't have to tell them. Trusting them. Practically every word they'd spoken to her had dripped with contempt, with their own assured superiority over her. They weren't friends. They never could be. They were, barely, allies of convenience in an arrangement that could be ended at any moment.

But those same two Mechanics had just saved her life.

Had there actually been a time when her life made sense? Or had she just been oblivious to how bizarre life really was?

On deck, Jules looked to see the boat already vanishing into the rain, on its way to the Mechanic ship.

"How'd you do it this time?" Captain Mak said from close by, the rain running in little rivers down his face and his oilskin.

"I guess I'm fated to live until I have that kid," Jules said.

"You promised to be careful."

"And I was, sir. Every step of the way."

Mak shook his head. "Were those really Mechanics in that boat?"

"Yes, sir. They got us through the Mages blocking access to the harbor."

"Friends of yours?"

"They'd be the first to tell you they couldn't be friends with a common," Jules said.

"That's what I thought. We'll talk more later. Right now we need to get out of Sandurin. There are Mages at the head of the pier. They showed up a while ago, but they seem to be waiting for something. We have to get out of here before they come down the pier to search us and the other ships."

She followed Captain Mak up onto the quarterdeck, the wind whipping at her. The crew was already taking in the lines tying the *Sun Queen* to the pier, but as Jules looked out over the harbor, she could hardly see anything in the pre-dawn murk. "Sir, maybe we should wait. It's going to be really hazardous navigating when we can't see past our own noses."

"I don't think waiting any longer is an option," Mak said. "Look down the pier."

She did, where storm lanterns provided some light that allowed more visibility. Figures moved on the pier. Figures wearing robes, coming this way.

Mages.

Had they sensed her arrival here somehow? Or just seen the boat pull alongside the *Sun Queen* and put two and two together?

The last lines taken in, the *Sun Queen* broke away from the pier, the wind pushing her away, as the crew fought against wind and rain to get the sails unfurled.

Jules stood by the rail, leaning out to try to see a little better, watching the Mages get closer, seeing one of them stop moving as the others kept coming.

The rail she was leaning on vanished.

Jules twisted her body wildly. The support she'd been leaning on gone, she was toppling over the side, grabbing frantically for anything that might stop her fall.

Another hand grabbed hers, her wet fingers slipping through that grasp.

CHAPTER THIRTEEN

J ules shouted a wordless cry, lunging to grab on to the arm again, this time the grip holding, her feet precariously on the deck, most of her body suspended over the water, her arms reaching back to hold onto the person who was taking her weight.

Captain Mak hauled her fully back on deck, breathing heavily from the sudden exertion. "I can't take my eyes off of you for a moment, can I, Jules?"

"Sorry, sir." Jules blinked rain out of her eyes, staring. Had she just seen the missing section of railing suddenly reappear in the air, to fall unsupported into the waters of the harbor? A long gap remained in the previously sturdy rail.

The *Sun Queen* swung about, the crew hauling on the lines to catch the wind. Jules, standing back from the railing at the rear of the quarterdeck, swung herself around as well to keep her eyes on the Mages who had reached the closest point on the pier to the ship. They stood in a group. Watching her.

It felt very oddly like when the legionaries at Saraston had stood on the pier, aiming crossbows at her.

Aiming.

"Get down!" Jules yelled. "Mak, get down!"

She grabbed his hand as she dropped, pulling him with her, seeing the sailor at the helm dropping to the deck as well at the frantic warning.

Intense heat bloomed just above her and the captain, as if the air from a roaring bonfire, or even hotter, had suddenly appeared in that spot.

The rain falling through the air above Jules vanished into a cloud of steam like that from a boiling pot.

Part of the wooden helm caught fire, spokes of the wooden wheel flickering with flames.

The back of Mak's oilskin blackened from the heat above it.

But the sensation of intense heat dissipated rapidly, blown away by the wind and more rain falling through the place where it had been.

Together, she, Mak, and the sailor at the helm beat at the burning part of the helm, aiding by the rain and the wet wood in rapidly putting out the fire. "What was that?" Jules asked Mak.

"The heat? I've heard Mages can do that, but I've never encountered it before."

"Why did they make that railing disappear instead of my head?" Jules said.

"No idea. Why not kill you directly? We'd have to go back and ask."

"No, thanks." Jules looked off the stern again. The pier had vanished in the gloom as the *Sun Queen* got farther away and picked up speed. The Mages were no longer visible.

"They say if a Mage can't see you, a Mage can't hurt you," Captain Mak said, standing beside her again.

"I hope that's true," Jules said. "Thanks for saving me from falling."

"Thanks for saving me from being burnt like overdone bacon," he said. "And for finally just calling me Mak."

"It was an emergency, sir."

"And there we go again." Mak waved forward. "Get up to the bow and see if you can spot any buoys."

"Yes, sir."

"Blazes, girl! You do that on purpose!"

"No, sir. I really don't, sir." Jules ran down the ladder and forward, splashing along the deck, narrowly avoiding slamming into the foremast when it loomed up suddenly before her.

She advanced cautiously along the bowsprit, only too aware of her slick leather bootsoles and wishing she'd thought to remove them. Having probably already run through several lives' worth of luck this evening alone, Jules kept a tight grip on the stays as she advanced.

When she'd gone as far forward as she dared, Jules hung on to the nearest stay, listening and staring into the dark, blinking constantly as the rain fell into her eyes.

The clong of a bell came from close to her right, to starboard. The wrong side when they were leaving the harbor. "We're too far to port! Come starboard!"

The *Sun Queen* swayed beneath her as the helm went over, turning the ship. Jules caught a brief glimpse of the buoy passing just under the bow as the ship went past. "Bring her back about one point to port!"

Another clang of a buoy bell, just to her left. Good. They were in the channel.

A sheet of rain swept by, blinding her for a moment. As Jules wiped the water from her eyes, she thought the skies above might be just a tiny bit brighter as dawn approached.

An anchor lantern on another ship came into sight to starboard, dim and wavering like the light of a ghost ship. Jules watched it as long as she could, trying to judge the movement of the *Sun Queen* by that marker.

Another buoy, this one appearing out of the gloom right under the bow, hitting and scraping along the hull. "Take her a point to starboard! We're too far to port again!"

It seemed to be taking a lot longer to leave Sandurin than it had to enter.

Another sound intruded on that of the storm. Jules listened, trying to sort it out. "I hear surf! We're nearing the harbor entrance!"

As the last word still hung in the air, Jules saw a large boat appearing out of the storm. Four men and women were at the oars, pulling for all they were worth.

And a Mage in the back, who stood up at the sight of Jules.

Blazes.

Jules reached back, drawing the revolver. She'd never tried anything other than a shot very close to her target. Could she hit a Mage a few lances away?

The boat bumped against the bow of the *Sun Queen*, the Mage steadying herself as she stared up at Jules.

Jules aimed as well as she could and pulled the trigger.

The crash of the shot echoed across the harbor.

She saw a spurt of water leap up as the shot missed both Mage and boat completely.

The Mage hadn't yet cast a spell, and somehow seemed frustrated.

Even though there was no way of telling how much time she had before the Mage finally acted, Jules forced herself to take her time to aim again, down the barrel of the revolver, waiting as the motion of the boat and the ship and the water carried the line she was aiming along across the front of the Mage.

The boom of the second shot startled Jules, who hadn't realized she was pulling the trigger until the cartridge went off.

The Mage jolted, took one wavering step backward, and fell back over the stern of the boat.

"Jeri!" Jules looked back to see Liv staring through the murk at her. "What happened?"

"A Mage. She must have ordered a boat to take her to the harbor exit so she could catch us." Jules saw the boat vanishing into the storm as the rowers fled the site of the encounter. "I shot her."

"Everyone in Sandurin must have heard it!"

"And what was it I was supposed to do instead?" Jules demanded. She looked to starboard as a vague line of white appeared, growing then vanishing. "We've got surf to starboard! About three lances I think!"

The *Sun Queen* heeled to port as that word was relayed to the quarterdeck.

Jules heard alarm bells ringing in the harbor and in the legion fort atop the high breakwater, the sounds fading as the *Sun Queen* found the open sea and fled west with the winds of autumn at her back.

* * *

By noon it was obvious that the storm was traveling with them, the westerly winds pushing it along in the same way they propelled the *Sun Queen*. That minimized the chance that any patrolling Imperial ships would spot them, but also maximized the discomfort aboard. Below decks was crammed with not only the *Sun Queen's* normal large complement of sailors but also all of the rescued prisoners, giving it a feel not all that different from the cell in the detention building. The mood was far different, but the surroundings were damp, cold, and very crowded.

They'd met the sloop carrying Loka, but the seas were too rough this day to risk transferring people between the ships. The sloop had veered close enough to the *Sun Queen* for Loka and some of his people to shout messages across to each other, but then the ships had opened the distance between them to reduce any chance of collision.

Not wanting to fight for enough room to breathe, Jules slumped on the deck, letting the rain beat on her. Her uniform was going to be a mess, but then the odds of getting away with using that uniform a third time seemed too long to risk it anyway. She wasn't sure that she'd have the nerve to try even if another good opportunity arose.

Someone stopped before her, kneeling on the wet deck, his head bowed. "Lady Pirate."

She squinted at him. "Oh. Aron. How's Lil?"

"Your healer says she should recover. Lady, I promised to be your slave and—"

"Don't finish that. I told you I wasn't looking for a slave."

He hesitated. "But, you—"

"I did what I did because I wanted to, not because I wanted a reward," Jules said. "Now drop it."

Aron gazed at her with a wondering expression that irritated her. "For you, of all people, to risk yourself for us when—"

"I'm telling you not to go there," Jules said.

He paused, choosing his next words with care. "How can we ever repay you?"

Jules looked away. "For getting there too late?"

"Lil told me what else would have happened to her. It wasn't too late."

"Are you still going to marry her?"

"Of course I am," Aron said.

Sometimes people didn't disappoint you. "Than I have my pay in full," Jules said. "Have a happy life. Have kids. Stay away from Mages."

"We've decided that we'll name our first daughter for you."

Jules shook her head. "That name hasn't brought me much luck."

"Not the real name. Can I say that? We know what that is, but it has a... a purpose." Aron asked. "Jeri. We were going to name her Jeri."

Jules laughed, surprised. "Fine. You do that."

She was still chuckling when Keli sat down beside her, looking tired. "How are they?" Jules asked.

"They'll all live," Keli said. "But their injuries serve as a reminder of why I left the Empire. You didn't happen to kill that prince, did you?"

"Sorry. He wasn't there."

"Shame." Keli grimaced. "What about you? Are you hurt?"

"Only my pride," Jules said. "I had a talk with some Mechanics."

"That'll ruin anyone's day," Keli said. "You killed another Mage?"

"I think so. There's no way to know for sure."

"Scared the blazes out of me, I'll tell you, when that thunder broke on our bow. Why are those Mechanic weapons so loud?"

Jules shrugged, feeling the rain running down her face. "I'd have to know how they work to answer that. But thanks for reminding me that I need to talk to the captain. I never did get a chance to give him a rundown about what happened ashore in Sandurin."

"You sure spend a lot of time in that cabin."

Jules felt an inner chill warring with the cold of the rain on her skin, her earlier levity vanished. "What does that mean?"

"Nothing," Keli said, having heard her tone shift and watching her with sudden tension.

"It meant something. Why did you say it?"

The healer paused, clearly thinking before speaking again. "I'm not implying anything improper."

"What does *that* mean?" Jules heard the steel in her voice and saw Keli swallow nervously. "Just what do you think is going on in that cabin? Because you clearly think that something is."

"Jeri, no one thinks that you and the captain have anything going on. If you were, it couldn't be hidden. People would know. We all like Captain Mak. You know that. He's happier around you. So that's good."

"What do you mean he's happier around me?" Jules pressed.

"Just that! No one thinks any more than that. It's easy to tell when a man and a woman want to touch each other, and that's not you and Mak at all. You're just comfortable with each other. That's all there is to it."

"We're not…" She'd been about to insist that she and Captain Mak weren't "comfortable" with each other's company.

But she did enjoy being around him. When they weren't arguing.

"I need to talk to the captain," Jules said.

She hauled herself up, suppressing a groan as she felt how her cold muscles had stiffened while she was sitting in the rain, and walked to the cabin. "Sir? I need to report."

"Come on in." She went inside, seeing Mak lying on his stomach in his bunk. "Are you all right, sir?"

"My back got a little scorched," Mak said. "Keli already put some salve on it. I'm too tired to stand, I can't lie on it, and I can't sit with my back like this."

"May I sit down, sir?"

"Blazes, Jules, just sit down."

She took a chair. "Sir, did you know that the rest of the crew thinks you and I are… comfortable together?"

"Comfortable?" Mak surprised her with a laugh. "That's life for a man. His whole life he's a threat to womankind, until the day he becomes old enough to be comfortable."

"Captain, you're not old."

"But I am apparently comfortable." Mak gave her a curious look. "Is that bad?"

"I don't know," Jules said. "Am I behaving properly toward you?"

"I think so. Except when you decide to run off on some mission you've just decided has to be done into an Imperial city swarming with Mages."

She looked down at the deck. "I'd hoped that you'd understand."

"I can't get into your head, Jules. No one else can. You're facing a situation that no other person has ever had to deal with. Was that also about proving you weren't just the woman of the prophecy?"

"No, sir," Jules said, looking back at him again. "It was about someone who needed help, and I could be that help. There wasn't anyone else. So I knew it had to be me."

He studied her closely before replying. "That matters a lot to you, doesn't it, Jules?"

"Yes, sir. I…" She waved an uncertain hand. "I know how it feels to want someone to come, to wait for help, and to never have it appear."

"All right, Jules. But there's something you need to think about. I know how unhappy you are with that prophecy. With what it did to you," Mak said. "But since that prophecy was made, the common people of the world have set their hopes on the help that will someday come in the form of that daughter of your line. If you die before you have a child, that help will never appear."

If anyone else had said it, Jules would have raged at them. But she knew that Mak wouldn't have said it unless he thought she needed to hear it. "You're saying I can't afford to take such risks."

"No, Jules, only you can decide that. But you do have to take everything into account when you decide. I'm sorry. It's an awful burden."

She sighed. "Maybe I'll just go ahead and find some guy. Someone who'll do. And get knocked up and have a kid and… stars above, that wouldn't solve anything, would it?"

"No," Mak said. "And if you don't mind your captain saying so, you don't seem the type of girl who'd settle for just someone."

"Oh, no," Jules said as something occurred to her. "What if another Mage sees some guy and says a daughter of his line will do those things? Wouldn't that mean that he and I would have to have children? No matter who he was?"

"That hasn't happened," Mak said, but she could tell he was unhappy at the thought. "The choice remains yours."

"But… no. You're right. The choice is going to be mine. No one else is going to decide who the father of my children will be. I hope he turns out to be someone you like, though."

Mak raised his eyebrows at her. "Why does that matter?"

"It just does. I guess because I respect your opinions. Although I guess you'll let me know if you don't think he's right for me, won't you?" Jules added, unsure if she was teasing Mak or not.

"I was right about Don," Mak said, smiling at her.

"We were both right about Don," Jules said. "The only person who thought he had a chance at me was Don. Sir, I actually came in to fill you in about what happened in Sandurin. I didn't get the chance to tell you a lot of things." She told Mak about the events of the night before, including what she could remember of what the Mechanics had said.

"That sounds like some serious infighting among the Mechanics," Mak said. "People have disappeared, she said? People like that Mechanic Karl, you think?"

"Probably," Jules said. "From what I saw of him, he probably didn't stay free for long before the Mechanics Guild snapped him up again."

"Are you sure you should have told those Mechanics all that you did?"

"No, I'm not. I need to learn to keep my mouth shut."

Mak put one hand to his mouth as he thought. "They will get weaker. Internal fighting never did anyone any good."

"But what about the Mages? How could they get weaker?"

"I don't know. You said the Mage on the boat just looked at you? No spell even though it seemed she had time for that?"

"Yes," Jules said. "I mean, I had time to shoot twice. I can't be sure of anything, but I felt like she was frustrated."

"Frustrated? Why would... do you think for some reason she *couldn't* do a spell?"

"All I know is that she didn't do a spell," Jules said.

"But the Mages on the pier definitely did, though none of their spells hit you directly. One more thing to think about," Mak said.

"There is no answer. There are answers beyond number," Jules said. "Sometimes I think that old Mage was just messing with me, and other times I think he really was trying to tell me wisdom as he knew it."

Mak nodded. "Thank you for everything that you told me. Get some rest, Jules. You look awful."

She grinned. "Thank you, sir."

"You're welcome. We're headed back to Kelsi to offload our new passengers. If things are quiet there we'll stay a few days."

Jules nodded wearily, seeing the water still dripping off of her onto the deck of the cabin. "Sir, you've been nice not to chew me out, but I messed up again. Everything was fine while I followed our plan, but then I went off to do something else and only luck got me through that."

Mak tried to shrug from his position lying on his stomach. "Plans are what you do before you encounter the situation. Once you're in it, sometimes you have to let your instinct tell you what to do."

"Should I have risked it? Going to get Lil?"

"Should you have?" He paused, thinking. "Despite what I said earlier about risks and the future, I think so. More importantly, Jules, *could* you have done otherwise?"

"I don't think so, sir," Jules said. "But I have to stop spilling my guts to people. You should have seen how those Mechanics looked at me when I said I'd had an actual conversation with a Mage. And I had an actual conversation with a Mage! Who does that?"

Mak looked over at her. "Jules, according to the prophecy that daughter of your line is supposed to unite Mechanics, Mages, and commons, right? She's going to have to talk with them to do that."

"Yes," Jules said. "But how?"

"The first step is to talk to them. Then you figure out how to understand them. Just maybe, Jules, your willingness to talk to people you're not supposed to ever exchange words with will prove to be a valuable skill for that daughter of your line. Maybe the most valuable skill."

Jules laughed. "You're saying that one of my weaknesses is something I should hope gets passed down to my descendants? How about my rushing into things? How about that?"

"Your instincts are good, Jules. I've told you that. The daughter of your line is likely to face a lot of danger. Being able to react like you do might save her."

She gazed at him, remembering other things she'd done. "What about my dark streak?"

Mak met her eyes. "That, I don't know. Perhaps somewhere along the way that dark streak will be softened."

"Thanks for not pretending it's a virtue."

"Jules, we don't know what that girl might have to do. Overthrowing the Great Guilds might require her to do some very ugly things."

She nodded, gazing at nothing. "It's why I went to get her. Lil. I think it came from the dark inside me, which at least partly came from that feeling of being abandoned. I don't know for certain. Maybe that daughter of my line will need that darkness in her. It's funny. I don't like her all that much most of the time, but I don't want to think of her having to do ugly things."

"You don't like her?" Mak asked, startled.

"Yes." Jules sighed. "She took my life from me. I'll never get all of it back."

"But she'll be your great-something-grand-daughter!"

"I didn't say I didn't love her," Jules said, looking at him so Mak could tell she meant it. "I do. I just have trouble liking her, because of what she did to me."

He nodded slowly. "I see. I suppose I can't find fault with that."

"You still love yours, don't you, sir?"

"You know I do. My daughter may never look on me with love again, but I won't change my feelings toward her. I do miss her, though," Mak said wistfully.

Jules forced herself to her feet, feeling awkward to see the feelings that Mak usually kept hidden. "Well… I'm here, for whatever that's worth."

"Yes. You are," Mak said, smiling at her. "But you shouldn't be. You should be getting some rest."

She grinned at him. "I'm going to get out of this sopping mess of a uniform, change into something dry, see if I can talk Keli out of a shot of rum, and get some sleep. Call me if you need me, sir."

"Jules."

"Yes, sir?"

"You did well in Sandurin."

She smiled. "Thank you, Captain." Others had said the same. But only when Mak said it did she really believe it. Because she knew he'd tell her when she messed up.

* * *

With the storm winds urging on the Sun Queen, they made excellent time, reaching Kelsi's settlement as dawn rose on the third morning after leaving Sandurin. Even better, Kelsi's once more proved to be devoid of Mages. "They left on ships headed east," was all anyone could say.

"Sandurin?" Liv wondered as she, Jules, and Ang looked at the city from the deck of the *Sun Queen*. "Like they expected you to be there."

"That one Mechanic said he thought more Mages were in Sandurin than usual. But if they knew that, why weren't they in position to catch me when I first went ashore, instead of barricading the pier after I'd already gone into the city?" Jules shook her head, puzzled. "It's like they knew I'd be here, but they didn't know when."

"It's more like they knew when, but only *one* when," Ang said. "They would have caught you then, that second time you came back to the pier. That seems to have been when they expected you to be heading for the harbor."

"That's weird, isn't it?" Jules said. "They knew pretty accurately where and when I'd be there, but only in one case. They didn't know that I'd be there earlier."

"Who knows how Mages know anything? Isn't everything about them weird?"

"Jeri!" Mak called. "There's a meeting ashore we should both attend."

The meeting proved to be in a large tent next to the under-construction masonry building that would become the town hall of Kelsi's settlement. Inside, the tent smelled musty as tents always did, the open flaps in the canvas sides allowing not enough air to circulate among the people crowding in, most of them men and women who'd been freed in Sandurin.

The leaders of the group of former prisoners turned out to be a couple who were aunt and uncle to Lil. The man, Gari, had a craggy face and stout body that made him resemble a boulder uprooted from its soil and looking for a new place to plant itself. His wife, Ihris, seemed more like a tree, slim and graceful. They had two children who had thus far survived their adventures, and Ihris showed signs of expecting another. Jules would have felt jealous of the happy family if not for a shadowy cast to Ihris' face. She'd made it out of the Empire, but from the way others treated her, the woman suffered from some relentless affliction that there was no escaping.

The Kelsi who'd founded Kelsi's settlement looked tired as well, her face that of someone long in years who'd poured her heart into building something but knew she'd never live long enough to see it stand on its own. Jules had no trouble sympathizing with her. "You can't stay here," Kelsi told the leaders of the group who'd been rescued by the *Sun Queen*. "The Imperials won't let up looking for you. And when they find you, they'll come to get you. Or kill you."

"Plenty of people have escaped the Emperor's dominion," Loka complained. "Why should we be different?"

"You got caught," Kelsi said. "And then you got away again, right out from under the hand of Prince Ostin. You flouted Imperial law and, more importantly to the Emperor, Imperial dignity. If you stay here, they'll find you, and they'll come for you," she repeated.

"Maybe Dor's settlement would offer you safety," Mak said. "If we can find it."

"Dor is building near the water," Kelsi warned. "The Emperor's hand would have to reach farther, but it's the same problem. He needs to make an example of you, if he can. Do you want my advice? You're all farmers, right?"

"Yes," Ihris said. "From the lands north of Centin."

"So you won't miss the sea." Kelsi shifted in her seat to point west. "There's a pass leading that way. Not an easy walk, but we just had a restless fellow come back from heading that way and looking around. It gives way to broad plains. He saw herds of wild cattle and horses. Rivers. No telling how far it stretches."

Jules saw the faces of the refugees light up at the news.

"Free land?" Loka asked. "There's no one already there?"

"No trace of anyone else," Kelsi said. "My advice is to take that pass, keep walking west until you find a good spot, and start building. You'll be far from the sea, which means you'll be far from any Imperial search parties, and a far, far walk for any Imperial expeditions." Her eyes lingered on Ihris. "You could stay. Just the one, they'd probably never notice you."

Ihris shook her head. "Where Gari and our children go, I go."

Gari frowned unhappily. "But the rest would be good for you."

"I'll rest when we reach the place where we'll build a city," Ihris said. She smiled and touched her stomach. "This one will be born there." The statement sounded oddly like a prophecy.

Jules left the tent as the meeting continued, walking out onto the street after carefully searching for any sign of Mages who might have shown up. She leaned against one partially-completed masonry wall, wishing that Mak would finish so they could return to the ship.

Eventually, Mak joined her. She walked alongside him silently as they headed back to the *Sun Queen*.

"What's the matter?" Mak asked.

"I'm awful," Jules said.

"Why do you say that?"

"Because I looked at that happy family, Gari and Ihris, and all I could think of was that those children had parents, and those parents didn't have to worry about the Great Guilds coming after their children just because of who their mother was."

"Their mother won't live another year, I'm guessing from the look of her," Mak said.

"Which makes me feel all the more awful," Jules said. She hesitated. "Do you think that child will be born?"

"There's a chance she can carry it to term before she grows too weak. She seems the type whose will can hold death at bay a while if need be. But if so, there's also a good chance that giving birth will kill her." Mak exhaled slowly, his eyes on the dirt road. "Parents will do a lot for their children. Even give their lives."

"Thanks for rubbing that in!" Jules glowered as she looked off to the side.

"Do you not realize that your father died for you?"

"He died in the Northern Ramparts, a long way from me."

"He died trying to provide for you and your mother," Mak said. "He didn't abandon you. He was killed."

"Does that make it hurt less?" Jules whispered.

"I don't know. Does being angry at others who are more fortunate than you make you feel better?"

"No."

"Then why do it?"

"I told you that I'm awful."

"I like you," Mak said.

Somehow he could always get a smile out of her. "You have terrible judgment. I mean, look at the kind of people you allow on your ship."

"Jules, having awful thoughts doesn't make you awful. It makes you a person. How do you think I feel when I see a father and a daughter together? But that father losing his daughter too wouldn't bring my daughter back."

"I would," Jules said, looking over at Mak. "I would, Captain. If I can ever figure out a way, I'm going to bring your daughter back."

He didn't answer for a long moment, causing her to wonder if she'd overstepped her boundaries.

But finally Mak looked at her and smiled. "You already have."

She gazed back at him, puzzled by the answer. "Do you mean when she came aboard the ship with those other Mechanics to give me cartridges? That wasn't the reunion I want you to have."

Mak didn't answer this time, and she didn't push it, reluctant to probe at what she knew was a source of pain for him.

Once back at the ship, Mak called over Ang and Liv. "You three should hit the town. Have some fun."

"Are they my bodyguards or are they supposed to keep me out of trouble?" Jules asked.

"Whatever needs doing," Mak said. "Jeri, when's the last time you had fun?"

"Last night." She saw skepticism and surprise on their faces. "Not that way! I played cards with some of the crew. It was fun."

"Come along, Jeri," Ang said.

He steered Jules and Liv past the waterfront bars to what had become the settlement's main street, a little way back from the harbor. "Better booze in the places away from the water," Ang advised.

"That's always the way of it," Liv agreed.

Jules looked ahead, seeing a patch of dark jackets sitting at an outdoor table as a small group of Mechanics enjoyed lunch. She, Ang, and Liv were on the opposite side of the street, so they kept on, walking past without talking. Commons always kept quiet near Mechanics, who had a tendency to assume that any whispered conversations in their vicinity had to be about them, and probably disrespectful. But even though she stayed silent, walking with her eyes set forward as if unaware of the Mechanics they were passing, Jules felt their gazes on her and on the revolver and holster she wore as usual.

"Brrr," Liv whispered when they were past the group. "Did you feel those looks, Jeri?"

"Yeah," Jules replied. "They didn't seem happy to see me."

"It's the weapon," Ang said. "I could be wrong, but I thought it made them angry to see a common with a Mechanic weapon, walking along as if she was a Mechanic herself."

"That's it," Liv agreed. "A common acting like she was as grand as a Mechanic. They hated seeing that."

"I'm not strutting along like they do," Jules grumbled.

"No. But they look at you and see that anyway."

"That's what they fear," Ang said. "Commons thinking they're as good as Mechanics. Jeri, you need to be very careful around Mechanics from now on."

"From now on?" Jules laughed. "Do you think I've been lounging back having a party when I'm meeting with Mechanics? I spend most of my time and all of my words trying to convince them that I'm as meek and submissive as they'd all like a common to be."

"You? Meek and submissive?"

"Well, I try," Jules said. "But I admit sometimes I do say some things I shouldn't. But mostly I act like what they want to think I am."

"How long do you think you'll be able to keep that act going?" Liv said. "Before you start telling them what you really think?"

"I don't know," Jules said.

"Let's go in here," Ang said, indicating a bar that actually boasted a name, TUIJA'S, painted carefully on a lacquered sign board.

The bar fell silent as Jules walked in with the others. She felt the eyes on her as she walked to a table at the back, conversations slowly, quietly, resuming in her wake. "I'm really tired of people watching me," Jules grumbled to Ang. "That's one of the reasons I stay on the ship."

Liv joined them with a full bottle of Emdin rum and three glasses. "Unopened," she said as she poured them drinks. "Sometimes you need that precaution."

Jules picked up her glass, sipping the contents instead of knocking it back. She looked up as three other sailors approached.

In the lead was the woman from the *Star Seeker*. She crossed her arms, looking down at Jules. "We found the gems. You spoke the truth."

Jules nodded in reply, taking another sip of rum.

"But the murder of Captain Vlad still lies between us."

Jules shook her head, seeing that Liv and Ang were both tensed for a fight but waiting to see what she did.

"Are you now denying you did it?" the woman demanded.

"I killed him," Jules said. "But why does that lie between us? What would you have done to him if you'd discovered while he was alive that he'd withheld those gems from the crew? That's theft from fellow members of the crew, isn't it?"

"Not the point, girl."

"Then say what you want and be done," Jules said, tired of her fate and of hiding her feelings.

The woman and her companions stared at Jules. "Are you asking for a fight?"

Jules set down her glass and sat forward, keeping her eyes on the woman. "Every Mage wants to kill me. The Mechanics will try to kill me as soon as they figure out I'm not actually doing what they want. The Emperor doesn't want me dead, but he does want me. I've lived with that for a while now. And yet you're trying to unsettle me with your hard words and hard looks. If it's a fight you want, we'll fight. I'd rather not. You've done me no wrong. But I said that night that no man will speak to me as Vlad did and live, and I meant it. You'll get no apology from me for that."

Ang gestured to the three sailors. "We're all sailors here, all off of free ships. Share a drink with us. Hey, three more glasses here!"

After a brief hesitation, the other three sat down. The woman nodded to Jules. "I'm Mab. Truth is, you did us a favor." She looked around the bar before gazing back at Jules. "They say you killed another Mage."

"Yes," Jules said.

"And went into Sandurin alone, into an Imperial fort, to rescue a girl from under the nose of a prince."

"Yes."

"Why?"

"She needed help."

"What of the prophecy?"

Jules picked up her glass again, gazing at the liquid in it. "Tell me, why would you believe that a daughter of my line could do what the prophecy said?"

"Because a Mage prophesized it," one of the men with Mab said.

"Who I am has nothing to do with it?"

Mab knocked back her drink before leaning forward to look closely at Jules. "You're saying that you're more than just the one whose line will produce that daughter?"

"I'm saying," Jules said, "that the Mage saw in *me* that a daughter of *my* line would do that." It was what Mak had told her, but Jules had finally put that together in a way that she could say to others. In a way that would make her believe in herself.

Mab nodded, keeping her eyes on Jules. "The sort of girl who could kill three Mages. But what if you didn't have that Mechanic weapon?"

"I talked the Mechanics into giving it to me, didn't I?" Jules said, which she knew was a big exaggeration of what had happened. But perhaps even Mak would forgive her that mistruth.

"And what are you going to do about the Emperor?"

Jules grinned. "Steal his treasure, free his people, and laugh at his legions."

The others laughed. "I'd think that the boasting of a girl trying to impress her elders," Mab said. "Except that you've already done it." She leaned forward, both hands flat on the table separating her from Jules. "Here's why we sought you out. First, to see for ourselves who you were. And if that played well, to express our thanks for seeing that the gems came into our hands. And to let you know that our crew has voted to invest some of that wealth right here, into building ware-houses and a new solid pier to hold and transfer cargo. Something to help handle the proceeds of piracy. Should we ever do such a thing even though we're all devoted to following the Emperor's laws, aren't we? A legitimate business for those tired of or too old to pursue the trade at sea."

Ang looked impressed. "I wish we had the money for that."

Mab nodded. "If you hang onto this girl, that might happen. Jeri? Is that the right name? Since we owe you for the gems, we also voted to give you an equal share in the warehouses and the pier. You could have kept those, never said a word, and none would have known dif-ferent. But you played straight with us." The two sailors with Mab nodded solemnly to affirm her statement. "You have our words on it, before witnesses."

"An equal share?" Jules asked, startled. "Just as if I was one of your crew?"

"That's it. If you shake on it, it'll be done." Mab extended her hand.

Jules reached and grasped Mab's hand, feeling the strong grip of someone used to climbing rigging and hauling lines. "I hope someone in Kelsi's settlement is also thinking about building some fortifica-tions," Jules said. "The more there is here, the more the Emperor's eye is likely to take notice of it."

"You're not the first to see that," one of the sailors with Mab said. "It's being discussed. A wall along the harbor side."

"Since you mention the Emperor's eye," Mab added, "and no offense meant, but are you planning to stay long at Kelsi's?"

Jules grinned. "No offense taken. I wouldn't have come ashore unless we were planning to leave before long."

Gord came in, angling over to their table. "Did you guys see those Mechanics?"

"The one's looking like someone washed their feet in their beers?" Liv asked. "What about them?"

"Something strange, is all." Gord gestured back and up. "I'm walking past, and I notice one of them is standing up on top of that building they were at. She's standing way up there, but instead of looking around she seemed like she was talking into this little box in her hand."

"That's all you could see? A little box?"

"I couldn't stop and stare," Gord said. "You know what those other Mechanics would have done to me if I had. I pretended I hadn't noticed anything and just kept walking."

"What are your friends up to?" Mab asked Jules.

"They're no friends," Jules said.

Ang sat, frowning. "I don't like the feel of this."

"We can't get spooked every time a Mechanic looks at us like we're something dirty on the bottom of their shoe," Liv said.

"I don't like it," Ang repeated. "Who was that Mechanic talking to up there?"

"There wasn't anybody else up on the building," Gord said.

"So who was she talking to?"

"They say Mechanics can send messages very quickly across long distances," Jules said. "The Mechanics I talked to at Caer Lyn claimed to know what was going on in the waters off of Landfall."

Ang looked at Jules and Liv. "I think we should get back to the ship. Don't you give me that look, sister!" he added to Liv. "I don't spook easy. You know that."

Liv sighed, nodded, drained her drink, and picked up the bottle. "Let's go then."

"Gord," Ang said. "Pass the word. Everyone back to the *Sun Queen*."

Mab and the sailors with her got up. "We'll help pass the word for you. When it comes to Mechanics, we're all on the same crew."

Jules, uncomfortable with apparently having cut short the fun of her friends, walked with a silent scowl beside them. They'd nearly reached the pier where the *Sun Queen* was tied up when the distant sound of a bell rolled down from a mountain east of the settlement. Jules heard three quick bongs of the bell, a pause, then three more, another pause, and three more.

The people around her were staring to the east. Jules spoke to one who was obviously a resident of Kelsi's. "What does that mean?"

The man she'd addressed licked his lips nervously. "Three bongs from the lookout on the mountain. That means an Imperial ship has been spotted headed this way."

Another nearby local interrupted. "Not just an Imperial ship! That's two bongs together. Three means it's an Imperial warship."

"Blazes," Liv said. "Good call, Ang. How 'bout we run the rest of the way?"

Jules followed as Ang and Liv broke into a run toward the *Sun Queen*.

CHAPTER FOURTEEN

As Jules dashed up the gangway a sailor on the *Sun Queen* yelled at her. "There's an Imperial warship on the way! Coming from the east!"

"I know!" Jules shouted back. She ran up onto the quarterdeck, where Captain Mak already stood. "Captain, to be here this quickly they must have left Sandurin during the storm. That's against normal Imperial practice, but Prince Ostin could have overridden objections and ordered them out despite the risks." She paused to look at the town behind her.

The formerly quiet settlement had erupted into activity. Sailors boiled out of bars and taverns and restaurants like ants from a disturbed nest, all dashing to their ships. None of them wanted to be in port when an Imperial warship showed up.

The residents of the settlement were hurriedly closing up shop so they could hide every item smuggled out of Imperial territory without the proper tax stamps and approvals. Others were heading inland, where they could hide until the Imperials left. Jules saw a column of people heading toward the pass to the west and guessed that they were those freed from Sandurin, making a quick departure since they were very likely one of the targets of the Imperial warship.

The *Sun Queen*, and Jules herself, surely being other targets. "Maybe

I should go with them," Jules said, indicating those heading for the pass to the west.

"You'd be seen," Mak said. "And that would ensure the Emperor sent a force after them, and you."

"But if I stay aboard the *Sun Queen*..." Jules shook her head at Mak. "What right do I have to demand that the crew of this ship be part of my distracting the Emperor?"

"I don't recall hearing any demands from you," Mak said. "Ang! How many are left ashore?"

"I think five, Captain!" Ang called back.

"Keep an eye out for them. If we don't see them in the next few moments we'll have to get underway and come back later when it's safe."

Jules looked around the harbor, counting ships. In addition to several small craft, fishing boats and long boats, there were two sloops and the three-masted *Star Seeker* in port along with the *Sun Queen*. "Four large ships. If we all reach the harbor exit at the same time we'll collide and block it."

"No one's going to want to wait for anyone else to go through first," Mak said. "We might have to shoulder aside those sloops."

"Mast in sight to the east!" the lookout called from the top of the *Sun Queen*'s mainmast.

"Ang! How many?"

"Two still missing! I say we go and pick 'em up later!"

"Take in all lines! Make sail! Jeri, keep an eye on the other three ships."

Jules stood at the rail, watching the frantic activity on the sloops and the *Star Seeker*. One mast. That meant an Imperial war galley.

The lines were coming in as the sails were unfurled and began catching the wind. One of the advantages of having a large crew for piracy was that in an emergency a lot could get done all at once. "One of the sloops is leaving the pier, Captain," Jules called.

"How's the *Star Seeker*?"

"She's starting to take in lines, Captain."

"Another mast!" the lookout called down. "Another galley behind the first!"

Two Imperial war galleys. "The Emperor may be a little upset with you," Mak told Jules.

"Him or Prince Ostin," Jules said. "Sir, two galleys means four ballistae, two on each. Plus at least twenty legionaries with crossbows and swords on each. And the oar-handlers."

"You're not telling me anything that I don't already know," Mak said. "We're going to do all we can to avoid coming to grips with them. If it comes down to close action, your knowledge of how those galleys operate could be vital. You're the only person on this ship who's actually served on an Imperial war galley. Stay by me, keep your eyes open, and tell me anything that you think I need to hear."

"The biggest thing our training emphasized," Jules said, "was thinking ahead as far as possible. You can maneuver a galley fast, but it burns out the rowers just as fast. Anticipate the other ship's movements, plan to be where they'll be, and use the galley's existing movement as much as possible without changes in course and speed that use up the rowers."

Mak listened, his eyes intent. "We need to mess with that, then, if those galleys get close. Make them think they know where we're going, then do something different. Jules, I need you to get in the heads of the captains of those galleys. Figure out what they're going to be thinking, what they're going to be planning, and tell me. Forget about this ship. I'll maneuver the *Queen*."

"Yes, sir," Jules said. "I'll try my best, sir." She grabbed hold of the quarterdeck rail as the *Sun Queen* left the pier, crew members pulling on the brace lines to shift the yardarms. "*Star Seeker* is moving away from her pier, and the second sloop is underway as well."

Mak stood for a moment watching the movements of the other ships relative to the *Sun Queen*, which was slowly moving faster under the push of the wind. "Blazes. Either we go through the harbor exit side by side with *Star Seeker*, which will make it all too likely that one of us will go aground, or one of us will have to hold back for the other."

"*Star Seeker* has a slight reach on us," Jules said. "We should follow astern of her."

"I agree. If I was in command of *Star Seeker* I wouldn't furl any sails to let someone else get past me. But I'm going to stay as close behind her as I can." Mak looked a little farther over. "Keep an eye on that second sloop."

Jules nodded, seeing how low the sloop was riding and how frenzied the actions of the sloop's crew seemed. "He's probably got a hold full of smuggled goods."

"Too bad for him," Mak said. "If we have to shoulder him aside, we will."

As the *Sun Queen* swung to port, lining up with the exit from the harbor, Jules saw the first sloop nearing the exit well ahead of the other ships. *Star Seeker* was to starboard of the *Queen* and just forward of amidships as both ships slowly picked up speed. The second sloop was behind both as it left its pier and tried to get all sails set. "We've also got a fishing boat coming out," Jules warned Mak. "Aft port quarter. He shouldn't be any problem for us."

"Good." Mak kept his focus on ordering the yardarms set to gain the maximum advantage from the wind on this heading.

Jules went to the port side of the quarterdeck, gazing to the east, where the masts of the two war galleys were now visible from this height. The galleys had their sails fully unfurled, running nearly even with the westerly wind. Even so they couldn't match the speed of the sailing ships, but if they got close enough their oarsmen could put on a burst of speed and catch the ships before they got clear.

She watched the masts coming closer, trying to judge if the *Sun Queen* would make it.

Jules grabbed onto the rail as the *Sun Queen* yawed to starboard, then back to port, coming in directly behind the *Star Seeker*. "I think we'll be good," she said to the Captain, spinning to check on the second sloop.

Which was coming in recklessly, trying to get ahead of the *Sun Queen* even though it was too far back to have any chance of that. "Watch out for the second sloop just aft of the starboard beam! He's coming in!"

"He's trying to make us back down," Mak said, as angry as Jules had ever seen him.

"Are we going to evade?"

"We can't! We'd run aground on the side of the channel." Mak judged the movements of the two ships. "Bring her a point to starboard!" he ordered the helm. "We need to meet that sloop on a course that won't shove us too far to port."

The *Sun Queen* swung a bit to the right, closing more rapidly on the sloop angling in from starboard. "Back off, you fools!" Ang shouted across the rapidly narrowing gap between the two ships. But the sloop kept coming.

A moment later the *Sun Queen* shook with the force of a collision, the deck heeling over to port, as the sloop struck her just aft of amidships.

Jules felt the *Queen*'s movement altering and looked up to see that one of the sloop's yardarms had gotten entangled with the rigging on the *Sun Queen*, holding the two ships together.

The *Sun Queen* slewed to starboard, slowing, as the sloop dragged at her. Sailors were hurling curses and threats back and forth between the two ships, the voice of Ang rising above others on the *Queen*. "Cut it free! Cut it free!"

Sailors on the *Sun Queen* ran up into the rigging, their axes attacking the lines holding the sloop's yardarm and the yardarm itself, trying to chop it free. On the sloop, sailors were making confused attempts to push the two ships apart.

Jules wrenched her gaze back to the galleys, seeing that the hulls were coming into sight. The oars were out, swinging in the slow cadence of assist to the sail, giving the galleys a little more speed without wearing out the rowers. She could see the ballistae on each galley, one mounted before the mast and one behind, swinging to aim toward the exit from the harbor. Legionaries were gathered near the bows of the galleys. She knew they'd be armed with crossbows.

Put herself on those galleys. Imagine herself standing by the helm, seeing her prey trying to escape the harbor. Seeing the two ships entangled. Seeing the *Star Seeker* about to clear the harbor. Two apparently certain catches, and one getting away. "They're going to target the *Star Seeker* with their ballistae!" Jules called to Captain Mak.

The *Sun Queen* lurched as the sloop's yardarm came free, the two ships drifting apart, Captain Mak shouting orders to get the sails trimmed again and the ship moving toward the harbor exit once more. Jules heard the sailors on the sloop yelling curses at the *Queen*'s crew but felt no sympathy as the *Sun Queen* began drawing ahead again.

The *thunk*s of two ballistae shooting came across the water. Jules could see the dark specks of the rocks they'd launched arcing over the water and splashing just astern of the *Star Seeker* as she made it out of the harbor. Moments later the second galley shot, its projectiles also falling just short of the target.

"We're not going to make it, Captain," Jules said, her eyes on the approaching galleys. "They'll be on us right after we clear the harbor."

"What do we do, Jules? Give me ideas."

The *Sun Queen* continued to pick up speed again, but the galleys were approaching steadily from the east.

Jules saw the *Star Seeker* veer south instead of running to the west, cutting across the path of the galleys. "Sir, instead of running out of range the *Seeker* is maneuvering to keep them launching at her!"

"We owe them," Mak said.

More *thunk*s echoed across the water. Jules saw one projectile splash just short of the *Seeker*, the second flying above the ship, ripping a hole in the mainsail, and on to splash in the water on the other side.

How long would the galleys spend trying to catch the *Seeker*? "They're going to keep coming this way," Jules told Mak. "Using their ballistae to try to hit the *Star Seeker* as long as they can while getting close enough to clear our decks with crossbow fire and then board us."

"What do I do, Jules?" Mak asked her, sounding calm, but his eyes telling her how badly he needed an answer that would save the ship.

She watched the galleys, imagining herself on them, remembering the ways they trained and fought. "They're going to sprint toward us as we clear the harbor. Trying to get on us before we can get the wind behind us and run. The oars will start attack rhythm when the galleys are about a thousand lances from us."

"All right," Mak said. "Can we outrun them?"

"No. That's exactly what they're going to expect us to try to do, though." Jules tried to sense the wind and wave, judging the sea outside the harbor as they neared the exit. "We need to do what they don't expect, what they'll have the hardest time countering."

"What's that?"

"Attack."

Mak took a moment to reply. "Attack?"

"Yes, Captain! When I give the word, we should swing the *Sun Queen* about to the east and tack as straight toward the galleys as we can!"

More *thunk*s as more projectiles chased the *Star Seeker*. Judging the distance, Jules knew the galleys would give up on that target very soon. "The ballistae may target us on the next volleys. Captain, did you hear my advice? We need to charge at the galleys."

"I heard," Mak said. "Give me the word when to do it."

"Yes, sir." Despite the tension riding along her skin, Jules felt a moment of joy that Mak was accepting her advice, taking her word on what to do, trusting in her.

But that also meant the lives of everyone aboard were riding on her. Possibly the future freedom of the world, if she died rather than surrender. Jules tried not to think about that, tried to focus only on what the galleys were doing and the feel of the *Sun Queen* and the sweep of the wind across her deck and the feel of the water and... "Here they come."

Strange how she could say that so calmly.

The oars of the galleys swept up and around, huge, graceful wings striking the water on each side, moving as if every oar were tied to the same mind and the same muscles, the oars hitting the water smoothly, sweeping back and up in a flurry of white spray, coming forward again, the faint sound of the drum beating the rhythm coming across the water to where Jules stood. *Boom... boom... boom...* Fast, putting the galleys into a sprint, using up the strength of the rowers as rapidly as water draining through a hole in a bucket. The *Sun Queen* had cleared the harbor, but Mak held her on course, waiting for Jules to tell him when to turn.

"Stand by," Jules said, her mouth dry. The galleys were nearly bow on to the *Sun Queen*, only the forward ballistae on each able to launch at the sailing ship. Jules saw the ballistae launch a moment before she heard the *thunks*, seeing two dark projectiles flying at the *Sun Queen*, flying toward her. One went slightly wide, splashing alongside the *Queen*. The other passed overhead with at least one tearing sound that marked a sail pierced.

The galleys were only five hundred lances away, legionaries with crossbows visible in the bows, looking over the curved, raised bow armor that protected them and the rowers behind them. There were other ranks of armor running across above the rowers, widely enough spaced to let the oars move and angled back to protect against projectiles launched at the galleys during their attack run. "Now, sir! Bring her about! As close to directly at the galleys as you can!"

The *Sun Queen* yawed as the helm went over hard to port, deck tilting, the masts leaning out over the water to starboard, Mak yelling commands to the sailors to shift the yardarms in order to catch any available wind as the ship came about.

As the ship swung about, Jules pivoted to keep her eyes on the galleys. The captains of the two Imperial ships would've been expecting the *Sun Queen* to turn. They wouldn't have been surprised when the turn started. It would take them a few moments to realize that the *Queen* wasn't turning away as expected, but toward them. A few moments of surprise. A few more moments trying to adjust to a very different situation than expected. A few more moments realizing what they needed to do. As both galleys raced toward their meeting with the *Sun Queen*.

She'd been on galleys practicing for such attacks. Been worried by how the attack plans assumed the targeted ship would behave in exactly one way. Been chastised for suggesting that maybe a ship would try something else.

They trained assuming the enemy would do as they wanted. With the enemy doing something else, they wouldn't react quickly, having to think through what needed to be done. Maybe their thinking and their reactions would be slow enough to save the *Sun Queen*.

Jules saw orders being called on the Imperial warships as the galleys were just short of passing the *Sun Queen* on each side. Even though the sailing ship had slowed as she turned into the wind, the galleys had kept charging, the rowers following their orders, the sails still drawing wind, while the captains of the galleys tried to understand what had happened.

The oars stopped, suspended in the air, as the galleys swept past the *Sun Queen* on either side. Only the captain on the galley to starboard had the presence of mind to order the crossbows to shoot, but because of the speed with which the ships were passing the bolts all went wild.

"Bring us around," Jules told Mak. "Head south on a beam reach."

Mak gave the order, the *Sun Queen* swinging to starboard to head south, the wind in her sails strengthening. But she was still moving slowly compared to what the galleys could manage in a sprint.

Jules kept her eyes on the galleys. One was using both sets of oars to back the ship down, the oars digging into the water to slow the galley so it could turn and go back after the *Sun Queen*. The second galley's captain was smarter, using the oars on each side in the opposite direction to turn the galley as quickly as possible. But both galleys had been going in one direction at the best speed they could manage. Turning them, getting them going in another direction, meant overcoming all the force they'd put into the galleys earlier. And their rowers were tired now, feeling the strain after the sprint to attack the *Sun Queen*.

The after ballistae on both galleys belatedly launched their projectiles. Jules felt a shock through her feet and heard the crunch of broken wood as one of the stones hit the *Queen*'s hull.

"As long as they don't hit a mast, I think we've got a chance," Mak said from beside her. "Blazes, Jules. That was some fine work. You called it perfectly."

"Thank you, sir." She pointed to the galley that had turned most quickly. "That one's still going to give us trouble."

"How much longer can he push the rowers?" Mak asked.

"That's a good question." Jules watched the galley building up speed. The other galley had fallen well behind, the exhausted rowers unable to get it moving at a decent clip and the single sail no match for the three-masted *Sun Queen*. But the *Queen* had lost speed turning into the wind and needed time to build up her own pace again, putting her in danger from the faster galley. "He's going to come across our bow to force us to either turn or back down. If we ram him we might cripple that galley, but that'd leave us helpless against the other."

"What's your advice?" Mak asked.

"We need to turn. But we also need to ensure he can't maneuver swiftly enough to catch us right after our turn when we're at our slowest," Jules said. She reached down to touch the revolver. "Sir, I'm going to need to go into the aft rigging."

Thunk. Thunk. Rocks passed just ahead of the *Sun Queen*, sending up fountains as they splashed into the water beyond.

"What are you going to do, Jules?"

"Try to make sure they can't turn, sir." Jules turned a brief, tight smile his way. "I'll be all right."

"You promise that?" Mak demanded. "This isn't some insanely risky thing?"

"No, sir, it's not an insanely risky thing."

"All right," he said, though she could see that his gaze on her remained worried. "Do you need to call the turn again, or should I?"

"You call it, sir. We want to pass close alongside them."

"Got it." Jules went to the shrouds farthest aft, climbing them until she was three lances or so above the deck. She put one leg through the rigging to secure her position, then untied the revolver holster.

She drew the Mechanic weapon, ensuring that the cylinder was set to shoot a cartridge. Four left. This would cost at least one.

Turning her head, Jules saw the quicker galley coming on fast, the oars sweeping as the rowers put what must be most of their remaining strength into getting just ahead of the *Sun Queen*. They were off the *Queen*'s starboard bow, moving closer with every stroke of the oars, aiming to cross just ahead of the *Queen*'s path.

Balancing in the rigging, Jules gripped it with one hand, the other holding the revolver.

Mak was cutting it close, Jules thought, as the *Sun Queen* neared the point where she wouldn't be able to turn in time to avoid a collision with the galley.

She heard Mak shout the order to the helm, felt the *Queen* turn hard to starboard, her bowsprit coming around to point west. The galley swung, too, the oars on the side facing the ship raised to avoid striking the *Sun Queen*, passing close to port. Close enough for Jules to look down as the two ships passed going in opposite directions and see the weary rowers and the startled faces of the legionaries and officers looking up at her. Seeing the galley going past, the canted armor meant to protect the rowers during an attack offering no protection to a shot from the rear, hearing the order called to the rowers, the order she knew would come, for the oars to help turn the galley swiftly and catch the *Sun Queen* before she could accelerate away.

Jules aimed the revolver. She knew hitting an officer, a legionary, even the sailor at the helm, wouldn't stop that galley even if she had a chance of striking a target at that distance.

All she had to hit was one rower in the ranks on the side closest to the Queen, as the stern of the galley went past the stern of the Queen and the raised oars began to sweep down in unison.

The revolver bucked in her hand as it shot.

Jules was still wondering if she should shoot a second time

when a single oar faltered in its smooth sweep. Other oars hit it, rebounding to strike the oars around them, those oars hitting others in rapid succession. In a moment, the graceful swoop of the oars on the near side of the galley turned into a chaotic tangle, many dragging in the water and slowing the galley instead of helping to turn it.

Breathing in deeply, Jules put the revolver back into the holster and tied it securely in place before coming down from the rigging.

Thunk. Thunk.

The slower galley was launching at them, still a danger, but a rapidly receding one as the *Sun Queen* picked up speed running with the wind.

Jules rejoined Mak just as a projectile slammed into the water just aft of the *Queen*. "You see, sir? That wasn't so risky, was it?"

Instead of answering, Mak started laughing.

She heard cheering and looked around, startled to see sailors on deck looking at her as they shouted and clapped.

"Well done!" Liv yelled, coming onto the quarterdeck. "That's showing 'em how it's done, sister!"

Jules laughed, too, relieved, as the *Sun Queen* raced away from the frustrated Imperial galleys.

It was perhaps only syrup on the cake to see that the second sloop was also making its escape, the galleys having spent so much time and effort chasing the *Sun Queen* that the sloop had been able to slip past them.

She turned a broad grin on Mak, feeling embarrassed to see the look of pride on his face. "Where to, Captain?"

Mak nodded south. "Once we get well clear of the galleys, I want to head down near Caer Lyn. I have an idea, but we need a town where some artisans have already set up business to test it. Blazes, girl, it's a good thing for us you're a pirate and not an Imperial officer any more."

"I've got a good mentor," Jules said, smiling again.

* * *

"Captain, can I ask you something?"

"Certainly." Mak smiled at her hesitation. "Is this a personal thing?"

"Sort of." They were a day short of Caer Lyn, far enough from Kelsi's settlement in both time and distance for the sense of euphoria at their escape to have subsided. Jules stood at the starboard corner of the stern rail of the quarterdeck, speaking softly to avoid sharing their conversation with the sailor at the helm. The rush of the water alongside the ship served to keep her voice from carrying too far. "Sir, there's something that's been bothering me since Sandurin. Do I look like the sort of girl who'd knife a guy?"

He looked surprised at the question. "Jules, you have knifed a guy. More than one. How many did you knife in Sandurin?"

"Only two," Jules said. "And they both deserved it."

Mak nodded, spreading his hands. "There you are. I've never known you to knife a guy who didn't deserve it."

"But do I look like that? If a guy saw me, would he think right off, she looks like someone who'd knife me if she got mad at me?"

Mak shrugged. "I think that would depend on what mood you were in when he saw you."

"Sir, I'm serious. This really bothers me. One of those Mechanics I talked to said I was like that, and I don't want to think that's me." She gestured toward the horizon. "I've got this hope that despite everything I can still meet a guy and have a nice relationship. But that's not going to happen if when I walk toward some guy who I think is interesting he thinks I'm going to knife him."

"You are serious. I'm sorry." Mak shook his head. "If that's your concern, then, no, you do *not* look like that. Any man you decide to approach should feel lucky and probably will."

"So you've never thought that?"

He laughed. "If I thought that you were the sort to knife men without good reason, would I have let you on this ship at Jacksport?"

"Maybe," Jules said. "This is a pirate ship. You might have thought that was a valuable job skill."

"No, that's not what I was thinking. Do you want to know what I was really thinking?"

"Do I?"

He smiled, also watching the horizon. "I was thinking that you were a young, scatter-brained Imperial officer who'd come from some high-status family in Marandur and would probably crumble under the first pressure, just as you were running from some Imperial superior who'd made it clear his interest in you was not purely professional."

"You did not," Jules said.

"I did," Mak said. "And then you ran up to the bowsprit to help get us out of Jacksport and I realized there might be a bit more to you."

"You know, I'm almost wishing you'd thought I was going to knife some guy. Scatter-brained?"

He looked at her. "You'd just heard that prophecy. You were a little rattled."

"I hardly remember anything of that night," Jules admitted. "Except every word of that prophecy engraved into my memory. Stars above. Scatter-brained." She heard Mak laugh. He went down to his cabin, but she stayed at the rail a little longer, gazing to the west.

* * *

The *Sun Queen* rode the waves to the south of Caer Lyn, sails furled, a sea anchor out to keep her drift slow.

A second ship had joined them, a craft so small that it almost qualified as a boat. Long and lean, with canted masts carrying a lot of canvas, it had *smuggler* written all over the design. In this case, though, what was being smuggled were people, and they were being brought out of Caer Lyn to this safe rendezvous at sea where neither of the Great Guilds should be able to find them or learn what was being discussed.

Three people came aboard from the smuggler. One was Kyle, a crew member whose trade before joining the *Sun Queen* had been that of a pickpocket. That experience made him the best for jobs that involved not being noticed, such as delivering messages to two people Mak knew in Caer Lyn.

"Did anyone take note of you?" Mak asked as Kyle came aboard.

"No, Captain!" Kyle said with a grin. "You do owe me for the hike I had to make into town from where you dropped me off on the coast," he added.

A man and a woman followed Kyle aboard, nodding in greeting to Mak. "What's this about?" the woman asked. "Your sailor said you had urgent need of a skilled jeweler."

"I do have need of your expertise," Mak said. "And of yours as a smith," he added to the man. "There's something I'd like you to look at."

The smith frowned. "Look at something? That's all you want? It'd better be something special for costing me a day of work."

"It is," Mak said. "Let's go into my cabin and talk."

There were only the two chairs in the stern cabin, so the two guests were given them. The woman wore her hair in long braids held by silver wire, while the man had rough features and reddened, calloused hands. Jules stood alongside the small table along with Captain Mak, facing the two.

"Jules," Mak said.

She brought out the revolver, producing gasps of surprise from the two visitors. Working carefully, Jules opened the cylinder and removed the cartridges, both those that had been shot and those that still held their deadly purpose. She laid the revolver and the cartridges on the table.

"Can I touch it?" After Jules nodded, the man picked up the revolver hesitantly, running a thumb across the metal. "I never thought I'd get to lay a hand on one of these. Nice. Steel." He looked it over, shaking his head. "This is better than any steel I've ever seen."

"How is it better?" Jules asked.

"Steel is made by combining iron and charcoal, smelting and working and hardening it. Quench it in water or blood and reheat it and it becomes tempered, like the steel in your swords. Do it wrong and the steel becomes brittle rather than strong. It's an art." He shook his head as he looked at the revolver. "This... they've done something else. I'm sure the parts of this are cast, not beaten into shape. And the steel itself..."

"Can you make it?" Mak asked.

"Not even close." The man examined the revolver from all sides, touching and even tasting the metal with the tip of his tongue. "There's oil on this."

Jules nodded. "It needs it. On the inside. There's none on the outside."

"Yes. It's where the parts move. The oil helps them move." The man sighed, putting down the weapon. "Let me tell you a story. I was an apprentice to a metalsmith in Marandur. One of the best metalsmiths in the Empire. He was trying some different things, messing around with metal the way a smith likes doing. I didn't realize it at the time, but looking back he was probably being paid by the Empire to try to make something stronger and better than the steel we use."

He sighed again, heavily, in the way of someone recalling painful memories. "One day I was out sick. The next day I went by the workshop and found a smoking ruin. The people who worked nearby told me that the Mechanics had come, killed my teacher, taken all of the metal samples and fragments from his shop, and set fire to the place."

The smith spread his hands. "My old teacher wasn't even close to metal of this quality, but the Mechanics found out what he was doing. Everything that he'd learned was destroyed. Every once in a while I hear a similar story. Some smith tries going beyond what we can do, starts trying new things, and dies. We not only can't make metal like this, we can't start trying to understand how to make it."

"How are the Mechanics able to know when someone is trying?" Jules asked.

He smiled sadly at her. "We've been able to figure out that to make metal like this requires more heat and different metals or other additions. Furnaces better than what any smith uses. Metals we don't normally work with. That sort of thing is impossible to hide. The Mechanics know how to do it, so they can tell when we're trying to do it just by watching what we're building and what materials we're looking for. Copper, that's fine. We can get away with adding that to the steel because copper is used in brass. So a smith acquiring copper doesn't stand out to the Mechanics—but it's worth your life to mess with other metals. I haven't been in Caer Lyn all that long, and I know the Mechanics are already watching me." He picked up one of the empty cartridges. "This now. This is brass. I can make you brass."

The jeweler with the silver braids nodded, an empty cartridge in one of her hands and an unfired one in the other. "Mostly brass. This rounded thing on the end of the whole one seems to be lead. Soft metal. A crossbow bolt is much harder."

The smith nodded as well. "Yes. The bolts are hard so they'll go through armor. This lead projectile wouldn't do that as well as harder metal would. The softer metal would deform. Spread." He frowned. "When it hit someone, that would make the damage worse."

"It moves so fast it still goes through armor," Jules said. "At least when you're very close, and the only times I've used it was when I was pretty close to my target."

"Why's that? The close thing?"

"It aims sort of like a crossbow," Jules explained. "And when it shoots, it kicks back really hard. So it's easy to miss anything that isn't close. If I had all of the cartridges I could carry, I might risk missing so I could learn how to aim better with the revolver, but not when each cartridge is so rare and valuable."

The woman made a face. "Each of these is worth more than any piece of jewelry I've ever created, precious metals and gems included. Why are they called cartridges?"

"I have no idea. The Mechanics never explained it. They never explain anything," Jules added, her voice getting harsher.

That earned her a sympathetic nod from the jeweler. "Every once in a while a Mechanic will ask me… I mean, *tell* me, to make a custom piece for them. It's never pleasant, and I never know if I'll get paid what the piece is worth, or paid at all." She looked over the empty cartridge in her hand. "I could make a copy of this. I can get the brass, and it would be like making jewelry. But what's inside? The whole ones must have something inside between the lead and the brass, don't they?" She sniffed at an empty cartridge. "Agents. I can't tell which."

"Agents?"

"Things that change other things," the jeweler explained. "Agents are used for things like tanning and dying."

"There's a smell when I shoot the revolver. Pungent, I guess you'd call it." Jules pointed to the flat end of the cartridge. "There's something different there in the center, I think, where this thing called the hammer hits. I heard a Mechanic call it primer. When the hammer strikes that, there's the loud noise, the smell, a little smoke, and the lead on the end gets hurled out of the barrel very, very fast."

"Some sort of reaction among the agents that is set off by the blow of the hammer," the jeweler guessed. "Like the smith, I find myself unable to guess how it works. But the Mechanics know what is involved."

"Which means," Mak said, "as with the metal, they would know if someone was gathering what was needed."

"Not just that. The loud noise these things make, like thunder. Testing substances to do that would also produce such noise. Where could we do that and not have the Mechanics notice?"

"What it comes down to," the smith said, "is that having this… what is it, again?"

"They call it a revolver," Jules said.

"This revolver. Having it doesn't mean we can copy it. I could over time produce identical-looking pieces of metal, with the help of a jeweler to shape them, but they wouldn't be the same. Not the same strength or other properties."

"Would that matter?" Mak said.

The smith shrugged. "I could make you a sword out of pure gold that looked like your cutlass. Would you want to use it?"

"Pure gold? It'd be too heavy and too soft. It couldn't hold an edge. Useless."

"That's my point. If I make an exact copy of this out of the best steel I can create, and our friend here," he nodded to Jules, "put one of those cartridges in it, I have no idea what would happen. But I do know that when metal isn't strong enough for the task it's given, it fails. And that can be a very bad thing."

"Even if we could duplicate the weapon, we can't begin to know how these cartridges work," the jeweler said. "Have you noticed this?" she asked, peering down the barrel of the revolver. "Look here, on the inside. You have to get the light right to illuminate it. There are lines carved in there. I think they're carved. Maybe they're also cast in. See how they curve around the inside until they reach the end? It looks somewhat like the curves inside a sea shell."

"Why would they put decoration like that on the inside?" Captain Mak asked.

"I have no idea. It must serve some purpose rather than being a decoration."

"Everything about this is much more complicated than it appears," Mak said, unhappy, "and we don't seem to be able to understand any of it. So much for my idea of making a lot more of these."

"The Mechanics are clever," the jeweler said. "They limit what we have and what we know so we *can't* make more of these."

"But we could," Jules said. "If we knew those things. It doesn't require some special skill we lack."

"I think that's true."

"What about how the Mechanics do their tests?" the smith said. "Every child takes those tests in school. And they find some who they take to train. There must be some special talent."

"They're people," Jules insisted. "Just like us."

"Sure," the smith said. "People just like us who can make things we can't. And who, if they catch us trying to duplicate their work, will kill us."

* * *

The smuggler had taken the artisans back to Caer Lyn, its sails dipping below the horizon, as the *Sun Queen* started south again. But that journey had barely begun when one of the metal Mechanic ships came into view.

The Mechanic ship circled the *Sun Queen* as if the sailing ship were standing still, before matching speed and coming close on the *Queen*'s port side. Mak had sent Jules below deck when the Mechanic ship approached, but as it hung menacingly nearby he called her up on deck again.

Some Mechanics held objects to their eyes, looking at Jules as she stood by the rail, the revolver in its holster on her hip. Those must be the far-seers Mak had spoken of. She stood, waiting, until one of the Mechanics hefted something and threw it across the gap between the ships. It landed with a thud, turning out to be a dispatch case tied to a strangely-shaped piece of metal with a crack running partway through it.

"Something broke, so they used it as a weight," Ang speculated as he brought the dispatch case to Mak.

He opened it, then passed the note inside to Jules. "It's addressed to you."

"Some Mechanics finally remembered my name?" She looked at it. "They want me to meet someone in Jacksport. Three days from now. There's instructions for the place I'm supposed to go in town. That's strange—why not their ship or near that Mechanics Guild Hall I hear they're laying out the foundation for?"

Turning, Jules waved to the Mechanics, indicating her receipt of the message.

The Mechanics didn't bother waving back. They went inside the ship, and soon afterwards it accelerated more quickly than the *Sun Queen* could have, racing away to the west.

"They must know how hazardous Jacksport is for you," Mak said.

"It wasn't an invitation," Jules said. "It's an order. They don't care how hazardous it is for me."

"But they did at one time," he said. "Now they're risking you in a town where we know Mages are present."

"Sir, what else can I do?"

"Not go," Mak said.

"But if I do that, if I cut and run without knowing what they intend, I won't know what they're planning." Jules tapped the revolver at her hip. "And hopefully they'll give me some more cartridges for this. I only have three left."

"I still don't like it," Mak said. "Jules, what's our plan if it all goes to blazes?"

"Run?" Jules said. "What else could we do?"

Mak hesitated, looking out to sea. "The *Storm Queen* should be around here somewhere. The last I heard, Captain Lars was going to try to operate near the Sharr Isles for a while. We need to meet up with that sloop of war."

"Why?"

"Because they owe you. And we need them. If you have to run, you won't be able to come back here. The Mechanics won't let us out of the harbor. You need another ship."

"But the *Storm Queen* can't outrun the Mechanic ships," Jules objected. "She'd get caught before she could get away, too."

"Not if she's not in the harbor. Come on." Jules followed Mak to his cabin, where he unfurled a chart. "Look here. See this small bay? It's a little way north and east of Jacksport on the island, only a few thousand lances. If you have to run, the Mechanics—or the Mages— will expect you to head for the harbor. But if we have the *Storm Queen* waiting over in this small bay, you can turn inland instead. Nobody will expect that. Head for the bay, and the *Storm Queen* can pick you up. Even if the water in the bay is shallow, the *Storm Queen* has a smaller draft and can send in a boat."

Jules looked at the chart. "It doesn't look like too rough a journey from Jacksport to that bay. And it's not too far. There aren't any cliffs behind Jacksport, are there? Higher ground but no cliffs. So it won't be like that last time when I was stuck in a strip of land near the beach. I can move inland and be hidden by the trees. Even if someone is chasing me, I should be able to stay ahead of them until I reach that bay."

"All we have to do is find the *Storm Queen*," Mak said. "And hope we won't need her services."

Jules heard the foreboding in Mak's voice and knew he didn't believe his own hopes. "I'll be all right."

* * *

Three days later, she was back in Jacksport. They had successfully rendezvoused with the *Storm Queen*, Captain Lars agreeing to wait in the small bay to the northeast.

She hadn't walked this street since the night the prophecy was made. Jules had on a long, light coat that went down to her knees, concealing the revolver at her hip. She wore a broad-brimmed hat against the sun, pulled down low to hide her face. The collar of the coat also helped conceal her, hopefully enough—along with a different braiding of her hair—to render her hard to recognize.

There weren't any Imperial ships in port, for which Jules was grateful. At least she wouldn't have to worry too much about running into Imperial soldiers or sailors, though she had to assume there were spies in Imperial pay everywhere. With any luck she wouldn't be recognized by them, either.

A metal Mechanic ship was tied up, though, its presence dominating the waterfront. Jules studied it as well as she could without being noticed. Outwardly, it looked identical to the other Mechanic warships she'd seen. Was that done to make it hard for commons to

304 ✧ *Pirate of the Prophecy*

track what the Mechanics were doing? There were still those who argued over whether the Mechanics had five of the metal ships, or only three. Most agreed on four, but keeping track of them was difficult. This might be the ship she'd been taken to, or a totally different one.

Jacksport's waterfront was crowded with men and women, as well as children, attending to morning business. In the light of day it felt respectable. The population of a solid and fast-growing community. It was only by looking beneath that outer appearance at the shuttered bars and taverns waiting for their night trade that the illusion of respectability was shattered.

So many people on the streets offered her good cover. She moved among them to keep from being spotted. Her greatest fear, encountering a Mage, didn't materialize. Jules caught an occasional glimpse of Mage robes on the street, altering her path to avoid coming close to them. That didn't attract any special notice. Every common person did that around Mages. And the Mages gave no sign that they knew she was anything other than an average common.

She passed a place where a building must have once stood, only charred wood remaining, the wreckage old enough that it must have burnt down some time ago, but no sign that any clearing of it had ever taken place. Why had it been left like this in the center of a street facing the harbor? The building had probably held a tavern like the other buildings all along this stretch, and it occupied a valuable spot where one could be rebuilt. Yet everyone else on the street was carefully avoiding even looking toward it. As if they were afraid to be seen taking interest in that place?

A tavern. Burnt down a while back. Left untouched.

Jules tried to keep her breathing steady and her expression calm as she realized what must have stood there. The tavern where she'd come face to face with the Mage and the prophecy had been spoken. Someone, probably the Mages, had set the tavern afire. Someone, maybe one of the Great Guilds, maybe both, had made it clear that nothing else had better be built there for common people to gather at and talk about what had happened on that spot. That no one should mark the place in any way, or even appear to take note of it.

If she hadn't run as quickly as she had, her charred bones would probably be resting under that pile of burned wreckage.

Jules walked on, trying to appear not to have noticed the ruin.

The instructions for the meeting took Jules a little farther down the street, down a side path, and into an open area perhaps three lances long by two lances wide behind a bar that was just opening for the lunch trade. Scattered tables and chairs spoke of outdoor seating for busy nights when weather permitted. Jules walked to the center of the area, looking around, feeling exposed. Where were the Mechanics she was supposed to meet?

The door in the back of the bar opened. Jules saw two figures in Mechanic jackets and headed that way as they gestured to her.

They stood back as she walked into the back room, which had no lights. With the windows covered, the room darkened as the door closed. But Jules heard a metallic click and a bright, steady light appeared from a squat tube held by one of the Mechanics. The male Mechanic waited as the female Mechanic put the tube on a small, four-legged table in the center of the room, the light shining up to the ceiling to illuminate the room. In that light, Jules saw that aside from the door in the back wall and the two covered windows, the only other exit from the room was a door in the front wall facing the interior of the bar.

Jules looked at them, initially pleased to see that the man was Mechanic Hal, but then surprised with renewed worry to see that the woman was Mechanic Gin, not the Mechanic Gayl who'd been with Hal in Sandurin. And Gin bore no trace of welcome in her eyes. If she had ever felt any good will toward Jules, it had vanished. "Good morning, Sir Mechanic," Jules said. "Lady Mechanic."

He nodded in reply. Gin just looked at her.

This didn't feel good. Tension seemed to be a fourth presence in this room. Both Mechanics had revolvers in holsters.

Hal finally moved again, dropping eight cartridges on the table.

Jules picked them up and placed them in a pocket of her trousers, wondering why Mechanics always avoided handing her the cartridges directly, as if reluctant to touch her.

"Eight?" Jules asked.

"That's doesn't mean the Guild is happy," Mechanic Hal said. "That's very likely the last you'll see of ammunition."

"Have I failed in what the Guild wanted me to do, Sir Mechanic?"

Hal shook his head. "The problem is the opposite one. You've been too good at it. The Emperor is so angry, the Guild is worried he might try to get away with directly defying us. And the Mages have made it clear they'll regard further killings of their own by you as an attack by the Mechanics Guild. Officially, you stole that revolver, but that story has been harder to make stick as you don't run out of ammunition for it. So, no more after today."

"That's why we're meeting you like this," Mechanic Gin said, her voice as hard as her expression. "No more public meetings. No more declarations on your part that the Mechanics Guild is some sort of supporter of your actions."

Jules looked from Gin to Hal. "Do you want me to stop doing anything?"

The pause that answered her didn't feel good at all.

Hal finally answered. "I'm going to be honest with you… Jules, right? Yes. The Guild is reconsidering everything. Including whether they want you running around freely."

"You are not authorized to tell her that!" Gin said angrily.

"She deserves to know," Hal insisted. "She's been doing the Guild's bidding."

" 'Deserves'? She's a common! Do you think a horse deserves to know where it's taking you when you go for a ride?" Gin fixed her gaze on Jules again. "Since we're being honest, the Guild's not happy with this whole prophecy thing. The Mages are still acting as if they believe every word of it, which gives it validity in the eyes of the commons. The commons are paying a lot of attention to what you do, and every petty triumph by the great pirate is making them believe in this garbage more than they did before. Which is making problems for us. *You're* making problems for us. Shutting down the whole thing might have some short-term costs, but in the long run it'll keep the commons compliant."

Jules stood silently, not trusting herself to speak.

In terms of her own safety, *shutting the whole thing down* sounded very, very bad. It looked very much as if this game was heading for a final result.

"Did you get that?" Mechanic Hal asked her.

"Why are you asking her that?" Mechanic Gin demanded. "Haven't you figured her out yet? She plays dumb, like some typical common without a clue about anything. But she's smarter than that! Look what's she's gotten away with. She's dangerous."

"I admit she's not stupid," Hal began.

"Look how closely she's listening to us while pretending to be a nice, obedient common!" Gin shook her head at Jules, one hand straying toward her own revolver. "We should just get rid of her now. No more risks."

"Gin, we're not authorized to do that! The Guild hasn't made a final decision yet."

"Oh, now you're worried about whether or not something is authorized." Mechanic Gin glared at Jules. "You're a liability. At one time, the Guild thought you were an asset. But now you're just stirring up the commons."

Jules had been listening, trying to stay calm and quiet, but at those words something finally snapped inside her. "How can you be so stupid?" she asked.

The two Mechanics stared at her in disbelief. "What did you say?" Gin demanded.

"You heard me," Jules said. "What, didn't you understand? I asked why you were so stupid. You claim to be so much smarter than us, but you don't have any idea who commons are. You think that without someone stirring them up, the commons would be happy and obedient little slaves for you. Listen up! We hate you. If every Mechanic died a horrible death tomorrow the celebrations would rock the entire world. And if we could kill every Mechanic tomorrow we would.

"We hate the Mages, too. But they're monsters. Made inhuman by whatever makes them Mages. We know that, so we understand when they act like monsters. But you! We can see that Mechanics are men and women like we are, yet you treat us like livestock. Wake up. The commons will never be quiet. We will never accept being slaves to the Great Guilds."

Silence fell as Jules stopped talking. Both Mechanics seemed too stunned by her words to speak.

Mechanic Gin recovered first, outrage running through her voice like a deadly wind off the waste. "That mouth of yours is going to get you killed, common. Orders or not, one more disrespectful word, and you're dead."

Jules smiled. "I know my mouth will get me killed someday. I also know that before I die I'm going to take down a lot of my enemies with me."

The threat hung in the air between her and the Mechanics for another moment.

"That's it! She's dead!" Mechanic Gin said, reaching for her revolver.

CHAPTER FIFTEEN

J ules kicked the underside of the table between them, knocking it up and toward the two Mechanics. The Mechanic light on the table flew off, hit the wall, and went out, plunging the room into darkness.

She'd already decided not to try shooting the Mechanics. Even if she succeeded in hitting both of them—and the odds would've been very much against her—Jules didn't want to shoot Mechanic Hal. He was a Mechanic, he was arrogant, but she did owe her life to him for helping her in Sandurin.

If she wasn't going to fight, she had to flee. Knowing she had only moments to move before the Mechanics recovered and shot her, Jules ran not toward the door she'd entered by, knowing the Mechanics would expect that, but toward the door opening into the front of the bar. She hit that door, pressing down on the latch and shoving it open.

Light streamed in through it. A Mechanic weapon boomed in the room behind her, and a hole appeared in the door not far in front of Jules' face.

She made it through and dashed between tables of men and women staring toward the noise of the shot. Not wasting a moment looking back, Jules darted out the front door.

And found herself facing a Mage who seemed as unprepared for that meeting as she was.

Jules rammed her elbow into the Mage's chest, knocking the Mage back to trip and fall. Having barely paused, Jules ran into the street and sprinted along it, her long coat flapping about her legs.

The sound of a Mechanic revolver crashed behind her, closely followed by two more shots. Jules heard something snap past her left ear.

But she barely noticed, seeing that as the people on the street scattered for cover they revealed others standing at the end of the street. Mages, all looking her way.

I am never coming back to Jacksport. Assuming I survive this visit.

Jules dodged to her left, into an alley between buildings, wondering in a frantic moment if it might be the same alley she'd fled through the night the prophecy was spoken. Dashing across the next street, she took another alley, then wove between buildings, heading inland.

Jacksport was still a long and lean city, sprawled along the harbor front, but not extending far inland. Jules cleared the last substantial building, finding herself in cleared fields of crops facing the wall of the forest a few hundred lances ahead.

She ran toward the trees, knowing how good a target she made out in the open like this.

A Mechanic weapon boomed, sounding different from the revolvers. Then another. Jules didn't look back until she reached the trees and paused to catch her breath.

At the edge of the town several Mechanics stood, two carrying the long weapons that one Senior Mechanic had called rifles.

Closer, Mages were coming out of the alleys leading to the cleared fields. They moved fast, long knives gleaming in their hands.

Jules turned and ran again, weaving among the tree trunks, trying to set a pace that she could maintain.

On the chart, this hadn't looked hard. Just a section of island. Running through the woods, Jules found herself facing a series of ridges that forced her to slide down one side and scramble up the other, fighting her way through patches of undergrowth that in some cases had wicked thorns on the stems. Her feet slipped on dead leaves. Fallen branches threatened to trip her up. She leaped them when possible, trying to avoid the spikes of broken segments sticking up into the air as if eager to impale a clumsy passerby. Compared to this, the land in front of the cliffs to the west of the harbor was ideal hiking territory.

Sweat streamed down her face as Jules ran, her breath coming in great gasps.

How far had she come? Straight inland so far, she thought. Or mostly straight, she corrected herself, using glimpses of the sun between the tree tops to orient her path.

Something growled far behind her. Something *big*. Jules had never heard anything like it. She discovered she could run a little faster.

It must be time to turn toward the coast, toward the bay where help was supposed to be waiting. Jules pulled off her coat, dropping it to the ground where it would hopefully mislead her pursuers, then ran to her right, trying to put as much distance as she could between her former path and her current route.

Struggling up another ridge, onto a cleared section where a tree had fallen, Jules paused to look back, her chest heaving with exertion.

Something was moving in the trees back there, down in a gap between two ridges, something tall enough to brush the limbs near the top of the trees. Jules caught glimpses of something shiny moving through the trunks, and saw one tree topple as if a giant had shoved it over.

Whatever it was, it seemed to be chasing her. And it didn't seem like a good idea to let it catch up.

She ran again, down the slope, relieved to see that she seemed to have topped off her flight. From here it was downhill, though that involved more than one more ridge whose side had to be climbed on the way down toward the water that beckoned through the trees.

A scream shattered the air of the forest, sending birds frantically flying in all directions. She looked back, leaning with one hand on a tree trunk as she gasped for air. The scream seemed to have come from where she'd left her coat.

What the blazes had made that scream?

Jules staggered down the slope toward the beach, knowing she was slowing down, unable to keep moving faster because of her exhaustion.

She heard something crashing through the trees behind her. Was it her imagination that the ground was shaking from the impacts of something very heavy running after her?

A branch fell before Jules, telling her it wasn't entirely her imagination. The ground really was shaking.

She ran out of the trees and onto the beach, almost sobbing with relief as she saw a rowboat resting a little way down the beach with two sailors standing by it. Out in the small bay, the sloop of war *Storm Queen* rested at anchor. At the moment, with some unseen terror at her heels, the *Storm Queen* looked like the most beautiful ship that had ever been built.

Despite the burning muscles in her legs and the rawness of her throat as she breathed in deep gasps, Jules managed to break into a run again. She gestured frantically with her arms toward the sailors with the rowboat, trying to get them to understand that they needed to go quickly.

The sailors seemed to get the hint, pulling the boat out into the water.

Another inhuman scream sounded behind her as a nightmare burst out of the trees.

Jules spared only one glance back, but that was enough to sear into her mind the image of the monster chasing her. At least three times her height, it stood on two massive hind legs tipped with claws. An equally massive tail stood out behind, balancing the creature as it ran. The creature's arms ended in hands that looked disturbingly human but were tipped with long claws. The head was a mass of sharp-edged bone interrupted by a huge mouth lined with teeth like daggers. The whole beast was covered in scales that shimmered in the light and looked very much like the scaled armor worn by some of the Imperial cavalry.

The monster's dark eyes searched the beach, alighting on Jules.

It screamed again, sounding like an eagle's cry made huge and terrifying, and began running after her.

Jules put on a burst of speed she didn't think she was capable of.

The sailors with the rowboat had seen the monster, too, and were pushing the boat into deeper water, clambering in and setting the oars into the locks with frantic haste. Out on the water, sailors had burst into motion on the *Storm Queen*, bringing up the anchor and racing up the rigging to unfurl the sails.

Not knowing how far the beast was behind her, Jules didn't pause when she got close to the rowboat, splashing out into the water with steps as broad as she could take before leaping the final distance and grabbing onto the stern of the boat as her body flopped onto the water. The sailors were already rowing, staring terrified at the monster behind Jules.

Jules pulled herself up and into the stern of the rowboat as it fled, her breath still coming in rapid, fear-driven bursts. She looked back, seeing the monster far too close. It began to run into the water after the boat, the resistance of the water slowing down its massive legs. But even though the panicked sailors were rowing so hard that the boat was practically leaping from the water on each pull, the monster was still getting closer.

Crouching in the stern of the rowboat, holding on as the boat rocked across the water, Jules knew that the Mechanic revolver wouldn't help her against this thing.

A thrown line with a weight on the end thumped into the rowboat. One of the rowers let off long enough to hastily tie off the line at the bow. The other was tied to the *Storm Queen*, which hauled the rowboat with her as the sloop slowly picked up speed. Sailors on the deck of the ship began pulling in the line, aiding the boat in getting closer to the ship and adding a little speed to its progress.

A huge hand tipped with claws grabbed the stern of the rowboat as the monster caught up. The two sailors from the *Storm Queen* bolted forward, hand-over-handing along the remaining length of line up to the ship.

Afraid that she'd be seized by those claws if she turned her back, Jules grabbed one of the oars out of its lock and thrust the broad blade like a spear at the dagger-lined maw lunging toward her.

The creature bit down on the oar, the impact knocking Jules back onto her butt in the bow of the rowboat. Splinters flew, leaving Jules holding only the shaft and handle of the oar.

She swung it high and brought it down on the head of the monster with all her strength.

The impact jarred her hands so badly that Jules dropped the broken oar. The monster seemed only momentarily dazed though, lunging at her again.

It went underwater.

Jules realized that the depth had increased enough that the creature couldn't keep its head above water. By now the rowboat had been hauled up right next to the ship. Terrified at the idea of the colossal beast swimming underneath her, Jules jumped off the bow toward the side of the *Storm Queen*, where hands caught hers and helped her over the side and onto the deck.

Jules got to her feet, barely able to move because of her exhaustion, staring back where the monster had last been.

It reappeared near where she'd last seen it, thrashing at the water as it screamed again, its eyes still fixed on the *Storm Queen*. Still fixed on Jules. It wasn't just hunting random prey. It had been hunting her.

"It can't swim," Captain Lars said.

Jules realized that he was standing beside her. "What is it?" she gasped between breaths, swaying on her feet.

"A Mage dragon. One of their monsters."

"That's a dragon?"

"It fits what I was told," Lars said. He was doing a good job of pretending to be unruffled so his crew wouldn't panic, but the tremors in his voice and his hands gave away his fear to Jules. "Not a lot of people survive their encounters with dragons to offer up descriptions. I've heard the size varies. How big they are, I mean. I have no idea why. Maybe it depends on how powerful the Mage is."

Jules sagged, only staying up thanks to the railing she was leaning on. "I nearly didn't survive my encounter with this one. I owe you."

"We're not clear yet." Lars pointed ahead. "See that cloud on the horizon?"

Jules looked. "That's from one of the Mechanic ships."

"And there's another," Lars said, pointing off to starboard.

"That second one is probably the Mechanic ship that was in Jacksport," Jules gasped, still short of breath. "Two of them? They sent two of those things after me?"

"You are, um, important, I understand," Lars said.

"Yay, me." Jules looked around the horizon. "You can't outrun them, but you can take the northwest channel between the islands. The *Storm Queen* has a shallow enough draft to get through there, but I hear those Mechanic ships draw a lot more water."

"One of them might be able to catch us at the other end," Lars said. "It depends how much they want to risk running aground."

"Yeah. At the moment, I don't think it's a good idea to test how badly they want me." Jules squinted to the north. "On your way to the channel, swing close by the north island. I'll drop off when they can't see me and swim ashore. That way they won't find anything on you if they catch you. I've got a mirror so I can signal the *Sun Queen* when she comes looking for me."

Lars rubbed his chin as he thought. "There are fresh springs on the north island. You should be all right for a little while. We'll do that." He was doing a very good job of not letting his relief show at being able to get Jules off of his ship.

"Can I borrow a cutlass?" Jules asked, her breathing finally moderating a little. Her legs still felt incredibly weak and wobbly.

"I think we can do that, too. What the blazes happened back there?"

"A lot of Mechanics and Mages were trying to kill me. And that dragon was trying to kill me, too. I thought that was kind of obvious."

"Was there any particular reason, or just general hostility toward a young pirate of some renown?" Lars asked.

Jules grinned for a moment at the memory, despite her lingering fear as she saw the dragon pacing on the beach far behind them. "I told some Mechanics they were stupid."

"To their faces?"

"Yeah."

"Oh, I wish I'd been there."

"Me, too," Jules said. "I would have tripped you while that dragon was chasing us."

Lars laughed, but Jules honestly didn't know if she was joking.

* * *

About a half hour later, having eaten and drunk some water, settled a cutlass at her waist, and been given a waterproof pack of hardtack, Jules eased over the side of the *Storm Queen* as the ship coasted close past the northernmost of the Sharr Isles. Jules slipped into the water with as little splash and sound as possible, her clothes and boots in an oilskin bag to keep them dry. The Mechanics might be using their far-seers to watch the *Storm Queen*, and who knew how far the far-seers could see? And no one really knew everything that Mages were capable of.

Jules swam ashore, grateful that the *Storm Queen* had been able to come close to shore so the swim was a very short one before her feet found the bottom. Wading through the shallows, she scuttled across the beach and into the trees.

Relatively small, with the roughest interior terrain and the only one of the Isles without a decent natural harbor, the north island had yet to attract any settlers. Maybe it never would.

It didn't take long for the breeze to dry her enough to get dressed. Jules made her way inland, traveling slowly both because of the rough landscape and because she was still worn out from her frantic dash to escape Jacksport. Climbing a slope facing south, she found an open ledge that provided a wide view of the waters, including the hills rising on the island where Jacksport was located.

She wondered if the dragon was still pacing on that beach.

How long would the dragon be there, waiting for her to come back?

It would have a long wait. She was never going back to that island.

With finally some time to think, Jules settled back against the slope behind her, chewing on some hardtack.

She wished the other Mechanic hadn't been Hal. Arrogant as he was, he had appeared open to thinking of commons as worthy of being treated decently. But even Hal had seemed to embrace the idea that Mechanic Gin had openly stated, that commons like Jules were the equivalent of horses. Useful, worth grooming sometimes, but ultimately a form of life meant to serve others. Hal had been just as shocked as Gin, just as outraged, over Jules' words.

The Mechanics wouldn't let up on her now. They wouldn't let her escape again. She'd have to avoid getting caught.

The Mages must be furious that she'd gotten away, too. If Mages could be furious.

The Emperor was mad enough to worry even the Mechanics Guild. If he got his hands on Jules now, she figured she'd probably end up chained to a bed somewhere in Marandur, the Emperor visiting once a year or so to get her pregnant again. She wondered how many such pregnancies she'd survive. And if having the children didn't kill her, once the Emperor had several heirs by Jules there wouldn't be any reason to keep her alive any longer. She would have fulfilled her purpose. Blazes, the Emperor would want her dead to ensure no other man had children with her.

Maybe he'd throw her to the Mages then. That would probably be a kinder and quicker death than anything else the Imperials or the Mechanics might do.

She tried to think things through as Mak would want her to do. The old plan, to be allied with the Mechanics Guild while actually working against it, was out the window. Once again it was her being chased by the Mages and the Imperials, only this time the Mechanics wanted her head as well. *Hazardous cargo.* The old words of Captain Erin applied once more. But had Jules' status changed as well? Certainly the crew of the *Sun Queen* respected her, saw her as solidly one of their own.

She was no longer just the young woman of the prophecy. A lot of people had heard of her acts of piracy. Her name meant something. Her reputation meant something. Jules didn't even think of herself the same way any longer. While the burden of knowing she'd give birth to a line that would lead to that distant daughter hadn't diminished, she'd taken to heart Mak's advice to build her own life apart from that. Mak hadn't always seemed thrilled by the risks she'd run, but he seemed happy with who she was.

She'd acquired a lot of friends among the commons. And there were more places to hide as new settlements went up and more people escaped from the Emperor's rule. If worse came to worse, she could always follow that pass west from Kelsi's settlement.

That would put her a long way from the sea, though. Jules looked out on the water, wondering if she could ever be happy if the sea wasn't there in sight, wasn't under the hull of a ship she was riding. She understood old Ferd, courting death when the prospect of leaving the sea grew too near to him. It'd be a sort of death, wouldn't it, to never ride the waves again?

She saw one of the Mechanic ships come through the waters between the north island and the southern island that held Jacksport. The Mechanic vessel moved slowly, cruising past the southern island, plainly searching its shores.

Would the Mechanics kill the dragon with that giant weapon on the front of their ship?

But if the dragon was still there the Mechanics ignored it, sailing on past back toward Jacksport, the smoke coming out the tubes or chimneys on top of the ship tinted by the setting sun just as if it were clouds.

The sun set, night coming on. Jules sat looking out across the night-darkened waters, hoping that the *Sun Queen* and all on her were all right.

She finally fell asleep, worn out by the day's labors.

The morning sun and a persistent insect combined to wake her. Jules grimaced, smacking her mouth and taking a drink of water to try to clear a bad taste. Maybe she'd inhaled another bug. Among other things, land had too many insects. The sea kept such creatures away where they couldn't pester people.

Her worries grew as the sun rose, lighting up the islands Jules could see. Where was the *Sun Queen*? Had the Mechanics seized her? Sunk her? What had happened to Mak and the others?

She caught occasional flashes of light from the island that held Jacksport. Sun reflecting off of metal or glass. Search parties? Were the Mechanics still looking for her there?

The sun was nearing noon when Jules perked up at the sight of masts coming around the island. She stood up, balancing on the slope, gazing anxiously as the masts grew higher, sails appearing under them, then the hull.

The three-master looked a lot like the *Sun Queen*. Was it?

The ship coasted past the small bay, clearly searching for someone ashore.

Deciding that she had to risk it, Jules pulled out her mirror and flashed reflected sunlight toward the ship.

It took a while for someone on the ship to notice, since they were all apparently looking toward the southern island. But eventually the ship tacked to the north and came toward her.

Jules waited as it got closer, deciding that if this wasn't the *Sun Queen* it was a ship that might as well have been her twin. She started down the slope toward the beach.

By the time she got there, the longboat was only a short distance off. Jules saw Ang waving to her and finally relaxed.

* * *

"Sorry it took us a while to get here," Mak said as Jules climbed up on deck. "The Mechanics warned us that if we left port yesterday they'd sink us. But this morning their ship came back and sent a lot of Mechanics ashore, so we felt it was safe to sneak out."

"Search parties," Jules said. "They think I'm still on that island."

"They probably let us go this morning in hopes that you'd go out onto a beach to meet us so they could find you," Mak said.

"Then they might have seen you pick me up," Jules said. "We need to get out of here. You do, anyway. Sir, I can't stay on this ship. You know that. The next time a Mechanic ship catches us they'll just sink the *Queen* right off. Get me somewhere I can hop another ship."

Mak turned to yell at the crew as they hoisted the longboat back aboard. "Jeri says she should leave the ship so the rest of us would be safer. What say you?"

They yelled back, booing the idea.

Jules stared at the others in the crew, startled. "Are you out of your minds? I'll be the death of you!"

Laughter.

"Captain—"

"Get us headed north, Ang!" Mak called. "Come and talk to me," he told Jules.

Inside the stern cabin, Jules stayed stubbornly standing, her arms crossed as she glared at Mak. "I won't have you or anyone else deciding my destiny, sir. Especially not with the lives of everyone on this ship now in great peril, sir."

"Angry again, are we?" Mak asked her as he sat down.

"No, sir."

"Let me tell you what we're planning. The crew has already voted on this."

"I didn't get a vote, sir!"

"You will. Let me explain." Mak rolled out part of the big map/chart. "While we were twiddling our thumbs in Jacksport, I was contacted by an old friend. You've heard of Dor and his settlement a ways out west on the south coast?"

"I've heard he found a good place. That would be the place you were once going to send me whether I liked it or not, sir?" Jules said.

"That place, yes." Mak tapped a spot about halfway along the southern coast of the Sea of Bakre between the Empire and the vaguely portrayed western boundaries of the sea. "It's about here. There are people, and cargo, in Caer Lyn that need to get to Dor. They'd pay us well to take that voyage, and it would also get us well away from any searchers for weeks. By the time we returned to these parts the fracas should have died down."

Jules glared at the chart. "In Caer Lyn? And how do we get passengers and cargo loaded at Caer Lyn without half of the Mechanics

Guild and a hundred Mages swarming aboard to kill everyone? Even if there aren't any Imperial warships present? Sir?"

"The plan is to loop around the Sharr Isles, coming in again from the north and east," Mak said, tracing the path with a fingertip, "and then pull into Caer Lyn near dark. We'd anchor well out from any of the piers, the passengers and cargo would come out in boats to be transferred to us, and we'd leave on the dawn tide."

She frowned, her eyes on the chart, thinking. "It's still not exactly safe, sir."

Mak leaned back in his chair, his gaze on her. "Jules, the crew voted to do it."

"I vote against it, sir."

"Then that's one vote against, all others in favor." He gestured to the other chair. "Why don't you sit down, Jules?"

"Because this ship cannot be my home anymore, sir! You and I both know that!"

"Where would be safer for you?" Mak asked.

Jules hesitated.

"There isn't anywhere, is there? Nowhere we know of, that is," he said. "Jules, I want to show you something." Mak unrolled more of the map to the west, spreading it out to show the western shores of the sea. "I want to show you places where no one else has gone."

Startled, Jules leaned forward and ran her fingers across that portion of the map. It showed, like every map of the west, the coastline from the north side of the Sea of Bakre curving down to meet the southern coast, enclosing the Sea in a vast prison of land. The farther west the map went, the vaguer the details, but the stretch where the sea ended in the far west was depicted as a welter of dangerous reefs finally ending on an inhospitable coast. The land beyond that was marked with the death symbol and notes about a lack of water and animals, a desert waste more severe than that facing the southern reaches of the Empire in the east. "Why go there? It looks like a death trap."

"Someone went there." Mak pointed to one marked object in the west, well inland. "Cap Astra. Someone named that."

"What does Cap mean?" Jules asked.

"That's a good question. Maybe it's someone's name." Mak gazed at the chart, his expression wistful. "I've always wanted to visit there."

"What? Visit a place in the middle of a wasteland beyond a maze of dangerous reefs?"

Mak nodded, his hand moving on the map. "Do you ever feel penned in, Jules? Like the whole world is a cage made for us? Look at it. The Empire to the east, controlling all the fertile land on that side of the sea, and ending in the coastline to the great Umbari Ocean. Maybe the Western Continent is somewhere beyond that. Maybe not. Rumors are that at least one Emperor or Empress tried to send an expedition searching for that continent and were told to forget it or else by the Great Guilds. Meanwhile, the northern and southern coasts of the Sea of Bakre are fairly forbidding except for occasional breaks in locations like Marida's harbor and Kelsi's settlement. And where Dor is setting up his place. Beyond that, the west is apparently uninhabitable and unreachable."

"Except for Altis," Jules said. "That's pretty close to some of these western coastlines, though. I wonder why we don't have better charts of those areas? It wouldn't be hard for ships from Altis to look them over. Everything is oriented to the east, though." She looked up at him. "Like you said, as if we're supposed to stay there."

Another nod. "Where the Emperor controls us," Mak said. "And the Great Guilds control the Emperor."

Jules ran her hand across the western portion of the map again. "I want to go there." Suddenly she knew that, felt it as deeply as if another Mage had looked upon her and prophesized that she would see the far west. "Why hasn't anyone done that yet?"

Mak pointed to where Dor's settlement was being founded. "No one has dared go beyond that. No one has dared it. Yet."

Jules smiled, her mind filled with visions of places no one else had ever seen. "I will."

Mak grinned at her. "Perhaps, Jules, you could even hide out there long enough for that prophecy to be carried out."

"I couldn't raise a family in a wasteland," Jules said. "Even if I found a suitable man out there. And if I stayed in one place, sooner or later the Great Guilds would find me."

"Maybe you should stay on a ship, then," Mak suggested. "I know one that wants you as part of the crew."

She looked at him, torn between laughter and tears. "I don't deserve this from all of you. For you to run these risks for me. Is this just about that prophecy? You all just want me to have that kid, don't you?"

"We want you to be safe, Jules," Mak said.

"It can't just be about me! Or about her! That daughter of my line! She's taken my life. I don't want her taking any other lives."

"At least you're not mad at me anymore."

"Sir, I do not call you sir when I'm mad at you, sir!"

He smiled at her. "Jules, will you at least ride the *Sun Queen* as far as Dor's? Once there, if your mind is set on leaving us, no one will stop you."

"That's a promise?" Jules asked.

"Yes." Mak looked at the chart again, seeming almost wistful. "I hope you think of me when you see Cap Astra."

"You'll be there with me, won't you?"

"I'd like to be, but…" Mak shrugged. "I'm getting a bit old for piracy, and for exploring uncharted waters and lands. Perhaps I'll stay at Dor's. Help make that place a strong home for free people, at least until the Great Guilds show up."

"Don't say that!" Jules protested. "You and me, we'll explore the western coast together. And find the Western Continent somewhere beyond that!"

This time Mak laughed. "I can't imagine anything that I'd like more, Jules. But just knowing that you'll go there someday is enough for me. You don't need me slowing you down."

She felt an odd disquiet at his words. "I don't need you, no. But I'd want you there."

"Thank you, Jules."

* * *

Jules held the helm as the *Sun Queen* steered east, the setting sun behind her turning the sails into sheets of gold. The day and the winds were gentle, so the helm needed little work, the ship clipping along placidly through the waves. They weren't in a rush, so the slow pace was no hardship, in fact welcome since it ate up time that otherwise might have to be spent closer to Caer Lyn where it would be more perilous to linger. With little required to do her job, Jules daydreamed about sailing west, daring the deadly reefs and finding places no one else had ever seen.

"Hey, Jeri," Liv said, coming up onto the quarterdeck. "How you doing?"

"Bored," Jules said. "To pass the time I was planning my expedition to explore the west."

Liv laughed, coming to stand beside Jules and looking up at the sails and rigging. "Mak talked to you about the West, did he?" Liv shook her head, smiling. "He's always been interested in that, but never made it."

"He's going to make it," Jules said. "We're going to go west and see everything."

"We? You and Mak?"

"Not just us alone," Jules said.

"Mak's getting on in years," Liv said.

"That's what he said. But how could we go west without the captain?"

Liv didn't answer for a while, gazing ahead. "You'd be safe there, wouldn't you? Way out in the west somewhere. Safe to have that family."

Jules shook her head, gazing somberly toward the bow. "No. It doesn't matter how far I went. They'd find me. They'd find the children. And they'd kill them. There'll never be a safe place for *my* children, Liv."

Liv paused again, frowning. "There must be a way to keep them safe. The prophecy says so."

"I know a way," Jules said. "I've thought of a way." Her heart felt heavy, as if a great weight had suddenly come to rest inside it. "I don't want to do it. I'm not sure I can. I hope whoever the man is who helps me bring those children into this world is strong enough to help me do what I'll have to do."

"I can't imagine you ending up with a weak man," Liv said. "But the heart does strange things, sometimes. You never know."

Jules, depressed by the turn the conversation had taken, tried to steer it onto a new course. "Liv? Speaking of strange hearts, have you and Healer Keli ever been a thing?"

She laughed. "Now and then. We've been more than friends more than once. But each time ended the same, both of us knowing we weren't going to promise ourselves to the other. So friends it was again."

"Keli's a good man, isn't he?" Jules said.

"To be sure. Even though I joke about him being a shark, he is a good man, and I'll break the teeth of anyone who says otherwise." Liv clapped Jules on the shoulder. "But even good men can have restless hearts. Good women, too. If I'm being honest, I'm the same. There're folks like Captain Mak, who set their heart on someone and never stray. And they're folks like me and Keli, as changeable as the sea." Liv studied Jules. "I think you're like Mak in that way."

Jules kept her grip on the handles of the wheel as she shrugged. "I don't know. My heart's never settled on anyone. What if it never does, Liv? What if I have to finally decide to just pick a guy and use him to get that child and then move on?"

"You won't do that," Liv said. "It's not in you to be like that."

"Why are you so sure?"

"Do you want the truth?"

"Yes."

Liv sighed. "You lost your mother and father young. You'll never go for something temporary, even as short as one night. You'll want someone who you know won't leave."

"My father didn't leave because he wanted to!"

"I know, girl. But, still, he left." Liv reached around Jules' shoulders to hug her with one arm. "There're two kinds in that regard, too. One is the kind who sees safety in avoiding promises, because that means they can decide for themselves what to do no matter what happens. And then there's the kind who sees safety in promises, in knowing what's expected of them and what others will do. You're the second kind."

"Am I?" Jules asked. "I violated my oath to the Emperor. That doesn't sound like someone who values promises."

"Why did you do it? Wasn't it because you knew the Emperor would violate his part of that oath, the one where he promises to look out for everyone in return for their service? You knew that. And if there's one thing you're certain death on, Jeri, it's betrayal."

"That's one thing, but it's not the only thing," Jules said, smiling. "Do you think she'll inherit that, Liv?"

"You mean the daughter of your line?" Liv frowned in thought again. "It may be a few generations, but she'll be your girl, won't she? I suspect that whatever else she is, that girl will also be someone who makes anyone who crosses her very sorry for their error."

"Maybe I'll be able to like her after all," Jules said. "Liv, tell me the truth. Why do I matter?"

"To me, you mean? Or to the world?"

"Both."

Liv scratched her head, gazing out to sea. "You matter because you're a sister, one who grew up in a legion home like I did. Because you're you, a loyal friend and one to be counted on. Because you do what's right when you can. Mind you, you might be a little too free with that dagger at times. But those who get it in the heart from you have always earned that, I think."

"You can't pretend the prophecy doesn't matter," Jules said.

"It does. It does," Liv admitted with a sigh. "I've seen it on you when you think of it. You get this shadow on your face and your shoulders bend as if the weight of every common person depending on you is resting there and your eyes look like those of someone seeing no good roads ahead. Then you pretend to push it aside and you laugh and you act like just another sailor, but it's always still there."

Liv paused. Her voice grew in strength. "But I see more than that. It's almost like I can see her sometimes, Jeri. Like I can see that daughter of your line standing behind you, and she's not all that different. You can tell she's from you, and you know looking at her that she'll do it, she'll overthrow the Great Guilds. Because no matter how many generations pass between, she'll be your girl. And I count it an honor to be beside you, and helping you, though my efforts are far too little, and I know that in a world that has never had hope there's some hope worth dying for now. So, yes, I look at you and I thank you for coming to this ship and giving me a role to play in that.

"And that's how I think of you and of the prophecy and now you may laugh at me for being such a fool. But I mean it."

Jules wiped her sleeve across her eyes. "I don't feel like laughing. Thanks, Liv." It was hard to think about leaving this ship, these people, who'd saved her after the prophecy was spoken and stood by her since.

Only until they reached Dor's. Then she'd have to go.

CHAPTER SIXTEEN

Jules pulled at the oars, driving the small boat through the entrance to Caer Lyn's harbor. Ang was in the boat with her, also pulling a pair of oars, the two of them getting past the dangerous waters around the point where Meg's shack stood, her feeble lantern gleaming in the growing darkness.

The boat that had come out to meet the *Sun Queen* as she approached the harbor near sunset had warned that one of the metal Mechanic ships was at the best pier. The Mechanics didn't seem to be particularly alert, but nevertheless they posed a danger. Best if the ship came in on the evening tide, and Jules followed behind just in case the Mechanics decided to search this late-night visitor.

Jules didn't think that too likely. The night was restless, erratic winds gusting across the harbor, scraps of cloud flying past above, even the waters inside the harbor choppy with agitated waves. The kind of night when anyone who had a choice would curl up inside near a warm fire, windows and doors closed against the feral winds prowling the dark.

It made the journey of the small boat not only dangerous but also a test of her nerves. The *Sun Queen* had set a second lantern near the stern of the ship to guide her and Ang to the right anchorage, an extra light that also conveyed the message that everything was safe for them to come to the ship. But Jules' eyes kept going to the bright, unnaturally steady lights of the Mechanic ship at the main pier.

Which ship was it? The one that carried Mechanic Hal and Mechanic Gin? Jules had no doubt what Mechanic Gin would do if she encountered Jules again, but what would Hal do? Would he pause to talk, to try to understand? *She'll have to talk to them*, Mak had said of that daughter of her line, speaking of Mechanics and Mages. Jules hoped that daughter would be better at such things than she was.

What was Mak thinking as the *Sun Queen* dropped anchor in the harbor of Caer Lyn? His daughter had been here. Might still be here, since she hadn't seemed to have come off the Mechanic ship. One of the Mechanics overseeing construction of their newest Guild Hall, probably. Lady Mechanic Verona.

Jules knew why she didn't like Verona: because the memories of his lost daughter hurt Mak. But she didn't know why she also felt a twinge of jealousy when thinking of Mak's daughter. Certainly not because she was a Mechanic. Perhaps because she had a father who was still alive and didn't know what a gift that was compared to what others had endured.

What had the Mechanics told Verona about Mak to make her so angry with him?

"It looks quiet," Ang said over his shoulder to Jules as they rowed. "Chancy weather, but as far as the Great Guilds or the Imperials go, it looks all right. The *Queen* is still showing two lights to let us know the coast is clear."

"I still want to get out of here as soon as we can," Jules said.

What were the Mages in Caer Lyn up to? Jules had her revolver with her in case Mages attacked, but using that weapon would alert the entire harbor. She didn't want to have to use it.

It felt a little odd to have so many cartridges for the revolver. She'd had three left when Mechanic Hal gave her eight more. Eleven. Enough to load the revolver cylinder almost twice over.

But there wouldn't be any more cartridges. Not unless she mugged some Mechanics.

The small boat, rocking in the unsteady waters, came alongside the anchored *Sun Queen*. Sailors watching onboard held out lanterns to be sure of who was in the boat, then tossed down a Jaycob ladder for Jules to climb while Ang hooked up the small boat to be hoisted back aboard.

Jules let out a sigh of relief when she reached the deck. Somehow being on the *Sun Queen* felt far safer than being anywhere else. "Where's the captain?"

Her moment of calm vanished as her question was met with guilty silence.

"Where's the captain?" Jules repeated, hearing the dangerous edge in her voice.

"They took him," Gord said. "Imperials and Mechanics together."

"You showed two lights!" Ang protested. "That meant it was safe!"

"The ship is safe," Liv said. "But they took the captain while he was ashore."

Jules inhaled slowly, trying to keep her mind working despite the red wave of rage threatening to swamp all else. "How?"

"Captain Mak was on the first boat to the pier," Liv said, her eyes fixed on Jules. "He had to be, to confirm the deal. When he stepped onto the pier, they came out of hiding and took him. Didn't touch anything else, like they didn't care about the people and cargo heading for Dor's."

Jules felt that coldness filling her, blocking the heat that had threatened to overcome her. "Where did they take him?"

"We don't—"

"Did they take him to the Mechanic ship?"

"No," Gord said. "They headed into town."

Jules pulled a cutlass out of the rack and checked the revolver at her hip. "Get the passengers and cargo aboard," she told Liv and Ang. "Be ready to sail when Mak and I get back."

"You can't—" Liv began, as Ang and some others moved closer to Jules.

She raised the cutlass, her gaze on the others. "I'll kill anyone who tries to stop me." She thought her voice was level and composed, but the others instantly stopped moving, staring at her.

"Jules, they want you to do this!" Ang said, his voice and expression pleading.

"You heard me. I mean it," Jules said, backing toward the ladder back down to the boat. She paused as a racked crossbow caught her eye. Keeping one eye on the sailors watching her, Jules pulled the crossbow free. "I'll be back with Captain Mak. Make sure everything is ready."

No one said anything else as Jules went over the side. She had to hastily sheath the cutlass, going down the ladder one-handed with the crossbow still tightly gripped. Dropping down the ladder perhaps a little faster than was safe, she landed in the small boat, quickly releasing the ropes that had been meant to haul it back aboard. Resting the crossbow beside her, she set the oars in the locks. She had only taken one stroke away from the ship when Liv called down, her voice despairing. "What of your line?"

Jules paused, looking upward at the faces staring down at her. "My line will be founded by a woman who stands by her friends. Be ready to go when I get back with the captain."

She aimed her course away from both the Mechanic ship and the parts of the piers illuminated by storm lanterns. Pulling harder on one oar, she headed toward the dark area where a new pier was being constructed. She wondered why she wasn't scared, why she didn't feel angry. Just the cold and the certainty that she had to do this.

Just as she'd warned Mak, he'd fallen into danger because of her. And just as she'd done at Saraston, she was going to get him out of the danger caused by her presence. Her fault. Her responsibility.

Grounding the boat on a patch of gravel near the landward end of the new pier, Jules made sure it was tied off and wouldn't float away when the tide came in. She paused in the dark near the water, gazing toward the lights and sounds of the town of Caer Lyn. Off to her right the bright lights of the Mechanic ship blazed, occasional figures in dark jackets passing near them. The errant winds teased and whipped at her hair, as if trying to provoke her.

Think. Make a plan.

They hadn't taken Mak to the ship. One of the other ships tied up at the piers might be the one that had brought the Imperials, but the crew members of the *Sun Queen* would have seen if Mak had been taken to one of those as well. That meant he was somewhere inland.

There wasn't any Imperial fort in Caer Lyn. The Mechanics were building a Guild Hall, though. It wasn't even close to being finished, but that's where they'd be. She felt sure of that, and also that the Mechanics would want to be able to keep a close eye on the Imperials so they could step in if Jules showed up.

She had the revolver, which she didn't dare use except in the direst emergency since the noise of its shot would alert the entire town. Also the crossbow, the cutlass, and her dagger. As Jules studied the darker areas before her she frowned, thinking that her shirt was too light for hiding in the night.

She saw a man walking past, wearing a dark, short coat.

Perfect.

Jules came up behind the man in a rush, her dagger coming around to hover in front of his throat. "Not a sound," Jules breathed softly in his ear.

The man stood silently, his body rigid with fear.

"I need a coat," Jules added. "Take off yours."

She stepped back, allowing him room to shed the garment and then stand again, waiting to learn his fate.

Jules dug in one pocket, pulling out a coin that should cover the cost of the coat, and shoved it into one of the man's hands. "Thanks."

He stared down at the coin, otherwise still not moving.

"Get out of here," Jules added.

The man left, walking quickly and not looking back.

She put down the crossbow and donned the coat, which was too big for her. But that was good. It hung down far enough to hide the revolver in its holster, and had enough room under it for her to partly conceal the crossbow.

Taking a slow, deep breath to calm herself, Jules began walking in a hopefully-not-suspicious way through the lighted parts of town, trying to stay to the less well-lit areas. Not that Caer Lyn had much in the way of street lighting yet. Most of the outside lights were those belonging to businesses like waterfront taverns.

Jules went through increasingly night-shadowed streets as she left the waterfront, heading inland. The buildings were mostly still raw and new, one or two stories thrown up using local lumber, but increasingly sturdier and more permanent structures either stood or were being constructed. The number of people on the streets fell off rapidly as she walked. Here away from the water, most of the businesses were the sort that operated during the day, and the houses were those of families or workers who were already settled for the night. Almost every light she saw now as she paced down the darkened streets was inside.

Until she reached the area she'd been heading for. Jules stopped in the lee of a building fronting on what would be a large, open plaza when finished. In the center, a massive structure was being built of stone and masonry, with piles of construction materials and loose earth scattered all about it.

In front of where the Mechanics Guild Hall was being built, large tents marked the temporary accommodations of the Mechanics sent to oversee the work and do those parts of the construction that required secrets of the Mechanic arts. Apparently lacking whatever fed their bright, steady lights, those tents were illuminated by lanterns both inside and out. Jules could see several Mechanics standing outside, gazing toward a nearby open area.

That area was also illuminated by lanterns set on the ground. One set of lanterns marked a perimeter with legionaries posted around it next to the lanterns, looking outward with weapons at the ready. Another set formed a much smaller circle, just large enough to surround a chair with someone tied to it. A few other legionaries stood near the chair. Jules, peering through the night, felt certain that the prisoner was Mak.

He couldn't have been more openly displayed. Couldn't have been more obviously bait for a trap.

What were the Imperials thinking? Probably that she'd put on the pretense of being an officer, hoping to bluff her way to Mak and then out again. She wasn't stupid enough to try that a third time. But there was no way to sneak through that lighted area to reach him, and any attempt to fight her way through the legionaries would also be doomed. Even the revolver couldn't help. Instead it would make things worse by immediately alerting all of the Mechanics.

The only good part, if it was truly good, was the small number of Imperials on the scene. Perhaps to keep the Emperor from thinking he could set up a permanent camp here, the Mechanics had allowed only about twenty legionaries into Caer Lyn.

But she couldn't handle twenty alone. And any force big enough to handle twenty, assuming she could assemble it, would also alert the Mechanics. No force of commons could stand against several Mechanics with their revolvers and rifles.

Despite her urge to rush to Mak's rescue, Jules forced herself to stand still and study the area, thinking. Twenty legionaries. How could she handle that many?

She watched the two legionary officers speaking together, a major and a lieutenant, and realized that maybe she wouldn't need to take out all of them.

Checking the pouch attached to the crossbow, Jules found eight bolts in it, each like a short, steel arrow with stubby fins on the back to help it fly straight and a nasty point on the front end.

Eight might be enough.

She moved cautiously, heading for the piles of construction materials, keeping them between her and sight of the legionaries and Mechanics as best she could, glad that she'd been wise enough to acquire the dark coat to help conceal her in the night. *I'm planning, Mak. Don't worry. I'll get you out of there.*

As she got closer to the legionary perimeter, Jules moved more slowly, trying to ensure that she made no noise. Reaching a sloping stack of bricks, she cautiously peered over it, seeing the prisoner in the chair. It was definitely Mak. One of the officers, a major, was standing not far from Mak, now talking to a centurion.

In the lights of all the lanterns, set to ensure that Jules would be seen if she approached, the legionaries themselves were easily seen, and well within accurate range for the crossbow. And the legionaries weren't moving around, making them stationary targets.

Get the centurion first, Jules decided. She slowly worked the lever on the crossbow, tensioned the cord, and set a bolt in place. Resting the crossbow on the bricks, she aimed carefully, waiting for the erratic winds to abate.

An instant of nearly calm wind, her finger tightening on the trigger of the crossbow, the bolt being released with a *spang* as the cord slapped the front of the bow, the centurion and the major beginning to turn at the sound, the bolt lodging in the throat of the centurion, the centurion falling back and down in a rattle of armor to lie still.

Jules was already moving, her steps masked by the sound from the legionaries as they reacted to her attack. Reaching a pile of dirt, Jules leaned on top of it, the crossbow once more ready, aiming at the major who was yelling orders at the legionaries and pointing toward where Jules' first shot had come from.

Jules launched another bolt. If the major had dropped at the sound, he might have escaped the shot, but instead the officer paused to look in the new direction.

The bolt took him in the chest.

The major fell, crying out with pain, as several legionaries knelt by him in a vain attempt to save him. The others stared fearfully or angrily into the dark, looking for their attacker. The surviving officer, a lieutenant, yelled orders in a nervous voice as she went to stand right by Mak, using his body to partially protect herself.

Jules had moved again, perilously close to where the Mechanics might see her, but she need a clear shot at the lieutenant. The Mechanics were watching the events with clear worry, but as of yet had done nothing.

Jules aimed carefully, once more steadying the crossbow, this time on a large squared stone.

Jules realized as soon as she shot that she'd over-compensated to avoid hitting Mak's seated figure, the bolt going high. But it was low enough to clip the side of the lieutenant's head with a crack that could be clearly heard. The lieutenant fell, maybe not dead but definitely unconscious for the foreseeable future.

Their leaders all gone, the remaining legionaries gazed around, seeking guidance and finding none. Looking for their attacker and seeing nothing in the darkness beyond the light of their own lanterns.

Jules, crouched in the shelter of another pile of bricks, tensioned the crossbow again and loaded another bolt. This time she aimed at one of the legionaries in the outer perimeter, standing next to a lantern.

The bolt took the legionary in the belly, punching through his armor to inflict a painful wound.

As that legionary flailed about, Jules shot another standing near a lantern.

She only had three bolts left.

But as she'd hoped, the leaderless legionaries finally did the obvious thing.

"Put out the lights!" one yelled, followed by others agreeing.

"But we need to watch!" another protested.

"We're sitting ducks with these lanterns beside us! Put 'em out! We'll cluster around the prisoner, and still see her if she comes for him!"

The lanterns were extinguished rapidly, putting the legionary area into the same darkness as the rest of the plaza. Looking over at the Mechanics, Jules saw that they were doing the same, realizing their own lanterns could make them targets for whoever was firing from the shelter of the night.

Dark fell, but quiet did not, the groans of the wounded legionaries and loud calls from the Mechanic tents filling the night.

Jules breathed in and out slowly, trying to think out her next step. Could she panic the remaining legionaries? Pose as an officer again? No. They'd have been warned about that. And sounds of a fight would draw the Mechanics in. Think. Think.

She looked down at her dark coat, wishing it were a magical cloak to make her invisible.

Wait.

Jules set down the crossbow and drew her revolver.

She stood up, moving carefully through the construction piles until she could approach the legionaries from the general direction of the Mechanic tents. Taking another slow breath, she stepped out and began walking toward to the legionaries, trying to swagger at the same time as she moved like someone worried about a sniper with a crossbow.

The faces of the legionaries, vague shapes in the dark, turned toward her as Jules strode up to them. She displayed the revolver, waving it about not in a threatening way but in a commanding fashion. "Release the prisoner. I'm taking him back to the tents. We'll watch him," she said, trying to sound as arrogant as the Mechanics who'd spoken to her, trying to match the way they talked. A dark coat, a revolver, and an arrogant air of command, combined with the cloak of the night. Would it all be good enough to fool the already rattled legionaries?

For a long, heart-stopping moment, the legionaries stared silently at Jules.

"But, Lady, our orders—" one finally began.

"Lady *Mechanic*," Jules snapped in a low voice.

"Lady Mechanic, our orders—"

"Didn't you hear me?" Jules demanded, waving the revolver again. "Do I have to make an example of you? Do as I say, common!"

It took all of her will power to hold still rather than flinch back into a defensive posture as the legionaries moved. She heard daggers sawing through rope, and saw another figure stand, staggering as he tried to balance after the time spent tied immobile.

Mak was shoved toward her. She took his arm, brandishing the revolver. "Come on, common," she snarled, trying to put Gin's contempt into the words.

They walked toward the tents, through the dark between the legionaries and the Mechanics, bearing to the right, until Jules could yank Mak into the area masked by the piles of construction materials. She pushed him onward, moving faster now, pausing just before they cleared the materials to holster her revolver, pull out her dagger, and saw through the bonds still holding Mak's wrists together.

It wasn't until they left the plaza, heading down streets toward the waterfront, that Jules spoke again. "It's too dark for the legionaries or the Mechanics to see what's happening to the others. Hopefully they won't dare light lanterns again tonight, so until dawn the legionaries will think the Mechanics have you and the Mechanics will think the legionaries have you. We should be well out of the harbor by then."

Mak's voice sounded rough. "Jules, of all the reckless, foolish things you've done—"

"You know what'd be nice, sir?" Jules interrupted. "If one of the times I rescue you I got a thank you instead of being chewed out. That'd be nice, sir, if it ever happened."

"I'm not worth the risk you ran to do this!"

"You're worth it to me, Captain," Jules said. "And you were only in this trouble because of me, which I warned you would happen."

He didn't answer for a moment as they hastened through the dark streets toward the water. "Jules," Mak finally said, his voice softer, "how do you think I'd feel if you got badly hurt, or killed, or captured, because of me?"

"I'm sorry," she said. "I have to do this."

"Why?"

"I don't know." Jules scowled into the night, trying to sort out her own motivations and emotions.

Mak sighed. "You did a great job. The Imperials expected you to do the sort of thing you'd done before, based their trap on you trying the same sort of thing, and instead you turned their own preparations against them. That was good planning."

She felt her mood lighten despite her worries. "I did it right?"

"You thought things through. Yes, you did a great job." Mak paused a third time. "Thank you."

"You're welcome, Captain," Jules said, grinning.

"Have you planned what to do if we run into any Mages? They might hear of what the Imperials and Mechanics were doing, and why."

"I'm hoping they don't hear in time to do anything," Jules said. "If worse comes to worse, I've got the revolver."

She shed the dark coat once they reached the rowboat. Untying the boat, Jules and Mak pushed it out into the water and Jules took the oars again. The water was still choppy and the winds still teased at her and the boat, but the night felt far less threatening.

"The Mechanics are going to be unhappy," Mak said as Jules rowed them toward the *Sun Queen*. "But not furious the way they would be if you'd shot one of them. Jules, if you ever openly kill a Mechanic, they'll come after you with everything they've got. Don't declare war on the Mechanics unless you're ready to deal with that."

"I understand," Jules said, breathing deeply as she rowed. "I didn't want to risk hurting any Mechanics here anyway. I might've hurt Verona."

"Thank you. Jules, it's possible you can work with the Mechanics again. They don't take the Mage prophecy seriously, you said. If in the future they decide you can once again be of use to them against the Mages and the Empire, I think they'll deal again."

"As long as I don't have to come back to Caer Lyn or Jacksport," Jules said. "They're too dangerous for me. And Caer Lyn looks like it's becoming respectable."

"I think so," Mak agreed. He seemed to finally be relaxing as they drew near the *Sun Queen*. "You don't like respectable towns?"

"No. Because respectable towns don't like me. Somewhere out west, Captain, there'll be a good harbor. We'll find it. And I'll found a city there. A city that'll never really be respectable, founded by a legion orphan and pirate with a lower-class Landfall accent. The sort of place that daughter of my line will need someday."

"Good idea," Mak said. "What'll you name that city?"

"Julesport," she said. "So that every time the Great Guilds see that name on a chart or hear it, they'll be reminded of the prophecy. Reminded that their days ruling this world might still have a while to run, but will be limited, and growing a bit less with each day that passes."

"Another good idea," Mak said, laughing for a moment. "And also reminding the world who you are. Not just the woman who founded your bloodline, but someone who challenged the Great Guilds and the Emperor and kept winning."

"Yeah," Jules agreed with a grin. "That prophecy is a curse as far as I'm concerned, isn't it? But I'm going to turn it into something that makes me mean something. Just like my captain suggested."

"I won't always be here," Mak said. "That's why it's so important that you planned things out tonight. I know you don't need me any more."

"Where are you going?" Jules asked, suddenly worried about that above all other things.

"People leave, Jules," Mak said. "You and I know that. We both lost people who were very important to us. Sometimes people leave, even when they don't want to. But we have to carry on as they would have wanted us to, just as anybody else has to."

"But…" Jules paused in her rowing, trying to think. "How will I know what to do? I'm not like anybody else. Not anymore."

"You never were like anybody else, Jules," Mak said. "And I mean that in the best way. You're going to have a hard course to steer in life. Sometimes it'll be hard to know which way to go. At times like that, remember what really matters. That's your guide star when all else fails. Remember that."

"Yes, Captain, I will. But how do I know what really matters?"

"You always know, Jules. People always know. They just have to listen."

"I'll try."

The boat came alongside the *Sun Queen*, anxious faces looking down and breaking into relieved smiles. Jules hooked up the lines to haul the small boat up, then followed Mak up the Jaycob ladder.

"We've got everyone and everything aboard, Cap'n," she heard Ang reporting to Mak.

"Any problems?" Mak asked.

Ang shook his head. "Do you mean aside from you and Jeri? Just nerves, I guess. Everyone's on edge. Feeling like we're bumping into people on the boats and on the deck who aren't there. That kind of thing."

"Get the anchor up and the sails set," Mak ordered. "We need to leave this harbor as quickly as possible."

Jules, the cutlass in her hand so she could rack it, stopped as Liv stepped in front of her. "Blazes, girl," Liv said. "How—"

Liv jolted aside as if she'd been pushed out of the way by a powerful blow.

Jules saw the air in front of her flicker, as if something was there and not there and then there. Two figures were suddenly standing before her. Mages. The hoods of their robes were down, revealing the expressionless faces of a male Mage and a female Mage, their gazes fixed on Jules in a way that reminded her of the eyes of the dragon. Both Mages had sweat on their faces, as if they'd been working hard and were tired, but both moved swiftly to thrust their long knives toward Jules while she stood momentarily frozen with shock.

In that moment, as the blades moved forward, a body slammed into Jules from the side, shoving her out of the way. She managed to keep on her feet as she staggered sideways, horrified to realize in the tiny moment of time before the Mages finished their thrusts that the person who had shoved her away from their knives was Mak. That he was now standing where she had been.

Jules felt the world stop as the long knives went through Mak from the front and out the back, red blood glistening along the blades. Mak still stood, held up partly by his own resolve and partly by the knives transfixing him.

"NO!" Jules screamed the word, the cutlass she still held coming up, her mind filled with rage, not caring that a normal weapon shouldn't be able to harm the two Mages. She swung the cutlass with strength multiplied by her fury, slicing completely through the neck of the female Mage, whose head fell to the side with no expression. The male Mage had yanked his blade free and was just beginning to turn toward Jules when she brought her sword back in a reverse cut through the man's neck, the blade jarring in her hand as it lodged in the Mage's spine. A trace of puzzlement appeared briefly in his eyes before the Mage toppled to the deck.

Jules fell to her knees beside Mak, her tears dropping to mingle with the blood spreading across his chest. "Mak. Mak. Keli! Where's the healer?"

Mak shook his head very slightly, his eyes glazed with pain. "Keli can't help. No healer could. Sorry… Jules."

"Mak, don't die," Jules sobbed. "Please."

"Sorry. My time. You'll be… all right. Listen… yourself."

"No, I won't be all right! Not without you here."

"You will," Mak said, his eyes searching hers. "Make us strong. Strong enough… for her. For… all of us."

"All right," Jules gasped, almost blinded by her tears. "I will. But for you. I'll do it for you. You'll be proud of me. I swear it."

He smiled up at her. "That's… my girl."

"Mak?" She shook him slightly, but he didn't react, the smile still there, but Mak's eyes looking somewhere beyond this life. "Mak!"

A hand fell on her shoulder. "He's gone from us, Jeri," Ang said.

She shoved the hand away, getting to her feet. "My name is Jules!" she shouted. "Jules of Landfall!" She went to the fallen male Mage and yanked her cutlass free, blood dripping from the blade. "And I am the woman of the prophecy! I'll hide that no longer from anyone! A daughter of my line will someday overthrow the Great Guilds! And she will do it so that no one else has to die like Mak! Do you hear me?" Jules ran to the side of the ship facing the piers, yelling at the top of her voice. "Here I am! Come try to stop me! I'll kill anyone who tries!"

* * *

An hour later she still stood there, the cutlass still in her hand. Under the direction of Ang and Liv the crew had followed Mak's last orders, getting the anchor raised, the sails set, and the ship out of the harbor.

"Jeri," Liv said.

"Jules." Jules turned her head to look at Liv. "I'm Jules."

"All right, Jules. You've got to snap out of it."

"Where... where's Mak?"

"We cleaned him up. Put him in the cabin. He'll need to be buried right, and we thought you'd want to help say the words."

"I do," Jules said, a great stillness inside her where feelings should be. "What about the Mages?"

"We already tossed the bodies overboard. You killed two Mages with a cutlass," Liv added as if unable to believe what she was saying.

"I know."

"I didn't know anyone could kill Mages that way. Maybe none of the rest of us could. But you did."

Ang walked up next to Liv. "Jules, is it, from now on? Jules, the ship needed a new captain. We've held a vote."

Jules nodded, not really caring about that. "They elected you, didn't they, Ang? You or Liv."

Ang shook his head. "We voted to make you the captain," he said. "Everyone in the crew voted for you, Cap'n Jules."

She stared at him. "Captain? I'm not experienced enough."

"We all want you to be the captain," Liv said. "Mak would've wanted it, too."

"Don't—" Jules felt pain coming, the pain she'd held off with numbness for the last hour. "I'm not Mak."

"You heard him at the last, Jules. We all did. You're his girl. The daughter he lost."

She felt tears again, running down her face. Jules blinked at the crew, who she realized were watching her. "What... what the blazes are you all looking at? Don't you have work that needs doing? Get to it!"

"What course, Cap'n?" Ang asked.

"Steer south. We need to lose any pursuers before we head west toward Dor's."

Ang saluted before turning back toward the quarterdeck.

Jules looked out over the water, nerving herself, before walking quickly to the stern cabin.

Mak lay there on the bunk, his body wrapped in canvas, but his face left exposed, the canvas that would cover it still open. She stood looking down at him. The smile had remained fixed on his face. The smile he'd given her with his last breath. "I'll take care of the ship and the crew, sir," Jules told him, tears spilling out again as she looked at him. "Just like you'd want, Captain."

* * *

The burial service took a while, everyone speaking a few words before the plank that Mak's body lay on was raised and his remains slid into the sea.

The canvas over Mak's face had been sewn shut after Jules and everyone else who wanted to had given Mak's forehead a farewell kiss. And after Jules had tucked in, next to Mak's heart, the book about wildflowers. She knew he'd want it with him. She'd also placed the reddish stone in one of his pockets. Whatever it had meant to him, he'd carry it forever now. The ballast stone tied to the canvas would take him down to the bottom, where he could rest without fear of storms to disturb his sleep.

Just before sunset they'd passed a ship heading for Caer Lyn, a respectable Imperial flagged merchant vessel that had nervously watched their approach. Jules brought the *Sun Queen* close enough to throw across a dispatch case with a sheet of paper inside, folded over and addressed to Lady Mechanic Verona of Severun. *Mak of Severun is dead. I thought you would want to know. He died bravely, still loving you and your mother who died long ago. Please remember him with love. He was a good man.*

She hadn't signed it. Jules suspected that if Mechanic Verona ever received the letter, she'd know who'd sent it.

Jules stood alone in the cabin, the captain's cabin that was now hers, looking aft out the windows, feeling a lack of life in this room where someone else should be. The drawing of Lake Bellad still hung on one bulkhead, a reminder of Mak. She thought he'd have wanted her to keep it, something to hold onto as a memento. At this moment, her fear of the prophecy didn't matter, the Great Guilds didn't matter, the Emperor in Marandur didn't matter, her fear for her children-to-be and that distant-in-time daughter-to-be of hers didn't matter. All that counted was the person who had filled an emptiness she hadn't known still haunted her. A person who was now gone but would never be forgotten by her. *I'll find Cap Astra, Mak. I'll explore the entire West. I'll make the common people so strong the Great Guilds will tremble. And I'll keep the West free no matter what the Emperor tries. When the daughter of my line comes, our people will be ready to follow her.*

Thank you for choosing to be a father to me. Your girl will make you proud.

No one's going to stop me.

ABOUT THE AUTHOR

"Jack Campbell" is the pseudonym for John G. Hemry, a retired Naval officer who graduated from the U.S. Naval Academy in Annapolis before serving with the surface fleet and in a variety of other assignments. He is the author of The Lost Fleet military science fiction series, as well as the Stark's War series, and the Paul Sinclair series. His short fiction appears frequently in *Analog* magazine, and many have been collected in ebook anthologies *Ad Astra, Borrowed Time,* and *Swords and Sadwdles.* He lives with his indomitable wife and three children in Maryland.

Don't miss the adventure that started
it all...

THE DRAGONS
OF DORCASTLE

PILLARS OF REALITY ✦ BOOK 1

JACK
CAMPBELL

NEW YORK TIMES BESTSELLING AUTHOR

FOR NEWS ABOUT JABBERWOCKY BOOKS AND AUTHORS

Sign up for our newsletter*: http://eepurl.com/b84tDz
visit our website: awfulagent.com/ebooks
or follow us on twitter: @awfulagent

THANKS FOR READING!

*We will never sell or give away your email address, nor use it for nefarious purposes. Newsletter sent out quarterly.